A SURE THING

MARIE HARTE

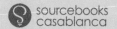
sourcebooks
casablanca

Published by Sourcebooks Casablanca, an imprint of Sourcebooks, Inc.
P.O. Box 4410, Naperville, Illinois 60567-4410
(630) 961-3900
Fax: (630) 961-2168
www.sourcebooks.com

Printed and bound in Canada.
MBP 10 9 8 7 6 5 4 3 2 1

To all the Marines who have served, are serving, and will serve—Semper Fi

And to D&R, I love you

Chapter 1

WORST DAY OF THE FRIGGIN' YEAR. SEATTLE HAD ITS doozies, but this one by far smacked of depression. In addition, it had been overcast and miserable all day, with rain continuing into the early evening. A glance around the surprisingly crowded gym made Landon Donnigan wish for a return to the scorching heat of Afghanistan. Better that than the danger of desperate singles looking to hook up on Valentine's Day.

God save me.

Though life in the Marine Corps had been fraught with risk—and not the bullshit emotional kind of risks—he'd enjoyed his time both overseas and in the States. During his service, he'd thought a civilian life behind a desk would be worse than anything he might imagine. Now he took his current job in stride, pleased to be useful once more.

But Valentine's Day surrounded by flirting singles, in *a gym* no less? Sacrilege. He did his best not to make eye contact with anyone, especially the small group of women who kept looking his way. With any luck, they hadn't noticed him, their attention on his supposedly charming younger brother standing next to him. He placed the hand weights he'd been using back on the rack, figuring he'd cut himself a break on his workout, just this once.

His brother glanced over his shoulder at several of the staring women. "Is it just me? Or do you feel almost hunted right now?" Gavin waved, and they waved back. "I mean, I *have* to be here. I'm a trainer. But shouldn't all these women be out with their significant others celebrating with flowers and chocolates? I thought lonely women on V-Day stayed at home, sobbing into their Earl Grey and fighting their twenty-plus cats for bonbons. Kind of like you on any night of the week—alone and lonely."

"You're an ass."

Gavin chuckled. "Yeah, I am. I'm kidding…about the women." He ignored the finger Landon shot him. "Seriously though, most of the women I know are either out with friends or pissed off at men in general and sitting at home."

"Like Hope, you mean?" Landon drawled. Their little sister had supposedly broken up with her latest dickhead boyfriend yesterday. God willing, the next guy she dated wouldn't be so toxic.

"Yeah. Like Hope." Gavin nodded. "No worries, Bro. Hope's situation will work out." Gavin took after their father in looks and temperament. Dark-haired, *too* laid-back, and for some reason, well-liked by the ladies, who continued to watch him.

Landon followed his brother's gaze to the attractive group. "They seem interested. Why not go ask 'em out?"

"No way in hell." Gavin frowned. "We don't fraternize with clients. Mac's orders."

"Really? Because you've got a mess of opportunity right over there."

"That group is way too loaded for my blood. And by loaded, I mean richer than shit. They're looking for a boy toy to play with. And rumor has it they break their toys." Gavin glanced around him, then murmured, "Mac didn't actually say I couldn't date gym members. But when I tell them that, they leave me alone. I mean, they don't want to get me fired from my job."

With any luck, Gavin would hold on to this one for a while. The last two jobs hadn't gone well. Landon wasn't the only one adjusting to civilian life after the Corps. He subtly leaned closer to Gavin. Good. No scent of alcohol on little brother's breath tonight.

"Smart excuse," he said, trying to cover the sniff check.

"Smart. That's me." Gavin didn't do smug as well as he thought he did. Not like their youngest brother, who'd come out of the womb smirking at life in general. "But why are *you* here? I'd have thought you and Claudia would be getting romantic. Hell, man, it's Saturday. You can't use work as an excuse."

Landon shrugged and retrieved his towel and water bottle from the floor. "I thought I told you we broke up. We were never more than friends anyway." *Intimate* friends. He'd been smart enough to end their casual relationship two months ago when Claudia had been hinting about changing their status to something much more serious. He'd been getting bored, and her constant neediness grated on his last nerve. As if Landon had time for more trouble when he had so much work to do fixing his dysfunctional family.

"Yeah? That's not what I heard." A pause. "From Claudia."

Crap. "She's been to the gym lately?" She'd quit when they'd broken up. Landon had only seen her once since then. Just last week. They'd exchanged a pleasant greeting, nothing more.

"Yep. Heard her talking to Marsha about you

yesterday, as if you two were still an item. Then she told me to say hi from her." Gavin smiled wide. "So hi."

"Shut up."

Gavin snickered.

Landon glanced around, praying the woman hadn't arrived tonight. He hated hurting anyone, and he'd been surprised she'd taken their "friend" breakup so hard. Which only reinforced the notion he'd been right to sever the relationship in the first place. Dating should be fun, not a minefield. He'd had enough of *those* to last a lifetime.

He scowled, feeling hemmed in. Jameson's Gym was supposed to be his refuge in this chaotic, civilian world. Landon appreciated the hell out of the owner giving his brother a job. Mac Jameson seemed to be a stand-up guy. He'd been a master sergeant in the Marine Corps before doing permanent damage to his knee, ending his time early. They shared that connection—common core values, an appreciation for discipline and order, and medical bullshit ending a guy's dream.

"Mac here?" he asked.

Gavin shook his head. "Seriously? You've seen his wife, right? She's hot as hell. No doubt they're hanging at home for some 'alone time.'" Gavin sighed. "I miss uncomplicated sex."

At his words, a pretty blond in tights stopped behind him and gave him a toothy grin. "Hey, Gavin. How's it going?"

His younger brother cringed, then turned around and gave her an insincere smile back. "Oh, ah, hi, Michelle. How are you?"

"Great. I just finished my workout." She eyed Gavin

the way a lion would a helpless gazelle. The comparison made it hard not to laugh, especially with the hunted look on Gavin's face. "Shouldn't you be out with your girlfriend tonight?" Michelle asked, her voice breathy. "Hope, right?"

"Hope's my sister."

"Oh, so you *are* single then. Megan and I were talking."

"I'm single, yeah, but I don't mingle with—"

Michelle grabbed him by the arm, her sharp nails a bright pink. "How lucky for me you're here. I could really use a spotter."

"I thought you said you were done with your workout."

"I mean I'm *almost* done."

Gavin couldn't rightly refuse to help Michelle train. Landon ignored the beseeching look his brother shot him and subtly stepped away.

"Ah, sure." Gavin blew out a breath. "Are all of you training together?" he asked, staring at the three women watching them.

"Yep. We need someone to show us the proper way to use some of the equipment." The same equipment she'd been using for as long as Landon had been coming to the gym. She tugged Gavin with her. "Then after, maybe you and I can do a casual dinner." She blinked at Landon. "How about you, Landon?"

Gavin hemmed, "Well, I don't know. My brother and I were supposed to—"

"Go ahead, Gav." Landon almost felt sorry for him. Then he remembered what Gavin had said and smiled. "Sorry, Michelle. I have plans. I'll be at home drinking Earl Grey and playing with my cats."

Gavin scowled at him. Michelle shrugged, her claws

still hooked into Gavin. "Oh well. Gavin, I know there's a no-dating policy, but it's not a date if it's just dinner. Or dessert," she purred.

Knowing his brother could take care of himself, at least when it came to women, Landon headed for the men's sauna before Michelle's rabid pack of singles decided not to take no for an answer. Not that he considered himself God's gift to women, but he'd been doing his best to avoid several of her friends since he'd been coming to the place. He'd never hurt for bed partners, blessed with his parents' good looks and a body built from constant exercise.

He didn't spend his free time at the gym to hook up. He wanted a workout.

As he sat in the sauna, he struck up a conversation with some other poor fool with nothing better to do on Valentine's Day. At least Landon wasn't the only guy not all that keen on hearts and flowers.

"Yeah, well, don't feel bad for not getting all the hype about V-Day, man. Frankly, I'd rather soak in here than deal with trying to figure out what women want."

"Or what men want," his companion griped.

"Amen." Landon chuckled, not surprised that any relationship could give a guy a headache. "Time for me to go. Later." The guy nodded, and Landon left to grab his stuff and head home.

The house he—and now Gavin—rented sat in the heart of Queen Anne. He lived close to his aunt and uncle and a bevy of annoying cousins, but a neighborhood over from his parents, who had a big home in Fremont. Since moving back to Seattle, he'd already been to an engagement party and had invitations to three weddings.

At least his cousins were getting married and growing up. To hear Linda Donnigan tell it, her own children
could take lessons from their McCauley cousins. The
Donnigans were seriously screwed up.

Frankly, Landon agreed.

He entered the house after locking up his car and
grimaced at the mess Gavin had *once again* left in the
kitchen. After doing the dishes and straightening up the
living room, Landon took his things into his bedroom
and put his laundry away before taking a quick shower.

Yeah, his mother had it right. She was a type A
workaholic, balanced by his mellow father who thought
the world would be all right with a little more love.
Landon snorted. If love came in the form of some hand-
to-hand combat or a grenade, then yeah, he agreed. It
never failed to amaze him that his father had served as a
Navy corpsman, taking care of Marines in combat, with
that peace-love attitude. But while Van Donnigan didn't
worry about much, Linda and Landon stressed for the
lot of them.

Landon finished his shower and dressed in comfortable sweats, dwelling on the mess his family had
become. Gavin had a bad case of PTSD he was trying
to drown in booze. Hope kept bringing home clones of
Jack the Ripper, and Theo had his head buried up his
ass, in denial that high school was over and he had to
grow the hell up.

With a groan, Landon settled on the couch and pulled
up a kung fu movie on television. After the week he'd
had, he deserved the break. Though he'd been relieved
to find transitioning to civilian life a lot easier than he'd
anticipated, his job had taken some getting used to. No

longer able to take long runs during lunch or bark orders at his subordinates, he'd gotten back into the swing of business management, landing a sweet job thanks to an employment recruiter and some old friends. Being an officer had its perks, even on the outside.

He could manage the employees of D&R Logistics with his hands tied behind his back. His biggest challenge had been learning the company's mission and getting on board with their management structure. That and convincing his buddy Daniel to stop treating him like a friend and act like a boss.

With a sigh, he ran his fingers through his cropped blond hair, aware it had never been so long, not in over thirteen years. But a high and tight haircut in Seattle, during the winter, was sheer idiocy.

He grabbed himself a beer and settled in for some amazing martial arts. Between one blink and the next, the show had ended, the room seemed much darker, and the front door opened. Gavin stumbled in. A glance at the clock on the mantel showed a glowing two in the a.m.

"Yo, Bro," Gavin slurred and chuckled. "What a night."

Landon sighed. "I thought you were done drinking."

"I was. But it's Valentine's Day! A night for lovers." He walked out of his shoes, dumped his bag on the floor, and tripped into the couch, sprawling next to Landon. "Michelle's a real snob, but she sucks better than a Hoover."

"TMI, Gavin." Landon shook his head, concern for his brother growing. "You didn't drive, did you?"

"Nah. Took a cab."

Thank God for small favors. "Come on. Let's get you to bed."

"Sure." Gavin grinned and closed his eyes. "Not gonna dream tonight. I'm plastered."

Landon dragged him to the nearby bathroom and nagged at him to piss. Then he half carried the idiot to his bedroom and covered him up in bed. Hopefully Gavin would get a decent night's rest. Then tomorrow, Landon would arrange for the family to plan that intervention his little brother needed, before it was too late.

He returned to the living room to lock the door, turned everything off, then went to bed. The world around him might be spiraling out of control, but he controlled his own environment.

He snorted. Valentine's Day with hearts and flowers? More like a drunken brother, a half-finished kung fu movie, and a beer. Yeah, that sounded about right.

Ava Rosenthal smiled at her date and did her best not to draw on preconceived notions of what a healthy beginning to a relationship should entail. *Turn it off, Ava.* She had a bad habit of overanalyzing everything, a holdover from constantly counseling her patients about their lives, no doubt.

Ten minutes into her date with Matt, she suspected he had narcissistic tendencies. But she was determined to give it time. She made it past the hors d'oeuvres and salads, nodding, smiling, and trying to interject a comment here and there, to show she was engaged.

"Yes, I agree, I—"

"Then I made sure he was satisfied. I mean, I won't get repeat clients if they feel like we're not working with their insurance companies." Matt smiled, and his dimples winked at her. Such bright blue eyes. He was slender, neat, and handsome. Just her type.

She took a deep breath and let it out, slowly. She could handle a chatty date. "Exactl—"

"So I told Alice to relay that to our providers. Then I created a new system where we…" His words ran together, and since he stared more at his plate, shoveling food in while he talked, he didn't notice her eyes crossing.

Good God, Matt, shut up for two seconds and swallow before you speak, at least.

He continued to discuss his dental practice, somehow segued into why he'd chosen online dating, and throughout dinner and into the dessert she'd tried to avoid, finally brought up his ex.

"They say you shouldn't bring up an ex on the first date," he said between bites of bread pudding, which she loathed. "But I figured we should get to know each other. I feel like we're really hitting it off, you know?"

How he could think that when he hadn't let her get a word in edgewise, she had no idea. Usually people asked her questions about what it was like being a clinical psychologist. Fascination with people and their problems she understood. This guy couldn't care less. Maybe her online profile had told him enough.

Stay positive. It's only a first date. "The food is delicious."

He nodded and smiled, and she saw more of his masticated dessert than she wanted. Now feeling a little queasy, she pushed aside her tiramisu and sipped from her water glass. *I am in a desert, thirsting for a meaningful connection, and I'm dying.* An image of her crawling through sand for water felt all too real.

She guzzled her glass.

"Want mine too? I haven't touched it."

She grabbed his water glass like a lifeline. "Thanks."

Matt talked through dessert, but he did pay the bill, for which she'd offered to go dutch.

"Nah. My treat. It's not often I get to go out with a beautiful woman."

Considering he'd already told her he only dated sexy professionals, the compliment had worn thin what felt like hours ago.

After the waiter brought back his card, she forced a frown. "Sorry, but I can feel my phone buzzing." She reached in, took the call, then ended it with a sigh. "I'm so sorry. A patient of mine is having a problem. She recently broke up with her husband. I know it's late, but I told her to call if she needed me." Ava stood in a hurry.

"No problem. Emergencies happen. Want me to wait for—"

"I'd better get to my office." She gave him a smile, thanked him for the dinner, and wished him a happy Valentine's Day. Then, before he could talk again, she darted out of the restaurant.

Once safely in her car and headed home, she put a call through to Sadie on her Bluetooth. Of her three cousins, Rose, the youngest, had married a terrific guy a year ago. Elliot, her confidant and only male cousin, remained single but had a hot date tonight. But Sadie, who'd sworn off men since her last ex, answered on the first ring. "How did it go?"

"I called an audible and made up a fake phone emergency. God, Sadie. He talked all through the meal. And I mean *all* through. I saw more of his food than I wanted and know all about his dental practice, his online dating disasters, and his ex-wife, who left him for another woman."

"Ouch." Sadie chuckled. "Hey, you wanted to start dating again. I told you to stay off the man train."

"Yeah, and Elliot told me to jump back on before I'm old and gray." She gave a quick glance at the rearview mirror, wondering if that gray hair she'd spotted earlier in the morning had been a trick of the light. She'd only turned thirty a few months ago. Yet after her disaster of a date, she felt decades older.

Sadie snorted. "Elliot's a player. You can't trust anything he says."

Ava grinned. "Jealous?"

"Hell yeah. His dates are hot." Sadie groaned. "More proof that all the good ones are gay or taken. It's a fact."

Ava immediately wanted to correct her cousin, to tell her to see the world in a more positive light. So she squelched the impulse, doing her best to stop telling everyone what to do all the time. "Yeah, well, we both know I'll get a social life eventually. Matt was only my fifth foray into the dating scene."

"Um, Ava? You're off the clock. You don't have to use big words like 'foray' with me."

"God, Sadie. Read a book." Ava huffed. "You do know what those are, don't you?"

"If it ain't got recipes, I ain't interested."

Sadie and her sister ran a successful bakery and catering service with Elliot in Green Lake, which explained why the girl always thought in terms of recipes—like Ava's recipe for that disaster date with Matt.

"Matt thought we had a 'connection.'" It was all she could do not to use air quotes while driving. "It kills me, because he was so handsome. Successful. I loved his smile." She groaned. "He had dimples, Sadie. But I barely had time to see them between watching him eat and hearing him blab. God." She pinched the bridge of her nose and pulled into her neighborhood.

"Sorry to hear that. But hey, at least you went out. I sat home, downed a pint of Ben & Jerry's, and watched *My Bloody Valentine*. Not that I'm complaining, since my night was better than yours. But at least you tried to get into the spirit of love and kisses."

"I don't know. *My Bloody Valentine* is a classic. It's got hearts, right?"

"Spurting blood, but yeah." Sadie laughed. "Time to see who the mystery killer is. TTYL…Dateless in Seattle." Her unfortunate nickname for Ava.

"Love you, too, dork." TTYL—*Talk to You Later*. Who else but Sadie would use abbreviated text lingo during an actual phone call?

Ava pulled into her parking garage and a few moments later stepped into her neat, sensible condo. Before the market had skyrocketed, her aunt and uncle had invested in some lucrative properties. The lady who managed it was a little rough around the edges but very nice, and Ava had never had a problem since moving in two years ago.

She stepped onto her porch and looked out over Lake Union, enjoying the cold temperature. The moon glowed overhead, outlining Gas Works Park and the sparkling lake water. Stars shimmered above, and had she been more fanciful, Ava might have imagined herself and Matt in the romantic setting. He could keep her warm, kiss her senseless, and let her bask in his metrosexual charm and good looks.

Unfortunately, the only thing that came to mind in regards to Matt was the droning of bees. Incessant and annoying. Embracing her negativity, if only for a moment, she noticed the rising tree line, which would soon obscure the view. The condo board continued to fight the city to trim the trees, but they seemed perpetually locked in a bureaucratic stalemate. No view, a bad date, and now she felt chilled.

With a groan, Ava let herself back into the condo and closed and locked the balcony door. After making herself a quick cup of tea, she sat in her favorite reading chair, grabbed her reading glasses, and picked up the paperback she'd gotten halfway through. A treat from the usual e-books she hoarded in her expanding virtual library.

Why was it that sexy, available men appeared so effortlessly to the heroines in the books she read? The men acted bossy in bed but reasonably sensible outside of it. They apologized when necessary, usually after making a real blunder, and always put the heroine at the forefront of their decisions.

Ava sighed. For someone so proficient in helping others help themselves, she felt lacking in her own life. She put the book down and took her tea downstairs, where the bedroom and study were situated. In her study, her favorite room in the house, she picked up her five-year plan and studied it.

She'd found an amazing job with a consulting group led by her mentor, Dr. Dennis Foster, and counseled patients who needed her help. Professional success— check. Her parents remained out East, but she kept in regular contact with them and spent time with her uncle and cousins in Seattle. Family support—check. Her feelings about herself continued to expand not only into pride but pleasure. And her exercise routine kept her in top shape. Self-worth—*mostly* checked.

Because in the personal column, a healthy relationship with a man (not related) remained blank. No husband, no babies. And she'd turned the big three-oh.

Not an X, a check, or a filled block.

"I'm deficient. I know." It felt healthy to verbalize the truth. She put her plan down, wondering what had gone wrong tonight. Then again, she didn't want to be too hard on herself. No sense in getting discouraged.

So what if her first four dates had been disasters? She'd tried again by going out with Matt. He'd been better than her previous tries. He might have been nervous about a date on Valentine's Day, which added more pressure to be happily coupled-up. And if he just wasn't compatible, she could lay the blame on the online site she'd tried. Her first dip into the dating world after her big move to Seattle. Not that she hadn't had the occasional dinner with a male friend, but she hadn't had time to seriously mingle since she'd begun working with Dr. Foster. But this year, she'd been trying. Her five-year plan called for it.

And she had to face it. Ava had difficulties engaging in intimacy with the opposite sex. She tended to be self-contained, which wasn't a bad thing. But it made developing healthy relationships somewhat of a challenge.

To push herself out of her bubble, she'd made a list, and she was determined to stick to it.

The time had come to date, to explore a personal

relationship that might hopefully wake up her woman parts. God knew they hadn't been used in forever.

Pathetic, Ava. Even Sadie's had more bedroom action than you, and she's been off men for months!

She turned on her computer and searched the dating site she'd been using. She had several requests from men wanting to chat. A good sign. After answering a few messages, one from a friend of Elliot's, she made a date for next week, in hopes she might have more luck the next time around.

It couldn't be worse than tonight, could it?

Chapter 2

"IT WAS WORSE. WAY WORSE." AVA COULDN'T BELIEVE how badly the date had gone. Elliot, her workout partner and never-again-matchmaker, had a lot of explaining to do.

Elliot blinked. "Seriously? Chris was so sexy and smart. I thought for sure you two would hit it off."

As they walked next to each other on their treadmills Saturday afternoon, Ava took a good look around the gym, making sure she didn't know anyone around her. Elliot loved to gossip, and she needed to get a few things off her chest. But as a therapist, she knew well the value of discretion. Elliot…not so much.

"You have to keep this quiet. I think he lives around here."

"So what? Tell me. You know I'm dying to know how the date went."

Ava felt the sweat pouring off her and started to relax. In retrospect, dating Chris "Handsy" Handsman was funny. Kind of. "Well, remember how I said I liked men closer to my size? Not huge or muscle-bound, but slender and scholarly?"

"Dorky Indiana Jones. I get it."

She frowned. "Not exactly. I just feel more comfortable with men closer to my height. It's easier to handle them if they get out of control."

"No. Way." Elliot paused his machine and leaned

over his railing. "Chris Handsman, Mr. Zen, got grabby? Do you need me to beat his ass?"

She flushed. "Yes and no." Her cheeks rivaled the surface of the sun for heat. "He acted like the perfect gentleman. He picked me up at the door. We had a lovely dinner. He actually asked me about myself and listened when I answered. It wasn't all about him. Not like with Matt. But after he drove me home, he turned off the car and went straight for second base." She lowered her voice. "And I hadn't once signaled him to steal."

"I know it's bad when you're using baseball analogies." He started up his machine again.

"Not funny."

"But true." Elliot shook his head. "Damn. Never would have pegged Chris for being the aggressive type. You sure you're okay?"

"I'm fine. I told him *no* in no uncertain terms, and he pulled away. Then I asked him what the hell he thought he was doing."

"Ouch."

She glared at her cousin. "It seems *someone* told him I was up for some 'fun.'" This time she did use air quotes. And it felt *good.*

"Oh. Huh. Well." Elliot blinked, his green eyes a mirror for hers. "I might have said you were looking for a good man to break a dating dry spell. Someone impressive. Hung like a horse…"

"*Elliot.*"

"Kidding. About the hung part, I mean." Elliot paused. "So was he?"

"Was he what?"

"You know. Hung?"

"Like a toy poodle." When he goggled, she huffed. "How the heck would I know? The minute he tried going for my shirt, the date was O. V. E. R."

"You're so dramatic, Ava."

"Me?" She set her pace faster. "It's one thing if I'm getting hot and heavy with a guy and he gets a little handsy." At her cousin's grin, she glared. "Yes, I'm aware of the play on words. Chris Handsman was *handsy*. Ha-ha. Hilarious."

He chuckled, then coughed. "Sorry. Something stuck in my throat."

"Your foot, maybe," she muttered.

"Come on, Ava. You have to admit you need help."

"Not from him." She arched a brow and looked down her nose at him, because she knew how much he hated that expression. "Or you."

"Seriously? Of the two of us, who gets more dates?"

"Having sex and dating aren't the same thing."

She must have said that a little too loudly, because the blond giant walking past her stopped and stared.

"What?" she snapped, embarrassed and not needing extra male attention after her recent dating disaster.

"Not a thing," the giant said, his deep voice giving her shivers. He gave her a less-than-subtle once-over, then moved on.

She and Elliot watched him walk away. For some reason, she fixated on his tight, tight glutes, trying to be clinical about his physique instead of infatuated. *Totally not my type. Too muscle-y.*

"Now *that* is an ass." Elliot sighed. "Too bad he's straight."

"How do you know?"

"My spidey-sense tells me things." He wiggled his brows. "That, and Jerry hit on him last week and got denied. That sexy blond Adonis is strictly into *madge vaj*."

"What?"

"You know. Madge vaj—the magical vagina."

Ava wanted the floor to swallow her when the young woman next to her laughed out loud and said, "That's hilarious."

She leaned closer to her cousin's machine. "Would you *please* lower your voice? I know people here."

"Me too." Elliot laughed. "Oh, relax. You know, getting horizontal with someone like that would be good for you."

Together they glanced back at the hulkish blond lifting a bazillion pounds with a man whose features looked enough like him to be a relation. Something about the blond interested her. He wasn't classically handsome. But he was so…masculine. A face of hard planes and angles, and a body that he'd definitely put a lot of time into.

Warning bells shrieked.

"Nope." She shook her head. "Not my type. He's too macho. I can tell just from looking at him. Anyone who needs muscles that big is compensating for something else."

"Oh? Want to bet on the size of his package? I say you're wrong about it being tiny. That man is totally rocking the hammock."

"The what?"

He grinned. "The banana hammock? You know, his stretchy underwear to make room for all that…maleness."

She felt winded, and not from exercise, because at that moment the giant looked over at her and winked. "You only say stuff like that to embarrass me." She casually looked back at Elliot, pretending she hadn't just been ogling a sexy stranger.

"Yep. You need to loosen up, Ava. Live life. Enjoy a hot man without thinking ten steps ahead. Try tossing that five-year plan, just for a little bit."

"Why?"

"Because you're thirty and your girl parts are starting to prune. You know they'll fall off if you don't use them soon."

"Why? Why do you say things like this in public?" Not exactly professional for Dr. Ava Rosenthal to be discussing penis size and things falling off in public. She absolutely refused to look at the muscle guy again, because for some reason her girlie parts demanded she take a harder look at all that maleness. Banana hammock. *Jesus, Elliot. Stop putting weird thoughts in my head!*

She left her cousin laughing. The woman next to her started up a conversation with him, and she knew Elliot would have a new best friend before the afternoon ended. He was like that, sociable and charming and everyone's funny pal. It was no wonder he never had a free evening.

Unlike her. Ava went to the free weights and decided to try a few of the exercises she'd viewed on YouTube the night before. Her arms seemed less toned than she thought they should be for someone her age.

As she lifted some light weights and did a few repetitions, she stared into the mirror but didn't see herself. Instead she saw last night's mistakes all over again. *Damn.* Chris had been so wonderful. So how had he become such a dud?

She had a new date planned for tomorrow evening.

A get-together for wine at a casual bar in Queen Anne on a Sunday night. Not a date that screamed "sex me up," rather one where she and her partner could get to know each other, *not* become drunk, then go their separate ways to get ready for work come Monday morning. With any luck, this new guy, Charles, would prove interesting and hands off, at least.

She sighed.

"You're doing it wrong."

She jumped and nearly dropped her weights at that deep voice. "Excuse me?"

A glance at the mirror showed the blond man she'd been ogling—*casually assessing*—looming behind her. He looked even larger up close. Tall and broad and so…muscular.

She had to swallow a bit of drool. *Sue me for being human. He's attractive—and* still *not my type.* "Are you a trainer?"

"Nope. My brother is." He nodded to the male she'd accurately pegged as a relation. They both had strong faces, but the brother had black hair, not dark blond, like Mr. Nosy.

"You're not a trainer, yet you felt the need to correct my form?"

He opened his mouth and closed it, then cleared his throat. "Yeah, your form. Don't mean to be pushy, but if you keep doing it that way, you're not going to get the full effect from your reps."

"But you don't mean to be pushy."

He either hadn't caught her wry tone or he chose to ignore it. "You can also hurt yourself by straining. It's bad posture. Not like that. Like this."

He straightened his stance and plucked a weight out of her hand. The brief contact where he touched frazzled her. *So bizarre.*

Yet she saw the difference in what he did as opposed to what she'd been doing.

"See?" He didn't seem to work hard at all, pumping her tiny weight with ease. "You keep your arms shoulder-height up and parallel to the ground, then slowly bring them back to your sides. That maxes eccentric contractions, building tone." He frowned at the weight. "Does this feel heavy when you lift it?"

"Why? Is it too light and girlie for you?" *Just try to talk down to me, you big Neanderthal. After the week I've had…*

He bit his lip, but she saw his smile. Despite herself, she liked the expression on him. *What is wrong with me?*

"I was just going to say you should lighten the load when you start, to get your form right. If it's too heavy *before* your reps, it's too heavy, period." He placed the weight back into her hand and curled her fingers around it. She ignored the sizzle this time. "You need any help with this, ask for Gavin." He nodded to his brother. "He won't give you a hassle, and he knows what he's talking about."

That said, he walked away. *So not trying to hit on me then.* She felt foolish for her snappish tone when he'd only been trying to help. Then she felt foolish for feeling foolish. Nobody had asked him to come help her. Not her fault she felt a little prickly with his gender.

"Oh, this is all Elliot's fault," she steamed, then grabbed a lighter set of weights and finished her set, this time using the proper way to lift.

———

Landon watched the prickly woman finish her reps—the right way—and smiled. Man, talk about fine. If he'd been in the market for a woman, which he wasn't, he'd have snapped her up in a heartbeat. Long, dark brown hair, a slender body curved in all the right places, and those light green eyes that had shot daggers at him. He loved a woman with fire, and he could totally imagine bossing her around in bed. Man, he'd give it to her but *good*.

He sat and reached for a barbell to curl, knowing it was unwise to think about sex while wearing thin shorts in a gym. Hard-ons and respectability did not go hand in hand while exercising. He wasn't some dog in heat. Even though for her, he could have been. *Totally*.

She put the weights back and returned to the guy she'd been treadmilling next to, joining him and some young redhead while they did crunches. Damn. Ms. Correct Form really did have an outstanding rack…

"Yo. You angling for a job?" Mac Jameson smirked at him. The guy looked like a pro wrestler, rivaling Landon for size.

"You wish. You couldn't afford me, Jameson." He set down the weight.

Mac laughed. "Right. I can afford Gavin, though."

"Yeah, but he didn't take over running this place inside of a few weeks. I'd already be hiring and *firing*." He pointedly gave Mac a look.

"Asshole." Mac held out a hand, and Landon stood to shake it. "So. Helping out one of my regulars, eh?" They both glanced at the brunette, now laughing at the people with her.

"She was doing it wrong." Landon shrugged, hoping he came off as disinterested. "Gavin's busy, so I thought I'd help." He frowned. "You should hire another on-hand trainer."

"Thanks for your unasked-for opinion. You're right. I am glad I never hired you."

"I never said you wouldn't be glad, just that you couldn't afford me." Landon forced himself not to glance over when the woman and her friends stood. "So what's up?"

"Nothing. Just came over to tell you Gavin's off tomorrow and the early part of the week. I had someone cover the hours."

Landon nodded. "Thanks." Mac knew what he needed his brother for, and the guy was all too willing to help. "He needs some time. Had a rough go overseas."

"I feel you." Mac understood. If not for that knee, he'd still be in the Corps, like Landon. "You're a good brother. You need my help, just ask."

"Will do." They shook hands again, then Landon left. He and the family had made their preparations. Tomorrow Gavin would get the talking-to he desperately needed. Poor bastard.

———

At eleven o'clock Sunday morning, Landon waited while Gavin joined the family at their parents' house, settling into the couch next to Theo, who sat next to Hope. Across from them in a love seat sat his parents, Linda and Van. Landon remained standing.

"Hope *and* Theo? Now I know it's a special occasion," Gavin teased.

His sister and brother exchanged a worried glance.

He'd get to those two later. Hope, especially, wasn't scurrying away until after he'd talked to her about her recent life choices. But not now. Not when they had Gavin to deal with.

His mother and father waited for him to start. Good. He'd worried Linda would try to take charge. That real estate agent she was battling must have been giving her a hard time, because she looked tired. He'd check into that, too. Later. Now, time to begin.

"So, Gavin."

Gavin turned to him. "So, Landon."

Theo chuckled, then ceased when Landon glared at him. Landon turned back to problem brother number one. "We're here for *you*, asswipe."

"Landon." Linda sighed. "What he means—"

"What I mean"—Landon assumed control before his mother ruined the intervention with too much understanding and compassion. Gavin didn't need empathy, he needed a kick in the ass—"is you're turning into an alcoholic, and we're worried." Bam. Blunt, effective…and *go*.

Gavin groaned and covered his face before lowering his hands and sighing. Theo and Hope started talking at the same time. Apology, concern, confusion. His father watched everything, kicked back in the love seat, one leg crossed over his knee, his hands steepled in front of his face. He wore his serious pose while their mother fretted and told Gavin how sorry she was and how much she loved him.

"Enough," Landon barked. Silence descended. "Okay. Hope, you first."

"Seriously? This is an intervention for me?" Gavin chuckled, trying to laugh his way out of it.

"Shut it, Gavin. You have a problem. We all know it. Now man up and deal."

"Fuck you." Not so happy anymore.

"Gavin," their father warned.

"This is stupid."

"You drove home from the gym last night. Remember, I saw you before you left, and I smelled alcohol on your breath," Hope said in a soft voice. For all that she resembled their mother, Hope didn't seem to have that core of steel inside her. And yet, she did. So sweet and pleasant, she often took people aback with her keen wit and intelligence.

No dumb blonds in this family. Good girl, Hope. Landon nodded at her.

"Not true," Gavin disagreed.

"So you weren't drinking last night?" Landon pounced, always able to catch his brother in a lie.

Gavin flushed. "Sure, I had a beer or two. But not until I got home."

"That's crap," Theo said. "I've seen you drink at work before. And man, Gavin. That's just wrong. You're always telling me not to drink and drive or do drugs. How is it you can do it and it's okay?"

That seemed to shake Gavin, because Theo had always looked up to him. "It's not okay," Gavin said, his voice rough. "It's never okay."

"Then cut the bullshit," Landon ordered. "And don't try telling us it's nothing. You lost guys. Men you've considered brothers. Guys you've known for years. Your friends. They're dead."

"Don't," Gavin whispered.

"Landon," Linda cautioned. "Be gentle."

He talked over her. "They died. You didn't. End of story."

"How can you say that?" Gavin asked, distraught. They didn't talk about his time in the service because it hurt him. But not talking about it hadn't helped, either.

"Because it's true?"

Gavin narrowed his gaze. "Yeah, it's true. Good men are dead. What's your point?"

"That it wasn't your fault."

"I know that." Gavin snorted. "Jesus, I'm not a moron. I wasn't with them when the bomb went off."

"No, you were back at camp smokin' and jokin'," Landon said, being deliberately cruel. He met his father's gaze and was surprised by the understanding there.

"Fuck you." Gavin stood, his fists clenched. "I was recovering from a bullet wound, you asshole."

"Exactly." Landon stood toe to toe with his younger brother, aware they had roughly the same height, the same anger for the wrongs they'd witnessed, the lives they'd lost. But they chose to deal with those emotions differently. "So cut yourself some slack, Gav. Drinking yourself into oblivion won't bring them back."

Gavin growled, "I know that. This little meeting of yours is pointless." He turned to leave, and Landon grabbed him by the shoulder.

"Wait."

"*Get off me.*"

Hope's eyes grew wide.

Theo sank back into his seat, looking nervous. "No, Gavin. You have to stay and listen."

"Why? So Landon can be the hero?" Gavin snorted.

"Ease up, big brother. You're always right, we're always wrong. Better now?"

"Nope." Landon swung Gavin around and socked him in the stomach. Not hard enough to do any real damage, but enough to wind the bastard.

His brother sagged back onto the couch and rasped, "What the hell?"

"Landon, stop it," his mother cried.

"Oh my God. You hit him?" Hope gaped.

Theo blinked. "Remind me not to make you mad."

"Hit him again if he gets up," their father said. Cool, calm, collected Van Donnigan had just prescribed violence?

The entire family stopped and stared at him.

Their father knelt in front of Gavin, still clutching his stomach. "Gavin, Son, look at me."

Gavin glanced at his father, his gaze guarded. "What? Are you going to hit me now too?"

"Avoidance won't change the fact that you survived and others didn't. That you should have been with that convoy when it blew up. Nothing can change you being here, with family who love you. Who can see you hurting. Drinking yourself silly only hurts you, and possibly others. How would you feel if you ran over John Schaefer's daughter because you were too drunk to drive? Or Micky Duncan's widow? Or Luke Barkley's sister? Would that make them being gone any better?"

Landon felt like shit seeing his brother pale, his eyes well up, but the truth had to come out. *Fuck.* It took all he had to hold back his own tears. He'd lost men over there. Had known others in 2nd Battalion who hadn't made it back. And every Marine gone left a hole, wide and deep, inside him. But drinking the pain away didn't solve a goddamn thing. And fuck if he'd lose his brother to a bottle of booze after Gavin had survived so much worse.

Gavin glared through tears at his father. "You don't know—"

"Don't tell me I don't know," Van said in a low, intense voice. "I patched up my share of Marines when I was in, and I saw plenty of loss."

Gavin quieted. Hell, you could have heard a pin drop in the room. Their father had never talked about the troublesome parts of a career spent in the Navy, caring for men in combat. But they all knew.

"It's sad, and it's tough to get past. Heck, sometimes you never get past it. You just deal with it." Van smiled, but his eyes showed buried grief. "I get past it by being positive, meditating." He gave Landon a wry glance. "By singing 'Kumbaya,' if that's what it takes."

Obviously his dad had heard some of his complaints about that carefree attitude.

"But, Son, you can't bury your grief, or it will eat you alive." Van clasped Gavin's hand in his.

Linda remained silent, tears streaking down her cheeks.

"Too many guys were lost over there," Landon agreed, wishing he sounded less gritty and more in command of himself. "Unfortunately, a lot are still lost over here. PTSD, booze, pills. Afghanistan was hard, man. No denying that. And you saw a lot of shit we'll never know." And didn't want to know. Landon had been in awe of Gavin's talents in the Corps, his skill with a rifle. He just wished Gavin would take to the civilian world and let go of that bottled-up pain.

Way easier said than done.

"Wouldn't tell you anyway," Gavin tried to joke and wiped his eyes.

"Yeah, well, I'm not cleared to hear it, no doubt." Landon smiled back, an image filling his mind of lifeless Corporal Leonard in his finest dress blues. Of visiting the man's wife and newborn, paying respects months later. Leonard had never seen his daughter cut her first tooth, or his wife trying desperately to hold it together. *Compartmentalize,* he ordered himself.

Landon clenched his jaw, cleared his mind, then continued, not missing a beat. "Point is, little brother, we're home now. For good. No going back." He added a bit of levity. "Now you only have to take orders from me."

Van sighed. Theo and Hope smiled. Even their mother snorted and gave a tiny, relieved laugh.

Gavin shook his head. "You're not the boss of me. And if you slug me again, I'll give it right back." He sighed. "But I guess I know I'm not right. Not yet."

"Gavin, I know someone you can see." Linda crossed to sit next to him, scooting Theo out of the way.

"Geez, Mom. Just ask."

She ignored her youngest and hugged Gavin, stroking his hair. "She's very good. She helped your aunt and uncle get back on their feet, and you know how stubborn your uncle is. She deals with problems people can't solve on their own."

"Not yet, Mom. But thanks. I will see someone when I'm ready."

Gavin said all the right things, but Landon didn't trust that easy compliance. "You can't fill that void with drink until you're 'ready.'"

"I'm not an alcoholic."

"Yet," Landon countered.

Gavin glared. "I know, okay? I heard you."

"Then you should be fine with staying away from booze, period. At least until after you've seen some counselor and gotten help. 'Cause I'm telling you, man, you hurt or kill someone while you're drunk, and you for sure will never forgive yourself." Landon stared into his brother's eyes, brown gaze to gray, and saw Gavin's ugly realization, his haunting guilt and self-loathing, come to the surface.

"I understand," came the hoarse reply.

Landon felt as if a weight had lifted off him. Gavin was by no means healed, cured, or better. But he was finally on the road to right. They'd keep a close eye on him, and Landon would make sure the guy saw a therapist. One *he* determined would help. Just because some shrink had helped Aunt Beth and Uncle James didn't meant the doc could handle serious PTSD, because sure as shit Gavin had issues.

But one thing to check off Landon's to-do list, at least. Gavin had acknowledged he had a problem, and that was huge.

"Good. That wasn't nearly as tough as I thought it might be," Linda said, trying to be positive.

Everyone just looked at her.

"What? Can I help it that I like life to be easy?"

Hope snorted. "Whatever."

"What does *that* mean?"

Before his sister could get into it with their mother, Landon nodded for Gavin to distract the family matriarch. Gavin smiled and charmed Linda into laughing with him, proving what Landon had suspected—that Gavin did better with purpose, something to take his mind off dire memories. Gavin and Linda occupied, that left Hope to her own devices. He watched her stand and try to sneak away.

Landon pounced. "Your turn," he murmured and cornered her while Theo argued with their father about what to have for brunch.

He closeted them in their dad's study, noting the pictures of his father with different Marines and sailors throughout the years. Always wearing a smile. Always handling his business with a laugh to hide the pain, apparently. Respect for his old man had always been high, but it went way up with his dad's confession.

Hope shook her head. "I never thought about Dad hurting. He always seemed so happy in his pictures. And he's the most easygoing person I know. Now I feel bad."

"Don't. Dad's at peace with his time in the service." *Someday I hope I'll be.* For all the heartache Landon too had seen, for all the bad that was out there, he missed his brothers-in-arms. Some days he ached with the knowledge of what he'd really lost because of one lousy gunshot. The camaraderie, the hard work and sacrifice, the sense he was doing something for the greater good…

Greater good.

That idea he'd had. *Hmm.* He glanced at Hope and stilled. "What's that on your arm?"

She glanced down. "Huh?"

"Is that a bruise?" His blood pressure shot through the roof at what that might mean. When she flushed, he had to force himself not to drag her closer and ask what the fuck she thought she was doing with her life. Then he said screw it and slowly, distinctly, asked, "What the fuck are you doing with your life?"

Chapter 3

HE'D ASKED IN THE CALMEST VOICE HE'D EVER USED with his sister. Because he didn't want to scare her. He wanted to scare the asshole who'd been manhandling her.

"Oh, please. That tone won't work with me. Save it for Gavin."

He put a hand on her shoulder, and she rounded on him. "Don't you dare hit me, you big bully."

"Jesus, Hope." He scowled. "Don't be stupid. I'm not going to hit you. Now tell me how you got that."

She pulled away and crossed her arms over her chest in the same pose of militant rebellion she'd always used to get her way. Now no longer a cute little towhead with dimples, she'd grown into a beautiful young woman—with dimples.

"It's not your business." In a less lofty tone, she added, "For your information, Greg and I are done."

"I thought you ended with him last week."

She sighed. "So did I. But apparently our breakup was confusing to him. We had words." She rubbed the small blue mark on her forearm. "It's not a big deal."

"He left *a bruise* on your arm." Landon planned to shove Greg's fat head up his ass.

"But that's all he left." She frowned. "Trust me. I'm not going to let some guy punch me and get away with it."

"He punched you?"

"No, no." She hurriedly slapped a hand over his mouth.

"Would you shut up before Mom or Dad come in here? I'm fine, Landon. I solved this problem all on my own. And for the last time, Greg wasn't physically abusive."

He caught her slight emphasis on *physically* and tugged her hand away. "So he was emotionally abusive?" *Totally going to maul the guy.*

"Controlling, more like. I ended it with him. Happy?"

"No. He was one in a long line of Gregs. Damn, Hope. I've been back for eight months, and in that time, this is the fourth dickwad you've dated. You're beautiful, kind, intelligent. What gives?" Tears swam in her eyes, and he felt like a heel. "Hell. Don't cry."

"You think I don't know I'm messed up? I have no idea why I'm attracting such losers. Maybe it's my d-dating p-profile." She hiccupped. "I know. Let's ask Mom. She can tell you *exactly* what's wrong with me."

Totally not going there. He blew out a breath. "Look. You want me out of your business?"

"Yes."

That idea he'd been toying with firmed in his mind, especially in light of Hope's loser exes, then overhearing that sexy brunette at the gym talking about some *handsy* guy. "I'll keep out of your business if you learn how to defend yourself."

"What?"

"I'm going to give self-defense lessons." At the gym if Jameson was on board. And this was totally something he could see the guy getting behind. "You promise to take them. I'll stay out of your love life."

"What love life?" she muttered, then seemed to consider the idea. "I don't know…"

"You don't take the lessons, I'll personally grill every

single guy you even look sideways at. And I have nothing but time." He smiled through his teeth. "I'm a civilian now, remember?"

"As if I could forget," she snapped. Then she frowned,
biting her lip like she used to do as a kid.

He thought her adorable but knew smiling at her
would only get her angrier. So he waited.

"Okay, fine. I take your stupid class—you keep out
of my life." She waved at the door. "You want to fix
someone else? Go fix Theo. He's thinking about joining Dad in pharmaceutical sales. Theo—stuck behind a
desk, selling things." Pause. "With Dad."

For their hyper-ass brother, probably not a good fit.
Theo's relationship with their father resembled the one
Hope had with their mother. Contentious, but in a weird,
laid-back way. Only their father could argue while
calmly smiling. "Oh boy."

"Yeah." Hope kissed him on the cheek, then gave him
a purple nurple, twisting his nipple.

He shoved her hand away. "Ow. Cut it out. That hurts."

"Sure thing, big brother." She laughed at him before
dancing out of the office.

Friggin' family. He rubbed his chest, annoyed yet
amused. Then he bellowed for Theo.

Sunday evening, Ava sat in the crowded restaurant with
Charles and smiled. So far so good. They'd grabbed
the last two seats at the bar, but the low conversation
and background music made it surprisingly easy to
hear. He'd waited for her to order her own wine, then
ordered his based on her opinion, since he was more of

a beer man. He worked in finance downtown but hadn't bragged about himself or the sporty, expensive convertible she'd seen him exit before entering the bar.

"It's so nice to meet someone who can carry a conversation." He smiled and toyed with his wineglass, keeping eye contact.

How refreshing to talk with a man who liked to converse, and who stared at more than her breasts. Ava had worn a light green sweater with a collar that brushed her neck, so no cleavage to give the wrong impression of wanting sex on the first date. Not that cleavage should mean that, but she'd found with a few of her dates that dressing sexy didn't seem to end well.

She'd also worn jeans and cute black boots to keep her look casual.

Charles had shown up looking, well, dapper. Dark jeans, a light blue button-down shirt, and a tan sport coat. He had styled, short black hair and nice brown eyes. *Nice.* The perfect word to describe him.

He finished a story about dealing with his neighbor's feral cat, which made her laugh. She added *funny* next to *nice* and *dapper.*

"So no cats for you?" she asked him.

"I have an older tabby. Rex is comfortable being king of my castle." Charles grinned.

She liked that he preferred Charles to Chuck or Charlie. A bit of formality never hurt anyone. Ava continued to enjoy her date, excited that she seemed to have found someone compatible for friendship at least.

"How about you?" he asked.

"Oh, no pets for me. Not yet."

"I keep thinking about getting a dog, but I don't

feel like I'm home enough to give it enough attention. Rex likes me best when I've fed him, then let him be." Charles chuckled. "Say, would you like to get anything to eat?"

They ordered a cheese and fruit plate to share, then he asked, "So what's it like being a psychologist on the dating scene? I'd think it's difficult not to overanalyze everything." He gave a self-deprecating smile. "Like me talking about the financial market with my sister over family breakfast. I have to do my best not to tell her and her husband how to invest. I drove my brother-in-law nuts before Shelly told me to stop. Oh, and he's in banking, by the way." He chuckled. "Took us all a while to get along."

She smiled. "It's not easy, especially if you love your job."

"Yeah."

"I keep telling myself to just relax and not read into things."

"Like?"

"Just because a man compliments himself does not mean he's a closet narcissist." Except for Matt, who she'd swear was. "It might just mean he's confident in his abilities. And confidence is a good thing to have."

"I see your point." He paused. "Trying to remember if I said I liked myself or not."

She laughed with him, then froze when she locked gazes with a man who stood directly behind him. The bossy giant from the gym. *Hell.*

His eyes narrowed. He glanced from her to Charles, then he smiled and settled onto his stool—right next to Charles.

"Problem?" Charles asked, not looking at Bossy Guy because he was turned toward her.

Since the restaurant had been filled with oenophiles eager for an extended happy hour before they'd arrived, they'd seated themselves at the only spot available. The place hadn't emptied since, and with nowhere else to sit, she and Charles had to remain in place, now next to a nosy, bossy, sexy—*strike that*—giant.

"Not at all," she said smoothly. "Just thought I saw someone annoying from my gym. But it wasn't *her*." *Deliberately not giving Muscle Man any importance to my night. Nope. Not looking at him at all.*

"Oh? Where do you work out?"

"Jameson's Gym. It's near my office in Green Lake."

"Nice. I go to a gym across the street. It suits my needs, and it's close to home." Which answered the question of where he lived. Queen Anne. Another good point in Charles's favor.

"Is it too forward to ask where you call home?" He grinned. "Don't feel like you have to give me an exact address. I'm hoping for a general area. You are from Seattle, yes?"

She nodded. "And you're asking because…?"

He sighed. "Online dating is hard. I once thought I'd hit it off with a wonderful woman, and it turned out she lived in Idaho. Mind you, we'd already gone out a few times and she'd never mentioned it. She was in town for a vacation and wanted to find someone to fill her down time, apparently."

"Not me. I'm never on vacation." They both laughed. "I'm definitely from Seattle. I live in Queen Anne too, as a matter of fact." Nothing dangerous about sharing that. A lot of people lived in Queen Anne.

"Something else we have in common." He lifted his glass, and she met it with her own. "Queen Anne and a love of conversation." They both sipped outstanding local wine. "Now how do you feel about architecture?" he teased.

She smiled. What a lovely—*drat.* Bossy giant gave her a funny look over Charles's shoulder. She deliberately ignored him, though it wasn't easy. "I can learn to love architecture."

After a surprisingly interesting talk about the Ballard Library and Chapel of St. Ignatius, she dug into the cheese plate the waiter delivered, surprised to find herself hungry.

They discussed different cheeses as well. "Fan of the creamy or nutty ones?" he asked as they devoured the plate.

"Both. I love Manchego, but I'm a Brie fan too. I didn't care for it when I was younger, though. My cousins are big foodies and like to host a monthly cheese and wine party." Well, Sadie had done it once then ditched the idea, but Elliot liked to charm new conquests with his knowledge of food and wine pairing. Said it made him look more sophisticated. "So you like cheese. What do you do for fun?"

The blond guy rolled his eyes.

What? The question wasn't creative enough for him? She focused on Charles's answer.

"I'm kind of boring."

Behind him, the blond guy nodded. She wished he wasn't so much taller than Charles. Then she might not be able to see him.

"…about reading." *Focus, Ava.* Charles continued, "And I'm a sucker for a quarterly prospective on my stocks." He laughed, and she joined him, though she secretly started to think Charles *was* kind of boring.

As the night wore on, she found she liked Charles because he seemed bland, safe. He acted polite, nice, and kind. But nothing about him made her want to jump his bones. A suitable candidate for life partner to a professional like herself. He knew how to make small talk, seemed comfortable in public, and didn't try to assert his authority over her. So far so good.

She took a surreptitious glance at the annoying yet attractive man drinking beer just behind him. Why did she continue to find herself interested in someone obviously wrong for her?

She thought about asking Sadie about her feelings, then thought the better of it. Sadie remained in her man-hating phase, despite her protests to the contrary. And Elliot had never met a man he didn't love. She wasn't sure she should ask him.

She took another hard look at Charles as he insisted on paying the bill. He fit all her physical requirements—to a T. He stood maybe an inch taller than her own five foot six, had a slender build but a manly feel. Nothing wussy about Charles. His confidence and sense of self-worth had been clearly evident all night without verging on arrogance.

All in all, a perfect late evening companion. Or he would have been, if the blond giant hadn't been making odd gestures behind Charles's back, causing her to wonder if she should look deeper into her date than the surface perfection he'd presented.

"I hate to leave, but work tomorrow, you know."
Charles shrugged.

"I know what you mean." She smiled. "I had a wonderful time, Charles."

He brightened. "Me too. Would you consider dinner some evening when you're free?" He handed her a business card. "You have my email, but here's my number." He gave a sheepish grin. "I confess I wrote my cell on the back earlier, hoping you'd be as lovely in person as you are online. You totally are."

"How sweet." She was touched.

Blond Guy sounded like he was choking on something. If only.

"Dinner sounds great." She pumped enthusiasm into her tone, because she meant it. Charles had fit all her criteria. No reason for her to feel let down by her night with him. She inwardly gave the blond giant a scowl while still smiling at Charles. No, no reason at all.

"Can I kiss you good night?" Charles asked. A gentleman to his bones.

"Please." She met his kiss on her cheek and blushed. "I look forward to our dinner."

"Me too." He looked flushed and brushed back a strand of hair that slipped over his forehead. "Can I walk you to your car?"

"I'm parked right next to yours." Which sat directly out front thanks to the timely departure of two couples earlier. "But I need to use the facilities before I leave. Go on without me. I'll call you later in the week."

He nodded. "Sounds great. Have a good day tomorrow, Ava."

"You too." She watched him leave, ignored the blond

guy staring at her with what seemed to be a smirk, then searched for the ladies' room. Once finished, she had every intention of leaving and not looking back.

But she paused next to the blond guy and, noting the still-open seat, she sat.

"You." She glared at him.

"Ava, huh? Pretty name." He turned in his seat and grinned down at her while guzzling a beer.

"And you are?"

"Landon." His grin nearly did her in, because his whole face lit up with joy, making it seem as if he'd brought the sun into the darkened restaurant. "But I'm sure there are a few other names you'd like to call me."

"What is your problem?"

"Me? I'm good." Before she could lay into him, he added, "But you're not."

She blinked. "What's *my* problem, besides you?"

"You and Boring Guy."

She frowned. "That's not a nice thing to say."

"Yeah, I'm not known for nice. But I'm honest. Honey, Charles is not the guy for you."

"Excuse me, but Charles was a perfect gentleman."

A jazz band started playing in the corner, making it harder to hear, so he leaned closer. Unfortunately, she got a good whiff of his cologne, and it went straight to her head. Just her luck Landon smelled like a dream.

She cleared her throat. "And my name is not 'honey.' It's Ava." She would have added *Dr. Ava Rosenthal* in a haughty tone, except Landon's breath brushed her ear, and her entire body locked up. Tight.

"Ava, you need someone who makes you hot. Boring is no good. Not for someone like you."

She'd swear his lips touched her, and her system seemed to go haywire. Her breasts tightened, she got a funny feeling in the pit of her stomach, and she clenched her thighs together, feeling a lower torso shiver from out of nowhere.

"Like me?" She felt weak and slowly pulled back.

Except that put her at eye level with the man a breath away. He was so close she saw gold flecks in the irises surrounding pinpoints of focus, directed at her. His cheekbones were high, his nose straight, arrogant, his chin square. Manly. His firm lips parted when he inhaled, as if breathing her in.

"Like you." He leaned closer and kissed her with the softest press of his lips, then pulled back as if he'd never been there. "Damn." He drained the rest of his beer then asked for his tab. After taking a deep breath, he let it out and turned to her once more. Landon stared at her mouth, then at her top, still visible because she hadn't yet zipped up her coat.

Despite the sweater that covered her from neck to waist, she felt almost naked as his gaze roamed her breasts before lazily working back up to her face. "When you come back to the gym, ask for me."

"Wh-what?" She put a finger over her tingling lips. "Why?"

He chuckled. "Suspicious little thing, hmm?" He pulled at her hair, tugging on the long strands.

She frowned and tugged it back.

His smile grew. "We're thinking of starting a self-defense class at the gym. It's a good thing for women in the dating scene, especially."

"To protect them from pawing men?" She glanced at her hair, then his hand.

His eyes glowed with mirth. "You should always know how to protect yourself." He leaned closer. "But never from a guy like me."

Especially *from a guy like you. Who can make a woman's knees weak when she's sitting—all from a kiss that's barely there?* If she hadn't been keeping an eye on her glass all night, she'd suspect she'd been drugged.

"I'm all about protecting people, honey." He paused. "Ava."

She hated that she loved the way he said her name, all growly and deep. "Landon." She stood, more than ready to leave. Unfortunately, the bartender slid him his bill. Before she could walk around him, Landon signed the slip and walked with her out the door.

She paused at her car and frowned at him. "Just why, exactly, should I believe you're a good guy who only wants to protect people?" She planted her hands on her hips, waiting for enlightenment. Anything to explain why she didn't want this man to go, not yet.

What a great question. Because right now, Landon could think of nothing better than bending pretty Ava over her car and fucking the hell out of her. Totally not what a modern, self-respecting woman wanted to hear. Or what a man in control of himself wanted to feel.

Thank God for tight jeans.

"I mean, you kissed me in there." She pointed to the bar behind him. "Without asking."

"What douche asks a woman who's into him if he can kiss her?" Landon snorted, thinking about what a pussy *Charles* had been. *Can I kiss you?* Puh-lease. Maybe a domme wanted a guy to beg. Somehow Ava didn't strike him as the leather-and-crop type. Though he'd kill to see her wearing something black and shiny. Or nothing at all.

Down boy.

"A *gentleman*," she emphasized, clearly not labeling him with that moniker, "would ask before forcing his attentions."

He stilled. "You saying I forced that peck on the lips?"

"N-no." She blushed, and man, she was hot as hell with her cheeks that color. It made him wonder if the rest of her would turn that pink. Like the tips of her breasts, her soft belly, her pretty little pussy...

God, he hadn't been this hard since his first time getting laid. Talk about some off-the-charts chemistry. He knew she'd felt it, because she still looked as dazed as he felt.

"So I was right, then. Only a moron would ask if he could kiss a pretty lady."

She frowned. "That's not the point."

"What is the point?" Was it wrong that he liked messing with this woman? He knew a little about her from what he'd overheard douchey Charles asking her. And he knew how she tasted.

Like melting vanilla ice cream over a hot apple pie. So delicious, and so perfect together. Her taste, his lips.

"Why are you looking at me like that?"

He blinked and tried to appear innocent, not like the sex fiend he'd become. "How am I looking at you?"

She blushed again. "Never mind."

The pull between them continued to deepen. Now if she'd just look lower, she'd see exactly what he'd been feeling for her. But the circumspect woman who liked a good Syrah, Manchego cheese—whatever the hell that was—and boring, wussy guys wouldn't look past his chin.

Smart girl.

He grinned.

"What are you smiling at?"

"You're pretty."

She blinked. "Thank you?"

"You're welcome?"

She covered her return grin with a frown, but he'd seen it all the same. "You never answered my question."

"Why am I trustworthy?"

"Yes."

"Well, you know I'm not some random guy. I'm Landon Donnigan. My brother works at Jameson's Gym, where we're both members."

"So serial killers can't work out?"

"Ah, sure. I guess." Hadn't she said she was some kind of counselor or something? Woman certainly had a brain, which only added to her sex appeal. The wind blew, and strands of her dark brown hair wisped over her face, covering those high cheekbones most models would kill for. But it was those light green eyes that had first captivated him. So soft yet profound, inviting him to look deeper while consigning him to hell because he wouldn't ask before doing it.

"I hate to turn to stereotype, but you're acting very blondish right now." She sighed. "Can't keep a thought in that pretty head, can you?"

So condescending. Yep. His erection refused to quit. He chuckled and invaded her space, pleased when she tensed. Then he gently tucked away that strand of flyaway hair behind her ear. And man, was it soft, smelling like flowers.

"Okay, Dr. Ava."

"Actually, it's Dr. Rosenthal." She lifted her pert nose.

He stroked her cheek, pleased when she trembled, yet she never backed down. "Well, Doc, I'm a Marine, or I was before a bullet took me out of commission. So you see, I live to serve and protect. Now I work for a logistics company protecting my boss's ass from inept employees."

"That's…" She blew out a breath. "That's not very flattering to your employees."

"Not mine. I just work there." He paused for effect. "Nah. Kidding. The guys and gals I work with are great. The ones who aren't I already fired."

"You have a controlling nature, don't you?" She narrowed her eyes. "Were you an officer or enlisted in the Army?"

No doubt she said that to needle him. *Army?* "Marine Corps, *honey.*"

She glared.

"Oh, sorry. *Doctor* Honey. So, was I an officer or enlisted? What do you think?"

"Officer. You're exceedingly bossy."

"You noticed." He sighed. "You *do* care."

She shook her head at him, but she was grinning again. "You really are obnoxious. And you're not even trying, are you?"

"Not yet. You should see me when I'm on a roll."

The wind blew again, and her teeth chattered.

"Okay, Doc. Enough flirting. Get in your car before you freeze your fine ass off."

She scowled, then opened and closed her mouth, as if not sure whether to be annoyed or flattered. He had mentioned her *fine* ass, after all. She gave a sniff, stalked around to the driver's side, and let herself in the vehicle.

She drove away in her sensible, compact little Prius, but he'd bet money she'd looked in her rearview at him before turning the corner.

Landon blew out a breath and wondered what the hell he was doing. He had no time for woman problems. Especially not the kind with an advanced degree and trouble written all over her. But he hadn't been able to get the gorgeous woman out of his head since seeing her at the gym. Then running into her at his favorite bar? What were the odds? It was like fate planting her in his sights. Because that dud of a date drooling all over her couldn't keep up.

Charles "I'm Boring Myself Silly" had no game. Not like Landon. Marines came, saw, and conquered. And he'd just decided he had a need to see what kinds of games Dr. Honey liked to play...between the sheets.

Chapter 4

AFTER THREE DAYS OF MARRIAGE/IDENTITY CRISES, AVA felt ready to call the week over, and she'd only reached Wednesday. Tired from expending so much energy on her patients, she de-stressed with a terrific aerobics class at the gym. Elliot joined her, sweating alongside the many women and men crowding the room. Heck, they'd had to kick out a few people for safety reasons.

The class ended, and they finished putting the steps away.

"Great class, Maggie." Elliot tussled the instructor's golden curls.

She mock frowned at him, always happy to see her favorite person in Intermediate Step. "Hands off, Elliot. Or I'll get my husband to geld you."

Elliot held up his hands. "Easy, now. Just paying you a compliment." He paused. "But if you want Mac to rough me up, you know, to set an example, I'll take one for the team."

Maggie chuckled. Her husband owned the gym, and he'd been Elliot's longtime unrequited crush since he'd first joined the place. Considering Mac had married the gorgeous, always in-shape Maggie, *and* the guy was straight, Elliot had never stood a chance. Didn't stop him from flirting though.

"One of these days somebody is going to rearrange

your handsome face," Ava said as she dragged him away from a laughing Maggie. "Then what will you do?"

"Find a hot doctor to fix me up?"

She tried not to laugh. "Seriously. You need to be more careful." If anything ever happened to Elliot, she didn't know what she'd do. She didn't have many people she could confide in, and he meant the world to her. He was her best friend, and of all her cousins—though she'd never admit it to Sadie—her favorite.

"Take it easy, Ava. I only play around here because I can." He grew somber. "Trust me. I know when to tone it down. This might be a city full of gay parades and rainbow flags, but not everyone's so enlightened." He wrapped an arm around her shoulders and dragged her down the hallway toward the front desk. "But just when you think we're a troubled city full of haters, Jameson's Gym comes through."

He grabbed a pen and shoved it into her hands, then nudged her toward a clipboard with a signup sheet. "What's this?"

"I thought you academic types knew how to read." He ran his finger under the words *Free Self-Defense Class.* "After hearing about you and Handsy, I think this is perfect timing. We're signing Sadie up too." He signed up his sister, then slid the clipboard toward her.

She signed up as well, then asked the girl behind the desk, "Who's giving the class?"

"Does it matter?" came the familiar voice haunting her dreams.

She jumped and spun around, her heart racing as much from shock as from Landon Donnigan's nearness. "Can you please *not* sneak up behind me?" Landon stood in gym shorts and a sweaty shirt that clung to him like a second skin. The man really did too much bulking up. She could see prominent muscles bulging all over the place.

At the thought, she felt overheated, refusing to look down past his neck. Unfortunately, she kept remembering Elliot talking about banana hammocks and maleness. A glance back at her cousin showed him similarly enthralled. He wiggled his brows and mouthed, *Big banana*.

"Ava?"

She whirled back around, blocking her cousin making size gestures with his hands. "You know, just once, it would be nice if you started a conversation the normal way."

Landon crossed his arms over his chest. "Oh?"

"Yes. Like this." She lowered her voice, pretending to be him. "Gee, hi there. I'm Landon. I'll be giving the gym's self-defense class. But don't worry. I know what I'm doing. I'm not here to boss everyone around. I just want to help. I'm every woman's *protector*."

Elliot moved next to her, watching her and Landon without blinking. She totally didn't trust the smirk on his face.

Landon grinned. "You know, I like you doing me." He paused to let that sink in, and when it did, her cheeks felt hot enough to impose third degree burns. "I sound pretty manly. Not at all...*boring*...like some guys we know."

She narrowed her eyes at his dig at Charles.

"'Every woman's protector.' I like it. Can I quote you on that?" he teased.

"Oh, I've got a quote you can use."

"Hi there," Elliot interrupted and stuck out a hand. "I'm Elliot, Ava's favorite cousin."

"Favorite?" Ava snorted. "Really?"

Landon shook his hand. "Landon Donnigan. My brother and I are giving the self-defense class over the next few weeks."

"Wait. Donnigan? So Gavin is your brother. Oh, I see the resemblance now." Elliot smiled. "Gavin's great. He helped me put on some serious muscle."

"Good for you. My brother's not half bad when it comes to building up others," Landon said while his gaze remained on Ava. Particularly, on her legs.

"I'm still stuck on the word 'favorite,'" she said, trying to gather her wits. Standing so close to Landon made it hard to breathe. Probably an allergy to arrogance, she thought with a bit of snark.

"Now what's that smile, I wonder?" Landon mused.

"Oh, that's her 'I just insulted you in my mind' look," Elliot explained. "I get it all the time."

"You're getting it now," she said, hoping she didn't look as red as she felt.

"I thought I told you to come see me," Landon said.

"I'm seeing you right here."

He just watched her. "Scared you away the other night, huh?" He shook his head. "Thought you were made of stronger stuff."

"Yo, Landon. I need you for a sec," Mac called.

Mr. Tight Ass turned and walked away before she could set him straight.

The nerve.

Before she could go after him and give him the piece of mind she had left after her exhausting day, Elliot dragged her to the side.

"What. Is. Going. *On?*" In a lower, yet still excitable

voice, he whispered, "That hot hunk of man was eye-fucking you all *over* the place."

"*Elliot.*"

"I know what I'm talking about. While you were doing your best to cut him down to size, he was staring at your breasts, ass, legs. I felt embarrassed just being near you two. So much heat." He fanned himself. "Now what the hell did he mean about 'the other night'?"

She grabbed his waving hand to hold him still. "You're imagining things."

"Am I?" He glared. "What have you been keeping from me, Dateless in Seattle?"

Great. Now Sadie had him calling her that. "Elliot, I'll tell you later. Not here." Where Landon might over-hear how she'd nearly lost her mind over a whisper of a kiss. For the past three nights she'd been dreaming about him naked, for goodness sake. And her dreams had nothing on the flesh-and-blood man parading around in those shorts. She'd never been drawn to muscular men before, and legs weren't exactly her thing. She preferred a big brain over hamstrings and glutes. But with Landon…

"You'll tell me now. There's no longer trust between us." Elliot sighed. "You've hurt me by holding back, Dr. Rosenthal. I'm feeling psychologically damaged. I think I might need therapy."

She pinched the bridge of her nose. *Such* a drama queen. "Fine. I saw Landon when Charles and I went out Sunday. Happy now?"

"And?" Elliot planted his hands on his hips.

"And nothing."

"Liar. *And?*"

Her cousin should have gone into psychology.

He could read just about anyone, her especially well. "Elliot. Come on."

He grew louder. "*And?*"

"And Landon flirted a little. There might have been a kiss, kind of."

"*A kiss?* So?"

"So that's it."

Elliot expelled a frustrated breath. "So does he have a big or small banana? Come on, Dateless. Share the good stuff. *Rawr.*" He clawed the air by her face.

She wanted to slap him. "Oh my God. You are *so* annoying." She walked around him and headed for the bathroom. "I'll see you tomorrow for dinner at Sadie's. Now go away."

"You'd better. And you'll talk or I'll make you," he added in his best aggressive voice.

She darted into the bathroom and waited a few minutes before thinking it safe to return to the gym. Once back in the main area, she spotted her cousin talking with Gavin and holding his gym bag in hand, heading toward the front door. Thank God.

A glance around the gym showed the object of her nightmares still talking to Mac by the aerobics room. She wondered if she could leave before he caught her again. Would that be cowardly though? It offended her that he thought she'd been avoiding him. She had, because he confused the heck out of her. But he didn't need to think that. She truly had been busy with work this week.

Landon saw her and raised a brow. *Hey, that's* my *move.* She frowned. Mac saw her and smiled, then stepped away to talk to someone else while Landon stalked back to her side.

No doubt about it. The man moved with purpose. Walk in front of him and be mowed down.

He stopped in front of her. "Wonder of wonders. You're still here. I thought for sure you would have hightailed it home by now." Again with the smirking.

"Okay, buddy. Explain that crack."

"We're buddies now? I'm moved. Truly." Landon put a big hand over his nonexistent heart.

"Why are you being so annoying today?"

"I'm never annoying. I'm honest, and, as I've come to find out, very few people can handle the truth."

"I'm way too tired to deal with you today."

Before she could add *I'm leaving*, he grabbed her by the arm and gently pulled her close. "It's obvious you've been avoiding the gym. Because of me."

"And you sound proud of that fact because…?"

"Because I'm getting to you."

"Like salmonella. Yes, you're pervasive in a germy kind of way." She ignored his low laughter. "For the record, I have been extremely busy with patients this week. My not being here had *nothing* to do with you."

"Hmm."

"What?"

"Your eye is twitching. Is that a tell?"

"Tell? I'll tell you something, mister, I—"

"When are you going out with Charles again?"

O-kay. Change in subject. "What?"

He shrugged. "You know. Charles. The poodle of the finance world. Pat him on the head and he'll roll over for you, might even beg."

She wasn't following. "I'm confused. You don't like poodles?"

He crossed his eyes. "Are you going out with him again or not?"

"Why is that your business?"

He paused. "I guess it's not. But I think it's a little tacky of you to date me and this guy at the same time."

She frowned. "We're not dating."

"Oh good. So it's just me?"

"No. I meant, *you and I*, we're not dating. And besides, dating doesn't imply anything intimate. It's okay to date more than one person at a time, *if* we were even dating, which we're not."

He gave her a sad look she didn't buy, because his deep brown eyes were still filled with amusement. "Our bonding over jazz and your wussy date meant nothing to you? I'm crushed."

Her lips twitched despite herself. "Are you done?"

"Ah. There's that smile." He tucked her hand in the crook of his massive arm and walked her back to the signup sheet. "Okay, I'm done harassing you. Mostly. So starting Friday evening, we run a three-part self-defense program. Come to the class. In all seriousness, the stuff we're going to teach could really help if you get into a problem." He gave her a look.

"What now?"

"Hell." He blew out a breath. "I overheard you last week talking about some handsy guy. So I'm just going to say it. If you're going out with Chuck again, make sure you meet in a public place."

"Thank you, *Dad.*" She tried to tug her hand free from the rocks he called biceps and a forearm, but he gripped her fingers and wouldn't let go. "His name is Charles," she corrected. "But I'm so glad to have a big strong man around to tell me what to do. However have I managed myself for the past thirty years without you?" She batted her eyelashes, aware she was interacting with Landon in a way unlike the manner she typically used when speaking with men.

Not cut and dried or soberly attentive. She thought she might be actually…flirting.

To her bemusement, she hadn't had such a fun conversation since the last time they'd traded barbs.

"Thirty, huh? Not bad, Doc. You have the legs of a twenty-year-old."

"You're a jerk, you know that?" Inwardly preening at his compliment, she still felt offended on behalf of thirty-year-olds everywhere. "I love being thirty." *And single. And childless.* Sigh.

Her five-year plan continued to tick away.

"I love being thirty-four." He shrugged. "What I don't love is wasting time in the gym." He glanced around. "You done working out?"

"I ducked into the bathroom to avoid my loud cousin. But I think he went home."

"If you hadn't been avoiding him, what would you have been doing?"

She sighed. "Toning up. My triceps need work." She glanced from her scrawny arms to his, envying his strength.

"Come with me."

Twenty minutes later, bent over an exercise ball, she finished doing a set of T raises. "My back is on fire."

"And you're all sweaty." He grinned. "I like the look, Doc."

"Do you think you might call me Ava?"

"I'll think about it." He paused. "Doc."

Gavin Donnigan joined them. "Um, Landon, you seem to be doing my job." Gavin looked like a dark-haired Landon, but with gray eyes and a slightly leaner build. He smiled. "Hello there. Need some help with your routine?"

"I'm good, thanks." She put the weights down and groaned as she started to stand, then gasped when Landon lifted her to her feet. "Warn a girl, next time."

"You don't weigh a thing."

Nice to hear, but his hands on her waist were doing odd things to her insides. She stepped back, flustered, and saw his brother grinning at them. "Actually, Gavin, I could use—"

"We're busy. Go away." Landon nudged his brother in the opposite direction. "I think Michelle wants you."

Gavin glanced over his shoulder and groaned. Ava couldn't blame him. She'd talked to Michelle before. The salon owner seemed nice enough, until she caught the scent of a single man in his prime. Then she followed the scent of fresh meat and attacked like a rabid she-shark. At the moment, the woman was shooting Ava some unfriendly looks.

"Oh hell," Gavin complained, seeing the woman coming their way. "Block for me, Bro. Please? She's stressing me out, and I'm trying to be all zen. Hey, if you'd rather I went out with her *to a bar* or something I—"

"I'll handle her," Landon growled. He stared down at Ava. "You, wait here."

She watched him walk away, wondering what he'd do if she just left. "He likes to give orders."

Gavin snorted. "Does he. But don't blame the Corps.

He's been like that my entire life. The Marine Corps just gave him an outlet to be the controlling jackass he's always been."

"I hear you." They watched Landon guide Michelle to one of the female trainers, her grabby, skeletal fingers clutched around his meaty forearm. "Michelle seems to like him well enough."

"More power to her," Gavin said. He looked down at her. Though average in height, around these Donnigans, Ava felt tiny. "But I get the impression big brother has his sights set somewhere else."

She didn't want to answer him, because honestly, she had no idea what Landon wanted. He wasn't her type. And she'd never been one for casual hookups. Maybe it was time to put her cards on the table and get him to commit to an answer or two.

She and Gavin chatted about the weather and the growing crowd at the gym. Those still working on their New Year's resolutions hadn't faded into the woodwork yet, but Gavin thought it was only a matter of time.

When Landon returned to them minutes later, she'd made a decision. "Landon, can I talk to you please? In private?"

He glanced cautiously from her to Gavin, who shrugged. "I have a session with Mrs. Litton. Later, and thanks for Michelle." He nodded to Ava. "See you, Ava."

She watched him go, then turned to Landon.

His wary look and taut stance pleased her for some reason. "Let's lay it all out."

"Let's." He crossed his arms over his massive chest. Defensive.

She liked that too. Made her feel more in control, and she needed that around this man. "What do you want from me?"

"What?"

"I asked what you want from me. You're a handsome man. You have large muscles that most women seem to like."

"Most women?" Now he was frowning. "What about you?"

"I doubt you hurt for companionship. Michelle seemed to like you well enough. So why are you coming on to me?"

"Now, Ava. Let's get real here. You're a beautiful woman who's currently on the dating scene. Is it so odd I'd like a chance to get to know you?"

"Well, um, I guess that's an acceptable response." She paused. "But you're not my type."

He blinked. "I'm not? Why not? What's your type, exactly?"

"Well, you're bigger than most men I date." She wasn't surprised to see him preen at what hadn't been intended as a compliment. "I like my dates more cerebral, not so physical."

"You calling me stupid?"

She blushed. Again. "No, of course not. It's just, in this environment, you don't seem so scholarly."

"I told you I work for a logistics company. I have to understand their vast array of spreadsheets and databases. And even with these fat, ugly fingers"—he held up long, hard hands that appeared surprisingly graceful—"I can type into one of them newfangled computers."

The hick accent annoyed her. "I'm not trying to talk

down to you. But you act like the very antithesis of what I'm looking for in a man." Another mental run-down of her five-year plan with its addendum of the right qualities in a mate flashed before her eyes.

"So let's have it. What's on your checklist?"

"Do we really need to do this here, now?" She glanced around, hoping not to see any patients. She always felt self-conscious in her daily life, away from the office. As if she shouldn't have a persona outside of Dr. Rosenthal.

"You'd rather go back to my place?" He shrugged. "Sure thing, Doc."

She blew out a frustrated breath. "I prefer a smaller man, one less than six feet, if possible. He should be well-read, a gentleman, well-mannered, and soft-spoken."

"Does he have strings you can pull? A lever for his mouth to open while you throw your voice?" he teased.

Apparently he wasn't taking her seriously. The man met none of the qualities on her list, though some women might find him appealing with that large frame and overbearing manner, she supposed. Oh hell. He was throw-down hand-some. *There. I said it.* It galled her to admit it, even to her-self, because he was wrong for her in so many *other* ways.

"Keep going," he prodded. "What else are you looking for in a man?"

"That's it." Wasn't that enough?

"Like, does he need to be rich?"

"No, of course not. I make my own money."

"Uh-huh." He stared at her. "What about looks? You said you want him small and mealy."

"I didn't say that."

"So yes or no on the sex appeal? Do you want him

super handsome or what? Or are looks not that important to you, being cerebral and all?"

She didn't like him poking fun at her. "You asked the
question. It's not my fault if you don't like my answers."

"True enough." He nodded, surprising her. "But you
haven't answered all *my* questions. Well? Handsome,
ugly, does it matter?"

"No. I mean, I suppose there should be a mutual physical attraction." To taunt him, she added, "If we're going to
have children together, we should be sexually compatible."

He seemed to pull back, as she'd expected he would at
talk of babies. She didn't know any man who didn't get a
hunted look on his face at the mention of procreation. Sex
for pleasure's sake was all fine and dandy. But add the
responsibility of a child to the mix and most men turned
the other way.

She crossed her arms, waiting for him to do just that,
and feeling a little disappointed she'd chased him away
so easily.

But Landon being Landon, he stood tall, watching
her from his formidable six-plus frame. "Kids, huh?
You're hunting for a baby-maker?"

"That's crudely put, but I suppose you're right.
I expect my future husband to be more than a 'baby-
maker' though."

"You think Charles will give you all that?"

She felt a sudden dislike for all his probing questions.
"I don't know him well enough yet to know if he'll suit
or not. That's why we're dating."

The dark look on Landon's face cleared. "Right. So
that's why *we* should date. You need to weed out your
baby-making candidates."

"Will you stop referring to them as baby-makers?"

"Plus, you can see if I fit your other criteria. We know I seem to be more man than you can handle, physically. But you've got nice tone." He looked her over and nodded. "I think we'll fit together when it counts."

She just watched him. "Seriously? This is how you go about getting a date?"

"A second date. We already had our first kiss, after all."

"That was not a kiss! It was barely a peck, and I wasn't expecting it."

"Yeah, I wasn't expecting it either. But hey, now that we're on the same page, I think we should go out again as soon as possible."

"What? Why?" How had she lost command of this conversation?

"So you can either immediately check me off your list or add me to it. I mean, you're a psychiatrist, right?"

"I'm a clinical *psychologist.* There's a difference." A big difference that he apparently didn't understand.

"You study social science."

"Well, my field has social science application, you could say."

"Right. So as a scientist, you know there are exceptions to every rule. Just because I'm physically intimidating doesn't mean I'll mentally outdo you."

She fumed. "I never said you were intimidating."

"Yet you avoided me for three days."

"Two," she muttered, annoyed that he had to be right about everything. Technically, only Monday and Tuesday had passed, because today—Wednesday—they stood talking.

Rather, she stood being annoyed.

"Right, two." He grinned. "So you admit you were avoiding me."

"I sincerely have no idea if this approach works for you with other women."

"What approach?"

"Annoying me until I want to brain you." She gave serious consideration to the tiny hand weights by her sides.

He chuckled. "It's funny, but my sister has the same response around me." He leaned closer. "But not the ladies."

"As in *plural*. Yet another strike against you. I require loyalty and fidelity in a mate."

"Me too. See? We have something more in common than just a mutual lust thing going on."

Sadly, he was right. She swallowed her retort, knowing he'd see through any denial. For some odd reason, she felt a real spark for this stubborn male. "What exactly do you suggest we do about this mutual admiration?"

He studied her. "Huh. Hadn't thought you'd admit you want me."

She sighed.

"But since you did"—he smiled—"how about dinner? Just you and me getting to know each other without Chuck between us."

She gritted her teeth, not sure why she allowed him to irritate her. Because that annoyance excited her, in a weird way. She truly engaged with him, on a level greater than that of doctor/patient or online date. She… liked…the conversational challenge he represented. She had to be on her toes, meeting a surprisingly intelligent adversary halfway.

Adversary… No, not an enemy. A test, a prick to her intellectual ego. A strong male presence that intrigued the female powerhouse inside her. And, well, he did have a nice ass.

She allowed herself to be charmed by his arrogance. "You know, I don't think anyone's ever worn me down this much into a yes. Not even Elliot, and he's considered a god when it comes to annoying women."

"I thought he was gay."

"He is. And that really annoys women because he's so cute and fun to go shopping with."

Landon chuckled. Then he caressed her cheek with one long finger. "Okay, Doc. So it's a date. After the self-defense class, which is Friday at seven. Then we'll get something to eat in town. Okay?"

She didn't want to appear too easy. "If I have to."

"You do."

She gave him a salute. "Yes, sir."

His eyes darkened, and that grin he shot her made her feel hunted. "Oh yeah, that'll do. See you Friday, Doc."

She watched him leave, wondering why her brains seemed to be sharing space with her pruning girlie parts lately. *Oh man. I think I might need therapy. A date with Landon Donnigan?* She glanced down at herself. *What are you girls thinking?*

Chapter 5

THURSDAY EVENING, LANDON SAT IN THE KITCHEN, watching his brothers horse around. Their mom had to work late, so their father had invited them over for some male bonding. Considering Landon had nothing better to do until tomorrow night, he'd looked forward to a meal he wouldn't have to cook himself. Plus, his dad had skills when it came to food.

Van had been the family cook for years while their mother kept order around the house. Linda Donnigan was a clean freak—where he'd gotten the tendency himself, according to his messy siblings.

Gavin shot him the finger, for no apparent reason, when their dad wasn't looking. Theo saw it and snickered.

"So, Theo. Where are you working now?" Landon asked. The little punk had managed to avoid him last Sunday.

"I'm delivering pizzas. But that's only for a few more days, until they close down. Then I gotta find something else, I guess." He shrugged, his lanky frame all skin and bones, though God knew he put away enough food to fit those size-twelve boats on his feet.

"You knew it would only be temporary when you took the job," their father commented from his spot behind the stove along the counter.

The kitchen was huge, and they sat at the large island in the middle while their dad cooked. With his back to them, he couldn't see Theo's resentful expression.

"Yeah, I did."

Theo and their father butted heads, which always amused Landon, because they seemed so much alike. Gavin, though, had the most in common with Van. Like carbon copies of each other, down to their looks. Theo looked like Van too, but he obviously had a lot of Linda in him. Stubborn to the bone, that kid.

"So what's the deal? Our cousins not giving you any love?" They had one cousin in town who owned a construction business with their Uncle James, another two who owned their own plumbing business, and a fourth who was a financial genius who'd given Hope a job. Landon wondered if Cam had room for another Donnigan, because Theo sure as shit needed the help.

Theo shrugged. "Mike and Uncle James are good, but I got bored hammering crap. And Flynn and Brody are fun to work with, but they're always making me go under the crawlspaces and do the jobs they don't like." He shuddered. "Do you have any idea what kind of stuff sticks in toilets?"

Landon and Gavin shared a grin. The McCauley cousins were good sports, but their families had always been competitive. So this discussion was a great reminder to think up more toilet jokes before the next big family get-together.

"What *is* your thing, Son?" Van looked over his shoulder and frowned. "You're twenty years old. Time to think to the future."

Theo rolled his eyes, but Landon thought his dad had a point.

So of course Gavin disagreed. "He's only twenty, Dad. Lots of time to think about what he wants to do. Now's the time for Theo to find himself."

"He's gonna find himself out of a house and food if he keeps mooching off Mom and Dad," Landon warned. Theo needed some tough love, and at least he and his father kept giving it to him. Left up to their mother or Gavin, Theo would be forty-nine and still living at home.

"Shut up, Landon." Theo glared. "We weren't all born knowing we needed to walk around with a sword up our Marine Corps ass."

"Oh, that's a good one." Gavin grinned.

Their father scowled at Theo. "Watch your mouth, boy."

"Or what? You'll spank me?"

Landon blinked. Even Gavin looked taken aback. Theo had never mouthed off to their parents before. Not blatantly.

Van gritted his teeth. Before he could say anything, Theo got to his feet.

"I'm leaving."

"Where are you going?" Van barked.

Landon gaped. His father, visibly angry?

"Out. Don't worry. I'm not going to do drugs or knock anybody up." Theo sneered. "And I'm not taking your precious car. I'll walk." He tore out of the kitchen. Their father darted after him, and Landon hurried to save the food from burning.

"Stir-fry. Yum." Gavin stood next to him, staring longingly at the contents in the wok.

"That been going on long?" Landon nodded to the exit way, where he could still hear his father yelling for Theo to return.

"Yeah. About a month. Dad's losing it." Gavin chuckled. "Sorry to say, but I'm enjoying it. Mr. Mellow has met his match. Who knew Theo could be so stubborn and rebellious? Makes me so proud." Gavin wiped a fake tear.

Landon shouldn't have grinned, but he hadn't realized Theo could be so assertive. Snarky, sure, but aggressive? He didn't care for little brother's disrespect, and he'd be sure to have a talk with the kid. But he liked Theo standing up for himself. Their parents were awesome people. But Linda could be domineering without meaning to be. And Van could be so chill he made a guy feel bad for ever disagreeing with what had to be the right answer.

Landon had never been outright defiant. He'd been a good little Marine from birth, to hear his parents tell it. But he'd left as soon as he'd been able, needing independence, to be his own person.

Van returned, looking frazzled. "That kid is making me gray."

"Not yet," Gavin said and put out some plates and silverware. "What did you do that's got him so pissed?"

Their dad sighed. "He doesn't appreciate my 'lectures.' I worry about him. He seems so clueless about everything. He has no idea what he wants to pursue. Hell, most of his friends are in their second year of college already. George Collins is at Washington on a football scholarship. That could have been your brother if his grades had been better. He's an amazing athlete."

"He has to make his own way, Dad. We're all different." Landon spooned a heap of food on three of the four plates, and put that last plate away.

Gavin dug into his plate. "Yep. Look at Hope. She never wanted more than an associate's degree in—what was that? She kept changing her mind. Basket weaving? Liberal arts? How to annoy her older brothers?"

"Gavin." But Van was smiling.

Gavin nodded. "But now she's rocking the business world as Cameron's secretary."

"Administrative assistant," their dad said around a mouthful.

"Don't seem so dejected, Dad." Landon patted his dad on the back. "We all wanted to get away from you and Mom at his age."

"Thanks, Landon. I feel *so* much better now."

Gavin chuckled. "Yeah, I'm not feeling that love either."

Landon sighed. "It's normal for a kid to want to be independent. It was easier for me. I went to college, then the Marine Corps. Gavin joined straight out of high school."

Gavin nodded.

"Hope, well, she's another story."

"My baby girl is just fine," Van said, a little defensively, in Landon's opinion. "She's got a terrific job with your cousin, and she's taking college classes to get even smarter." He beamed. "Not that she needs it."

Landon snorted. Gavin rolled his eyes. Their father was such a sucker for his daughter. Hope had been manipulating the guy since she'd learned how to smile. "She has her own problems, but she's fixing them herself."

Gavin's eyes narrowed. He knew about Hope's exes, and this Greg asshole especially, because Landon had shared. They both agreed Greg needed to be taught a lesson.

Landon continued, "In fact, Gavin and I are teaching a self-defense class at the gym, and Hope's taking it. She's a smart girl."

"Of course she is." Their father cleaned his plate, but Landon didn't see an ounce of fat on his old man. *Old* didn't seem to fit Van Donnigan. The guy ran four miles daily, looked like Landon's older brother, ate right, loved his wife and kids, and worked from nine to five every day in the business he now had a share in with his rich partners. Talk about living a clean life.

Landon wondered if he'd ever have that kind of domestic bliss. An image of Ava unexpectedly popped up in his mind's eye, and he ignored the weird sensation in his gut that seemed to accompany thoughts of her. Had to be all her talk of babies and baby-makers that brought her to mind when it came to domestic bliss.

Then again, considering how Theo had stormed from the house, *bliss* might be the wrong word to describe his father's state of being.

"I just think it's funny you and Theo are butting heads." Landon finished his dinner. "You never had that problem with any of us."

Van shrugged. "What can I say? He's complicated."

"Theo?" Gavin looked surprised. "Kid's easy enough to read. He wants to be as successful as his mom and dad. His older sister is out of the nest, leaving him all alone at home. He has big shoes to fill when it comes to his oldest brother." Gavin sighed. "Then he sees me drinking my problems away, and he's freaked out that joining the Marine Corps might turn him into Gavin 'The Loser' Donnigan."

"That's not true," Van denied.

"Yeah. I wouldn't call you a loser. A dumbass, maybe, but not a loser," Landon said to take the sting out of Gavin's idea of how others perceived him.

He had to give his brother credit, though. Pretty insightful for a guy who just the other day had pantsed Landon in their living room like a fourteen-year-old. Gavin had a point. Theo had written him a ton of letters about possibly joining, back when Landon had been overseas. And then Landon and Gavin had come home.

Landon couldn't blame Theo for being confused. One brother put out of commission by a stupid, unfortunate bullet while another suffered from issues caused by death and destruction in the desert. Not a great endorsement for becoming a Leatherneck. Yet Landon wouldn't trade it for the world. There was so much good to being a Marine, so much to learn and share. He still felt great pride for his service.

Yet he knew serving in the military wasn't for everyone. Maybe it wasn't for Theo. Who the hell knew?

Van stared at Gavin. "Do you really think that he wants the Marine Corps, and now he's afraid to join? Or is he just scared of making the wrong choice, so he's not making any decision at all?"

"With Theo, who knows? Maybe the latest episode of the *Clone Wars* has him wanting to be a pilot?" Landon joked, and they all laughed. But his father looked introspective throughout the rest of their dinner.

He and Gavin soon left Van to his thoughts.

"Got plans tonight?" Landon asked as they departed in his SUV.

"Not particularly." Gavin shrugged. "Why?"

"I was thinking we could pay Greg a visit."

Gavin straightened. "Yeah? You know where he is? I asked Hope a bunch of times, but she only told me to shove it."

Landon snorted. "And Dad thinks she's a dainty little lady. Yeah, right." He had hope for his sister. Just as long as she finally stopped dating jerkwads. "What's up with her, anyway?"

Gavin sighed. "I think Mom's on her ass again. It's funny to see Linda and Hope as twisted as Van and Theo. We're lucky to be the ones they left alone."

"Mom's always been harder on Hope than the rest of us. Still, Hope's smart. Why the hell is she dating these losers? I can't believe that fuckhead put a bruise on her."

Gavin scowled. "Think he did more than that, but she won't say?"

"Who knows?" Landon saw red just thinking about it. Then he remembered Ava talking about some guy trying to steal second base. He wanted to beat the shit out of any guy who'd take advantage like that. And of Ava? Hell no.

"So where are we heading?"

Landon turned south at the next street. "Some dump on Rainier. I heard that's where he was going to be tonight."

"You heard how?" Gavin looked interested. Good.

"I called Cam, told him about it." Their cousin might be a roughneck McCauley by name, but he seemed the most enlightened of the bunch. "He dug a little into Hope's business and gave me a full name and picture to go with it."

"Gotta love Cam." Gavin chuckled.

"Yeah. So I just happened to be driving by the guy's place of business and saw him arguing with a woman. She stalked away after giving him a hard time, and she and I had a little chat." Landon grinned, remembering the many names she'd called Greg.

"What place of business?"

"Greg works for a heating company. The chick he was arguing with is his steady girlfriend. She had no idea he was cheating on her with Hope. When Hope found out, she dumped his ass. That's when he got grabby, apparently."

"What a dick."

"Yeah." They drove past several warehouses that looked either run-down or deserted. Landon pulled behind a neon sign missing some letters that should have read *Mazatlan*. But the clientele hanging around out back didn't seem in the Mexican food frame of mind. A lot of motorcycles, rusted pieces of crap, and muscle cars littered the lot.

"This is it? Jesus. Hope was scraping the bottom of the barrel with this guy, huh?"

"I don't know what her problem is. She's cute, right? I'm not just thinking that because I'm her brother, am I?" Landon asked as he parked the car.

He and Gavin got out, and he made sure to lock the thing tight. With any luck he'd still have wheels when he and Gavin returned.

"Nah. She's hot. I mean that in a brotherly, not incestuous, way."

Landon cringed. "Thanks for adding that."

They glanced at the place. "You sure this is it?"

"Yeah." Landon took a deep breath then blew it out. "It's a bar now. Been Ray's for over ten years."

They looked at the sign, then back at the place.

"Great."

Landon paused, wondering if maybe he should have left Gavin at home. "It's a bar, but we're not going in there to drink."

Gavin sighed. "I know that. I'm not a drunk, Landon. I just had some issues the beer made go away."

"Uh-huh."

Gavin glared. "Okay, so I still have those issues. I'm not drinking anymore. And I have no urge to drown myself in cheap beer. No shakes, no seeing things. I'm not detoxing, you jackass. I'm just dealing."

"I'm getting you a therapist." No question about it.

Gavin stared at him, then glanced away. "Fine. But can we not talk about this now? You're making me want to drink just to forget you."

Landon smirked. "After you." He waved toward the degenerates hanging out by the back door. Leather and denim and tattoos. Oh joy.

Gavin cringed. "Shouldn't you go first? Whatever happened to age before beauty?"

"Not hearing you. Move out, Marine."

―✺―

Gavin glared once more at his overbearing brother, said a few less-than-considerate things under his breath, then took the lead. He could handle this type of trouble. Beatings and fights, no sniper fire or IEDs, thank God. He hadn't been in a good brawl for a while, not since those special assignments, like the one that had landed him in the med bay with a bullet in his lung.

The dark thoughts threatened to overtake him, drowning him in nightmares of memory, so he pushed them aside, focusing on bringing the pain to the asshole who'd put a finger on his sister.

Thoughts of golden-haired Hope always made him smile. Their poor sister, the only girl in their house of testosterone. Hell, their mother had bigger balls than their dad, or at least, he used to think so. He hadn't forgotten his dad's deep talk about losing people. Still, Linda Donnigan could be one scary voice of authority. You didn't piss her off and hope to escape notice. No, sir. No how.

Hope had been the gentle, calm soul in the household. So girlie. So cute and happy and caring.

For this guy to have bruised his precious sister? *Hell no.* With that thought in mind, he made straight for the back door. He and his brother dressed casually, enough to blend in, he hoped. He proudly wore his favorite Seahawks sweatshirt and jeans. His brother had on some old flannel shirt over a white T-shirt with black denims. Nothing special.

The expression on Gavin's face must have warned people not to screw with him, because they gave him wary looks but didn't say a thing as he approached the door.

They entered Ray's and paused. The place seemed a lot more decent on the inside. It still smelled like a bar—stale beer, sweaty guys, greasy food—but it looked halfway decent. Cleaner than he'd have imagined, and no one lay bleeding or shivved on the sticky floor.

The bouncer who let them in gave them a long, hard look. The guy looked like he picked his teeth with trees instead of toothpicks. The shirt that read *Bouncer* strained over his broad chest and steroid-induced biceps.

"Problem?" Landon asked, his balls bigger than his brain, as usual.

"Won't be if you keep it clean, hero." The guy smirked at Landon.

"Sure thing, Bouncer." Landon grinned back, though the expression didn't reach his eyes. The bouncer had read him right, though. With Landon's ramrod-stiff posture and still-short hair, he looked ex-military. Even if they didn't meet Greg tonight for a few rounds, Gavin had a feeling his brother might rub someone else the wrong way. He was good like that.

Gavin brightened. A fight might allow him to let go of the constant tension that was making life practically unbearable. He'd been supplanting his alcoholic deluges with workouts at the gym before he headed home each night. Even if he didn't work a shift, he still showed up to work out. He slept like a baby lately, too tired to think about much.

He rotated his shoulders, appreciating the burn in his lats.

"There." Landon didn't wait. He moved straight to a dark-haired guy sitting with two bald dudes and a red-haired idiot with questionable taste in fashion. Seriously? A mullet in the twenty-first century? Despite the hair issue, all four looked like ex-cons—tatted, brawny, with mean eyes.

Quite the place Greg liked to frequent. "Landon, hold on."

They hadn't discussed how they'd planned to handle this, but big brother, as usual, took charge.

Sometimes Gavin appreciated Landon telling him what to do, where to go, how to handle himself. He'd learned a lot from his older brother throughout life. But Landon could also get on his last fucking nerve, rushing into situations before thinking them through. Dominant, aggressive, and focused, Landon could have gone as far as general with no trouble. Except for one pesky little bullet that had managed to lodge in his knee and do enough damage to permanently fuck up his joint.

No coming back from that. As healthy and buff as his brother seemed, Landon would never be able to discount that possible weakness in his joint. At odd times his knee just gave out on him. Landon didn't know it, but Gavin had seen him rubbing the injury when he thought no one was looking.

Maybe I'm not the only one with anger issues. He caught up to Landon in time to hear his brother mouthing off.

"None of this involves you three." He gave the others a dismissive look. "You Greg?" he asked the dark-haired guy. The man wasn't as tall as Landon or Gavin, but he had some muscle on him. A man larger than Hope for sure.

Gavin stood next to Landon, his arms crossed, waiting for the dickhead to pull something.

Apparently the people close by thought the same, because the crowd around them quieted and backed up, watching.

"Yeah, I'm Greg. Who the hell are you?" Greg stood, still drinking his beer. He seemed sober enough, but he looked a little anxious.

"A friend of Hope's," Landon said clearly, his voice deep, angry.

The others at the table stood as well. Would it be four against two, then? Gavin prayed for a yes.

A pretty African American woman with bouncy light brown curls came over. "Trouble, guys? Can I get anyone something to drink?"

Gavin smiled at her. She smiled back. Oh man, this bar had more than a fight going for it. *Nice.* "I'm good, thanks."

She winked. "You are so cute." She thumbed at Landon. "How about you, handsome? Something to drink?"

Mullet frowned. "Back off, Rena. This ain't a good place for you to be."

"Sorry, Rena," Gavin agreed. "My brother and I have something to say to Greg, and you'd probably be better off back by the bar."

Rena's eyes widened, and she left.

"What the fuck does that bitch want now?" Greg snarled, trying to sound mean. His eyes told a different story. He kept glancing around, looking for an escape.

"You calling my sister a bitch?" Landon asked softly.

Mullet had a brain under that bad haircut, because he and one of the bald guys backed away. "You stepped in it now, Greg."

Unintelligent Bald Guy smirked. "She was a hot piece, I'll give you that."

The giant bouncer returned just as Gavin launched a fist at stupid and bald, who went down and didn't get up, moaning and clutching his nose.

Greg tried to punch Landon. A mistake.

The bouncer sighed. "Shit. I knew you two were going to be trouble."

Before he could intervene, in seconds, Landon had Greg in a chokehold. "Next time you mark up my sister, asshole, I won't just choke you out. I'll break your goddamn neck. Got it?"

Greg tried to plead—for his life, mercy, something. Then Landon squeezed, and the bastard passed out.

Landon dropped him like the sack of shit he was. Then he turned a mean look on the bouncer.

So not smart.

Before the bouncer could turn Landon's head into a punching bag, Gavin stepped between them. "We're leaving. We just wanted to let Greg know it's not cool to mess with our sister."

The bouncer studied them. "I think he got the message. No problem with what you're saying, guys. But maybe you ought to leave now."

Landon hadn't moved, so Gavin turned to see his brother assessing the bouncer. And shit, but Landon looked seriously dangerous, if not a bit psychotic. Badass with a capital B. Even had Gavin not known what his brother was capable of, he'd have steered way clear of the guy.

"Yeah, okay, we're going." Landon cracked his knuckles, then glanced down at Greg. "Fucking pussy."

Others around them laughed and went back to the business of drinking and talking. They made room for Gavin and Landon to pass by. He caught the glance of the sexy Rena and paused. Maybe he could get her number and—

"No. Just no." Landon grabbed him by the collar and dragged him out. "This place is nothing but trouble. Trust me."

Gavin sighed. It might have been worth it for another look at that cute waitress. But oh well. He followed Landon out to the SUV and got inside after his big brother unlocked it. "We were there maybe five minutes, and you destroyed the guy." He sat in a huff, now bored once more and needing something to take his mind off his coming nightmares.

"I noticed you put down your own jerk with one punch. Not bad." Landon grinned. "We did what we came to do—accomplished the mission."

Gavin shook his head. If he let him, Landon would start mouthing five-paragraph orders and mission statements.

"We let Greg know," *Major* Landon continued, "in no uncertain terms, that you mess with one Donnigan, you mess with us all."

"Hmm. All of us? Maybe we should have let Theo come with us."

"Yeah, that's funny. No."

They laughed together at the thought. Theo would have been shitting his pants but putting on the attitude like being in that place didn't bother him. Gavin had pride in his brothers. They might annoy him, but damn, none of them liked to back down.

He mulled over a thought he'd been having. "I've been thinking."

"Damn. You okay?"

Gavin flipped him off. "Theo and Dad aren't getting along. Maybe he should come live with us for a while."

Landon groaned. "I'm only letting *you* live with me out of pity." He paused. "For Mom and Dad."

"That's not nice."

"Hell, you know if you lived with them you'd go nuts. I love 'em, but Mom is worse than I am about keeping the house clean."

"And you're a major pain in the ass to begin with." He ignored Landon's scowl. "I get it, but Theo's in a hard spot right now. I feel like I let him down." Not a lie. He had. "I don't want him to hate the thought of joining the Marine Corps because of me. Despite the shit I went through, I miss it. Not the fighting." *Or the killing.* "I miss my friends."

"Yeah, me too." Landon sighed. "I don't know. Maybe joining up isn't for him, Gavin. What if he lost more than his knee over there? Got more than a punctured lung?" He referred to Gavin's own run-in with an enemy projectile.

"I know. But it's got to be his choice. I don't want it colored because he thinks I'm a big fuckup."

"But you are." Landon smirked. "With women, I mean."

"Please. I'm not the one currently striking out with the sexy Ava Rosenthal." Gavin saw his brother's surprise. *Oh yeah, I pay attention when it counts. Gavin knows and sees all. Plus I listen when Elliot speaks.* "What's the deal with you and the hot shrink?"

"She's not hot." Before Gavin could contradict him, Landon added, "Not to *you.* And what I want with her is none of your business, numbnuts. So stay out of it."

"That a threat?"

"No. It's a condition of letting Theo live with us for a while. Oh, and he's sharing your room and bathroom, so clean up."

"Fine." Like hell he'd keep out of Landon's love life. "So if I can't ask about Ava, can I at least ask if you and Claudia are back together?"

Landon's fingers tightened on the steering wheel. "Why the hell would you ask that?"

"Um, remember last week? When she told me to tell you hi?"

Landon groaned. "I'd forgotten about that. I haven't seen or talked to her since. Have you?"

"No. But it might be awkward if you're sniffing around Ava and Claudia steps in, don't you think?"

"Good point. Guess I'd better talk to her." He shook his head. "I don't get it. We were just fuck buddies for a while. Nothing serious. She didn't want anything more, and neither did I."

"What happened?" Poor Landon. He had no idea how the women talked about him in the gym, every chick wanting to be bossed around by the dominant Marine who had a habit of looking *through*, not at, people. Landon didn't help matters by choosing seemingly flighty bed partners.

The guy had no clue what he wanted in a woman. So this Ava Rosenthal had been a pleasant surprise, at least to Gavin's way of thinking. She had her own mind and didn't seem the type to let his big brother run all over her.

"I honestly don't know what happened with her. Claudia, out of the blue, announced she wanted us to get closer. She wanted me to be 'emotionally vulnerable.'" He snorted. "A load of bullshit and boyfriend/girlfriend crap I don't have time for."

"But you have time for it with Ava."

Landon turned to scowl at him before focusing again on the road, and Gavin fought a grin. "I'm just seeing where this thing with Ava might go. I'm not trying to put a ring on her finger, for God's sake." A slow smile worked over his mouth. "But I'm trying out for the position of baby-daddy."

"*What?*" Gavin straightened.

"That's what she's angling for. I'm all wrong for her. We both know it. But I can damn sure show her what great sex is all about." He smiled kindly at Gavin. "Need pointers? Or is Michelle all the woman you can handle?"

Gavin blushed, still embarrassed he'd succumbed to that barracuda. "Hey, I was desperate."

"And drunk."

Gavin glared. "And horny. Friends don't let friends beer-goggle."

"But brothers let brothers learn for themselves. See how destructive booze can be?"

Gavin wanted to be angrier, but Landon was right. As usual. "Yeah, yeah. Now stop busting my balls and figure out how to handle Claudia—before Ava has to."

Landon's sour expression restored his good mood.

"And I'm bored. How about we hit that arcade downtown, and maybe grab something for dessert? That stir-fry left me hungry not twenty minutes later."

Chapter 6

LANDON HAD WANTED TO PUT OFF THIS CONVERSATION with Claudia forever. Because he shouldn't have had to have it, not again. His simple "We're over because we want different things" should have sufficed. Succinct, straightforward. Impossible to misunderstand.

Right?

He stood inside her condo downtown and did his best not to fidget. He wanted to pace. He did his best thinking pacing, putting together strategy and mission and delivering the best possible outcome.

Instead, he waited while Claudia fetched him a friggin' glass of water, because he wanted to be social and let her down easily for *the second time.* He could be a total hard-ass and had no problem being honest. To a point. He really hated hurting women's feelings. And he blamed that shit on his mother.

Linda Donnigan had raised him to protect his younger siblings, but Hope especially. *Never hit girls. Hold the door for them. Be a gentleman.* He'd once tried to argue that Linda sounded anti-feminist, because shouldn't he be treating women equally?

She'd forced him to listen to his father's long-winded lecture about the male agenda in America and about the spiritual balance of the masculine and feminine essences within oneself, then had to watch a Gloria Steinem interview. Scarred at the age of twelve. Never again had he questioned his mother when it came to dealing with women.

He waited politely for Claudia to speak.

"I gather Gavin told you I said hello?"

He accepted the glass she gave him and nodded.

"I've missed you, Landon."

Hell, her eyes looked misty. A pretty redhead with curves and bright blue eyes, she'd been just the diversion he'd needed after returning to the States. After a few months seeing other women, he'd found her at the gym. Their on-again, off-again sexual play had energized him while giving him the emotional distance he'd wanted from anything resembling a relationship. And she'd been down with the same. Until she hadn't been.

"You're looking good, Claudia." He smiled. "Nice to see you're going to the gym again." *Not really.* "I was hoping our past wouldn't affect your workouts."

Claudia avoiding the gym because of him? He'd had no problem with that. Had Ava taken one more day to show up, he'd have sought her out and demanded she return. Claudia desired a closer relationship. Ava was on the hunt for a husband and kids. Yet he hadn't wanted Claudia anywhere near him when it came to true intimacy. With Ava, he kind of seemed to crave it.

Strange, and something to worry about *later.* When he no longer had Claudia to deal with.

"I've seen you at the gym," she said softly. "I hear you're not seeing anyone."

"You're asking about me?" *Shit.* "Claudia, we're over."

"But we don't have to be." She drew close and put her hand on his arm. Then she looked up at him from under her lashes and bit her lower lip, giving him The Look.

All innocence, demure but slutty underneath—how she'd once described herself.

Before, her actions would have been the prelude to sex. Mind-blowing for her, boring for him at the end. She was a nice woman but way too needy.

Not at all like Ava.

He blew out a breath, determined to put Ava out of his thoughts, at least until later tonight. He had another hour before the self-defense class, then magic time with a stubborn psychologist.

"Claudia, it's not going to happen. We had fun together. I like you." He tried to pull away.

She gripped him tight. "I like you too. A lot." A tear slipped down her cheek. "I think I might lo—"

"*It's over,* Claudia," he said forcefully, not wanting to hear what she desperately wanted to say. He felt itchy just thinking about it. "You're sweet and beautiful and smart. Any guy would be fortunate to be with you." She refused to let go, so though he wasn't proud of himself for it, he did the cowardly thing. He lied. "But I'm with someone else now. I'm sorry. I don't want to hurt you."

She released her hold on him, and he stepped back and set down that stupid glass of water he hadn't even wanted.

Her tears stopped and her eyes narrowed. "Someone else?"

"Yeah. We met and clicked right away."

"Emotionally, you mean?" Part of what had driven him away was her inability to shut up about them talking and oversharing every damn thing in his life. Hell, they'd hooked up because they both wanted sex. Then she'd started changing the rules.

Problem was, Landon didn't like giving over control

to anyone. Not when he wasn't ordered to. And now as a civilian, he sure as shit didn't have to. "Yeah, emotionally." Wouldn't Ava get a kick out of that?

"How did you meet her? Or is this a lie to keep me away? I hope it isn't, for your sake. You need softness in your life, Landon. You're such a great guy, but you're too hard."

Never seemed to have been a complaint before. He shrugged the crude thought away and concentrated on getting the hell out of her place. "Look, Claudia. We were friends. I wanted to give you the courtesy of a face-to-face after talking to Gavin. But I don't owe you an explanation. About anything. We had a good thing, and it ran its course. We're over." Then, because even he knew he sounded dickish and her eyes looked shiny, he added, "But we can still be friends."

"Friends, huh?" Did he detect a note of bitterness? "Okay. I'm sorry if you felt like I was trying to force something that's obviously over. I still plan on going to the gym, though. I can't wait to take that self-defense class you and Gavin are offering. I hope that won't be awkward."

Fuck me. "Great." Maybe she could stand next to Ava and they could become best friends. *I'm in dating hell, wanting in one woman's pants while desperate to stay out of another's.* "Look, Claudia. It was nice seeing you, but I have to go."

"I'll see you at the gym in an hour. And Landon, no hard feelings. Okay?"

He decided to take her words at face value. Relieved, he smiled. "Great, thanks." Then he left, heading to Jameson's with one thought in mind, getting through the damn class so he could figure out why Ava figured so prominently in his mind lately.

———

Ava stood with Sadie, both of them dressed in shorts and T-shirts as opposed to the many women in the class wearing flashy tights and sports bras. She'd never seen so much makeup in the gym before. Eager women chatted amongst themselves, and the name Donnigan continued to buzz around the room.

"This is too funny," Sadie murmured, standing close. "Apparently our instructors are single and super handsome. Maybe my unlucky streak is about to end."

"I wouldn't count on it." She'd been reluctant to share her history with Landon to Sadie, who still thought men the devil in disguise.

"Oh? Is that because you have a date with our blond instructor after it's over?"

Ava groaned. "Elliot told you."

"Of course he told me. It constantly amuses me that you think you can hide anything. What he won't get from you, I will."

Ava had wiggled her way out of dinner last night, legitimately busy catching up on paperwork at the office. "How was dinner with the playboy? You do know he's now dating Mitchell and Tony, at the same time."

"Gotta love that dedication to *amour*, huh? We didn't have dinner together, because, what a coincidence, he was out with Mitchell. We just gossiped about you over the phone." Sadie's wide grin did nothing but alarm her. "So I hear your guy has a big banana?"

"Shut up." Ava blushed and whispered, "I have no

idea about *that.* We're going out to dinner tonight. And that's it. I'm sure it'll be over when he realizes I don't intend to have sex with him on the first date."

"Second date, actually, the way I hear it."

Ava frowned. "Where *are* you hearing all this, anyway? I never told Elliot I had a date tonight."

"Must have been something in the wind. Now shush. Our instructors are here."

Landon and Gavin had walked in, and a new energy filled the room. Everyone centered their attention on the double dose of testosterone bundled up in tight T-shirts and shorts showing off some fine, manly legs.

"Oh wow. I just blinked and had an orgasm." Sadie laughed. "Elliot wasn't kidding. Nice, Cousin. At least you have good taste under all those repressive degrees."

"Shut up, Sadie."

Sadie laughed. The noise in the room returned to the volume it had been before the overwhelming Donnigans entered. Then Mac walked in, joining them, and Ava heard the collective sighs. Talk about a lot of male candy to look at. Not the most professional thing to come to mind, but Ava had ovaries, after all. She could think it, she just couldn't say it.

Landon glanced around, saw her, and smiled. Then he said something to Gavin that had him grinning as well. An annoyed blond woman joined them. The only woman in the room who appeared unhappy to be there.

"Don't look now, but there's a lady eyeballing you." Sadie nodded to their left.

Ava turned a subtle glance that way and saw that Sadie hadn't been lying. As soon as she made eye contact, the redhead glanced past her and smiled and waved.

"She was eyeballing someone else, I guess," she said to Sadie.

Mac called the class to order. "Ladies, thanks so much for coming. It was pointed out to me that we've done you a disservice by not offering this class sooner. With the amount of singles in the dating world, and the growing number of scumbags to choose from, guys that look like Prince Charming can turn out to be anything but."

"Truth," a woman called out.

"Sadly, yes," another agreed, and several in the audience laughed.

Sadie gave Ava a big grin, made even bigger when her cousin nodded toward Landon, who was staring at them. When she frowned back at him, he winked, then turned to the blond girl by his side and whispered something, to which she elbowed him in the stomach.

Ava stared at the girl, then realized she looked like Landon, just feminized. His sister maybe? She ignored the relief that came, surely not the least bit jealous Landon might have an ex-girlfriend in the room. Because she had no claim on him other than an hour of his time for dinner. That was it.

"Pay attention," Sadie said and tapped her arm. "Hunky Mac is still talking."

"…so in essence, when you can't run away, and yelling for help hasn't done you much good, this is where the class comes in. Again, violence is never the answer."

"Until it is," Landon added.

"And that's my cue to go." Mac shook his head. "Good luck, everyone. Let me know what you think when it's over. And be honest. The Donnigan brothers can take it." He waved and left. Mac was known and liked by just about everyone.

Ava had liked him the moment she'd seen him staring at his wife with such love in his eyes. Right before he'd told Maggie to move her ass to the aerobics class and quit dicking around. That dichotomy of soft affection and tough handling had amused her. Oddly enough, that dichotomy seemed to exist in Landon as well. Perhaps that's why she found him so fascinating?

"Profound as always, Landon." Gavin snorted and took over. "I'm Gavin, a trainer in the gym. This is my mouthy brother, Landon. We're going to be teaching this class. We come to you with knowledge gained from being guys, who are in essence reactive, and not always the brightest or nicest creatures on the planet."

"You got that right," the blond with them said.

"Our sister Hope is going to help demonstrate some holds," Gavin added, by way of introduction. "In all seriousness, Landon and I know what we're talking about. We're both former Marines. We learned hand-to-hand defense as part of our training, and we've modified it for you. Because on average, women have less muscle mass than men. That's a biological fact, not a sexist statement."

"There are smaller men out there too," someone added.

"Yes, there are. And if they were smart, they'd be in here taking this class," Landon growled, which shut the lady right up. "We want to teach you ways to leverage your weight to your best advantage. To seek out the soft, vulnerable points of your opponent and take him off guard, to give yourself time to run.

"This isn't an MMA class. We're not going to teach

you how to take down your attacker and pin him to a mat. You don't get points for a hit to his ribs or a glancing right off his cheekbone."

A few ladies chuckled.

Gavin continued, "But we *are* going to show you how to give yourselves time to get away, to get help. I have a lot of female friends in the dating pool. I know I'm preaching to the choir, but it's not always the ones you don't know that you need to be wary of. A lot of the time, it's the guy sitting across from you at that table in the restaurant. The one you drove with because he was so funny and charming online."

The room quieted.

"Our methodology is to get you to respond without thinking," Landon said, commanding the room. "Instinctively, quickly. The more you practice, the more it becomes muscle memory. So learn from the class and practice at home. Then if you're unfortunately put in a bad position, you can recognize and exploit your opportunity to take the bastard out." Landon gave a half grin, mean yet sexy. "Then call me and I'll come kick his ass."

Laughter filled the somber room, releasing the building tension.

Gavin shook his head. "Ignore my brother. This is about you guys learning to take care of yourselves."

Hope spoke up, her voice light but firm. "Dating can be and should be fun. But when it isn't, I want to be able to defend myself, or least get the hell out of Dodge and find help before my date comes on too strong. You know?"

Several women nodded. Hope turned back to Landon and whispered something that had him frowning.

Gavin directed them. "So, let's all partner up. If you haven't already, give yourself some space."

The redhead who'd earlier been looking her way stood with another lady next to them. "Hi. I'm Claudia. This is Bridget."

Sadie nodded. "I'm Sadie. This is Ava."

"Nice to meet you. I'm so glad I'm taking this class," Claudia said.

"Yeah, me too." Sadie sounded a little too chipper for Ava's peace of mind. Sadie stepped closer and leaned in to whisper, "Your man is looking over here and scowling big time. I don't trust these two."

Always suspicious of everyone. Poor Sadie. But Ava didn't want to lecture her cousin. "Okay." Easier to just agree with her.

"Just keep an eye on her."

Whatever. Ava nodded.

The class started in earnest.

Gavin used Hope, grabbing her by the wrist. "You can see I'm bigger than Hope. I'm holding her tight. There are several ways to get free. One, break his grip by ripping your arm free where his thumb and forefinger meet. Like this." He nodded to Hope, and she pulled her arm free. To the group, he said, "Go ahead and try it, ladies. Switch off in your pairs, so you each get to practice."

Landon walked around while the groups alternated getting free.

"Great." Gavin nodded. "Okay, now watch this." He pulled Hope in again, grabbing her wrist. "Do it, Hope."

Hope tugged and pulled as instructed, but this time she couldn't break free. "Crap."

"The release we just learned will usually work, so

long as your opponent doesn't have a *really* strong grip. I do, and my sister is kind of wimpy."

"Hey." Hope glared.

Ava couldn't help but laugh with the crowd. The Donnigans were entertaining, to say the least. She noticed Landon out of the corner of her eye smiling at something two older women said.

"So another way to get free. Watch," Gavin ordered. "Hope's going to squat down, keeping her weight centered, and move her elbow *toward* my arm, breaking the angle of my grip. By doing so, it's physically impossible for me to hold on. But this move isn't easy. It goes against instinct to go toward danger, which is what Hope is doing by leaning toward me and not away. It's got to be a fast move too, because as soon as she's free, she needs to run."

They watched Hope execute the move twice. Then Gavin ordered them to try.

Landon helped a few people. By the time he stood next to her and Sadie, watching, Ava thought she'd already mastered the move.

Sadie wore a smirk when she saw him standing there. "Good class."

"I hope so. Long as it helps keep my sister safe, I'm happy."

Ava realized there might be more to this class for the Donnigans than strutting around in shorts acting authoritative. Not that she'd given much thought to the reason behind his giving the class in the first place, but knowing Landon wanted to protect his sister, she softened toward him without meaning to.

"I'm Sadie, by the way," her cousin introduced herself. "Ava's cousin."

Landon smiled. "Landon. Ava seems to have a lot of cousins."

"Three, but Rose is busy at home canoodling with her husband, and Elliot's out whoring around town, so it's just me tonight."

"Sadie." Ava couldn't believe the mouth on her cousin.

Landon laughed. "I've met Elliot." He said no more, one circumspect person in the room, at least. "Okay, Sadie, let's see you get free from me." He gripped Sadie's wrist.

Sadie escaped easily.

"Good job." He smiled, then gave Ava an arched brow. "Now, let's see you in action, Doc."

Ava smiled through her teeth. "Bring it."

He gripped her wrist, and she felt that tingle of connection he seemed able to engender each time they were together. She tried to pull free the first way they'd been taught, but he only tightened his grip. Annoyed, she glared at him.

He smirked. "What's wrong, Doc? Can't get free?" He leaned closer and whispered, "Or don't you want to?"

She reviewed what they'd learned and squatted low, then moved toward him, until her elbow touched his forearm, forcing him to let go. But he didn't make it easy. She was breathing hard by the time she'd scuttled out from under his massive body.

"Nice job. I didn't want to let go, but you made me." He nodded and moved on before she could question why he'd been tougher on her than her cousin.

It didn't escape her notice that Claudia had watched their interaction closely. The redhead smiled at Landon, and he smiled back, but he didn't go over to help her or Bridget with the move.

The class learned two more stances, one that aimed for the bridge of the nose, another that involved a wrist lock and knee to the face.

The hour seemed almost up when Landon and Gavin decided to show the ladies what a real assault might look like. But instead of using Hope, they used each other.

Landon looked over the crowd, lingering on her, it seemed, before shifting his gaze. "Violence isn't pretty. We're not trying to scare you, but you need to be aware it won't be like the classroom. It won't be measured, slowed enough for you to react. We're going to demonstrate, and it's going to get a little rough, so be warned." He turned to his brother. "Gavin, you're the girl, here."

"You're an ass," Gavin muttered and turned pink while everyone laughed. "Okay, ladies. I'm on your side. He's the enemy." He faced his brother and raised the pitch of his voice. "Thanks for dinner, Landon. I had a great time. And you know, I'm surprised you paid. Rumor has it you're a cheapskate."

More laughter.

Landon sighed. "You're welcome, Gavina."

"Gavina?"

"Work with me, honey." Landon closed the distance between them and put his arm around his brother's shoulder. "Let me walk you home." Then, before Gavin could take two steps, Landon had him in a headlock, dragging him toward the doorway.

It happened in the blink of an eye, and Ava watched in astonishment as Gavin struggled violently to be free, his face turning red.

Then Gavin sagged.

Sadie gaped. "Oh my God. I think he actually passed out."

Landon relaxed, just enough, apparently, because Gavin exploded into action and soon had Landon at arm's length, his fists cocked and ready to punch.

Then both men stopped.

"See how quickly it can happen?" Landon asked, not even winded. "Just like that, I had him in my hold. And just as fast, he was out of it, faking unconsciousness before jumping at me. We'll work on lulling your opponent before turning the tables next week. But no choke-holds for real," he said, a slow smile making Ava question how she'd ever thought him not classically handsome.

The class clapped as the group broke up.

"Man, that was hot." Sadie fanned her T-shirt at her collar. "Your man is fast, for sure."

"Not 'my man.' Would you stop saying that?" Ava was all too conscious of Claudia once again watching her. "But I think you're right. Claudia keeps looking at me."

Landon walked over to her and whispered, "Let's go. Claudia's getting on my last nerve." He put a proprietary arm around her. "Nice meeting you, Sadie."

"You too. Be good. Because I'll know all about your date tomorrow."

"Is that so? You kiss and tell, Ava?" he asked as they left the room.

Ava wanted the floor to swallow her. Too many people remained behind to overhear him, and the specu-lation and envy she sensed as they moved toward the lockers felt oppressive.

The speculation she didn't care for, but a prideful part of her reveled in the envy.

"Who, exactly, is Claudia?" she found herself asking even after she'd told herself not to care.

"An ex from hell." Landon sighed. "I'm sorry about this."

"About what?"

"I had to tell her I was seeing someone else to get her to finally understand we're through. I didn't want to hurt her feelings, but we broke up two months ago and she's not getting the hint."

"Two months ago? Did you have sex with her since then? Because that can muddy the waters."

To her surprise, his cheeks turned pink. They moved down the hallway before stopping outside of the ladies' showers. He pulled her aside, away from the many gym patrons coming and going. "No, I didn't sleep with her again," he said in a low voice. "I'm not a dog, Ava. I'm a stand-up guy. When she and I dated, we wanted the same thing. Then we didn't, so we broke up."

"You mean, she wanted more, so you broke it off." She'd nailed it, because he nodded.

"I swear, I wasn't trying to lie or put you in the middle of any of it, but she kept bugging me to get back with her." He rotated his neck, twitchy. "Then she cried. I hate crying, I'll just tell you that now."

She wanted to smile at his fierce look. "If it makes you feel any better, I only cry when I'm in pain. Although tears can be an emotional release, so it's actually very healthy to cry. Just not all the time."

Landon stared at her. "Good to know."

"Yes, well, you mentioned it first."

He lost his nervous edge. "Okay, Doc. Just wanted to apologize if I put you in the middle of my mess. I saw her staring at you in class, so she must have guessed you're the rabbit I'm after."

"Excuse me?" She frowned. "Rabbit?"

"Tender morsel? Hot, sexy psychologist? Do you wear glasses? 'Cause I'd love to see you in them."

"Um, yes. But they're just for reading." How did the man turn an insult into a compliment so easily? Rabbit to sexy in the same breath?

"I dig smart chicks. Just so you know."

"You mean intelligent women."

"That's what I said." He brushed his finger down the slope of her nose. "Man, you are so pretty when you're all red. I'll meet you out here in twenty minutes, then we'll go to dinner. Okay?"

"Yes, fine." She reached out to make a point of her own and grabbed his wrist. "But stop being so grabby. I'm taking a self-defense class, and I have it on good authority that if you even try roughing me up, my instructor will, and I quote, 'kick your ass.'"

He stopped smiling and drew her hand to his mouth for a kiss she felt all the way to her toes. "Ava, I swear I'll never do anything to intentionally hurt you. And putting my hand, or any other part of my body, on you isn't gonna happen if you ever say no. I mean it." He paused. "If you really don't want this date, we don't have to go."

The sudden seriousness took her aback. "Ah, I was just teasing." She released his wrist. "Unless you'd rather not go, I can—"

"Dinner it is." He looked relieved. "I'm heading for the showers. See you soon." He leaned close and breathed her in. "Yep. Flowers. Damn." He sighed.

"Hurry up, Doc. I'm hungry for dinner. Last one to the front desk buys the first one a drink."

She watched him jog toward the men's locker room, then she turned to get her own shower.

He'd given her an out. She could have taken it, said that all that talk of predators and self-defense had freaked her out. He wasn't her type. Heck, if he ever tried a real wrist lock and meant it, she didn't think she'd be able to get herself free, no matter what moves she made.

She didn't know much more about Landon than his name. And that he had a brother and sister. That he worked downtown. That he'd been a Marine. That he loved his family and was a protector of the innocent...

Landon, you are killing me.

She checked the clock by the entrance and swore under her breath. She wouldn't be late and give him the satisfaction of holding that over her during their dinner. One she very much wanted to attend, to her bewilderment. He still wasn't her type. She'd seen him physically overpower his brother in seconds. And he had sarcasm down to a science. That didn't stop her excitement from building, nor did it stop her from imagining what a long, slow kiss with him might feel like.

Her shower lasted for all of five minutes. It took Ava ten more minutes to dry off, dress and apply makeup. Just as she'd finished setting herself to rights in a pair of dove-gray slacks, an emerald-green blouse and a scarf to match, Claudia entered.

"Hi, Ava. Can I talk to you for a minute?"

It appeared Ava would be buying the first round after all.

Chapter 7

Ava waited while Claudia shored her nerve. "Yes?"

"I know we just met, but I thought you should know something." The redhead didn't appear to be scheming, angry, or bitchy. She seemed…sad.

"That you and Landon used to date?"

"He told you?"

"Was it supposed to be a surprise?"

Claudia blinked. "I guess not."

They stood in silence. A subtle glance at the clock told Ava she'd missed the twenty-minute mark. Darn it. "Was there anything else?"

Claudia's eyes watered. "I'm sorry. I shouldn't have come in here to talk to you. It's just that… I can't…"

Ava grabbed a few tissues from a nearby dispenser and handed them to Claudia. "That's okay. What's really wrong, Claudia?"

"I l-love him, and he ended us too soon."

"Recently?"

Claudia nodded. "B-before Ch-Christmas."

Two months ago, like he'd said, so not *too* recently. But Claudia didn't appear to see it that way. "I'm so sorry. I know it takes a while for the heart to heal. But you're a beautiful woman, so you…"

Claudia sat on a bench, crying harder.

Ava sighed and joined her, unable to ignore someone in need.

"I thought I was over him. We had a strictly physical agreement, you know. But then I started falling for him. That smile, the way he loves his family. That protective instinct." Claudia nodded.

Ava nodded with her. "Every woman wants a responsible, loving companion." Ava paused. "If this is really hurting you, maybe you could see someone to get over—"

"He came over today. I knew he would, because I manipulated Gavin into giving him a message for me." She didn't sound upset over the fact she'd used trickery.

"Okay." He saw Claudia, *today*? Not pleased but now wanting to know more, Ava waited.

"He told me it was over. He told me before, but I didn't believe him. He holds a lot back, emotionally. He saw things in the Marines. Oh, we never talked about it. But if I ever mentioned the news, he'd grow cold, distant. I tried to get him to share with me, but he never would. And when I tried to tell him how I felt about him, he broke it off." She sniffed. "Then today, he told me about you."

"Oh?"

"Not you, exactly. Just that he'd met someone. And I could see it in his eyes, so I was curious. I wanted to talk to you, to meet you. I heard from a few friends that he was into some woman at the gym."

"Okay." What the heck to say to that? What exactly did "into" mean, anyway? And why were people gossiping about her? That didn't sit well. At all.

"I'm sorry. I know I'm imposing. I just… I don't know what I want. I miss him, but I want him to be happy. I just wish it was with me."

Ava stood and patted Claudia on the shoulder. "Breakups can be hard, especially when it feels one-sided. If time hasn't helped you get over him, maybe think of seeing someone who can counsel you through it. I know therapy has helped a few friends of mine." Elliot, years ago, had talked to her extensively about losing the love of his life. At the time, it had seemed as if he'd never move on.

Until months later, when he came out of his shell and accepted himself and the gay community. Now there was no stopping him. She thought about him juggling Mitchell and Tony. Hmm. Perhaps they should have another discussion about the merits of monogamy and deepening a relationship.

She smiled to herself, because Elliot would love this drama at the gym. Knowing she'd been involved in a my-man/your-man discussion in the locker room, of all places. And before her big date with said man? Priceless.

Even Ava could see the humor in the situation, though not in Claudia's pain.

"Therapy. I might do that." Claudia gave a wan smile through her tears. "Just know that if you and he don't work out, I'll be waiting."

"Is that supposed to make me feel better?" Ava might be a therapist, but she was also a blood-and-bones woman. Claudia was starting to seriously annoy her.

"No." Claudia blew her nose. "I just wanted to be honest."

"Do you feel better for having done so?" Ava asked. *How about I be honest right back and tell you I want to punch you in the face?* Ava breathed deeply. She felt much better imagining Claudia's cute little nose askew and bleeding. Then she tucked the feeling away, having accepted her irritation as her due.

Claudia nodded. "I also feel stupid for bothering you." That said, the woman bolted into a bathroom stall.

Ava sighed and grabbed her bag, then met Landon at the front desk.

"Well, well. You sure took your sweet time, Doc. Not that you don't look like you put the time to excellent use"—a direct once-over that set her blood ablaze—"but man. You took an extra twenty minutes." Landon ribbed her.

"I'm so sorry. I was speaking with *Claudia* about something." She took great satisfaction in his shocked expression. "Let's discuss it over dinner, shall we?"

———

Shit, shit, shit. Man, try to give a woman compassion, let her down easy, and she craps all over your dinner plans. Damn Claudia, anyway.

Landon kept watching Ava for any hint she meant to dump him during dinner. It was killing him, all this polite conversation about his work, his day, his fine fucking job teaching the self-defense class.

They sat in Toulouse Petite, his favorite restaurant for Cajun cuisine in Seattle. As usual on a Friday night, the place was packed. So looking on the bright side, if she just walked out on him, no one would notice.

"Do you like managing people?" she asked and munched on her salad. She had a healthy appetite, which he appreciated. Nothing worse than going out with a woman who picked at her food.

"Yeah. It's like being in the Corps, except here people cry when you yell at them." He shrugged. "But once I let

Kyle know I wasn't serious about ripping his throat out, he calmed right down. Set a good tone for the office though."

She just looked at him, and he could totally imagine her in a pair of sexy glasses, peering down her nose at him. He mentally added a super prim skirt suit with garters and crotchless panties underneath. Then she'd ask him to lie back on her couch and confess his fantasies while she slowly stripped down...

"I'm kidding," he confessed, and she looked relieved. He actually *had* made Kyle cry, but not from threatening the guy bodily harm. More like, if the idiot didn't improve his efficiency, stop taking two-hour lunch breaks, and get his head out of his ass, Landon would openly fire the dumb shit in front of his fiancée and the entire office. Kyle had been a model employee since.

"You said you were a business major in college, and you're used to managing people. Sounds like you're a perfect fit for your job. So what's your office environment like?"

He responded, trying to sound interested. But good Christ. This polite chitchat was driving him insane. What the hell had Claudia said to her in the locker room? He kept waiting for Ava to bring it up. But for some reason she wasn't.

"Do you think it might snow this weekend?"

He couldn't take any more. "Are you going to tell me what Claudia said or what?"

She paused in the act of sipping her water, then set it down. The waiter chose that moment to bring them *more* water and to inquire about refills on their drinks. So Landon waited through excessive inquiries from an overly smiley guy about to get a fist in his face if he didn't hurry the hell up. Once Smiley finally left, Ava took a few bites of her salad, prolonging the agony.

In a calm voice, she mused, "You seem a little bothered, Landon."

"You think?" he snapped. He'd lost control of the situation, and it aggravated him. He couldn't do damage control if he had no idea what needed to be fixed. She hid a smile, but not fast enough.

He scowled. "You think this is funny?"

"Actually, I do." She laughed and finished the wine he planned on paying for, even though she'd lost their earlier bet. Delayed by his *ex*. Talk about a bad way to start the night.

He tried to hold onto his irritation when the waiter returned—friggin' guy—and dropped off their drinks and entrées. Ava wore a devilish grin, her full lips utterly kissable. Her hair looked silky under the soft light overhead, and he wondered what it would feel like brushing his belly while she kissed her way down his body.

He was dying to get his hands on her. She made it worse, because every time she smiled, his heart threatened to race out of his chest. Snarky, intelligent, sexy. She had it all, the trifecta of just-his-type, and he wanted a real kiss this time. So badly he could taste it.

With a loud sigh, he rested his elbow on the table and sank his head into his hand. "Okay, I give up. What the hell did she tell you? It's eating me alive not to know."

Ava's laugh warmed him. "Relax, Landon. She had nothing but lovely things to say about you."

He straightened in his seat and waited for the ax to fall.

Her compassion, and mirth, unnerved him. "In fact, I think she's in—"

"Don't say it."

"—love with you. Or maybe she just thinks she is. Because even after two months, she still misses you. Oh, and according to her, you don't emotionally share like you should. But then, your relationship with her was just physical, so maybe that's all you were invested in to begin with."

He groaned. "She told you that?"

"Yes. You should also know she's waiting with her arms wide open whenever you decide to go back to her."

Did Ava have to take such joy in the telling? Her eyes sparkled, and her cheeks looked so pink and pretty. Her lips were a glossy red, a deep, rich color that invited him to lean closer and take a sip. Would she taste like her wine? Or like the spicy dish she'd ordered, a saucy gumbo that smelled like heaven?

At that moment, his stomach rumbled. "You can keep talking, but I've got to eat. My stomach's about to collapse on itself." He swallowed a moan along with a healthy bite of his sandwich while she dug into her food. He finally relaxed, realizing she had no intention of ditching him. At least, not until after dinner. "I'm, uh, glad you're enjoying tonight."

"Oh, I am. It's not every night I see the great Landon Donnigan out of sorts with a woman." Ava's smile widened. "And being that woman, why, I never want the experience to end."

Neither did he, oddly enough. Wanting to sex her up made sense. Wanting to sit and talk and make her laugh? That went deeper than the physical. It was something to think about.

They ate in silence for a few bites, and he felt it safe

to change the subject. "Ah, so all that talk about the self-defense class. Did you like it?"

"I did."

"Don't sound so surprised. We know what we're doing."

"What surprised me most was that you two never talked down to us. You never tried to act tough and manly, as if you know better. You explained, you broke things down, and you put the power to act in our hands." She considered him, and her intensity stripped him bare. "You're doing the class for your sister."

"I mentioned that." Not in so many words, but Ava was smart. She'd put the clues together.

"Not in so many words."

Like she read my mind. He cleared his throat and pushed his po'boy aside. "Hope is my little sister. Lately she's been dating some real bozos. I don't want to see her get hurt, so we're teaching her how to physically stand up for herself. I mean, hell, she's smaller than you."

"I'm not small."

Ava was perfectly proportioned, to his way of thinking. "You're about average in height, right? Five-six? Five-five?"

She frowned. "Five-six and three quarters. I like to round up to an even five-seven."

"You're so cute pretending to be taller." He laughed at her, pleased at her blush. "Yeah, so, Gavin and I talked Hope into taking the class. And I realized it would help a lot of people, not just her." He gave her long look. "Like you. I mean, who knows what the next yahoo you date will be like?"

"There is that." She gave him a disdainful once-over. "Who *knows* what I'll be dealing with?"

He chuckled. "That's what I like about you." *Besides that mouthwatering body.* "Your sense of humor."

"And wit."

"Yeah, brainy babes do it for me." He deliberately laid on the macho attitude. The thicker the better.

Except she smiled at him again. "I know you're putting me on. I can tell when you try to get a rise out of me."

"Are you shrinking me, Doc?"

"Shrinking is not a verb, Landon."

He liked her saying his name with that combination of vexation and amusement.

"Technically it is."

She frowned, then sighed. "So it is. My point is I don't 'shrink' people. I talk to them. I observe. I offer therapeutic advice and counsel to my patients." She drank more wine. Moderate but consistent. Ava remained fully in control of herself. He liked that about her too. "I try not to beleaguer my dates with armchair diagnoses."

"Tell me about your dates." Finally a place he felt on even keel. "You told me you're looking for a baby-maker and future husband."

"I knew you'd bring that up again." Her eyes narrowed. Hot topic, apparently. "Why? Are you auditioning for the role?" she snapped.

"For baby-maker? I'm sure game to try." He smiled. "Though I'm surprised you're so casual about your future baby-daddy."

"I am *so* sorry I mentioned that to you." She finished what remained of her merlot. "To be honest, I only added the baby part to throw you. I'm dating because I'd like to find someone to share myself with. To be intimate with, yes, but for much more than mere sex."

Mere? "Sex is an important part of any relationship. Anyone can have friends. But sex is something you only have with someone special."

"Like Claudia?"

He saw her flush the moment the words left her lips. "Jealous?"

"I'm as jealous of her as you are of Charles." Her smug retort made his erection return full force, and just when he'd relaxed enough to be able to stand up without embarrassing himself.

He took a long drag of his beer. "Well then. I'd say you're pretty green, Doc."

She blinked. "What?"

"'Cause I didn't like the dickhead sitting anywhere near you. He's not in your league, and we both know it."

"But you are?"

"Hell yeah. I'm starting quarterback. You're easily a wide receiver." He pursed his lips and gave her a deliberate once-over. "Well, not wide so much as built. Sexy. Hmm, what's a complimentary word for 'killer rack'?"

Her pretty pink cheeks made it impossible not to reach for her. He stroked the back of her hand on the table, taken with her softness. So delicate, and so *tense*. He needed to do something about that.

They finished eating and waited for the bill.

"I'll pay my own way." Ava pulled her purse in front of her.

"I asked you out. I pay. Besides, you had to deal with Claudia." Her name felt bitter on his tongue.

Ava gave him a straight look and said, "You do realize buying my dinner does not entitle you to my body," just as the waiter arrived with the check.

Landon grabbed it from him, ignored the guy's wide eyes, and grinned at her. "Well then. How about if I let you leave the tip? My generosity should get me a kiss at least." He looked up at their waiter. "What do you think? Your service was stellar. I'm thinking a big tip for you, my man."

The guy turned on his heel and left. Landon glanced at Ava and saw her fighting not to laugh. "Something I said?"

She burst into laughter, and the sound of her amusement filled the empty spots inside him. Who knew making her feel good would make him feel twenty feet tall? Granted, he liked taking care of his dates, but seeing to Ava's—what she'd call—*emotional needs* felt as vital as breathing.

"He was fine. Twenty percent. What do I owe?"

"I was kidding." He tried to move the bill but she dragged it from him too fast.

She stuffed some cash in the card folder. "So our date…I have to tell you I wasn't bored. Not at all."

"Gee, Ava. Stroke my ego, why don't you?" he muttered and handed off the bill to their waiter, who darted off with it like a deer chased by hungry hounds. "So."

"So." She sipped her water, looking completely composed.

He didn't like that. He wanted her flustered, impassioned, her lips parted and begging for more. "What's the verdict?"

"I'm sorry?"

"You should be. You said you weren't bored. So did I charm you into another date or what?"

"I don't know that I'd use the word charming. At all." She snickered. "But you're interesting to talk to."

Interesting. Right up there with *nice.* The dating Kiss of Death. Might as well go for broke. "Well, let's make this plain. I want to go out with you again. You intrigue me. Don't think I didn't see how you deflected most of my questions, either. Every time I asked you about you, you turned it around and made the question about me. You'd make a hell of an interrogator."

"Thanks." She seemed genuinely pleased.

And that. There. She was so damn adorable. How many women liked being praised for their devious inquisitive skills?

"Shall we go?" he asked after the waiter slipped the card folder back on the table. He'd pester her outside for their next date, which they *would* have.

"Yes, let's." They stood, and he rounded the table to help her with her coat. She looked startled, then gave him a warm smile and accepted his help.

"I'm not completely hopeless."

"Not completely."

"You're a real smart-ass, you know that?"

She beamed.

Again, that attitude. He buttoned up his coat, glad it and his dark jeans masked his erection. They went outside, in the cold wind, and hurried to her car. She slipped on a patch of ice and would have fallen to the ground, like her purse, had he not grabbed her.

"Thanks," she gasped. "Fast reflexes."

He grunted, straightened her on her feet, and knelt to grab the stuff that had fallen out of her handbag. When he handed it to her, still on one knee, she put a hand on his cheek.

"My hero." She leaned down to give him a kiss, and he froze.

The warmth of her mouth, the sweet taste of woman and wine, made it difficult to swallow a moan, but he did, not wanting to come off as easy. A simple kiss and he was ready to beg.

Fuck.

She lifted her head, and he saw she'd closed her eyes. Her dark lashes looked thick, a forest of intrigue hiding the light green eyes of a temptress. Good thing they were in public, or he for sure would have tried to get her naked. Stat.

She blinked her eyes open and stared into his, and he swore he felt something snap between them. Then she hurriedly pulled back and clutched her purse to her chest. "Uh, th-thank you."

He rose and stared down at her. "You're welcome." He cupped her chin and returned the gentle kiss, still not sure how something so benign could make him feel as if he'd been hit by a two-by-four. He lifted his head and saw her looking starry-eyed. "So I'll see you again. Tomorrow?"

"Yes. Tomorrow. Right." She didn't blink, her gaze honed in on his. "What's tomorrow?"

He smiled. Good. The woman was scattered. It wasn't just him. "Tomorrow's Saturday, Doc. How do you feel about college basketball?"

"Watching it?"

"As opposed to…?"

"For all I know, your family gets together to play. And I never played."

"Washington is playing Oregon tomorrow. Want to come to my place and hang out? Take in the game on a big-screen TV? It'll be some casual fun, so you can continue screening me, see if some of my other qualities make your list." He smiled. "Besides, you know you want to see where I live. Consider it research, checking me out in my natural habitat."

"You make it sound like I'm heading into the jungle to study gorillas. Though the comparison seems apt."

He chuckled, not at all offended. "Yeah, sometimes my sister calls me a big ape."

"Not surprised. And I could have guessed you'd have a big-screen TV. You seem the type."

"Not that tough to figure out." He helped her into her car, then leaned down to confess, "I'm not compensating either, in case you were wondering."

"Compensating?" She started her tiny car. He doubted he'd be able to fit his arms in the thing, let alone his whole body.

"You know. A big-screen TV to make up for my *small banana*."

Her face paled.

"For the record, I rock a really big hammock." He winked. "See you tomorrow, three o'clock. I'll text you directions." He stood back, once more in control of this fledgling relationship, and watched her try to regain her composure before she drove off.

Laughing, he texted her directions to his place. Near him, something beeped. He glanced around and saw a pale blue phone on the sidewalk. "Hell." It must have fallen out of her purse.

He'd panic if he lost his phone. Despite not liking to talk to people in general, his cell was a necessity. With his family and work associates, people needed to get a hold of him. And Ava was a psychologist. She'd definitely need her phone.

He scrolled through it with a sigh, adding to his to-do list—*Remind Ava to password protect her cell phone. Tech Security 101.* Damn. He found her contact information easily, scoring her home address.

Landon whistled and walked to his car. His night had gotten even better. Now he had an excuse to see the doc at home. With any luck, she'd be wearing a negligee as she got ready for bed.

"Oo-fucking-rah." He grinned the whole way there.

Chapter 8

Ava HAD ALREADY PUT ON HER FAVORITE FLANNEL sleep shirt, her purple fuzzy socks, and washed up for bed when she realized she had yet to charge her phone. But when she rooted through her purse, she couldn't find it.

"What the heck?" She looked everywhere before she remembered she'd dropped her purse. "Oh no."

Beside herself because her life was on that thing, she hurried to find her tablet and had just rattled off a message to Landon, asking if he'd seen it after leaving her, when she heard a knock at the door.

She froze.

The doorbell rang, and she hurried upstairs to answer it. It had taken her a while to get used to having her bedroom and office downstairs. But with this layout, she had spectacular views of Lake Union off the main living space. A glance out the peephole showed Landon standing with his hands in his pockets, looking larger than life.

She yanked the door open then dragged him inside, locking up behind him. "Do you have my phone?"

He smiled and held it out, making the thing look tiny in his large hand.

So grateful she could weep, she took it and grabbed him for a tight hug.

He didn't move, and she felt a little silly. When she pulled back, she tried to go get her robe, but he latched on to her wrist and refused to let her go. A hysterical part of her wondered if she should use her self-defense move, to see if it would work in a real-world situation.

"What are you wearing?" His slow smile turned into a laugh. "I'd imagined something a little different. Are those tiny snowmen on your socks?"

She frowned. "Yes, they are."

"I like them."

"You do?"

"Yeah." He let her go after caressing the inside of her forearm with his thumb. A tiny touch, yet it felt overwhelming.

She prayed he couldn't see her nipples beading under her sleep shirt. She'd removed her undergarments, planning on going to bed. A big believer in airing out at night, Ava now wished she'd been a little more buttoned up.

She cleared her throat and crossed her arms over her chest. A pitiful defense, but it was all she had. "Thanks so much for bringing this by."

"I had a feeling you'd need it."

"Yes." They stared at each other.

"Well, I guess I should go," he said, at the same time she said, "Would you like a cup of tea?"

His slow grin heated her up from the inside. "Sure. That'd be great."

"I'll be right back." She hustled downstairs to get her robe, then returned and found him studying some of her family photos in the living room. "What kind of tea would you like?"

"You pick." He lifted a frame and studied it, then her. "How long ago was this taken?"

She stepped closer and took it from his hands with a smile. "Ah, that was right after college. A vacation to Germany with my parents."

"You look a lot like your mom. She's pretty."

Ava blushed. "Thanks. What about you?" She put the frame back. "Do you look like your parents?"

"A lot like my dad, but I have my mom's coloring. And personality, according to my brothers and Hope." He shrugged. "Mom's type A, and so am I. We're effective go-getters. Kind of like you." His sly smile unnerved her, and she made a pretense of turning away to make him tea when she was really trying to escape the strange heat filling her.

"Moroccan Mint okay?"

"Whatever. Sure." He followed her into her tiny galley kitchen and stood at the doorway, blocking her in. Probably not his intention, but with his size and the small space, he pretty much had her pinned to the room. He took off his jacket, still staring at her.

"You can toss it on the couch."

He stepped out to rid himself of the coat, and the kitchen again felt bigger. Until he returned.

He leaned against the open doorframe and crossed his arms over his broad, broad chest. The dark brown sweater he wore only enhanced his golden coloring. But she'd bet her last dollar he had no idea of his impact.

Landon seemed at ease with his masculinity and had no reason to play up his impossible-to-ignore maleness. Her girlie bits did flips of joy just being near the man.

She swallowed a sigh and turned on her electric kettle.

He frowned. "Seriously? You plug it in and turn it on? What happened to the old-fashioned whistle kind?"

"It's called technology. Your water will be ready in three minutes. Your tea in eight, after it's had time to steep."

His lips quirked. "You're a very precise kind of gal, aren't you, Ava?"

"Precise is good. It's difficult to get things wrong when you're precise."

He nodded. "I one hundred percent agree. I wasn't being critical, just making a point."

"What point?"

He stepped closer, and her pulse raced. "That we're a lot alike. We're both professionals. We're driven. We like to be *precise*," he said in a low voice as his gaze traveled over her body and lingered on her breasts—once again nearly exposed because her stupid robe refused to stay closed.

Damn, the things felt heavy, her nipples like tiny pebbles.

"R-right." If she crossed her arms now, he'd know she meant to hide her chest. And with a man like Landon, it paid to look in control. She'd pretend she suffered from the cold. He would be none the wiser, especially if she didn't react to that sexy, slumberous look on his face.

God, his eyes had half closed, his lips had parted, and he seemed to be breathing faster.

Considering her willpower seemed to be at an all-time low when it came to *not* kissing the man—*what had she been thinking after the restaurant?*—she sincerely hoped she could *not* sleep with him as well.

Not wearing any panties didn't help, because her body seemed to be readying itself to receive him even now. *I am not growing wet because he's here. No. Not that desperate. Am I?*

Before she could unfortunately answer herself, the timer dinged.

She sagged with relief. "Water's ready."

He nodded, still watching her like a hawk. She turned and poured them both a cup of tea, then looked for her timer that refused to shut itself off.

"What's wrong?"

"I can't find my apple timer. It's cute. A little red timer shaped like an apple. It turns when it's ticking." She found it behind the coffee grinder and hit a switch.

"Uh-huh. Why don't you just watch the clock on the microwave?"

Had he stepped closer?

"That's a good idea." She turned and found him standing in her personal space. But she couldn't back up because she had the counter directly behind her. "Landon?"

"You know, something else we both have in common. We love our families. I could tell by that picture, by the way you mentioned your parents, that you guys are close."

"We are." She sucked in a breath when he toyed with the hair on her shoulder.

"Are they in town?"

"N-no." She concentrated on being cool. "They're out East. My uncle and cousins are here though. You met Elliot and Sadie. So I have a great support system. Lots of family, friends." Her family were her friends, really, but she didn't want to look pitiful. "I have a great life."

"Yeah?" He leaned close, inhaled, and closed his eyes for a moment. When he opened them, the gold flecks in his irises mesmerized her. "You smell like flowers."

"It's my soap."

He nodded. And somehow his hands were on her shoulders, one of them stroking a length of her hair *so close* to her breast. "While we wait for our tea to be ready, maybe I could get that kiss you paid for."

"What?" She couldn't look away from his descending mouth.

"You know. You paid the tip. I figure I owe you for it."

"Tip?" Now just a mass of desire, she moaned as he laid his mouth over hers.

Hot. Not warm or cold or in between. The man was flipping *hot*, his lips like silk as they teased hers to open farther. Then his tongue was there, coaxing, delving deeper. She wanted to pull him closer, to fuse them together until she felt only him. Nothing made sense but Landon kissing her, touching her.

She ran her hands up his strong arms, gasping when he lifted her and hugged her tight, then sat her on the counter and spread her legs so he could step between them. He slid the material up her thighs while he kissed her into an almost-orgasm.

"Yeah, Doc. You taste like I thought you would."

The man could think? She sure as hell couldn't. "Uh-huh."

She arched her neck while he ran his lips over her throat, to her ear, then nibbled on her earlobe.

A burst of pleasure coursed through her body and centered between her legs. She ached, wet and aroused to the point of mindless desire.

"Like honey. So sweet. And sticky. And addicting." Landon stuck his tongue in her ear, and she gave a breathy moan.

He kissed her some more, his hands moving up and

down her inner thighs, stroking but not close enough to where she really wanted him.

"*Landon.*"

"What, baby? What do you need?" His low voice sounded more like a growl.

She felt him, hard and insistent, pressed against her inner thigh. His erection enormous, and doing her no good so far away. Ava drifted in a fugue of pleasure as Landon played her body as if he owned her.

"You're so pretty. So soft." He ran a hand from her leg up her belly and cupped her breast. "So fucking perfect," he rasped.

He held her breast, and she shifted, needing him inside her.

Then he pinched her nipple, lightly grinding the heel of his hand against the nub.

She yanked him by the neck closer and kissed him, ravaging his mouth.

She felt him breathe into her. Sensed the shiver pass over him, and then his hands were there, sliding up her thighs, pushing her sleep shirt higher. His fingers grazed her slick folds, and he swore.

"In me," she breathed, on fire to have him. Never so desirous of anything in her life. But she felt like she'd die if he didn't *do* something!

"Oh fuck. Yeah, that's what I want. You, Doc." Landon pulled his hands away, and she could have cried. But then he was between her legs, his face pushing closer, and he sucked her clit with deep draws.

She cried out and clutched his hair, trying to get closer.

Landon licked and sucked, throwing her into an orgasm with little effort.

Ava came hard, crying out as she rocked over his amazing mouth while he continued to lick and tease her into a second, even more powerful climax. This time he added a thick finger, and she swore she lost awareness of everything for a moment.

When she could think again, she felt his kisses on her thighs. He rose to his feet, his large hands gripping her legs hard enough to leave bruises, and the pain felt surprisingly pleasurable.

"God, Ava. You look fucking sexy as hell right now." He stared down at her, seeing her face sans makeup, no doubt slack with the bliss she could feel to her bones.

Landon kissed her again, and she tasted herself on his lips. So sexy, that he'd kissed her there. So intimate. She'd claimed a part of him, and she wanted to claim even more.

But Landon swore and stepped back, his erection impossible to miss. Talk about huge.

He saw where her gaze had gone and sighed. "I should go." He glanced at her, sitting on her kitchen counter with her shirt still hiked high enough to see everything, her robe doing her absolutely no good untied and parted, and moaned. "I want to fuck you so hard. Bend you over and just take you until we're both screaming." He sounded hoarse.

So do it!

"But I didn't bring any protection with me. And if I get anywhere near that pussy, I'm coming inside."

His frank language did nothing but turn her on all over again.

Landon surprised her by moving once more between her legs. This time he pulled her sleepshirt down and retied her robe, covering her back up. Then he kissed her with all the passion inside him and left her unable to do more than groan and beg him to continue.

"That's what you need to remember, Ava." He kissed down to her throat and sucked. Hard.

She gasped, stunned at the painful pleasure.

"Me. My mark. We're going to have so much fun when we finally hit the sheets." He leaned back to stare down at her. "I like being in charge in bed. You liked me eating you out, baby?"

She could do no more than nod.

"Then just think how good I'll make you feel when I'm driving into you." He leaned closer and whispered right into her ear, "When I'm coming and you're gripping me tight with that pussy. Or when I'm thick and hard and between your lips. When my mouth is sucking that sweet clit until your cream rushes down my throat." His hand crept to her neck, and he gave a little squeeze. "I'll never, ever hurt you. But I'll show you so much you never knew you liked. You'll beg for it and love when I give it to you."

She couldn't believe how aroused she was from hearing his bossy talk. *Oh. My. God.* What was this man doing to independent and powerful Ava Rosenthal?

He lifted her from the counter and stood her back on the floor. Then he tugged her with him to fetch his coat and walk to the door.

He stopped to put on his coat, then he took her chin in his hand.

By this time she'd gathered her wits. What the hell had she done?

His satisfied smile belied the tension in his frame and the erection she could still see. "You liked what we did."

"So what? You did too," she said, no hesitation.

He nodded. "I loved it. Tasting you, seeing you come. I've never seen anything sexier in my life." He continued to hold her chin, still taking charge.

Because she'd let him.

She tugged her chin free, and his smile deepened. "Don't get any funny ideas. It was great sex. But you don't own me."

"Not yet." He licked his lips. "But I think we could have a lot of fun together. Exploring." He paused. "You liked me taking charge, didn't you?"

"I did." No point denying it. Ava refused to be ashamed of her sexuality. "As much as you liked dominating."

He nodded. "I want that with you. I want sex. I want a lot of it."

She could have slapped herself. *On the first date, Ava? Really?* "It got out of hand. I hadn't expected this."

"Me neither." He pointed to himself. "You see this, right? I didn't bring any condoms with me."

She flushed. "Yes, yes, I see it. You don't need to point."

He chuckled, and the sexual tension lowered but didn't dissipate. "So you still coming to the game tomorrow?"

"Yes, but I'm unequivocally stating I refuse to have sex with you on the second date."

"Actually, it'll be our third date. But I'm fine with that." He shrugged.

"Really?" She nodded to his groin.

"I'm not driven by my hormones. I'm in control of myself." He lifted his chin. "I can wait until you're ready."

"I'm not making babies with you," she said bluntly.

"Good, because I'm not ready to be a father yet." He continued, "I'm clean. Always use protection. And I'm assuming you do too."

"Of course I do." She paused. "Shouldn't we have had the safe sex talk before you went down on me?"

He blinked. "Wow. Went down? Yeah. I sure did. Didn't think you'd want to talk about it though."

She raised a brow. "I'm a therapist. We're allowed to talk about sex."

"And glad I am about that." He chuckled. "Relax, Doc. Just because you came, hard, doesn't mean I'm winning any contests."

"Do tell."

He laughed again. "And yeah, I should have asked first. But you made me so crazy. We have some seriously hot chemistry. I want to eat you up all over again." His eyes darkened.

Ava wanted the same thing, and she had no idea what to make of her suddenly overactive libido. "That was nice."

"Good. I was striving for nice."

"Oh, shut up."

He laughed. "I should go before you start avoiding me again."

"For the last time, I wasn't avoiding you."

"Liar." He kissed the tip of her nose. "Okay, gorgeous. Here's the deal. You say when we have sex. But I say how we have it. I get to be in charge. But you set the pace. Third date, fourth, tenth, your call."

"Hmm." She liked the idea. A little too much. "Well, I don't know…"

"What's not to know? Don't you want to feel me inside you the next time you come?" His eyes widened. "*Now* you're blushing? Seriously?"

"Would you hush for a second?" She took a deep

breath and let it out, trying to be rational. "I'm very attracted to you. I admit it. But I'm also out on the dating scene, looking for compatibility in a man."

He frowned. "Your point?"

"I have a date with Charles on Sunday. A follow-up."

"Follow-up. Sounds like a dental appointment," he huffed. "So break it."

"No."

His frown turned into a scowl. "Look, I'm not interested in you sexing up the male population to see who fits you best."

"Neither am I." Seriously irked, she shoved him back a step. Or at least, she *tried* to shove him back. The mountain of a man wouldn't move. "Look. You're not my type, but I'm giving you the benefit of the doubt. Something I'm right now regretting."

He grabbed her by the arms and turned her around, then backed her up against her own front door. Pinning her there, his hard body against hers, she felt his heartbeat racing, his cock grinding against her belly. He was forceful but not scary. In a word—sexy.

"Regretting, huh?" He kissed her, showing her no mercy, until she panted and clawed at his shoulders for more. "Regretting that too?"

She wanted to slap him, but his arrogance was having the opposite effect. She wanted him again.

"You want me, Doc. As much as I want you. I don't share. You want to play around with some wussy wannabes? Fine. But this mouth belongs to me. So does this pussy." He cupped her between her legs, and kissed her.

By the time he'd finished, she'd come again while he seemed even more frustrated.

"Well?" he rasped. "You want me to take this to Claudia?" He ground against her.

She didn't have to think about her answer. "*No.*"

"Then we agree."

"Yes. Wait. What?"

"You can have your date with *Charles,*" he sneered the man's name. "But you're still coming over for our game tomorrow. We're going to enjoy it, get to know each other better."

She nodded, wanting nothing more, oddly because of his angry attitude and protective, overpowering strength.

"And when boring Charles doesn't turn your brain on like I do, you dump him. Deal?"

Had he not said the word "brain," she might have been able to reject his claim. But Landon did more than arouse her body. That he did stupendously. The jerk also aroused her mind, and he knew it.

"You're on."

He pulled her hand to his crotch then and closed his eyes. "One more thing."

"Yes?" She gripped him, unable to help herself, and saw his grimace as her tribute.

"Are you on any birth control?"

"I, um, yes. Why?" It had been over a year and a half since her last sexual encounter. A casual date that had had the potential to go further, except the sex had been awful, their connection even worse. Another reason to focus on her work instead of a man. But she'd continued to take her pills because she liked regulating her cycle.

"Because I'll be getting a checkup. You and me...I don't think we'll want to use condoms when the time comes. But tell you what. I'll leave that decision up to you too."

"You're so generous," she mocked, wanting to be annoyed. She sure as hell planned on making the decisions when it came to sex. But every time he conceded something important, whether he knew it or not, he conveyed that he valued her intelligence, her worth, and her *right* to decide.

"Want to see how generous I really am? Don't wear panties again tomorrow." The manipulator ran a finger inside her thigh and into her sex.

"God." She gripped his shoulder, worn out yet wanting another go.

"Yeah, feels like heaven to me too." He groaned and withdrew his finger, then sucked it clean. "I want more. Don't make me wait too long."

"Or what?"

"Or my balls might turn blue and fall off," he growled, kissed her, then set her back. "Now I have to go before I come in my pants. Hope you're happy." He left and shut the door behind him.

Ava stared at the door, motionless, slippery between her legs, and so incredibly sleepy.

Landon Donnigan gave me three orgasms. For free. The thought made her laugh. Then she remembered him tonguing her and she shivered. He had skills. No question. She totally knew why Claudia wanted him back, and the notion didn't sit well at all.

Landon had a gruff charm, despite what she'd said to him. He was protective and commanding at turns, tender and selfless at others. He hadn't demanded she get him off, nor had he even considered unprotected sex. *At least, not until he gets himself checked out by a doctor.*

The idea of Landon and her having sex, skin to skin, set her into another round of erotic fantasies, many of them where she took control in bed. Would he let her? Would she want to, after the pleasure he'd shown her by being in command?

Ava's phone buzzed, distracting her. She picked it up and saw his address, along with an order to be on time tomorrow and bring chips and salsa.

"Jerk." She smiled. She felt weightless. So good and relaxed. Poor Landon. He had to be hurting. And yeah, he did rock a big hammock.

Ava turned everything off and cleaned up before going to bed. But once there, she couldn't fall asleep, thinking she needed to make a few moves of her own to keep Landon where she wanted him. She just wished she knew where that might be. And why the idea of another date with Charles now felt…wrong.

Chapter 9

LANDON NAGGED HIS BROTHERS TO HURRY UP. HOPE was coming too, an unexpected addition after her Saturday plans had fallen through.

He still wasn't sure why he'd invited Ava to a family gathering, but at least his parents wouldn't be in attendance.

You know why you want her here. He frowned, because he did. With his siblings present, he'd be tempted, but he wouldn't fuck the woman over the couch. Or go down on her in the kitchen, though maybe the dining room table would be at a better height for—

No. He'd completely lost it last night. What kind of guy went down on a girl on their second date— because he was totally counting that night next to her and Charles as their first—and hoped to get a third? He'd totally pushed her boundaries, with her consent of course, but still. Landon knew better. There was a certain pacing that went with courtship. Had he and Ava been looking to bounce and nothing more, then sure, a one-night stand worked.

But he wanted more, and now he had work to make up for having no willpower to resist her last night. From Ava, he wanted laughter, teasing, her approval. *Fuck.* The woman had bewitched him, even after dealing with her attitude and hearing all her nonsense about dating and babies. Plus, she was a therapist. Landon had to be a masochist to want to date a woman who psychoanalyzed everyone she met.

Yet she hadn't done that to him. Hadn't asked him a million questions and demanded he share crap the way Claudia and a few others throughout the years had.

"You going to stand around staring or help out?" Gavin groused as he sprayed glass cleaner on the TV screen.

"Are you using the microfiber cloth?"

"For fuck's sake." Gavin grabbed the microfiber and dusted.

"Just make sure there aren't any pee stains on the toilet and you're done," Landon ordered.

"Theo, go—"

Landon cut him off. "No, Gavin. *You* made the mess, *you* clean it up."

"Asshole."

Theo grinned, but his smile faded at Landon's glare. "What? What did I do?"

"You're going to be on your best behavior today. And you keep Hope in line. You get me?"

"Oh, sure." Theo smiled. "I won't let her badger Ava, I swear. I even wore my best sweatshirt. Look. No holes."

Landon grunted.

"So what's the deal?" Gavin asked. "Are we just impressing her until you get laid or what?"

"Nice mouth." He glanced at Theo, still just a boy in his eyes.

"Please. The kid's twenty. He might be all virginal, but he's had the sex talk by now."

Theo glared. "Screw you, Gavin. I don't need any protecting from anything."

"Is that so?" Landon studied his youngest brother. "Popped your cherry, huh? Theo's not a virgin anymore, are you?"

Theo turned bright red. "What the hell kind of question is that to ask?"

Gavin blinked. "Oh my God. You aren't, are you? Theo, you dog. I'm so proud."

"Stop talking. Please."

Landon smiled. "It was that girl you took to the prom, wasn't it?"

"So what if it was? She's nice."

"You two still hooking up?" Gavin asked.

"Nah. She went away to school."

"You miss her?" Landon asked.

"No. We were just friends."

"*Friends*-friends." Gavin winked, being a horse's ass without even trying.

Theo expelled a loud, annoyed breath. "Does he have to be here?"

"I'm keeping an eye on him, so yeah."

Now it was Gavin's turn to be annoyed. "The hell you are. I'm fine."

"You're sober, but you're still not sleeping well."

"You don't know shit."

"No, you have a lot of nightmares, Gav." Theo obviously felt bad about narcing on him, but between them, he and Landon had agreed to care for their brother, whether Gavin wanted it or not.

"Nah." Gavin huffed. "I was probably just talking in my sleep or something."

Landon would have said more when the doorbell rang. Crap. The house still needed some sprucing up.

"I'll get it," Theo sang and bolted for the door.

Landon shoved Gavin toward the bathroom. "Hurry up with the toilet."

"Aye-aye, Major Pain in My Ass."

He told Gavin to shove it, then took another quick glance around. The room looked neat. He'd cleaned most of it last night. After coming home and jerking off, *twice,* with the taste of Ava still on his lips, he'd been too keyed up to sleep. But after his head hit the pillow, he'd slept hard...and late. Waking at nine-thirty on a Saturday? He'd wasted too much time on dreams about Ava, when he'd be seeing her soon enough.

She entered with a chatty Theo, holding a bag.

"Chips and salsa." She handed the bag to Theo. "I was ordered to bring them."

"'Told to' bring them. I'd never order you, Ava." Landon grinned.

Theo snorted. "He's always bossing everyone around. Not surprised he got to you too." He left for the kitchen.

Ava looked Landon square in the eye without a blush. Nice. He'd expected her to be flummoxed, embarrassed, a little shy maybe. Apparently his doc was made of stronger stuff.

"Landon."

He stifled a grin at her formal tone. "Ava."

"Theo told me this is a family event?"

"Sometimes. I like to watch the games with friends," he said as Gavin walked back in the room.

"But today I figured I'd go with family instead, since Gavin's so pathetic lately."

Gavin frowned. "Quit being an ass." He set down the bin of cleaning crap he should have left under the sink in the bathroom. "Hey, Ava. Brave of you to join us."

She smiled. "Well, who am I to miss a college basketball game? Who's playing, by the way? I forget."

"Oregon State against Utah. I thought it was Washington, but they play the Ducks later tonight. My bad." Landon rubbed his hands together. "But the Utah game is going to be even better. I can't wait."

"He's biased," Gavin said. "Landon played football for the Beavers."

"Middle linebacker," Theo added. "It was actually pretty cool. We went to some of the games, and when he played in college, he stopped tackling us at home."

"Funny." Landon smirked.

"Landon went to college?" Ava blinked. "I didn't know he could read."

His brothers laughed, and Landon knew a sense of satisfaction that Ava would fit in just fine with his family. Today wouldn't be awkward or weird, and he had a feeling she wouldn't try too hard to be liked. She'd be her genuine self, and everyone would love her.

Landon glared at his brothers. "If everyone's done mocking me—"

"Not yet." Gavin smiled and moved to Ava. He took her hand in his, kissed the back of it, then led her toward the kitchen. "What can I get you to drink? You'll probably need something strong since you agreed to be with Landon here for the game. Or did you agree? Did he force you into coming? It's some kind of blackmail, right?" He sighed, loudly. "I've been trying to get him help for his criminal tendencies."

Gavin was such a dick.

Landon didn't hear what Ava said back, but he heard his brother's laugh well enough.

The doorbell rang again.

"That's Hope. I'll get it." Theo once again darted to the door.

Landon took the opportunity to hide the cleaning stuff, straightened up in the bathroom since Gavin had forgotten to set out a clean hand towel, and returned feeling more in control of himself. He hadn't jumped Ava, thrown her up against the wall for the kiss he was desperate to have, or made a fool of himself. Yet.

So far so good.

He returned to the living room to find his brothers on either side of Ava on the couch. Gavin smirked at him. "Hey, Bro. Bring in the chow, would you?"

Landon frowned and swallowed the *Get it yourself* he wanted to snarl at his brother. Instead, he played host and fetched the chips and dip tray, as well as the mini pizza pockets he always ate on game day. If the Beavers lost, he refused to take the blame.

He saw Ava and Theo drinking sodas. To his relief, Gavin had a glass of water in front of him on the table.

Following his stare, Gavin rolled his eyes, no doubt tired of what he perceived as Landon's unasked-for interference.

Everything seemed perfect. Except… "Where's Hope?"

"I'm here. Don't get your panties in a twist." Hope hurried down the stairs. "Sorry. The bathroom was occupied so I used the one upstairs. In your room," she said to Landon. "Gavin, yours is gross."

"Hey, it's not me, it's Theo."

Hope just looked at him. "Please. We all know you're a slob."

Ava grinned. "It feels like I'm at my cousins' for a Sunday dinner."

Hope shoved Gavin off the couch, forcing him onto a chair so she could sit next to Ava. "Hi. I'm Hope."

Even better.

"Ava." Ava held out her hand and they shook. "I saw you at the self-defense class. You were great demonstrating techniques."

"Yeah. I've had a lot of experience dealing with idiots who can get grabby." She shot her brothers a look. "That means you too, Theo."

"Hey, I'm the *good* brother." He smiled at Ava. "I'm the baby of the family."

"He gets away with more crap…" Gavin shook his head. "Sad, really."

Landon wanted a beer but in deference to Gavin grabbed a soda instead. He took the remaining chair next to the couch, doing his best not to heave Theo out of the way and plant his ass next to Ava.

He could handle sitting near her, but he couldn't tolerate the chatter. "Okay, everyone shut up while they announce the start."

Ava said in a low voice, "When he says come over and watch the game, he's not kidding."

"Shh." He glared at her, as well as the peanut gallery laughing at him.

The game started, and though he tried to be absorbed into it, he couldn't help spending most of his attention on Ava.

"I don't get it." She sighed. "My cousins watch football

for the tight pants and manly looking uniforms. But basketball is all giants rushing around to sink an orange ball in a net. What's the point?"

"I'm with you. I especially don't like how they play." Hope shoved a bunch of chips in her mouth, obviously at ease with Ava. She wasn't using any of her "guests are here" manners. "Like that guy. He's clearly not going to get through the mob of people standing in front of the basket. So why doesn't he pass it off?"

"To draw the foul." Theo shook his head. "We've been through this, Hope. Seriously. It's not hard to follow."

Ava sipped her drink. "It's ridiculous. Why keep plowing through so many people? I'd pass the ball, then move where there's no one, yell for someone to pass it to me, then shoot. That's if I didn't dribble out of bounds. Frankly I find bouncing a ball in place tedious."

"I know, right?"

"Yes." Ava took some chips. "I mean, that guy right there. He's shoving the guy right next to him. That can't be legal."

"It's called playing a physical game." Theo frowned. "Have you ever played sports?"

Ava nodded. "I suppose tennis doesn't count. But at least in tennis, I never shoved anyone out of the way."

Hope agreed. "Good point. It's so much more civilized."

"And not so pushy." Ava pointed. "See? That guy is open right there. Shouldn't someone be passing him the ball?"

Theo sighed. "That's the referee."

"Hey, you two armchair quarterbacks." Gavin frowned. "Can the chatter."

"Isn't that football talk?" Ava asked.

"It fits," Gavin answered.

"Seriously." Even Theo looked annoyed.

Landon saw the tiny smile Ava tried to hide. She was *such* a pain in the ass. Man, he really liked her.

Hope shrugged. "Just calling it like we see it. I mean, why doesn't that Oregon guy just launch it down the court to number fourteen?"

"That's a good point." Ava asked.

"Because he can't," Gavin disagreed. "Utah will pick if off if they try. See? Number thirty-three? He's guarding twenty-two, who's right in front of fourteen."

"Why don't they just throw the ball up and let everyone jump for it?" Ava suggested. "It looks like Oregon is taller."

Landon struggled not to laugh out loud. "Just because a guy is tall doesn't mean he can jump. And throwing the ball away is just stupid." He paused at something one of the announcers said and glared at the TV. "*What?* That wasn't offensive. Are you kidding me? He friggin' moved his feet!"

"Nah. Totally charged." Gavin pointed to the replay. "See? Utah is planted."

"Bullshit."

Theo jumped in. "I'm with Landon."

"Of course you are, brownnoser." Gavin snorted.

Landon argued the call, enjoying the hell out of himself.

"You ask me, there are too many rules. They keep blowing the whistle every three seconds." Ava turned to Hope. "Hey, do those pizza rolls taste good?"

"Try some. I love 'em." His sister handed her the bowl.

The girls talked appetizers while Landon and Gavin dove into another shouting match, this one about the reversed call on the charge.

"Seriously?" Gavin yelled. "What bullshit. That wasn't a foul. It's called good defense."

Theo scowled. "Sorry, Landon. But in slow-mo, even I can see that reverse call is crap."

"Traitor."

"Whatever. I hope Utah takes the game," Gavin announced.

"You're such an asshole," Landon growled.

"Such language." Gavin tsked and sipped his water, sticking out a pinkie as he did so. "Ah, water. How refreshing." His sarcasm was enough to choke a mule. "Would anyone like refills on drinks?"

Landon choked on a laugh. "You're a moron, you know that?"

"Why? Because I think Utah's got a better defense than your stupid team?"

"*Stupid?*" Not funny. He rattled some stats off the top of his head, because he knew Gavin had nothing to come back with.

Then Theo joined in for another rousing argument while Hope and Ava sat watching them as if baffled by their behavior.

Yeah, college basketball was the absolute best.

Ava watched the guys argue, volleying back and forth without taking a breath, and getting louder with each statistic and swear word.

"Then you have people like *him*," Hope said, nodding to Landon, "who think anything they say will influence what happens on TV." She sighed. "It's sad, really. My brothers always seem much more intelligent before watching one of these games."

"Don't tell, but my cousins aren't the only ones who like football games for the tight pants and shoulder pads," Ava admitted.

Hope laughed. "Don't forget soccer and their strong thighs."

"Good point." Ava watched the game. "Hmm. Some of those players aren't bad. Too young and too tall. But not bad-looking."

"I like 'em tall. And big." Hope wiggled her brows and gave an evil laugh.

"Ha." Ava had expected to like Landon's family. But she hadn't anticipated feeling so at ease with them. It really did feel like being with her cousins at Sunday dinner.

More, she liked the way Landon behaved with them. He wasn't showing off, acting any differently than she'd imagined he would, or seemingly trying to impress her. Which in itself impressed her. She'd met too many people who cared more about looking grand or important than being decent. Not Landon.

As he argued with his brothers, he seemed to be enjoying himself. And that joy was easy to see.

Ava faced Hope again. "So your brother played college football?"

"Yep. Full scholarship. He was really good, but he only used college as a stepping-stone to join the Marine Corps as an officer." Hope eyed her brother with amusement. "He's a scary guy."

"Oh?"

"All that focus. When he wants something, he goes after it full tilt." Hope turned to her, the pretty blond with deep brown eyes a carbon copy of the picture of the woman on the mantel.

Ava glanced at it, thinking Landon and his siblings would age well. *What a handsome family.*

It took Ava a moment to realize Hope's amusement had settled on her. "Why are you grinning at me like that?"

Hope leaned closer to murmur, "Landon doesn't bring girls home to watch basketball games. And he sure doesn't act all goonish around his conquests."

"Conquests?" Was Hope referring to her? And conquests, with an S?

"My brother is a decent guy, but I'm sorry to say women come kind of easily to him." Hope sighed. "All my brothers are like that. Even Theo, and he's just out of high school."

"Well, you're an attractive family." Ava glanced once more at the picture on the mantel.

"Thanks. We do kind of take after Mom and Dad. Fortunately, we just *look* like them. If I was a carbon copy of my mother, I'd shoot myself."

Ava chuckled. "A common mother-daughter complaint."

"You too?"

"No, but I'm a therapist. I hear a lot of things in my office. And that complaint is as commonplace as fathers and sons butting heads."

"That would be Theo and Dad, which is funny because my dad is the easiest guy in the world to get along with."

Landon swore. "Theo, you can't seriously think that. Are you a moron? You—" Landon broke off as his team scored twice in a row. "*Yes!* Did you see that?" All three men now stood in front of the TV, so Ava couldn't see a thing. Not that she particularly cared.

"I have eyes, Landon." Theo glared. "Now I think I'm going for Utah too."

"That's it." Gavin hugged him. "Come over to the dark side."

Hope chuckled. "Gavin's a master at getting under Landon's and Theo's skin. But not mine." She took a pizza roll and nibbled. "See how goonish big brother is acting? I love it."

"I don't know that I'd call it goonish."

"Neither would I," Landon said, proving he'd been listening to them. "Don't be a pest, Hope."

"Whatever. Look, you big ape, we can't see the screen. You're all blocking it with your enormous fat heads."

"Another commercial. This sucks." Theo stomped back to Ava's side and sat.

Landon plucked him from the couch, dumped him on the floor, and sat next to Ava instead.

"Landon, damn it."

He put an arm behind her on the couch. "Hey there, Doc. How are you?"

"Oh, you have time for me now that a commercial is on?" She found him endearing in a dopey, male-stereotypical kind of way.

"Yep. And these last for at least five minutes. So talk."

"I'm using the head," Gavin announced and darted down the hallway.

"TMI, dude." Theo frowned at the near-empty bowl of pizza rolls. "Aw, man. Hope, you ate them *all*."

"Nope. That was Ava."

Ava flushed, because she'd done her share of munching. "Um, it might have been me because—"

Theo shook his head. "Nice try. But I saw you chowing down, Hope." Theo's eyes widened. "God. I'm so sorry. I forgot."

"What?" Hope sounded wary.

"That you're eating for two. Explains why your hips have been getting wider. Better for the baby."

"Hope?" Landon's eyes widened. "Are you—"

"You'll pay for that, Theo*dork*." Hope raced after Theo, who ran laughing all the way up the stairs.

"Lovely family." Ava chuckled. "Will she hurt him if she catches him?"

"He's big but he's spry. My sister, however, is evil. She can pinch like nobody's business. And if you try to retaliate, she runs to Mom and Dad. She's so annoying." He wore a wide smile while saying it, then whispered something.

"What?" Ava leaned closer to hear him and found herself succumbing to a kiss that was over too soon.

"Been wanting to do that since you walked in," he admitted and tucked her hair behind her ear. He kissed her again, this time slipping her some tongue. She wanted to protest that his family was too close for this kind of intimacy, but she couldn't find it in her to deny a simple kiss.

"Get a room, you two," Gavin said.

She could hear his smirk.

Landon quickly disengaged and stood, glaring down at her. "Seriously, Ava. *My family* is here. Hands to yourself."

Seeing Gavin's wide eyes, she blushed. "Oh please. He was all over me and I—"

Gavin yelled for Theo and Hope, who soon appeared. "Hey, guys, Ava's mauling Landon. Come see."

"Gavin, you are an ass," she seconded Landon's opinion of his brother, who laughed like a loon.

"What? What did we miss?" Theo asked, breathless. His hair was askew, his sweatshirt rumpled, while Hope didn't seem to have a hair out of place.

"Nothing but your brother bothering me," Ava growled, torn between embarrassment and laughter.

"With his *mouth*," Gavin emphasized. "No funny business here, people. This is a family party."

"Yeah, Ava. Really." Landon looked horrified. "I mean, not in front of my brothers and sister. Oh, the shame."

"I can see why no one likes you," she said in a flat voice, causing his siblings to burst into laughter.

"Well, I really like *you*, Ava." Gavin gave her a thumbs-up. "It's like you see the real Landon under all that testosterone."

"You should talk," Landon bit back, now looking less than amused.

Theo pointed to the TV. "Oh hey, commercial's over."

Like magic, the brothers settled back down to watch and argue.

She and Hope exchanged a look.

Hope shook her head. "Men."

Ava nodded. "An alien species, all right."

Chapter 10

DURING HALFTIME, LANDON TOOK HER ON A TOUR OF his place at the prodding of his brothers, who were still whining about all the cleanup they'd had to do.

Ava thought it was sweet that he'd wanted the place to look tidy for her. "How nice of you, Landon."

"Stop calling me nice, damn it."

"Nice is bad?"

"Nice is terrible. Now, the tour." He grabbed her by the hand.

She glanced down at it.

He smiled. "I don't want you to get lost while you're here."

"So thoughtful of you." Ava bit back a grin, surprised to find herself having a fabulous time. "You're not taking me to see your etchings, are you?" His palm felt warm around hers.

He chuckled. "Nah. I'll show you something much better." They walked up the stairs.

"You mention the words banana or hammock and I'm out of here."

He laughed long and loud. "Jesus, you're funny. Come with me, Doc. I'll show you around." He stopped at the top of the stairs. "This is our hallway. Note the clean carpet. That's all me. I love to vacuum."

"I'm not surprised." Landon was a discipline-and-order

kind of guy. She couldn't see him living in a mess. They walked down the hall.

"And here, the guest bathroom. The *clean* bathroom, unlike the one downstairs known as the pigsty Gavin funks up on a daily basis." He opened another door to show a room full of boxes. "Gavin's crap. He's temporarily staying with me until he gets his own place. His room is downstairs. He and Theo are sharing right now."

"Theo lives with you too?"

"We're giving him a break from Dad." Landon shook his head. "Family drama. It's tiresome."

"But someone's got to handle it, so why not you, hmm? I'm sensing that's your role in your family. The peacemaker."

"You *are* good." He gave her a look she had a hard time deciphering.

"I am."

"Okay, Doc. Just no shrinking me unless I ask for it."

"You're always asking for it," she said under her breath.

He must have heard her because he laughed. "I am, aren't I?" He paused in front of a closed door and turned the knob. "And this, good doctor, is the ultimate in bedrooms. A master for the master. A glorious area for my splendor to be showcased, where my magnificence is only matched by the size of my—"

She shoved past him into the room and froze.

They stared, her in amusement, him in shock that soon turned to anger.

"Gavin! Hope! Theo! *Get your asses up here.*"

"Do you really want your family seeing this?" She

had difficulty keeping a straight face. "I mean, your proclivities are nothing to be embarrassed about."

"It's not mine, damn it."

"But still, you're sharing the house with Theo, and he mostly likely hasn't been exposed to these kinds of things."

"I have no idea who put this here."

His cheeks rivaled the red of her favorite apple.

"Are you sure? It's nothing to be embarrassed about. And if you think about it, using…that…is a way to promote safe sex."

"Christ." He dragged a hand through his cropped hair, and she coughed so as not to laugh.

What sounded like a herd of elephants tramped up the stairs before Hope, Gavin, and Theo rushed in behind them.

"What…?" Hope was aghast. "Oh my gosh, Landon. What is *that*?"

Gavin and Theo started laughing. Hope joined in.

Ava could no longer contain her mirth. "No wonder you think you're popular with the ladies!" She held her ribs. "They never say *no*, do they?"

"Ew, that thing looks like Ava," Theo said when he could catch his breath.

Ava wiped tears from her eyes. "Well, this is awkward."

The blow-up doll in the middle of Landon's bed had long dark hair and neon green eyes. It wore a pair of shorts and a Jameson's Gym T-shirt. And by its left hand was a flyer for the self-defense class that had written in marker over it, "SIGN ME UP."

"Man, Landon. I had no idea." Gavin shook his head.

Landon glared. "*You* did this."

"Not me, Bro."

"Hope, Theo?" Landon stared with suspicion at his brother and sister. Then he turned to Ava.

"*Whoa.* I certainly didn't do this. I mean, I guess I should be flattered. She's oddly attractive in a rubbery kind of way."

Landon clapped a hand over his eyes.

Ava bit her lip not to laugh again. "Do you do this often? Substitute dolls for real women? Because, Landon, that's not exactly a healthy relationship in the making. I could recommend someone you could see if you wanted to talk about—"

"*Out.* Everyone—*out.*"

Ava followed his family down the stairs, watching them high-five each other.

"Hey, I didn't do it," Gavin said, "But that was hella funny."

"Bust-a-gut funny," Theo agreed. "But it wasn't me."

Hope frowned. "It wasn't me either."

They all turned to Ava. "Don't look at me. I just came for the game and the pizza rolls."

Theo looked back at Gavin. "You're lying. It had to be you. But don't worry. I won't tell."

"Narc, of course you will. My money's on you, though."

"Me? Why make trouble? I don't want more prank wars."

Hope shuddered. "Not that."

"Prank wars?" Ava settled back on the couch with the group. Her cousins would love these guys.

Hope explained, "It used to happen when we were all living at home together. Someone would prank someone else, then the jokes would get embarrassing and out of control. Pantsing someone in high school, writing weird notes about them in the school paper. Once, Theo blamed

Gavin for something Landon did—for five bucks—and my parents grounded Gavin for two weeks."

"I'm still not over that either," Gavin groused.

"It's funny, but evil. I want no part of it." Theo shook his head. "I'm not looking for a buzz cut or a mohawk, and I sure as heck don't want my hair dyed pink again."

"Seriously?" Ava gaped.

Theo rolled his eyes. "When I was a kid, I wanted a mohawk. Mom said I couldn't get it. Then I woke up one morning missing most of my hair except for a long strip in the middle. I was eight, and it grew back fast, but man, I was in so much trouble. Dad just laughed." Theo grinned, then frowned. "Back when he was a forgiving man. A decent father and nice guy."

"So dramatic." Gavin put Theo in a headlock and gave him a noogie, ignoring his younger brother's protests.

"Before you ask, yes, they're always like this," Hope admitted.

Landon came down the stairs with a deflated doll in his arms.

"Oh look," Gavin said, "Landon sucked all the air out of her. Where was the valve? Where *did* you put that mouth, Bro?"

Ava had been taking a sip of soda, and when she heard that she choked.

"Asshole," Landon growled and disappeared into the garage.

They laughed so hard they were crying by the time Landon returned. It took much cursing and threats of violence before they settled back down to watch the rest of the game.

An hour and a half later, Ava followed Hope to the door.

"See you, squirt." Landon hugged his sister, then shoved her out with a push to her butt.

"*Hey.* I'll get you for that."

"You and what army?" he sneered. Then he turned to Ava.

"Ava, I…" He paused, glaring over her head.

Ava looked over her shoulder to see Theo and Gavin standing there, staring at them.

Landon pulled Ava with him through the house to the garage and slammed the door behind them. "So."

"So." She grinned.

"You know, it's really annoying when you do that."

"I know."

"You're so cute one minute, then sexy and evil the next. I like it."

"Evil?" That was a little harsh.

"Conniving. Better?"

"Not much." She wondered if she should ask, then went for it to see his expression. "Landon?"

"Yeah?"

"Was that doll really a prank? Be honest. It was yours, wasn't it?"

As expected, he turned bright red. "*Oh my God.* It was *not* mine," he ended in a low growl. "That was one of my idiot brothers or sister pulling a fast one. Trust me. I don't use a doll. I used this last night." He held up his hand, and now it was her turn to blush.

"You do tend to overshare, you know that?" Now she couldn't stop thinking about him masturbating, and she shivered.

His slow smile made her warm all over. "Yeah? Well let me share some more." He brought her hand to his crotch, and she felt him huge and hard. "I've been on fire for you since you showed up. But I'm keeping it in my pants, under control." He leaned closer and nipped her earlobe, then whispered, "I keep thinking about going down on you. How fucking good you tasted. I want more."

He leaned back, and she wished she could control her breathing better.

"You said it was my choice when."

"It is. No harm in letting you know I'm game. The earlier the better." He gave her a shark-like grin. "But I guess you should go. I wouldn't want to keep you when you need to get ready for your big date tomorrow. You know, with *Charles?*" His grin turned malicious. "Be nice when you dump him, Doc. You wouldn't want to cause irreparable harm."

"Yeah, because then I'd have to see him as a patient," she retorted, giving as good as she got.

But Landon only smiled. "That'd be fine by me. Because you're the type who follows the rules."

"Oh?" She planted her hands on her hips so she wouldn't wrap them around his thick neck. With her track record, she'd start with the intent to choke him and end by pulling him in for another kiss.

"Yeah. You'd never sleep with a patient, would you?"

"Of course not." She felt offended at the very thought.

"Exactly. So I retract my earlier statement. Do as much harm to old Chuck as you want. Reject the poor bastard. Then call me when you're done so we can set up our fourth date."

"Third," she automatically corrected.

"Whatever you say, dear."

His smug grin irritated her, because it also turned her

on. She yanked him down for a quick kiss, nipped his lower lip and caused him to start, then walked around him and stalked back through the house to the front door.

"Ava?" Gavin watched her go, confused. "You're still here?"

"Your brother is a horse's ass. That's my official diagnosis."

Theo snickered. "She called that one."

She grabbed her purse from the front table and slammed her way out the door. But she continued to think about the big oaf and what he'd said all the way home. Because as much as she wanted to give Charles a real shot, she couldn't help thinking Landon was right.

Charles didn't stimulate her mind, or her other parts, the way Landon did.

———

Sunday afternoon, Ava sat with Charles in Queen Anne at one of her favorite coffee shops. This time she'd paid for the small treat, making her feel a little more in control of the occasion. She understood why men usually offered to pay. For some reason, holding the money and dictating what was purchased made her feel as if she were in the driver's seat.

Interesting. She'd make a point to talk to the group about it at work. Ava was fascinated by social dynamics.

"I'm so glad we're out today," Charles said with enthusiasm. He sipped a black coffee, no milk or sugar. And he'd asked for a plain croissant as well.

She could almost hear Landon saying, *Plain being the key word* and hastened to put him out of her mind. Today was about her and *Charles*. Not Mr. Know It All.

"So what did you do yesterday?" she asked as she drank her latte.

"Nothing much. I worked out, spent dinner with my sister and brother-in-law. Oh, and I cleaned up the house. Sounds kind of boring, huh?"

Yes. "Not at all. It's tough to find time for the menial chores when you work long hours."

"Exactly." He smiled. "You understand, don't you? How much do you work a week, do you think?"

"Easily sixty hours."

He shook his head. "I'm more like eighty. But it's really my fault. I'm addicted to my job."

"Me too." *See? We have that in common. And he has such a nice smile.*

Someone tapped on her shoulder. She turned. "Yes?" Then she blinked. "Theo?"

He wore an apron around his waist. "Hello, ma'am." He nodded to Charles. "Sir. Just bringing you some donuts, on the house, to thank you for being a customer." He lowered his voice. "We got two extra boxes by mistake, so the boss gave everyone a few extra. I offered to give them to the customers, and he gave me big kudos for it. Pretend you don't know me."

Ava smiled as he placed two donuts in front of them. "Thank you, young man."

Theo made a face, then brought a donut to the guy sitting at the table next to them.

Charles, she noted, put the sugary treat on her napkin.

"Not a fan of sugar?"

"It's not good for me." He sighed. "It's not good for anyone, actually. But I'm on a health cleanse, so I'm abstaining. And it's not easy."

He had discipline. Another mark—*against* him? Did the man do anything fun? Not that Ava could throw stones, but geez, even she could allow herself a cookie or donut once in a while. Landon would have… *No.* Not going there.

She gave Charles a wide smile. "Good for you. I'm afraid I don't have the same discipline."

Charles blinked. "Oh no. You don't need to lay off anything that I can see." He flushed. "I mean, you mentioned before that you work out a lot. You could probably eat two dozen donuts and be fine. I'd gain ten pounds."

She nodded. "No, me too." *And why is it not okay that he's concerned with his weight? I am. Most women I know are. A man can care too.*

Yet he sounded so…wussy…being worried.

She waited for him to say something else. Oddly enough, they'd seemed to come to a standstill in their conversation. When he simply drank his bland coffee and smiled, she took charge. One thing Ava could do, talk and put people at ease.

"I watched a college basketball game yesterday with friends."

"Did you?" He seemed eager to pursue that venue.

"Yes. I'll admit I'm not a huge fan of the sport, but it was fun hearing my friends razz each other. There was some pretty good trash talk going on."

He laughed. "I'm a soccer fan myself. Go Sounders."

"Sounders?"

"The Seattle Sounders, our pro team? I played a little in college. I love the sport."

He didn't look like a soccer player. He had skinny legs. "Oh. I'd have pegged you more as a runner."

"I am. I run competitively. Keeps me in shape and it's something I look forward to, to get me out of the office."

"Good for you." She bit into a donut, needing something sweet to revive her fading attention span. "So, not to change the subject, but I'm curious. What do you think about online dating?"

"It suits me. Sounds weird, but you know, I'm so busy at work, and I wouldn't think about dating a colleague, so finding ladies online is the only way I can meet people. There's the gym or market, I suppose. But I go there with a specific purpose, not to talk to women."

"Good points." Except she'd met Landon at the gym. *Ack. No. More. Landon.*

It didn't help that she spotted Theo glancing her way. The young man looked too much like his brother for his own good. She might have thought he'd come to the shop to spy on her, except he was working behind the register.

She glanced back at Charles to see him watching her.

He still said nothing, waiting once more for her to pick a topic to talk about. Truth be told, being with him felt a bit draining. And she desperately wanted him to be interesting, if only to prove He-Who-Will-Not-Be-Named wrong. *Oh my God. Now I sound like I'm in a Harry Potter novel.*

"Have you read Harry Potter, by chance?" Well, at least it spurred the conversation.

Charles waxed poetically about the books versus the movies. Then he transitioned into other book-to-movie series he liked and disliked. Much like their conversation the previous week, this one felt natural and smooth. It was fun, until it wrapped up. Then another long silence sat between them. Charles seemed fine with not speaking.

Normally, this wouldn't bother her. But today it felt like a huge waste of time.

She wondered how long she might sit there, not talking, just smiling back at him, before he'd become uncomfortable.

A minute and a half, apparently.

"This was really fun." He consolidated all his trash into his empty cup. "Let's do this again."

How to let the man down? She hadn't truly considered she might have to, determined to prove Landon wrong. But for some reason today's date had been excruciating.

Ava fiddled with her cup. "My schedule is pretty crammed lately. I think people are gearing up to be stressed for tax season."

They both smiled at that.

"But I'll text you when I get the time." She decided to add a dose of honesty, in the hopes it would scare him away. "Just so you know, I've been seeing a few people from that dating site. Just for drinks or coffee, but I didn't want to in any way be dishonest about my intentions. I'm trying to get to know people better."

His smile dimmed, but he answered with a cheery, "I think that's smart. And I appreciate you being open with me."

"What about you? Are you seeing other women?"

"Not yet, but I'm sure I will. I've been happy out with you, to be honest."

What could she say? "You're fun to talk to." *When you talk.*

He seemed relieved. "Good. Well, call me when you can."

She wanted to kiss him, to see if perhaps her

desperation had made Landon seem so right. But doing that now would send the wrong message. And honestly, she felt less and less attracted to Charles the more she spent time with him.

They stood together, and this time she hugged him good-bye.

He left with a spring in his step. She sank down to her seat and groaned.

Theo came by. "Can I get you a refill?"

"Personal service?" She arched a brow.

He shrugged. "You looked like you needed it. How was the date with Chuck?"

"Charles." She mentally cursed Landon. "It was nice. You can tell your brother that from me."

Theo blinked. "What? Oh, hey. I'm not here to spy on you or anything. This is my new job, and I'm just trying to be friendly."

"I'm sorry." Great. Now she felt bad, all because Landon had put suspicious thoughts in her head. "I'll take an Americano." She slid him a five. "A small one. Keep the change."

Theo grinned. "All right." He left and returned minutes later with a steaming cup.

He handed it to her but remained standing by her table.

The caffeine hitting her system felt more than welcome. She'd drunk half when she realized Theo hadn't moved. "Yes?"

"I'm on break. Do you mind if I sit?"

"Please." She nodded to the chair Charles had vacated.

He longingly eyeballed the remaining donut.

She slid it to him, and he bit in and sighed. "I love these things."

"Me too." She watched him. "Theo, is something on your mind?"

"What? No." He finished the donut in what looked like two bites. "Well, maybe."

"Ask."

"Um, you're a therapist, right? So anything we say is confidential? You wouldn't tell Landon?"

"If you were my patient, then yes, what we discussed would be confidential. But because I'm in a—something resembling a relationship—with your brother, it would be unethical for me to take you on as a client."

His crestfallen expression affected her more than it should have. But Theo was so cute, and looked so much like Landon. No way would she consider giving Theo any therapy. She was too biased to be truly helpful. But…she could listen.

"However, you're not my client. You're a friend. I'm more than happy to listen."

"Will you keep this between us?" he asked, his cheeks pink.

"Sure. But only because you gave me a donut," she teased.

He relaxed, his over-six-foot frame sagging into the too-small chair. Dark-haired like Gavin and just as handsome, Theo would be a real heartbreaker when he got older. Though according to Hope, he was already breaking hearts. No doubt girls fell for those deep brown eyes, eyes so like his oldest brother's.

"It's…well, it's a lot of stuff. But it's hard to talk about with anyone, especially my mom and dad. My brothers don't get it, though Hope kind of does. But she's got issues with Mom, so she's not the easiest person to talk to." He paused. "My friends are all in college and moving on. And my cousins are so annoyingly settled and getting married and stuff. None of them remember what it's like to not know where you're going."

Ah. This was about Theo's future. She might have guessed. "So what's the problem?" She'd let him do the talking. The most effective part of therapy, sometimes, could be found in letting the patient discover what he or she had known all along. They just needed guidance to find their own answers.

"I'm stuck. I'm twenty, almost twenty-one, and I'm still living at home, bouncing from job to job, while my buddies are playing football at college and joining the service or out there working for a living. But the jobs I've found don't fit. And it's hard, because everyone in my family is so successful and smart. And I'm just Theo."

"Do you think they started that way, successful, I mean?"

"Landon did." Theo nodded. "Gavin didn't have any issues. Right out of high school, he joined up. Dad retired from the Navy, and he's a bigwig salesman. Mom too, except she sells real estate, not drugs."

She must have shown him her puzzlement, because he amended, "Dad works for a pharmaceutical company."

"Ah."

He grinned, then sobered. "Everyone's got something to look forward to. For a while, Hope was as scattered as I am. But then she went to work for Cam, my cousin, at his megabucks investment firm. Now she's doing good, and I'm still…me."

He looked miserable.

"But you're working. It takes skill to find job after job."

"I guess. Except a few weeks into any job, I get bored."

"What do you want to do, Theo? If you could do anything, what would it be?"

He paused. "You won't tell—"

"I swear. This is just between you and me."

He blew out a heavy breath. "I want to join the Marine Corps. So bad. But Landon got shot. Gavin too, and he's all messed up. It's different than it was in Dad's day, according to Dad. He's always on my ass about being sure about everything. How the hell can I be sure? I'm twenty years old."

"Or maybe he's acting cautious because two of his sons were hurt in the military. And he was in the Navy, so maybe he saw combat."

Theo nodded. "Oh, he did. He was a corpsman, spending all his time patching guys up."

"Right." She understood his father's unease, though of course there might have been much more behind the elder Donnigan's reservations. "So maybe your dad is worried about you too, that you'll be hurt if you join the Marine Corps. Or it could be he's worried that he's putting undue pressure on you to join the military because he did and your brothers both did."

Theo frowned. "Hmm. I never thought about that, that he might think he was pressuring me into joining. He's always acted the opposite. He's pretty chill, and that can be super annoying when you want a straight answer on stuff."

She nodded. "Yes, direct people tend to give you the straight yes or no."

"Like Mom and Landon." Theo sighed. "It's just… For a long time I wanted to be a Marine. But it's not an easy choice now."

"Because your brothers got hurt?"

"Yeah, and because I'm afraid if I go overseas, I'll be all messed up when I get back."

"Is Landon messed up?" She hadn't seen that in the stubborn man, but he did hold things in.

"Not really. Oh, his knee isn't right anymore, but he works hard at the gym to make it stronger. It's more Gavin. He and I are a lot alike. And he got mentally fragged from stuff he did. He won't talk about it." Theo bit his lip. "We had an intervention for him because he was drinking a lot. Like, a lot-lot. But he's not drinking anymore."

"That's good." She wanted badly to delve into that, but it wasn't her call to make. The fact that Gavin's family had stepped in to help him, and that he'd listened, told her Gavin was doing much better than he might think.

"So will I?" Theo asked.

"Will you what?"

"Will I be like Gavin if I join the Corps? What do you think?"

He looked so hopeful, wanting an answer. "What I think is that you'll know."

"Huh?"

"When the time is right for you to make a decision regarding your future, you'll know. Theo, there's no time stamp saying when you need to make a big decision like this. You have to do what's right for you. But I can tell you that everyone reacts to things differently. Gavin went through some difficult situations, and it affected him. Landon did too, but your brothers process differently.

"You and Gavin could be in the same war conditions, and you'd each handle them in your own way. You come from a dedicated family, one that has served and sacrificed. One that is close, sharing love and acceptance.

That you guys had an intervention for Gavin instead of tossing him out, that you could see he needed help and you acted on it, tells me your family is actually pretty good at dealing with conflict. As a whole."

"I guess."

"And you're a part of that. But only you can know what you can handle. Do you want to join the Marine Corps only because your family did?"

"No. I love the Marines. They're the best of the best. They train hard. Man, those guys are mean, and they don't take any shit—ah, stuff—from anyone."

She nodded.

"I'd be proud to be a part. You have to go to boot camp. And you have to be physically fit. I've been running hard, lifting weights at the gym. Gavin was training me."

"Was?"

"Still is, now. He was a little rough a few weeks ago, but I kept going anyway."

"So you give him purpose, letting him train you, and you benefit because you're getting in better shape. The fact you're still training, even though you're not sure of what you 'really want,' should tell you something."

He nodded. "I know. It's just… I'm afraid."

She took his hand in hers and squeezed. "We're all afraid. Heck, I was afraid of wasting tons of money and time on a degree I might come to hate. I spent eight years between schooling and interning to get licensed to practice. And now it's my job."

"Do you like it?"

"I do. But I had to go through it to find out. Same as you can't know if you'd like the Marines or not until you do it. But I understand it's a big commitment. Once you sign that dotted line, you have a good four to six years before you can get out, right?"

"Yeah."

"It's a risk you have to be willing to take. Only *you* can know if you're willing to take it."

He nodded. "I think I always knew the answer, I'm just giving myself time to think about it." His mood had lightened, the process of unburdening himself a healthy step in the right direction.

"Good for you. And Theo, don't be afraid to feel uncertain. I bet if you asked Landon, he'd tell you he's had the same feelings."

Theo snorted. "Landon? You have met my brother, haven't you?"

She grinned. "You have a point. But even Landon had second thoughts about his decision. I guarantee you."

"I'll think about talking to him. But you won't say anything?"

"Not a word. This was just a coffee and donut between friends."

He smiled. "Thanks, Ava. Now I'd better get back to work before I get fired." He saw his boss glancing at their table.

"No problem. And thanks for the donut."

He hustled back to the counter. Ava sat, sipping her coffee and letting the beans have their way with her. Her brain started buzzing, getting that jolt she needed.

She wondered how best to let Landon know he'd been right about Charles without admitting he'd been right. Hmm. A conundrum. And a challenge. But first, she'd have to arrange their next—third—date. How to disarm the man. What should she do, she wondered?

Chapter 11

"I KNOW IT'S OUR FOURTH DATE AND ALL, BUT TAKING me back to your place to have your wicked way with me... It's been done, Doc. Not very creative." Landon smirked.

"First of all, it's our third date. And second, there's nothing wicked about garlic chicken. Note the garlic in the recipe. Not something you serve when you want to kiss your date afterward."

He sighed. "You got me there. But hell, a free meal? Who am I to complain?" He accepted the beer she gave him. "Besides, you owe me."

"How is that?" She checked the chicken in the oven.

He had to admit, it smelled delicious.

"Well, I let you put me off about your date with Chuckles. So what's the verdict, Ms. I'm Too Busy with My Job to Talk to You?" He took a large swallow of beer. "That excuse isn't working anymore. It didn't work when you avoided me at the gym, and it's not working now."

He laughed at her scowl. He'd played along, of course, giving her until Wednesday night to see her, because Theo had hinted that she hadn't seemed overly thrilled on Sunday. Granted, he'd had to choke the information out of his surprisingly close-mouthed little brother, but he'd heard what he wanted to hear.

"For your information, I enjoyed my time with Charles."

"Really?" He waited until she stood and looked into his eyes. The liar.

"Well, I enjoyed my coffee."

He smiled.

She scowled and turned to the oven once more when it dinged. Ava bent over, and he had to work not to drool. The woman filled out a pair of jeans better than anyone he knew. She'd also worn a light-blue shirt that molded to her curves, and he was dying to unbutton the thing and peel it apart.

Instead, he guzzled more beer and watched her putter around in the kitchen. He knew it was throwback, and hell if he'd ever admit it to his mother or sister or anyone else with two X chromosomes, but he liked watching a woman in the kitchen. He especially liked Ava and her cute pink fuzzy socks.

He leaned over the small window in her tiny dining room to see her feet. "Do the pink ones have snow-men too?"

She looked down at her feet. "Nope. Just lots of pink fuzz. I like my feet to be warm."

"They'd have to be in those things."

She smiled at him. "Yep. Not sexy at all, are they?"

The minx. She wore her hair down, and as usual, he wanted to caress her. She seemed so soft all over. She'd been especially soft between her legs, where he'd stroked that velvety slick cream and licked it all up.

Shit. He tried to ease his dick from poking through his jeans, uncomfortably aware of how she could get to him without even trying.

"So when do you wear glasses?" he asked. Not smart to change the subject to another of his sexual fantasies, but he was dying to see them on her.

"When I read." She fixed their plates. "I hope you like a Caesar salad, because I made one."

"So garlic, anchovies, what else is on the menu? Some stinky cheese? Doc, I get that you don't want to make out."

"Shut it, Donnigan. And go sit down at the table."

He grinned and sat, pleased she'd lit candles and had the table all prettied up. "This is much fancier than my basketball party."

"That was not a party. That was a free-for-all with pizza rolls." She served him a plate that made his mouth water.

"Damn, Ava. You can cook." He glanced up to see her looking satisfied. "Or did you have your cousins come make this so you can look like you know what you're doing? Yeah, I know all about the masterminds at Sofa's." A terrific coffee shop in Green Lake. He'd met friends there once or twice and been bowled over by their homemade soups and sandwiches.

"I'm insulted."

"Really?"

"Yes, because this was a lot of work." She frowned. "You know, I should have had Sadie cater this."

"I, for one, am glad you worked your pretty little fingers to the bone."

"Patronizing much?"

"Hey, I'm trying to be complimentary about your stinky food."

She shook her head and laughed. "You are such a jerk. Well? What are you waiting for? Dig in."

He did and fell straight into heaven. He cleared his plate while she was in the middle of hers. "Damn, woman. Can I have more?"

She blushed with pleasure. "I'll get it." She reached for his plate.

"No, no. Eat up. I can help myself." He noticed she'd emptied her water glass, so he took it with him and refilled it. After he piled up his plate once more, he returned to the table, placing her water in front of her.

"What?" he asked at her odd look.

"Nothing. Thanks." She drank half the glass. "I was parched."

"I gotta say. This is some fine eats. I mean, really good." He sighed as he bit into more chicken. "I love the dark meat."

"Me too." She smiled. "My mom gave me that recipe. My dad is the one who came up with the green bean concoction there."

"They cook together?"

She nodded. "One of their many passions. They're also both medical people. Dad's a doctor, Mom's a nurse."

"So that's where you get it. That need to help people."

"I guess. I just knew I didn't want to work in a hospital. I'm not a fan of blood."

"Me neither."

"You're not afraid of needles, are you?" she asked.

"Get that excited look off your face. No. I also don't faint at the sight of blood. Sorry to disappoint."

"That's okay. I'll find your weaknesses and exploit them another time."

He chuckled. "See? That's why we get along so well."

"Don't call me evil, devious, or conniving."

He paused in thought. "How about scheming?"

She sighed. "Whatever."

"I mean, you've manipulated me all night with amazing food, fine beer—"

"That you brought."

"And you served."

"And still, you haven't told me about your date with Charlie. Well?"

She threaded her hands through her hair. "Do you have any idea how annoying you can be?"

He pretended to pause in thought. "Hmm. I think so. Yes."

She groaned. "Fine. If you must know, it was awful."

"Really?"

"Yes," she snapped. "And it doesn't help that you sound so cheerful about that fact, either."

"Sorry."

"Not buying it." She toyed with her salad. "He was boring. I don't understand it. On our first date, Charles was nice and funny. But today, he followed my lead on everything."

"Yep."

"What?"

"You don't want a wuss."

"I also don't want a macho headcase who thinks he can tell me what to do twenty-four seven."

"Gee, Ava. You seem aggravated."

To his surprise, she stood and started pacing, running her hands through her hair. He was captivated, because the woman seemed genuinely frustrated. He'd never before seen her this way. So human. So fuck-all sexy.

Every time she paced by the table, her breasts heaved and her hips swayed. That ass was begging to be spanked, he'd swear to it. And once again, he was hard as a rock, watching Ava.

"You have to be right, don't you?"

"Not always."

"Well, you are," she snarled. "I thought he and I were doing well together. But he bored me. And why is that, you ask?"

"Why is that?"

"Because he wasn't *you*."

Landon sat dumbly, unable to believe his good fortune.

"You're incredibly annoying."

"I think we covered that." He sounded hoarse, he couldn't help it. He hadn't known the woman long, but what he knew, he liked. A lot.

"It's taken me a long time to be comfortable with the idea of dating. I've been so busy with my career that men have taken a backseat. And I was okay with that. But now I'm thirty, and time is ticking away."

Was this a biological clock thing or something? And why wasn't he more panicked at the thought it might be?

"It's time I crossed off a few more items on my list. I'm financially set. I'm supported emotionally by family and friends. My job is amazing, and I love it. But my social life, when it comes to intimacy with a man, is lacking. So I decided to try dating. And after some really bad dates, I met you."

Meaning, I'm not a bad date. Score.

"The worst of the bunch."

"Excuse me?"

"You're arrogant, too muscular, handsome in an unconventional way, and coarse."

"Yeah?" Okay, she was starting to irritate him. Mostly because the table separated them when he wanted to pull her into his lap and kiss the breath out of her.

"You're a family man. You protect your own and

those you consider needing protection. You're not afraid to love others, even if you don't like to talk about your feelings."

He frowned. "What's the rule about not shrinking me, Doc?"

"And yet, despite you being totally not my type, you turn me on. It's like my body isn't mine when I'm around you."

"All good things." He nodded, wishing she'd come closer so he could sit her over his raging hard-on and help her turn *off*. A few orgasms and she'd be feeling just fine.

"I'm supposed to set our tempo when it comes to sex, but I get the feeling you're herding me in the direction you want me to go."

"How's that?" Okay, so she was *really* good at reading him.

"That blasted basketball game, where you showed me how natural you are, how loving, with your family. Giving me orgasms without taking any for yourself," she hissed.

God, she was so fine. She spun on a heel as she raged, and her hair flared around her breasts. He could see the tight buds of her nipples through the blouse, and he could only too well imagine how wet she might—hopefully—be.

"It didn't help that you played me."

"Played you?" He sounded like he'd swallowed a bucket of gravel. "How'd I do that?"

"By 'giving me' the control. Please. You've been doing your best to seduce me, and I see right through you."

"Um, Ava. You're a little out in left field here." *Totally spot on.* "I wanted to introduce you to my family, but in a comfortable setting. Hence the basketball game. What we did together that night wasn't scripted, honey. I wanted you, bad. Letting you set the pace is only right. I don't want you to feel rushed."

"Bullshit. You liked taking charge through the rest of it. Why stop there?"

"Huh?" Man, he was so hard. He wanted her mouth over him in the worst way.

"Did you get that checkup?"

"Wait. What?"

"That checkup you mentioned. Did you get it?"

"Not yet. I scheduled it, but—"

She stalked over to him and grabbed him by the arm. She tugged, and he went with her, mesmerized by her tirade. An angry Ava was sexy personified. So hot with those light-green eyes shooting daggers at him. She seemed mussed, and that was just the way he wanted her.

"You okay?" he asked. "You seem a little—"

"Shut up. And stand right there."

He was amused despite his erection. He stood next to the table, wondering what the hell she planned next. Maybe a striptease? Would she wrestle him to the ground and try to beat on him? Poke him in the chest? Get right up into his face? Foreplay, by his standards. But let the poor thing tire herself out—then he'd pounce.

Landon crossed his arms over his chest, waiting.

She just watched him with those witchy green eyes. "Do you practice safe sex? Or is that a lie too?"

He glared. "Hey. I'm not sure why you're getting so pissy. I never lied to you. I'm always safe. Damn, Ava. I left you after going down on you because I didn't have a condom."

"Because you don't want to get me pregnant. But what about STDs?"

"Hell no. First off, when we fuck, it's not gonna be about babies. We're going to have fun, period. No kids. Not until I'm married, because that's the way I'm made. Sorry if you don't agree."

"Why are you talking about babies?" She crossed her arms over her chest, tapped her foot, and glared back.

"Second, I've never gotten a disease because I always wear a condom. And before you ask, blowjobs count. If I don't know her, she's not kissing jackshit with a dirty mouth. Got me?"

"Yep." She stalked over to him, and he braced himself for a slap, a punch, a kick, even. He hadn't prepared himself to watch her drop to her knees in front of him. Every dirty thought he'd ever had came rushing to his mind.

"Ava?"

"Shut up." She put her hands to the waist of his jeans, and he froze, unable to move. She unbuttoned him, having to work to maneuver around his erection. Then she pulled his jeans down to his thighs, while he stood there like a stiff, his arms locked tight across his chest.

He blinked, sure he'd imagined it, but no, she remained on her knees, busy getting his cock free. *Christ.*

"Ava, you—*oh fuck.*"

She'd pulled his underwear down and cupped his balls. Still in shock, he could do nothing but watch as her cherry-red lips took the tip of his cock into her mouth and sucked him but good.

A wave of pleasure consumed him, and he felt a spurt of come leave his body. *Hell.* If he came in two seconds, she'd think him a lightweight for sure. But the woman was on her fucking knees. He wasn't strong enough to withstand the sight of her, let alone the feel of her lips sucking on his cock.

She bobbed over him, massaging his sac while she worked him with a mouth that knew what it was doing. Her clever little tongue stroked just under his cockhead, and he rocked into her, helpless to stop himself.

"Ava," he groaned and rested a hand on her shoulder, the other going to cup her head. "Please. Oh fuck. I'm so hard."

He felt her smile around him, before she pulled away. "Now who's in charge?"

He'd say and do *anything* to get her to continue. *So close...* "You are," he breathed and moaned when she put that hot mouth back around him. She sucked and stroked, laving him as she took him deeper to the back of her throat.

"Ava. Baby. Oh fuck. Gonna come." He was down to one- and two-word sentences, his grasp of language fading as his body took charge.

He expected her to pull away at this point, finish him off with her hands. But she only rubbed his balls faster and sucked harder.

He thrust, in and out, watching himself fuck her mouth, and he couldn't stop. "I'm coming. Oh yeah, swallow me. All of me," he said and came so hard he saw stars.

He could only pump, letting her suck the life from him as he jetted down her throat. Weeks of frustration and desire rushed into her hot little mouth.

She moaned as she swallowed, and her desire made

it all so much better. He remained half hard when she
eased away from him. He watched her wipe her lips,
then suck her finger.

"See? I told you we wouldn't be kissing tonight."
She looked so pleased with herself, and he could barely
stand without shaking.

"You happy with yourself?" he rasped, so fucking
replete.

"Yes, I am." She tucked him back into his underwear
and pulled up his pants, but she didn't button him up.
She stood, but when she started to back away, he moved
with her until he had her pinned up against the wall.

"I don't think so."

"You have a problem with what I just did?" She narrowed her eyes, but he could see her excitement.

"Yep. I didn't get any dessert."

"Dessert?"

"I want something sweet, like honey." He didn't give
her a chance to protest as he unfastened her jeans and
shoved them down her legs. He continued to stare into
her eyes, daring her to object. But she kicked her pants
off. He yanked her panties down and tossed them aside,
and she let him, then widened her stance.

"You want it, don't you? Let me hear you say it."

"I admit nothing." Her lofty tone didn't fool him in
the slightest.

"You're a brat." *And I love it.* "Take off your clothes."

She blinked. "Huh?"

"All of them. Get naked, Doc. Now."

She seemed uncertain, but he didn't care. She'd
pushed the rules of the game. And he'd never been so
thankful in his life.

"Want some help?"

She seemed to come back to her senses. "You want me naked? You do it."

He had her shirt and bra off, followed by those goofy pink socks, in seconds. And when he stood to admire her, his breath stopped.

She was amazing. Gorgeous. Generously built and all fine lines. She had full breasts, a nipped waist, and flared hips, just right for riding him until they both came. He wanted to take her, right now, no question. But she'd started this game, and she'd play by the rules.

"Spread your legs, beautiful."

Blushing yet defiant, she still did as told.

"There you go. You're wet for me, aren't you?"

"Yes."

He smiled and stepped closer. Instead of getting to his knees to return the favor, he bent to suck her breast. He took the tight nipple between his teeth and gently rolled it, sucking hard to bring her more pleasure. Her hands gripping his hair told him he'd done all right. So he did the same to the other breast.

Meanwhile, he stroked her belly and the thin strip of hair between her legs, then kissed his way to her cheek.

She tried to kiss him, but he turned his head, not giving her what she wanted. So she kissed up and down his neck like a starving woman. Only the fact that he'd just come down her throat gave him the measure to hold himself back. He fingered her, sliding between her folds and grazing that sensitive nub that had her arching and moaning his name.

"You're one hot piece, Doc," he murmured and shoved his finger inside her. Damn if she didn't grip him, making him wish he had something else to put inside her. But not yet, not now.

There were other ways to find pleasure.

She twisted, trying to get him to move faster. But he wouldn't be rushed. He added another finger inside her while rubbing her clit with the heel of his hand with each push. He kept thrusting his hips, unable to stop the instinctive reaction, needing to be inside her.

"Touch me. Get me off with your hand," he ordered, panting as she dug her hand under his boxer briefs and wrapped her fingers around him.

He stared into her face as he finger-fucked her while she jerked him off, their movements faster, desperate, and so damn good. Watching each other while they played felt almost voyeuristic, removing another layer to deepen the connection between them.

Landon came close, could see her veering on an orgasm. He pinched her clit before shoving hard inside her with his fingers.

She gripped him tighter and like a vise, clamped her body down while she climaxed.

He swore and shot hard, drenching his underwear, and her hot hand, with a mess of seed.

When she finally stopped shivering, he removed his hand. She took hers away as well, but he gripped her wrist. "Wipe it over you," he demanded.

She stared at him, then shuttered her gaze and wiped his come on her belly. Not as good as being inside her, but it satisfied some primitive part of him needing to stake a claim.

"Was your dessert satisfactory?" she asked, breathless. Her nipples were taut, her breasts round and pretty.

He would always have this memory of her now. And sure as hell, it would make being around her even more difficult. The fantasy of bringing her to orgasm had been arousing, but having her lips around him… Permanent hard-on for sure.

"I loved my dessert." He planted kisses along her throat, her upper chest, then one for each berry-red nipple. "But I didn't get that cream I was hungry for."

"Maybe next time." Her breath hitched, and she sagged into him. "What did you do to me?" she mumbled against his chest.

He smiled and lifted her in his arms.

"Don't drop me," she said on a gasp.

"Honey, you don't weigh enough to worry about." He kissed her this time, giving her the full tongue before he pulled back with a grimace. "And yeah, that garlic chicken, not so great for kissing."

She laughed, her eyes sparkling. "Told you so."

He set her back on her feet and put her shirt on, minus the bra, followed by her jeans and fuzzy socks. "No underwear when I'm around."

"Oh please." She huffed.

He shifted and grimaced. "Man, I made a mess."

"Yes, you did seem pretty pent-up. That's a lot of come, isn't it?"

Only Ava could make him feel self-conscious about a body he hadn't been self-conscious about in forever. "Do you have to talk about it?"

"Why not? I swallowed more than a mouthful, remember?"

At the thought, his cock stirred. "Oh yeah. I remember."

She turned pink. "You liked it."

"You mean I loved it. And okay, that's one round to you."

"We're not keeping score, are we?"

"Not yet." He grinned. "I'll be right back. Bathroom?" He followed her nod and returned somewhat cleaned up. "Um, you might want to replace the hand towel in there."

"Noted." She laughed at him. "I totally had you begging me, didn't I?"

"Yeah, garlic breath. You did."

"You should talk." She waved her hand in front of her nose, still grinning.

That smile hit him right in the feels. Good God. What was she doing to him?

"You okay? You look a little sick." She smirked.

If it were possible, he would have heard his heart drop at that very moment, locked onto her smug smile. "I think I need a doctor. Preferably on her knees."

She snickered. "Dream on. Sucker."

"Say that again. The suck part." He hugged her to him, loving the feel of her unbound breasts against his chest. "So when's our next date? 'Cause at this point, I'm thinking we're dating. You know, like, going out."

"Is this where we quantify what we are to each other? With labels?"

"Yes, Dr. Obvious. It is."

She sighed and squirmed out of his arms. "So traditional."

"Deal. You are now"—he bowed, giving her the royal wave of his hand—"Landon's girlfriend."

"Really? All this pomp and circumstance for what?"

"Amazing oral sex?"

"Well, when you put it that way." She tugged him close by the ear.

"Ow."

"Okay, Ava's boyfriend. We're now dating, exclusively. So no Claudia or any of the other gym bunnies you've no doubt bounced around with."

"Hey, you know the word 'bounce.' Nice." He pulled his ear away and rubbed the offended appendage. "Yeah, that goes for you too. No more Charles or Preston or Chipper for you."

"Seriously? You're poking fun at Charles's name, and you dated *Claudia*?"

"Point is, we're exclusive. You said it." He gave her his best grin. "And I'm getting that check-up tomorrow. The doctor's a friend of mine, and I plan on getting those results rushed."

"Fine, but remember I'm in charge of when we do it." She crossed her arms, hiding her pretty breasts.

"Fine," he mimicked her, enjoying the hell out of this date. "But I'm in charge of *how* we do it." He gave her a wicked grin. "And baby, I can't wait to suck those tits while I'm pounding into you." He leaned closer. "By the way, I know your tells. Doc, you are a huge fan of dirty talk."

She groaned. "I am." She took him by the hand and sucked his forefinger in her mouth. In spite of his exhaustion, his dick twitched. She pulled his finger out. "I know your tells too, Landon. And you're a fan of my lips around your cock."

"Just…yeah, I am."

"Now who likes dirty talk?"

"Not the talk. I like a dirty girl." Landon kissed her

again, garlic breath and all. "And baby, you are one dirty, dirty doctor."

He helped her do the dishes and clean up, then they watched a movie on television. No screwing and skating for this Marine.

Oddly enough, he was hard-pressed to say what had been the best part of his evening. The sex that wasn't sex, or just sitting with Ava and laughing over a dumb sitcom.

Chapter 12

"THAT'S GOOD, ROB. I THINK YOU'RE REALLY STARTING to break through." Her first Monday client typically drained her for the rest of the morning, but Rob seemed to have reached a turning point.

His anxiety had lessened to such a degree that he could openly talk about his worries without showing visible signs of his unease. Mostly he seemed contemplative. And all without medication.

Rob Hill was her age, tall and thin, and when he smiled, he made everyone around him smile. Unfortunately, his doom-and-gloom attitude had pervaded every aspect of his life for the past six months. They hadn't been able to peg the cause as any one thing, more a cumulative downpour of several bad incidents seeming to converge all at once.

The death of a favorite uncle, a good friend moving away, his girlfriend leaving him for another woman. All things that even taken individually would get a person down. But happening within the span of a few months, the effects had snowballed.

She might have chalked up his signs as depression, but he refused to take medication for his issues. After meeting with him for a few weeks, she'd agreed. He seemed to do better when he had "homework" from her, usually something that helped spark his creativity and put him in a balanced state.

Rob smiled at her, his blue eyes sparkling. He was

blond, his hair longer than Landon's, but she'd never mistake this man for her larger-than-life, supremely confident boyfriend.

Just thinking the word *boyfriend* made her tingle, and she smiled back. *Stop it and focus on your patient, Ava. This is not about you.*

With a silent apology to Rob, she continued the session, nearing the middle of their hour. "Continue to take the art classes. I think they've been a good outlet for you. We all have a creative self needing expression. And you found yours."

He gave her a shy grin, then moved to his knapsack. "I have something for you."

"Now, Rob, that's not necessary." And not acceptable. Ava took nothing more from her clients than payment for a session, a smile, or a thank you.

"I don't need to. I *want* to. And besides, I made it."

He handed her a charcoal sketch of herself, and she was blown away. "This is amazing, Rob."

It looked exactly like her. Right down to the tiny grin on her face.

"Yeah. You're so…" He trailed off, just staring at her.

And a huge wave of *uh-oh* smacked her full in the face. She was always careful to maintain a professional distance from her patients, but sometimes transference couldn't be helped. Patients could too easily confuse gratitude with deeper affection.

"I'm so…?" she prodded, a polite smile on her face.

"Helpful." He swallowed. "I'm glad you're my doctor."

Doctor. Not friend. So long as that line was never crossed, Ava felt as if she kept her patients safe from an unhealthy relationship with her.

"I'm glad you're finally seeing your self-worth." She nodded at the picture. "This is incredible. You should put it with your portfolio."

"Nah." He shrugged and sat back on the couch, slouching down. "It's just a hobby."

"You have to do what you think best. But I have to tell you, I think this is more than a hobby. You have genuine skill, Rob." Ava continued with positive reinforcement. "What did your mother think?"

He smiled. "She liked it. You should see the one I did of her."

"Do you have it?"

They went through more of his art, and in each picture she saw a different emotion expressed. With his mother, she saw love. With herself—she hated to admit—she saw admiration and attraction. With his brother-in-law, arrogance. He'd also drawn a few pictures of his ex-girlfriend, none of which had been flattering, and his uncle, which showed a robust man engaged and joyful.

"I like that he's not sad," she said, encouraging Rob to talk about the man who'd been such an integral part of his life. "Tell me something quirky about him. Did he do anything that could make you laugh and scratch your head in puzzlement at the same time?"

Rob lit up, and as he shared, his animation buoyed her as well.

The session ended on a high note, and Rob stood to leave with a smile, as opposed to his usual hangdog expression and air of solitude.

"Enjoy your dinner with your mother," she told him.

"I think I will."

When she tried to hand him back her portrait, convinced it was too good to accept, he shook his head.

"No, please. Keep it. I want to see it when I come back and remember how I felt when I created it."

That sounded healthy enough, but she'd keep a closer eye on him during her sessions. And she'd discuss this with her mentor, Dr. Dennis Foster, as well.

"I will. And thank you." She'd get it framed. Because yeah, it was that good. Flattering, yet the picture represented all she'd ever wanted from her job. To help others. This was a great progression toward a healthy sense of self for Rob.

He gave her a wave and a last look that she almost called him on, then he left.

"Damn." She set the picture on her desk and made notes in his chart. Ava always did her best to consolidate her thoughts after a patient departed, though depending on her schedule, sometimes she had to wait until the end of the day.

Now, fresh and with another hour until her next patient, she took the time to write down Rob's session and progress. After saving what she'd written into her computer, she sought help from the one person she considered her go-to when it came to just about anything. Dr. Dennis Foster had taken her under his wing two years ago and continued to treat her the way he did his grown daughters.

Dennis ran Mind Your Matter—MYM—Counseling, a consulting group. Four of them, including Ava, each focused on a certain field while overlapping with the others. Between Dennis, Ava, Lee, and Emily, they had psychologically based dysfunction treatments well-covered.

Like her, Dennis preferred family and individual

counseling. Ava dealt with a lot of anxiety disorders as well, like Rob this morning.

She'd never been happier, and she loved collaborating with the others if she needed a sounding board. Like she did today.

She found Dennis in the communal break room at the back of the house down the hallway—where they normally met once a week to discuss patients in crisis. The first floor of the remodeled Craftsman consisted of hers and Lee's offices, a bathroom, a waiting area for clients, and the kitchen. Upstairs, Dennis had one office, Emily used the other, and an additional waiting room, bathroom, and filing/storage area took up the rest of the home. It was the ideal place for a four-person consulting group.

She grabbed a cup of coffee and joined him at the table.

"Ava. How goes it this morning?"

Dennis had dark gray hair, a goatee trimmed to perfection, and glasses over bright brown eyes gleaming with intelligence and wit. She felt comfortable discussing any and everything with the man. In a lot of ways, he was like a surrogate father and mentor all in one. He provided a safety net in a place where mental stimulation and confusion could overwhelm.

"Things are good, but I think I might have a situation." She explained about Rob and her perceptions, not surprised when Dennis agreed with her.

"Yes, you're going to have to be careful there. I'd continue your course of therapy, as it seems like it's really helping him. But he does seem to be developing an attachment. If it continues, you're going to need to address it carefully. He needs to know a personal relationship can't go anywhere."

She nodded. "I don't want to make him uncomfortable or set him back, but yes, he needs to see me as his doctor and nothing more."

"Good." Dennis sighed as he finished his cup. "I love my coffee. I'm a proud addict. What can I say?"

She chuckled. "Maybe you should get some counseling for that."

"Funny." He grinned. "So how's your nonexistent social life doing?"

And like clockwork, he brought up her least favorite topic. He'd been bugging her for a while to get out and mingle. But she finally had good news to tell him. "As a matter of fact, I'm dating someone."

Dennis blinked. "Oh?"

"Yes. I met him at the gym. We clicked, even though he's completely not my type." She felt the need to focus on that aspect of Landon a lot, and she started to wonder why. A sense of self-preservation maybe? Because she felt more for the man than she felt comfortable feeling after such a short time?

"All of us have a preconceived 'type.'" Dennis shrugged. "Greta was just my type. Beautiful and mouthy."

They both grinned.

"But she was more outspoken than I was comfortable with at first. And her family is a nightmare. She'll tell you the same thing. I'm not talking out of turn.

"But you know better than most that it's best to judge someone on his or her own merit rather than what we think they are." Dennis stood and put his cup in the sink. "And that's all the advice I have to spare today. Not that you asked for it."

"Not that I asked for it, no." She drank and waited.

"But about this man…"

She groaned.

"Has your uncle met him? Your cousins?"

"No and yes." Dennis worried like a mother hen, but she loved him for it. "Actually, Landon is coming with me to Elliot's for dinner tonight. Sadie will be there too." She crossed her fingers her cousins would behave. "Landon's a solid guy. He was in the Marines, but an injury forced him to retire early. And he's only a few years older than me."

"I like him already." Dennis had a soft spot for ex-military. His brother had served and been killed in the line of duty. "Unless he doesn't treat you right. Then we'll give him to Lee and turn him into a complete basket case." Lee, another of their consultants, specialized in PTSD trauma. Dennis lowered his voice. "But I never said that out loud."

She winked. Dennis left to get ready for a patient, while she nursed her coffee, with time to spare. Landon and Lee had many of the same attributes. Self-confidence bordering on arrogance. Large personalities, big laughs, and great senses of humor. Yet Landon never made Ava feel like she had to prove herself. With Lee she sometimes felt on the defensive.

Landon seemed easy to understand. On the surface. If he was hungry, he ate. If he liked you, he'd tell you. If he didn't, she had the feeling you'd know that too. He didn't pull his punches, and she appreciated that about him. Yet he also kept her off balance. For a woman who prided herself on being in control of her life, Landon had come in and swept her off her feet. Literally.

He could lift her without a struggle. He took charge,

sexually, and she liked it. For once she didn't have to be in command, and that submissiveness excited her. Sexually. She'd been studying that part of her psyche since that first time in her kitchen with him.

Though she understood why she'd reacted that way to him, it disturbed her a little. It also unnerved her that she'd never even dreamed of behaving submissively with another man. Not the way she had with Landon.

Landon Donnigan—a commanding individual who all of a sudden was not so commanding.

They talked and laughed, but never about anything deep. They didn't discuss politics and never discussed his time in the Marine Corps. He seemed insistent that she not "shrink him," and though she knew he probably needed to talk about his time in the service, she didn't push.

He puzzled, frustrated, and aroused her. And not in that order. Since their date on Wednesday night, where she'd "blown" his mind—and that naughty play on words continued to amuse her—they hadn't had sex. Hadn't even fooled around a little. Just a few pecks on the cheek.

Her amusement died while she wondered at his game. In the days since that explosive night together, they'd gone to dinner with her cousin Rose and Rose's husband, Joe. They had really liked Landon. He'd been an ideal dinner date, surprisingly enough. He had entertaining stories but didn't monopolize the conversation. He didn't try being a bigger man than Joe, but listened and laughed at all the right moments.

And he acted caring and protective without smothering. He'd held her hand or put his arm around her shoulder, but he hadn't pulled her into his lap or shoved his tongue down her throat—much to her disappointment.

The big man was truly letting her say when.

Just terrific. She glumly considered their pending evening. With any luck, it wouldn't end the way their movie date had. Saturday night they'd gone to a movie together. It had been an awful film. They'd complained the whole time they were watching. Afterward, they'd hit an all-night arcade and battled it out over Space Invaders and Galaga. She'd won both, but he'd defeated her in the silly fighter games that had too many buttons to figure out.

What had she received for her wins? Not kisses. Pats on the back and smirks, because he knew what she wanted. Hell, he wanted it too. He'd been aroused for most of the night. But Mr. Discipline refused to come down off his high horse and make choices for her. Because he respected her.

"Screw that."

"Ava?" Emily entered and glanced around. "Are you talking to yourself?"

"Yes." Ava sighed. "It's my new boyfriend."

"Ah." Emily nodded, sagely saying nothing more than, "Enough said."

Ava took her coffee back to her office. She straightened up then checked her emails and phone messages. After booking four more appointments, she readied for her eleven o'clock.

Ava centered herself, focused inwardly, and let all her emotions just…go. Landon, her cousins, her coworkers, her patients, nothing mattered but the present.

She opened her eyes, glanced at the clock on the wall,

and nodded. Then she left her office and walked down
the hall, where she found Mr. and Mrs. Davis sitting on
opposite sides of the room immersed in their cell phones.

"Hello." Ava smiled and called on her patience,
because Mr. Davis liked to yell and Mrs. Davis liked to
mimic her husband, just to annoy him. Ava drew on her
calm. "It's good to see you again, Alan, Amy. Please,
come on back."

Monday evening, Landon glanced around Elliot's place,
one of several apartments in a modern complex in Green
Lake. They were on the first level of a totally open floor
plan. Elliot and Sadie stood behind the giant rectangle
of a kitchen island, which divided the kitchen from
the living room. The kitchen cabinets had been done
in white and gray, and Elliot worked at one end of the
island hovering over the stove while Sadie leaned at the
other end, critiquing him.

Functional, simple décor, mostly in gray, chrome, or
white, filled the living room. Splashes of color in the pil-
lows, a throw over the couch, and in the curtains livened
the space. His mother would have a field day in here,
because the damn home looked like something on one of
those home and garden channels she watched.

If Landon hadn't already known the guy was gay,
this incredible bachelor pad would have given him some
strong hints. No straight guy had such a sense of style, at
least, none he knew. And yeah, he felt lacking. For just
a second. Because while he might not be all that great
when it came to decorating, he felt totally comfortable
in his house with furniture designed to fit his frame. No

way he'd sit in that white boxy chair that probably cost a grand or more but appeared too damn tiny for his ass.

"Looks great, Elliot." Ava smiled as she studied the area, still standing in the living room with Landon.

"Of course it does. I had Jason reconfigure everything."

"Wait. Who's Jason?"

"That's right. Not Tony or Mitchell. Jason is Elliot's good friend," Sadie said. "And why are they good friends?"

Ava answered for her cousin while Landon placed their jackets over the couch. "Because Elliot hasn't tried to sleep with him. Yet." She shared a glance with him, reminding him of their conversation on the way over.

Unfortunately, a bad breakup some time ago had sent Elliot into healing-through-sex mode. No matter how many times Ava tried to help him, her cousin continued to go through men, as if seeking validation through his physical appeal, while keeping his heart locked down tight.

Man, Landon *so* didn't want her shrinking *him.*

"So hurtful, you and your words." Elliot wiped his hands on his white apron, looking like a master chef as he concentrated on the wonderful smells coming from the sizzling pans before him.

"What's for dinner?" Landon asked, more than ready to eat.

Elliot had agreed to host dinner on the condition that Landon had to come and be prepared to answer questions. He liked the guy's attitude. Protective of his cousin and snarky. From what Landon had seen of him at the gym, Elliot would have fit in well with his own family. He had that annoying younger brother vibe going for him, a lot like Gavin.

And like Gavin, he had his share of groupies, though Elliot's seemed mostly male.

"We're having fajitas, handsome." Elliot glanced over at him. "But we haven't properly welcomed you. Sadie, put on your manners. Ava, Landon, so glad you two could make it last minute."

Considering her cousins had pestered her into the dinner—according to Ava—Landon knew to be on his guard. They wanted a look at him. Fair enough. His family had already gotten a look at his *girlfriend*. He took her by the hand, feeling warm inside. Damn, he liked being with her. Even among the enemy.

"Last minute? That's funny." Ava dragged Landon with her into the kitchen and leaned on the island next to Sadie. Sadie pulled away to give her a hug, then she treated Landon to a long, full-bodied embrace that was a little uncomfortable.

Ava tried not to smile. "Sadie. Don't do the anaconda thing, please."

An apt description. Sadie had just about wrapped herself around him. And she was strong. Taller than Ava and more muscular, the woman looked like a champion kickboxer. He'd seen her leg sweeps Friday night and had been impressed.

"What?" Sadie finally let him go. "Wow. He really is all muscle." She wrapped her hands around his biceps.

"I feel dirty," Landon said in a loud whisper.

Elliot snickered. Sadie wiggled her eyebrows.

Ava said drily, "You should. Sadie feels up all my boyfriends."

"Yeah, that's why you got a *major* hug, Landon. Get it? Major?" Sadie chuckled. "Sadly, it's been a year and a half since I groped anyone new. Dr. Dateless was going through a dry spell before you. Those recent losers she met for coffee don't count."

Ava glared. "Was that information really necessary?"

"Yes. Yes it was." Sadie gave him a cheeky grin, and Landon couldn't help laughing.

Of the two of them, Ava clearly had a prettier face and, in his opinion, a better body. But Sadie was no slouch. More cute than pretty, and with a mouth that didn't quit, Sadie would more than hold her own on the singles scene.

"Just be glad she didn't grab you and tell you to turn your head and cough," Elliot said.

Landon's brows rose. "Really?"

"She does it to all my dates," Elliot complained with a twinkle in his eye.

"To *one* date," she enunciated, "and that didn't even happen that way. I accidentally tripped into the guy and hit his, well, touched his you-know-what. But Elliot told him I was gropey, so in the process, I actually helped him lose a clingy boyfriend." She said to her cousin, "And yeah, you still owe me."

"It was an ugly scene," Ava confided, then laughed. "By the end of it, Sadie was all red, Elliot wouldn't stop laughing, and his date had a hissy fit. Literally hissing and shrieking, because Elliot wouldn't finish what Sadie had started."

"It was so gross." Sadie shuddered. "Elliot's kinky boyfriend using me to turn him on with Elliot. Just so you know, I don't care how hot you are. I'm not feeling you up so you and Ava can get it on."

"For God's sake." Ava looked like she wanted to be anywhere but there.

Landon laughed out loud, enjoying himself immensely. "I think you're safe with me. I like my time with the ladies to be pretty private."

"Good for you." Elliot nodded. "I'm not against certain kinks, but I like my lovers one-on-one. And I'm not a fan of seeing my junk on the big screen either. Because some guys like to take pictures and post them, know what I mean?"

Ava's cheeks had turned pink.

"Guys can be scum. I think we all know that," Landon admitted, trying not to laugh as Ava covered her ears.

Her cousins nodded.

Ava let out a loud breath and dropped her hands. "Do you guys think we could get something to eat or drink and have a normal conversation *without* mentioning sex? We just walked through the door!"

Sadie shook her head. "You know, for a clinical psychologist, you can be quite the prude."

"Quite," Elliot reiterated.

"I have to use the bathroom." Ava shook her head. "You're on your own," she told Landon and darted down the hallway.

"So Landon, quick," Elliot urged in a low voice. "Ask me anything you want before she gets back."

Landon was *so* glad he'd agreed to dinner with her family. He would have come anyway, simply to get to know more about her. But this was an opportunity not to be missed. "So a year and a half?"

Sadie and Elliot nodded. "He was a bad lay," Sadie confided. "And boring. But safe. Ava has a thing about safe guys. Same as her recent online dates. Bland seems to be a thing with her." Then she and Elliot gave him a once-over and exchanged a look.

"Yeah, you're totally against type." Elliot nodded.

"That's what I've been hearing." And every time Landon heard it, he grew more annoyed. "So what qualities am I missing, exactly, from being Ava's 'perfect man'? I know I'm a little bigger than she's used to." He hadn't meant that to come out wrong, but from the smirks on Sadie's and Elliot's faces, he knew he'd already misspoken. "You guys really do live in the gutter, don't you?"

"Yep," Elliot said without pause. "So, to reiterate, you're too big, you're not an academic"—Elliot ticked off his fingers—"you don't have a PhD. Don't dress in slacks and loafers. Gag, but yeah, she even has a dress code on her stupid list. Are you a family kind of guy?"

"Huh?"

"Like, are you close with your family?"

"Yes."

Sadie nodded. "That's a plus. And you're somewhat intelligent."

"Gee, thanks."

Elliot continued in a rush, "Mr. Right has to be funny, smart, handsome—because physical chemistry is important to Ava—have life goals, make his own money, oh, and he has to like *us*." Elliot grinned, showing his teeth. "You can't be abusive in any way, and you have to want marriage and family down the line. And most importantly, you can't be intimidated by Ava."

"Because her brain and her mouth can be scary," Sadie said. "You might not see it now, because you're all about the boobs and the hair, but she has a tendency to cut through all kinds of BS. So if being with someone who's a real brain and can tell when you're lying bothers you, bail now, buddy."

Before he could respond, Ava returned. Her cousins both watched him, waiting for…what?

"Still here."

"Good." Elliot looked pleased.

"What did I miss? The warnings? The STD talk? The 'I'll break your legs if you hurt poor Ava' speech?" She grabbed the bowl of pita chips and hummus from Sadie and slid them toward Landon.

"Nothing poor about you that I can see." Landon had no problem with her family looking out for Ava. And her list made a sort of sense. It was practical and on point for a woman who wanted a decent guy in her future.

Landon just wished she'd throw out a few of her stupider requirements. Who cared if he was big and muscular? And why the hell should a PhD matter anyway? That bothered him. He knew he could and would eventually rock her world in the sack. The sexual chemistry between them was like nothing he'd ever experienced. Sexually, they'd be gold once the stubborn woman gave him the go-ahead. But he had no intention of getting an advanced degree. Ever.

Would she then consider him her intellectual inferior? *Him?* Major Landon Donnigan? Nah. No way.

He looked down at her, pleased she'd worn her hair down over that pretty pink sweater that accentuated her curves. She also wore a long tan skirt and boots. Professional chic. And damn, he wanted to see her in her office wearing those glasses while she counseled him. The fantasy refused to leave him.

"Landon?" She grabbed a glass of water from Sadie. "Did you want something?"

A hard fuck would be nice. "How about something to drink?"

"Sadie," Elliot ordered, "get the man a...beer? Wine? Iced tea?" He went back to those amazing-smelling fajitas.

"Iced tea works." Landon salivated, and his belly rumbled.

Elliot snapped his fingers at his cousin and pointed to the fridge. Sadie gave him a dark look even as she fetched then slid a glass of tea to Landon.

"So, Ava. Now's your chance," Sadie said. "What do you want to ask Landon that you haven't yet? Because we can ask for you while we're getting to know him. It's our right as family."

"And doesn't count as me being nosy because I'm not asking." Ava turned to Landon. "Aren't they funny?"

"Hilarious. However, you will recall that my family didn't ask you fifty questions."

"No, they just blamed me for mauling you on the couch and for possibly putting that blow-up doll in your bed."

Elliot dropped his spatula. "Say that again?"

Landon groaned. "You just had to bring that up, didn't you?"

Her wicked grin had his heart racing. The light over-head made her green eyes brighter, her lips darker. She was so damn pretty, and smart, and sexy, and... He had to stop. This obsession with the woman—one he hadn't even properly sexed up yet—was getting to him.

Hell, he now had a girlfriend. Instead of feeling hemmed in by the title, it curbed him of any desire for anyone else. Well, *she'd* actually curbed him, but still. And he loved the title, because it told others she was taken, no longer available.

"Ahem. Blow-up doll?" Sadie watched him and Ava, her eyes narrowed.

"It wasn't mine," he denied, as he'd been doing to the great hilarity of his siblings. "My brothers and sister are still blaming each other, but I'm going with Gavin as the culprit. And man, the payback will be such a bitch."

"Nice." Elliot nodded. "No wonder you and Ava get along. She's as deceitful as you are."

"Why does everyone talk about me as if I'm not here, and in such unflattering terms?" Ava scowled. "And stop hogging the hummus, Sadie." She tugged it back.

Seeing Ava with her cousins added a dimension to her that Landon could have done without. Because it made him crave her all the more. He wanted to see that loving grin on her face directed his way. To feel her accepting all of him, his foibles, successes, everything, simply because he belonged to her the way her family did.

Somehow, he'd gone from wanting a date and sex to wanting much more.

Had to be her lists getting to him.

Landon dragged a finger down her nose, amused when she whipped her head back and glared. "See? That's mean Ava coming out. I don't know. It's just so perfectly you."

"That is really insulting."

"No, it's honest. I don't like 'em nice. I like 'em mean. Strong. Intelligent." He told her the unvarnished truth.

She blinked. "I guess that is nice."

They watched each other, saying nothing, only the sizzling of the food to be heard.

Then Elliot sighed. "Oh man. I think she found a keeper. You'd better rock the hammock, man."

"Big banana all the way," Landon agreed, just so he

could see Ava turn bright red and bury her head in her hands on the counter.

Elliot and Sadie laughed and laughed. And Landon realized he'd crossed a hurdle without realizing how much it would mean that her family approve of him. He could check one more mark off Ava's stupid list. Now how to get her to see that a PhD meant nothing in the face of smokin' hot sex…?

Chapter 13

TUESDAY NIGHT, AVA WAITED IN HER KITCHEN FOR THE water to boil, needing a hot cocoa and marshmallow fix until she could take out all her frustrations on Landon "I'm Impossible" Donnigan.

She still couldn't understand it. She loved her cousins dearly. But they usually made her life miserable when dating someone new. In the brief time she'd dated while in Seattle, they'd run off one man before her sexual dud of a date ran himself off. Of her recent dip into the online dating pool, the few men she'd actually brought to coffee with her cousins had been scared off without much effort. Matt and Charles didn't count, because she'd dealt with them herself.

But Landon didn't seem to care about Sadie's mauling, her gorgeous body, or her dry sense of humor. He liked her sarcasm and Elliot's snark. Even more baffling, he'd turned aside all of Elliot's flirting and designs to make him uncomfortable. Not a homophobe in any sense of the word, and this from a military guy. Though she hated to generalize, the military-minded tended to be rather conservative. But not Landon.

They'd argued city politics and religion at dinner. She'd been beyond thrilled to see him open up. Then she'd played devil's advocate, just because. Landon, like her and her cousins, seemed to thrive on conflict. Talk about a loud, rousing, angry yet fun-as-heck dinner.

The kettle whistled, and she prepared her hot chocolate with six tiny, perfect marshmallows, all bobbing in steaming cocoa. Chocolate—a remedy to heal all ills.

After another night of pats on the shoulder and a platonic kiss to the forehead, she'd had enough. Though she'd never been an overly sexual person with any of her previous boyfriends, she'd become a sexually crazed idiot when it came to Landon.

Just being around him made her want to kiss the man, to touch him, stroke him. She loved feeling the hard muscle, loved feeling him cage her in those arms. He could pick her up without breaking a sweat. The last time she'd been held by a man, it had been her father fifteen years ago, saving her from falling into a creek. Men didn't lift her in their arms. They didn't swoop in to save her from anything, because Ava had never been that damsel in distress. Had never once felt that way.

But with Landon, she *wanted* to feel protected, cared for. She could more than take care of herself, but on some level, she wanted to submit to a stronger male.

So weird. She'd read up on the submissive tendencies in people. But she knew herself, or thought she did. She would never be a slave to someone, couldn't accept a lifestyle of domination or submission for herself. But in no way did she discount the appeal to many.

She liked the play in bed, though. Not with whips or chains, though restraints might be fun. But letting Landon go all caveman on her and tell her what to do? *Sign me up.*

That's if the blasted man would stop playing hard to get.

Oh please. He's not the one playing hard to get. It's you, you needy therapist.

Ava groaned and sucked down a marshmallow,

needing the comfort of something sweet. She both hated and loved the fact that she couldn't lie to herself.

No, none of her frustration was due to Landon, but to herself for questioning what she felt. If any of her patients had asked her what to do in this situation, she would have told them to follow their instincts, lead with the heart.

Ava's instincts told her to experiment with a man who treated her with respect and turned her on. No one would be hurt, they genuinely liked each other, and she'd started to seriously care for him on an intimate level.

But Ava felt like she had to wait. Why? She didn't know why.

Yes, you do.

She frowned and sucked down another marshmallow.

Because he means something to you, and that *means he has the capacity to hurt you. For all that he says he can handle you, you're afraid he can't. Physical strength and mental strength are two different things.*

She drank her cocoa, wondering at her truth. The few times in her life she'd been serious about a man, it turned out that man wanted a different woman. Once they realized she would only settle for a true version of themselves, and that she didn't need saving or protecting, just loving, they bolted or she'd cut them loose.

Landon still wanted to protect her, but he seemed to view her as a woman who could also protect herself. A contradiction, except defending others seemed a part of his makeup, what made him Landon. So he'd always want to protect her, no matter what. She thought she could live with that, so long as he didn't get too clingy. And he didn't seem the type.

But they hadn't gotten close enough to that sharing part, where they told each other secrets and cuddled in the night. She didn't know if she could see herself doing that with him, because it would be all her secrets and none of his.

Yet that didn't stop her from wanting to have sex with the man and call him her boyfriend. Getting serious with someone who really didn't meet the list?

What the heck, Ava? You're not acting rational. No, I'm following my heart.

And wasn't that a kick? The distant, cool professional feeling giddy in the presence of a big strong man. Just the thought of him sent a shiver down her spine, caused those butterflies in her belly to flutter and desire to flare inside her.

A loud knock shattered her already shaky nerves.

She glanced down at herself. She'd worn her hair in a ponytail tonight. A pair of gray lounge pants and a sweatshirt capped off with red fuzzy socks. But no underwear or bra. Her concession to seduction.

Did Landon suspect what tonight would be about? Sex on their seventh date? Didn't good girls wait for their tenth date? Or was it a length of time? A month before proper women had sex? Three months? Six?

She sighed, because she didn't really care. Just more fodder to keep her from her true emotions about Landon. Fear, excitement, affection bordering on something deeper…

She took a deep breath then let it out. He rapped on the door again. Impatient man.

"Yo, Ava," he barked.

She forgot to be nervous as she stalked to the door and yanked it open. "What?"

He grinned down at her. "Aw, you dressed up for me." He pushed her inside and slammed the door behind him.

"What—"

Then he kissed her. He tasted minty fresh, so he'd either been chewing gum or just brushed his teeth. As usual, his large hands pinned her down while he ravaged her mouth. She lost track of thought seconds after the mint hit her.

His tongue and lips took and gave, leaving her panting, wet between her legs, and on fire to have him inside her.

So of course, the contrary man pulled back, breathing hard, and smiled down at her, his joy easy to see.

"Miss me, Doc?"

She blew out the breath balled inside her and tried to calm down her raging desire.

"You mean, since last night?"

"Yeah. I missed you." He handed her…flowers? She hadn't even seen them in his hand, so done in by one freaking kiss.

"Oh, how nice." She loved flowers. Cliché, and she knew it, but Ava thought flowers to be terribly romantic. And he'd brought them. For her.

"You can put them in that vase under the sink." He grinned. "I looked around last time I was here."

"I'm adding nosy to your list."

He blinked. "*I* have a list?" His smile took up half his fat head. "Am I on your perfect man list?"

"Yes," she drawled, unable to stay annoyed with him right now, and put her flowers in a vase, then added water. "Right up there next to 'Must Live with His Mother' and 'Needs Someone to Drive Him Around.'"

"Whatever floats your boat, sweetheart." He rubbed

his hands together and looked around. "So what's on for tonight? Board games? TV? Another movie…though I'm thinking we're staying in since you're wearing…" He leaned closer, seeming to stare through the chest of her sweatshirt. "Oh." He'd noticed the no bra. He swallowed audibly. "Right."

"Sit down, Landon. We need to talk."

His gaze narrowed. "So talk."

"In the living room please. This is serious."

He didn't argue. He sat on her couch as directed, but stiff and slow moving, like a rabid wolf debating when to tear out the throat of his handler.

She needed to think, so she paced in front of him, aware he watched her every move.

"Yeah?" He sounded a little snippy, she was surprised to notice.

"I've done a lot of thinking."

"You do like to think." He snorted. "Must be all those fancy degrees."

She frowned. "I've come to some conclusions."

He sighed. "Go ahead." He kicked back, took off his shoes, and put his feet up on her coffee table. Then he spread his arms out on either side of the cushions. Wearing jeans and a flannel shirt unbuttoned at the top, he looked like an advertisement for a romantic getaway. Especially because she had the gas fireplace going in front of him.

Just need to get a fake bearskin rug and lay him naked on top of it…

He sighed again. "Still waiting."

"You really are aggravating."

He didn't grin with her, the way he normally did

when she criticized him. "Yeah, and I'm too big and dumb apparently."

"What?"

He leaned his head back, not looking at her. "Is this the part where you break up with me? Because I don't have all night."

Interesting. In an effort to save himself from hurt, he was pretending this didn't matter. She didn't even try to peg his uncaring attitude as sincere. She'd seen the flash of panic, then dismay in his eyes before he'd averted them.

Odd, but in all her musings about where her relationship with Landon might be going, she'd never considered *he* might be the vulnerable one. And wasn't that…fascinating.

She felt worlds better about life. She had the power. The control. Though tonight she'd be giving that—physically—over to him, right now, emotionally, she held the reins. Over a big, strong, could-break-her-in-half Marine.

Ava needed to be gentle and planned to ease into her seduction slowly.

She kept her grin to herself, her heart racing so fast she swore he'd be able to see her breasts bouncing all over the place if he'd just look at her. That he didn't made it easier to proceed.

"We've talked many times about us—you and me—and our status."

"Yep." Still not looking at her.

"And you kindly stipulated that I be in charge of when we had sex. *If* we had sex."

"Yep again."

She fought a grin. He started tapping the cushions, impatient to get dumped, apparently. "But you never did get yourself tested."

He stopped tapping and lifted his head. "Excuse me?"

"I'm taking birth control pills, and I had a physical last month, before I even met you, declaring me safe and sound. I still have the paperwork, as a matter of fact. I haven't had sex in a year and a half, so I know I'm not carrying any diseases." Enthralled with his intent expression, she continued, intentionally trying to rile him, "But you and Claudia, and who knows how many other women, have been having a lot of sex."

That number of women no longer bothered her, because as she'd come to know Landon, she realized faithfulness was an integral part of who he was. And right now, he was hers.

"That's not something you should worry about," he growled. "I always used protection with them. I *told* you that." He stood, no longer content to sit and watch. As usual, he had to command with his presence. And presence he had. Wow. "For your information, Dr. Rosenthal, I got my test results back yesterday. I'm clean as a whistle, and I brought the damn paper to prove it."

"Oh?"

He grabbed a folded piece out of his back pocket and shoved it at her. "Here."

She made a big production out of looking it over, glancing at him, frowning, glancing back at the paper...

"What now?" he snapped.

"I was considering having sex with you, but your attitude is a little disconcerting."

He froze, must have sensed himself looming over her, and sat so fast he rocked the couch.

She bit her lip to keep from laughing and held her hands behind her back. "I know I mentioned babies before, in an effort to scare you away, but you have to understand I'm not ready for children yet. I'm not ready to be married either. Like you, I prefer to marry then have children."

"Right." He had such a deep voice.

"This exercise in dating is to find a compatible mate. A boyfriend, and hopefully at some point after we've known each other, a fiancé."

A subtle glance showed he had a prominent erection. He widened his legs, making no effort to hide it.

"But I refuse to be rushed. On this, our seventh date, I—"

"Eighth."

She'd known he wouldn't be able to let that go. The fact that she knew that made her decision impossibly easy. "Again, your numbers are wrong."

Now he was smiling, and her heart did a funny dip seeing it. His hair continued to get longer, and he hadn't cut it yet. He was so sexy, so manly. And that body of his didn't quit.

"My point. If we're going to have sex, I need to lay some ground rules."

"Please do." He shifted his hips, as if to seek release from the pressure no doubt growing.

"I am on birth control. The pill, to be precise."

"Precise. Right." He chuckled.

"No interruptions."

He nodded. "That's why you say, 'Hold all questions

to the end,' before you begin. But continue. I'll shut up." He unbuttoned his shirt, the bastard, showing off all that muscle.

She had to swallow around a dry throat. "You probably didn't bring condoms. But your note states you're safe, so I'm willing to forego them."

He groaned.

She frowned. The groaning stopped, but the flush on his cheeks was real. This man wanted her. And that heady knowledge hurried her words. "We have to be safe though. You told me you would dictate what we did together. And I trust you. But I also have to trust that you'll stop at any time I tell you to. No matter what."

He nodded. "I swear. I'd never hurt you."

"But you might think you're not hurting me, and you might be."

"My cock is big, but I'm pretty sure you'll fit me."

She licked her lips, nervous all of a sudden. "Right. But, well, you're not planning anything too weird, are you? Just normal sex?"

His eyes softened. "Ava, I want inside you. But nothing too kinky. I'm a pretty vanilla guy, to be honest. I just like to be in charge. Nothing too weird. But I can't promise you won't get spanked at some point." He winked. "You have been pretty naughty."

She exhaled the breath she hadn't realized she'd been holding. "Okay."

"Is that it?" He didn't leave the couch.

"Almost. I just wanted you to know that I'm looking forward to it." She nodded. "Yes. That's it."

"Okay." He closed his eyes, breathed evenly, then opened them. "I'm going to fuck you until you beg me

to stop. Because once ain't gonna cut it with you, sweetheart. And we both know it."

She nodded.

"No, tell me you know it."

"This is where you get bossy, is that it?"

His panty-melting grin answered for him.

"Fine. I know it."

"Good." He stood and stared at her. "Lift your shirt."

She did, no question, liking him taking charge.

"No fucking bra. I knew it." He cupped a breast in his
large hand, and the moment he grazed her nipple, heat
shot straight to her core. "Pull down your pants."

She did.

He swore and let her go, stepping back. "You're a
cruel tease. You knew I thought you were canning me,
and you stood there without underwear? No bra?"

"Now, Landon. How can I know what you're thinking? I was told not to 'shrink you.'"

A mean look came into his eyes, and she grew slicker
because of it. "Oh man, I can't wait to teach you a few
lessons, Doc. Now go get on your business gear. A blouse
and skirt, one with access, so not too tight. Put your hair
down and grab your glasses. I'm going to lie down on this
couch and wait. Because I need some therapy, ASAP."

Oh wow. He wants to play.

She stared at him for a moment, then raced downstairs
and put on a short, stretchy black skirt she normally
wore going out to a bar or club with Sadie, but it could
pass for work clothing if need be. She also selected an
aqua-colored silk blouse. She brushed her hair out, put
on a bit of makeup, spritzed some perfume, and grabbed
her glasses as she started back up the stairs.

I'm missing something…

"You better not be wearing any underwear," Landon called out.

She remembered and hurried to her closet again. There, she found a pair of high heels she'd never wear to work, but which showed off her legs. She returned to him slowly, so as not to cause bodily injury when she broke an ankle in her four-inchers.

Once at the top of the stairs, she put a little sway into her hips, slid on her glasses, and joined him at the couch.

He was lying down, but when he saw her, his eyes grew wide. He looked her over from top to bottom and licked his lips. "Oh fuck, yeah." Then he lay back and laced his hands behind his head. His bare feet hung over the end of the couch, because he was too long.

She sat in the chair by the couch and crossed her legs, showing off her heels.

He groaned and shifted. "I am so fuckin' hard."

"And I'm wet," she announced as if talking about the weather. "Now shall we begin, Mr. Donnigan?"

He slanted a dark look her way. "Oh yeah, Doc. I need to tell you about my fantasies. I'm having problems."

"Tell me." She hadn't thought he'd want to wait. That they'd have sex in a hurry and put out the erotic flames making her so darn hot. But this… *So much* better than she could have dreamed. Landon had a real flair for sex.

"You see, I have these fantasies about my therapist."

"What's her name?"

"We'll just call her Doc. I wouldn't want to make her uncomfortable. Everyone likes her. She's funny and smart. And she has the prettiest green eyes. Now when I see anything in that shade, it reminds me of her."

She blinked. She hadn't expected this. Raunchy, sexy talk, sure. But complimenting other parts of her? Admitting to deeper feelings? Her heart raced even faster, her emotions deepening despite her inner warnings to be cautious of falling too far too fast.

"Continue," she rasped.

He turned his head to watch her. "In my dreams, she's sitting there, waiting for me to open up." He licked his lips again, his gaze on her breasts. "But while she's waiting, she toys with her shirt, unbuttoning it so I can see her breasts. Her nipples are hard."

She followed his direction, unbuttoning the shirt bit by bit.

"And they're a cherry red. So tasty." He stared at the silk gliding over her flesh, making her more aroused. "Her skirt rides up, you know? But she's not wearing any panties. She spreads her legs while she watches me through those sexy glasses. I can see her pussy. She's all wet, like she's dreaming about me too."

Ava shivered, not feeling the cold but a desire so deep it was like an aching throb. She uncrossed her legs, hiked her skirt in slow increments, until it hit the tops of her thighs, then spread her legs and scooted so he could see her better.

"Damn." He expelled a loud breath. "Just, damn."

"Does she touch herself?" she asked after she came to the last button on her shirt. She pushed it apart, exposing her breasts. Her pussy on display, herself wide open, she waited.

"Oh yeah. She fucking does. She slides her fingers through all that wet skin, and she makes her clit all big and hard." She did what he said, coming closer to orgasm, and mostly from having him watch her touch herself.

"But what about him? Shouldn't he be naked while she slides her fingers in her pussy?" she asked as she slid one inside her.

He swore again, gripping the back of his head. "Nah. I watch, and I get ready to come. But I don't get naked, not until she takes my shirt off. She only unbuttons my jeans and pulls down my underwear. I'm not supposed to be naked, because we're in her office. But she can't help herself. She strips down, except for the heels."

Ava stood on shaky legs, took off everything but her heels, and crossed to him. Then she leaned down and unbuttoned his shirt. He let go of his head to cup her breasts and stroke her belly, and she gasped.

"Then she tells me how good it feels," he whispered, "and she leans closer, so I can suck her tits while she's telling me she wants more."

Ava bared his chest entirely. "I want more. I want your mouth on me, Landon," she urged.

He pulled her down, just enough that he could suck the tip of her nipple into his mouth.

She couldn't help the small cry that left her, because his mouth felt like an inferno. Her pussy ached, so empty. And soon she'd have him, all of him, inside her. That big erection straining at his jeans, so close she could touch it.

He moved to her other breast, and she went off script. She put her hand over his cock and squeezed.

He stopped moving. "Doc, what do you think you're doing?"

Chapter 14

LANDON WAS TWO SECONDS FROM LOSING IT. SERIOUSLY coming in his pants for his first time with Ava. Oh, hell no.

She stopped moving. "I'm b-bracing myself. I'm so sorry, Landon," she apologized in a breathy voice. "Did I hurt you?"

The liar. "Move your hand." She did, and he wanted to tell her to put it back. Instead, he forced himself to follow his fantasy, because hell yeah, he wanted it to play out. "Now take off my shirt all the way."

Ava watched him from behind those killer glasses. Her breasts were spectacular. No question. Wearing only high heels, she looked like a walking wet dream.

She leaned over him, brushing her tits against his chest. He swore he felt zipper marks against his cock as he swelled even more. *No. Have to hold on until she comes, then I'm inside her.*

He leaned up so she could remove his shirt, then she placed it on top of hers. He didn't have to tell her twice to free his cock. She moved with gentle fingers, though she had a difficult time getting the fly unbuttoned because he'd gotten so big.

She didn't touch his dick, but she did scoot his jeans down his hips, hampering his legs while exposing his cock and balls. "You aren't wearing underwear." She arched a brow, and that whole naughty therapist vibe crushed him.

"Fuck no. I had hopes for tonight." He groaned. "Get away from there." When she stood, he put his hands behind his head again. "Now spread your legs for me."

She proudly widened her stance, bringing his attention to her toned legs and that sexy strip of hair guarding her sex. Without encouragement, she put her fingers between her legs and brought them out for him to see.

His voice was low and hoarse. "So wet, aren't you, Doc?"

"Yes, I am. I need my own kind of medicine, I think."

"I have it right here. Come sit over my face." *Bam. Right there.* He'd wanted this since he'd first seen her. With any luck, he wouldn't come yet, because God knew he was ready enough without even touching her.

She walked over to him in those fuck-me heels, and he scooted down on the couch, tossing the back cushions to give them more space. She knelt over him, her knees on either side of his head.

"Yeah. Lower that cunt, that's right."

She moaned. That was his Doc. She loved his coarse talk, the dirtier, the better.

"That's it, baby. Let me lick you up. What a hard little clit. Yeah. Work yourself over me. Come on."

She slid over his lips, so slick, he knew it wouldn't be long before she came. The taste of her. *Fuck me, she's perfect.* He licked and thrust his tongue into her, wanting to get so deep. He had to touch her, and he gripped her legs, wanting her to move faster, so he could get more of her when she came.

"Landon," she moaned. "I'm going to come. Oh, please."

Thank God. Because all this play had made him crazed. He wouldn't last much longer either, but she had to come first. Because the minute he entered her, he'd explode.

He held her by the hips, grinding her over his tongue and teeth.

She cried out as she came while he lapped her up like a fucking drug. She continued to moan, still caught in her pleasure, but he couldn't wait.

He yanked her off his face and straddled her over his hips while he positioned himself to receive her. Then she slid right over him, all that heat gliding down, and her body, still seizing…

"Fuck. I'm coming. Oh shit. *Ava.*" He gritted his teeth as the most intense orgasm of his life jetted out of him. She rocked over him while he emptied inside her in the most blissful moment of his existence.

It felt like forever as he released, until the black spots behind his eyelids faded and he could see again. He hadn't realized he'd been holding her so hard until he let her hips go. "Fuck me." He blew out a breath, stroking the red marks on her skin.

"Oh my God." She'd braced her hands on his chest at some point, because the scratch of her short nails over his nipples set him off again, and he groaned and jerked as another spurt left him.

"Oh man. That was so damn good." Could anything come close to that? Ever? Landon stopped her when she would have gotten off him. "No, stay."

She sighed and leaned over him, pressing her breasts against his chest.

"Ava, honey, that was the sexiest thing. I mean, I

came the second you put yourself over me." He swore. "I'll do better next time, I swear."

She laughed against his chest, her body still snug, holding him tightly inside her. That he'd come without a condom, skin to skin inside Ava, aroused him anew. He'd poured a lot inside her, no doubt. But he had a feeling he could go again if he found the right rhythm… He carefully nudged his jeans down farther.

"Don't feel bad, Marine. I came pretty hard over your mouth, and that was right away too."

"That's true." He wanted a kiss. "But we're missing something."

She leaned up on her chin.

"Have I told you how much those glasses turn me on?"

"I think you convinced me." She squeezed her insides and he felt her, all up and down his cock.

"You little witch. You owe me a kiss. More than a kiss." When he'd thought she was breaking up with him, his despair had been all too real. And scary as hell. "I thought you were dumping me."

"When I wore no bra?" She scoffed. "And I thought you paid attention to detail."

"I wasn't sure. The sweatshirt fooled me." He growled. "Now kiss me."

She tried to scoot up his body, but that would have meant pulling off his cock.

"Wait." He sat up with her, so suddenly she gasped. But she also settled onto him, driving him deeper inside her. "That's it."

"You're still hard?" She blinked at him. Then she took off her glasses and tossed them to the side. "Sorry. They're for reading, really."

"Yeah, sure. Whatever." He pulled her head down for a kiss and rocked into her, holding her waist while he flexed inside her. She tasted like chocolate and sugar, and he wanted more.

He stroked into her mouth with each thrust deeper into her body. Like magic, he grew harder, his kisses fiercer. Deeper. He couldn't get deep enough. With each push and pull, her breasts raked trails of heat over his chest. Her thighs settled around his, their body heat an inferno.

He kissed down her throat, holding her by the hair, and she whispered his name. A plea or a curse, he couldn't be sure, because he was ready again, hard and excited, and he needed her there with him.

Landon edged his hand between them, seeking her clit. When he found it, she slammed over him, and that pressure built in his balls.

"Yes, yes," she pleaded and rode him hard, clutching his hair while she kissed and licked, sucking his tongue deep.

Sensations abounded. Memories of her blowing him while he drove deeper inside her, of how she'd looked while staring into his eyes through those sexy glasses...

He stabbed his tongue into her mouth, on the edge, needing her to come. And then he couldn't wait.

He pulled his mouth away and pressed his head to her shoulder as he drove inside her and came. By some miracle, she climaxed as well, clamping down on him and giving more pleasure than he could handle.

He was shaking, outside himself, yet always conscious to keep the precious treasure in his arms safe, protected.

You are so mine, he wanted to say. Instead, when he

could put his words together once more, he managed, "So was it good for you too?"

———

Ava thought she'd gone blind, and then she blinked and the spots dancing in front of her eyes cleared. "Um, yes. Except I don't think my legs work anymore."

Sex like this wasn't supposed to be possible. At least, she'd never imagined it could be. Like the books and the movies, with orgasms so intense people blacked out? He remained inside her, starting to soften, finally, like a mere mortal. She'd seen him aroused, but feeling all that steel inside her? He was so big and thick, he filled her, almost painfully so.

Almost.

Instead, any time he moved, even breathed, he touched another part inside her that would cause tingles of ecstasy to ravage her body. She toyed with the hair at the nape of his neck and heard him groan. Like a big beast under beauty's touch, she thought with a touch of whimsy.

"You are one amazing fuck," he said bluntly.

She burst into laughter.

She couldn't help it. The least romantic words on the planet, yet equally true of him. "Back at ya, Casanova."

He laughed as well, and then they had to move, *fast*, because he'd made a huge mess. *Twice.*

They quickly rose, and he shoved a towel between her legs. "I borrowed it from the bathroom under the sink while you were downstairs. Didn't think you'd mind." He held the towel and stared down at her, his expression intense.

"Um, no. I don't mind." She let him take care of the mess, then wasn't sure what to do. "Now what?"

"Now we wait until I get my second wind."

She blinked. "What?"

He put her hand on the towel to hold it while he stripped out of his jeans. He stood naked and just…

"You are a specimen of maleness. I just have to say." He had all the lines the Greek statues had. Cut, muscular… She sighed.

"Go ahead and touch me. You know you want to."

"I really do."

He chuckled. "It's okay. I feel the same way about you. Your breasts are just amazing." He cupped one, rubbing the velvety soft tip, and it sprang to attention. "You're soft but hard underneath. I like your tone, Doc."

"And I like your imagination. Where the heck did you come up with all that?"

He flushed. "I've been wanting that since I first saw you."

"Well, *I* might need therapy before I see my clients again. Just so you know, I have never and will never offer that kind of therapy to my patients."

"Good." He kissed her, this time with a tenderness that shook her.

"Oh." She cradled her hands against his chest. "Speaking of second winds, how did you do that? Twice like that?"

She felt his rumble of laughter in his chest. "Liked that, did you? I've been thinking about doing you for a while. Yeah, I was pent-up. But I'm in my prime, baby. You got a sex machine for a boyfriend." He sounded deeply satisfied. "But it's all good, because my sex kitten girlfriend milked me dry. Seriously. I need some food and tender care before I can fill you up again." He rubbed her back. "And I plan on doing that a few more times tonight."

"Wow. The floodgates open, and I'm bowlegged after one night. Imagine that."

He laughed again. "Come on, woman. Feed me some hot chocolate and marshmallows. Then, if you're lucky, we'll hit some doggie style and a sixty-nine."

"On a school night?"

"Hell yeah, on a school night. See what you created? This is all your fault."

"My fault?"

He wrapped her in his shirt, which came to her knees, and she fixed him some hot cocoa. He remained naked, however, and not too shy about it either.

"See this?" He gripped himself. "Ever since meeting you, I've had to release the dam at least twice a day. Sexual frustration is not good for a man." He looked sad. "I can't believe you made me wait so long."

"Seriously? You know nothing." She handed him his cocoa and popped another marshmallow. *Addicting little things, a lot like Landon.* She wanted to lick him up all over again. "I was high and dry for over a year."

"That's because you hadn't met me. I'd have had you out of those panties in no time. And then we'd have been doing it nonstop." He smiled. "In fact, let me finish this hot chocolate and…" He wiggled his eyebrows.

She blinked. "Seriously?"

He downed the cup. "Oh yeah. That shirt of mine on you? Unbuttoned like that?" He groaned. "I have more fantasies, mostly about you wearing *me*. Now about that sixty-nine…"

Chapter 15

GAVIN DIDN'T KNOW WHAT TO THINK. LANDON HAD always been a ladies' man. Not one of Gavin's caliber, but big brother worked his biceps, flashed that Donnigan know-how, and typically had women eating out of his hand.

But Landon had never looked at any of them the way he looked at Ava. It was like she'd put a spell on him, and he knew it but had no idea how to get out of it.

They sat at his parents' for a Thursday night meal. Their mother had finally sold that home out from under her rival, and she wanted to celebrate. A savagely exultant Linda Donnigan was no one to mess with, so Gavin had shown up early with a bottle of her favorite wine to congratulate her—unopened of course, or God forbid they'd think him off the wagon. He'd have dragged Theo with him, except Theo was working.

He sat to his mother's left, while she sat next to Van, who occupied the head of the table. His parents had always taken their meals together, sitting close and sharing a smile while watching over their brood. That they still liked to be close gave Gavin the warm fuzzies.

Hope sat on the other side of Ava, talking about something, while Landon watched on with satisfaction. A big, lazy lion keeping watch over his pride.

Oh yeah. Big brother had gotten a piece of Ava, for sure. He had that "this woman is mine" look that meant he'd staked a claim. Plus, those little blushes Ava made when she caught Landon's eye were telling.

She was beautiful. So smart and strong and independent. Gavin contained a laugh, just barely. Landon had no idea what he'd done by snagging the hot doc. She'd tie him in knots, no doubt.

"So dear. How's your work going?" his mother asked him while his father regaled Hope and Ava with some story about a juggler downtown that morning.

"Fine." Gavin tried to hear more, but his mom leaned closer.

She whispered, "Is this Landon's girlfriend? The one he told us about?"

Why the hell was she whispering? "Yeah."

Linda leaned back, her gaze shrewd. She turned to Ava and said, "Dr. Rosenthal, I am just *thrilled* you and Landon found each other. After all that work you did for my sister and her husband, I was hoping that wouldn't be the last we saw of you."

The table grew silent. Ava's eyes grew round. "Oh my gosh. Now I know why you looked familiar. You're related to Beth McCauley, aren't you?"

Landon blinked.

Hope glanced from Ava to her mother.

Gavin tried not to laugh, now realizing why the name Rosenthal had rung a bell. "Ah, so Ava is Uncle James and Aunt Beth's therapist? Oh man, the stories you could tell…"

"I had no idea." Ava gave a strained smile and a subtle look at Landon that promised trouble later. "I haven't seen them for a while, actually. I hope they're doing well. Oh, and call me Ava, please."

"They're wonderful," his mother gushed. "Did you know their son Cameron got married and had a baby?"

"I thought Vanessa had the kid?" Landon cut in. "Or did the genius somehow manage to reproduce all by himself?" Landon grinned. "Like a spore. I can see Cam doing the whole asexual reproduction thing."

"He is kind of like a fungus," Gavin agreed, always game to make fun of their annoying cousins. The McCauleys liked nothing better than to prove they were better at everything. Unfortunately, Gavin and Landon dove into the competition headfirst. To this day, the cousins still fought about who had been the best at sports in high school, though it was no contest who had gotten the best grades. Taking the brainy Cameron out of the equation, Landon and Hope had kicked some serious ass. But Gavin had to hand the wrestling win to Mike, not that he'd ever admit that out loud.

Linda ignored them, focused on her favorite subject lately. "They had a baby girl. Beth is a grandmother twice over now." She sighed. "Not me. I'm still *so far* from having my own grandbabies." That tone meant bad news.

Gavin, Landon, and Hope exchanged wary glances.

Landon straightened in his chair. "Uh, Mom? We're just here for dinner. Not to repopulate the family tree."

Ava blushed. "I had no idea you were related to the McCauleys. The subject never came up."

"How did you two meet?" Linda asked, as if she didn't already know.

"Landon and I met at Jameson's Gym."

"Technically, Landon was *bothering* her at the gym," Gavin corrected. "Out of desperation, and to get him to quit stalking her, Ava gave him a pity date. Now she can't shake him."

His sister snickered. "That sounds like Landon."

"Yes, Beth now has Colin and baby Eleanor." Linda had departed reality for her own world, one in which nothing existed but babies and future progeny. "Such a gorgeous little girl."

"James is so excited." Van laughed. "Colin, their once one-and-only grandson, not so much. He's still pretty anti-girl, the poor kid."

"I feel for him," Landon added, with a look at Ava. "Girls can be a real pain."

Like Linda, Ava ignored him too. "You're young yet, Linda. You have plenty of time to be a grandma. I still can't believe Landon's your son. You don't look old enough to have Theo, let alone these three." She looked around the table at them all.

Linda fluffed her hair. "It's my stylist. She's really good."

"That and the thrill of victory," Hope said while pushing her food around. "Mom drinks the blood of her victims, keeping her eternally young."

Van hurriedly interrupted. "Actually, I'm wondering myself what you three are waiting for. I'd make a stellar grandfather."

Linda gave her husband a wide smile.

Gavin scowled at his dad. *Suck up.*

"Exactly," his mom agreed. "Ava, what do you think? Are my children afraid of commitment or of growing up? Or maybe both? Is that why I'm grandbaby-less? You're a smart woman. In your professional opinion, what would you say?"

Man, Hope was right. His mother was totally out for blood tonight.

Everyone waited for Ava's response. Gavin had to hand it to her. She didn't seem intimidated by Linda's toothy smile at all. But he wanted to hide somewhere, away from all those sharp teeth.

"Actually, Linda, I don't know your family well enough to make even a guess. It seems to me they're smart enough to wait until they're ready."

Linda turned to Landon. "Yes, but when will that be?" She looked from him to Ava, a big question in her cunning brown eyes.

For once, big brother was in the hot seat. And poor Theo was missing this! Gavin and Hope gave each other an air high five.

"I saw that." Landon frowned, then turned to Ava. "This is the real Linda Donnigan. Don't get taken in by the savvy professional eating up the competition. This crazy woman demanding babies is my mother doing her best impression of 'unhinged and baby-obsessed.'"

"That's a terrible thing to say." Yet Linda laughed. "I'm teasing you, Ava, and at Landon's expense. My sister thinks the world of you, and so do we. They were having some problems, but now they're doing so much better."

Gavin noticed Ava had yet to comment on his aunt and uncle. The woman took her job seriously, not spilling any beans. And knowing his aunt and uncle, he was sure plenty had been spilled in therapy.

"Have you helped Landon with his issues yet?" Gavin asked.

Ava turned to him, her green eyes bright and full of

mirth. "You'll have to be more specific. Landon has *a lot* of problems."

"You got that right," Hope muttered.

"Hope." His father coughed to hide a grin. "Landon's just fine. He's managing Daniel's company well enough. And every time I see Mac Jameson at the gym, he's bugging me to get Landon to come work for him too since Gavin's doing so well there."

Landon snorted. "Yeah, right. Work for Mac and that ego?"

"*Who's* got an ego?" Gavin asked.

"And working with my little brother?" Landon continued. "No way in hell."

Gavin hated when Landon called him that. Theo was the little brother. Gavin was just younger by two friggin' years. Big deal. "Yeah, because I could never work with you either. You're too controlling. It's all I can do not to plant you on your ass in self-defense class. You tend to take over, you know."

Landon raised a brow, and Ava tried to suppress a grin.

"What's so funny?" Gavin asked.

"You. You two are very similar."

"Wait. Gavin and *me*?" Landon frowned. "Have you been drinking?"

Van grinned. "No, she's right. Gavin might act like me a lot, very chill"—his father saying *chill* made Gavin want to cringe—"but they both like to control their worlds. Gavin's just more subtle about it."

"No way." Gavin glanced at Hope. "Back me up?"

"Actually, you've all been bossy since the day I was born." Hope snorted. "Trust me, Ava, being around so many boys has its drawbacks. The smells. Dear God."

Ava chuckled, as did Van and Linda.

"Nice, Hope." Landon rolled his eyes. "I think we're getting off track here. Ava hasn't helped me with anything. Well, except for making me happy."

"In bed," Gavin murmured, loud enough so that Landon could hear him but the others couldn't, he didn't think.

"Don't be a dick," Landon warned in a low voice.

"It's okay, Landon. I'm not ashamed of our relationship," Ava said, quite clearly. "I enjoy Landon's company, and I find him very attractive."

"Well said." His mother rubbed her hands together, and Gavin imagined her planning the pair's nuptials as Ava spoke.

"He has his drawbacks, but then, we all do."

Landon's smug smile faded. "Drawbacks? Like what?"

"You do tend to be a little *too* bossy," Hope said.

"And a little too rigid at times," Van offered. "But I'm sure Ava can work around that. You two are dating, after all. You obviously find each other compatible. Landon, you truly lucked out. Ava's not only pretty, she's smart and well-spoken. A keeper, hmm?"

Ava blushed. "You must be where Gavin gets his charm."

"You mean where *I* get *my* charm." Landon frowned. "Charm? Um, no."

Gavin couldn't help but laugh as she stymied Major Arrogant.

Ava returned to the topic at hand. "Yes, we're dating. Landon's intelligent and funny. I always enjoy myself with him." That seemed to mollify the big bastard, until she added, "But he is somewhat emotionally distant, as he well knows."

"What did I say about not shrinking me?" Landon growled at her.

Ava didn't appear anxious in the slightest. "I'm not 'shrinking you,' Landon. Your personality is an open book to those who know you. And I'd think your family knows you best."

"That's true." Van smiled and refilled Hope's water glass, then Ava's. "I think of Landon as Superman, with a heart threatened by kryptonite."

"Not the superhero rhetoric," Hope protested.

"Rhetoric?" Gavin was impressed.

"It's on my Word of the Day calendar." Hope sighed. "Forgive them, Ava. My parents aren't used to us bringing people home."

"Is that so?" Ava gave Landon an innocent look. "Not even Claudia?"

Gavin whistled. "And score! Three points, Ava. Field goal on that one."

She sent a smile Gavin's way while Landon hemmed and hawed under his mother's twenty questions.

"Who's Claudia?" Linda wanted to know for the fourth time.

"Not that redhead from the gym. Landon." Van sounded disappointed.

Back to Linda. "I thought you were just going to the gym to work out. Not to meet women."

"It wasn't serious, obviously." Van played peacemaker. "And he is a grown man. The boy has needs, honey."

"*Dad.*" Landon glared at their parents.

Hope rolled with laughter until Landon turned that dark look on her.

"I'm sorry. Was that a secret?" Ava asked. "I just

assumed you were close to your family and shared details
of your life. I apologize if I shared too much."

"You'll pay for that later," Landon promised. Then he
turned to his parents and fobbed them off with a story about
Claudia and him just being friends.

Gavin snorted. His parents were older but not stupid.
Damn, son, learn how to lie, at least. Boy Scout that he
was, Major Donnigan was shitty when it came to fibbing,
and he always had been.

"Totally just friends, nothing more," Landon emphasized.
"Not like me and Ava, my girlfriend with the big mouth."
He smiled at her through his teeth, but she only smiled back.

Man, she really was hot. And brainy. And sarcastic. Just
like Landon.

Gavin liked her a lot. He wasn't used to liking Landon's
girlfriends. Not that he'd met that many since they'd joined
the Corps, but the few he'd met never left a lasting impression. Ava was different.

"I was just teasing," Ava said as Landon started to
argue once more with their father, who was clearly poking
fun at his son. She raised her voice. "But I did want to say
one thing, and that's thank you for inviting me to dinner.
Linda, this pesto recipe is fabulous."

That shifted the conversation to food and deflected
both Van's and Linda's attention. Clever Ava.

Gavin raised a mental toast her way.

Linda smiled. "I'd love to take credit, but Van does
all the cooking."

Their father grinned, not too proud to enjoy a pretty
woman's flattery. "That's true. I do."

"Wow. You're amazing." Ava chewed another bite,
just to prove it.

"That's true too. I am."

Ava swallowed then laughed. "Now I see where Landon gets his confidence. From his mom *and* his dad."

"The confidence is all me," Linda corrected her. "But the arrogance? That's Van, for sure."

"Ah. I see." Ava then turned to answer something Hope said.

Gavin wondered if Ava was processing it all, making note of the family dynamic and assessing them. Was she even now counseling them internally, seeing the dysfunction that existed between mother and daughter, who hadn't said much of anything to each other? Or did she concentrate instead on the warped middle son who couldn't hold his liquor and had stupid nightmares because he was too much of a pussy to get over Afghanistan?

At the thought, images flashed in his mind's eye. The sound of the grandfather clock in the other room boomed a bit too loudly. A mortar exploded. He could almost hear the whisper of wind through sand, the thuds of bullets hitting the ground, then bodies...

He sucked down his water, wishing for a beer right now. His father shot him a look, and Gavin forced himself to relax, to breathe deeply. He'd been getting better at putting it all away, enough that he could poke fun at Landon's possessive arm over Ava's shoulder.

"Damn, Landon. Afraid she'll bolt for the door if you let her go?"

Hope snickered.

Van relaxed and winked, then leaned closer to whisper, "I like this one. I think Landon's going to have a hard time handling her. Not the other way around, for once."

Gavin chuckled. "No kidding. Big brother's met his

match." He paused. "But I like her." Maybe enough to talk to her later about getting some help. He didn't want anyone else to know, though. Ava had helped Aunt Beth and Uncle James, and she didn't share their secrets. Maybe she could unscrew his brain and help him, and since she was doing—*dating*—his brother, perhaps he'd get some kind of family and friends discount.

Gavin took a second helping of chicken pesto and wondered when he could get Ava alone to talk to her. Without looking suspicious…

Ava hadn't enjoyed herself so much in a long time. Sure, her cousins and uncle could be amusing, but the loudness and constant back-and-forth barrage of trash talk and family fun in the Donnigan house was new and engaging. Landon was *a lot* like Linda. Ava had expected that from everything Landon had described about his mother. A go-getter, type-A personality, a barracuda in business and a blond to boot. Just like her son.

But Landon shared several traits with his father as well. The elder Donnigan seemed calm, unflappable, and he had a palpable protective demeanor. She could easily envision him as a commended Navy corpsman. So like his oldest son. Van Donnigan was dark where Landon was light, yet with classic good looks. Between Linda and Van's genes, she knew Landon would age very, very well.

And time to stop thinking about sex around Landon's family, you hussy.

"…if you'd like a copy."

His father had mentioned something about giving her the recipe?

For the chicken pesto. "Oh yes, please. I love to cook."

"She makes a mean garlic chicken." Landon sounded proud, and he kept his arm around the back of her chair. She supposed she should be glad he hadn't peed around the base of it to prove she belonged to him.

Primitive, but kind of cute. Landon had labeled her his girlfriend, and he meant it.

She carried the conversation without forcing it, at ease with the Donnigans. But as always, she found it impossible to turn off her counseling hat. She hadn't missed Gavin's dark expression, the sudden shift to tense and anxious, or how fast he'd come back. Some issues there he'd have to deal with, but it wasn't her place to interfere, she knew.

And Hope. Now that girl was interesting. A dynamo full of energy. Blond, pretty, even perky, she resembled her mother to a T—except for the eyes. Linda Donnigan had the eyes of a predator. A tough businesswoman, a protective mother. Hope, however, had a softer expression. A dreamer, perhaps, a woman still finding herself. Those comments thrown her mother's way seemed to have gone ignored, yet Ava saw Linda watching Hope with…what? Determination? Exasperation? Worry?

Ava wanted badly to dive into that relationship and forcibly refrained. Her ties to Landon made personally helping his family a no-go. But she could recommend help if asked.

Not that they would. Linda might ask on Gavin's behalf. But she was the type who'd handle her own issues herself. It hadn't escaped Ava's notice that Linda had sounded a bit holier-than-thou when mentioning her sister and brother-in-law getting help. Because Linda would never need assistance in fixing *her* family.

Ava glanced at Landon, noting the same confidence, the same arrogant tilt to his head. Oh yeah, she'd have her work cut out for her, dealing with him later. Intentionally needling him about Claudia had been childish, but so satisfying. He hadn't given her any warning that they'd be coming to his parents' for dinner until they'd been standing on the doorstep.

Had he thought she might run away if he'd told her ahead of time?

She rose from the table and excused herself to the restroom, thinking about all she'd learned.

Everything about the Donnigans made her like Landon even more. *Hmm. What to make of that?* The affection she felt for Landon, combined with the sex and the more she got to know of him, had her feeling something deeper. Something more serious.

She finished in the washroom and exited, still lost in thought about her stubborn boyfriend. They were so new. She shouldn't feel this way yet, not for a man she'd technically only had eight dates with.

Of course, Landon would tell her they'd had nine, because he liked to irk her like that…

"Ava?" Gavin approached her. "Can I talk to you for a minute?"

"Um, sure, Gavin." Had something happened while she'd been in the bathroom?

He glanced behind them, then walked down the hallway toward what appeared to be a craft room.

"My mom sews. She used to do it a lot, but with her so busy with her job, she's slowed down," Gavin explained. "But hey, if you start popping out grandkids for her, I bet she'll sew you a baby blanket. Maybe knit you a hat or booties." He laughed at her.

But he looked tense.

"Very funny." She gave him her best you-can-trust-me expression. "Now what did you want to talk about?"

He glanced at the doorway again. "I, ah, I was wondering if you could help me."

"With what?"

"I kind of need to talk to someone. Like, a therapist. But I don't want anyone to know." He sighed. "And I don't have a lot of money. But my job at the gym is good."

"I know." She felt for this man, knew what it had cost him to ask her. "I can't help you, Gavin."

He looked crestfallen, then stoic as he nodded.

"But not because I don't want to. Because Landon and I are close, and I'd feel a conflict of interest in treating you. But I know someone who can help." She paused. "This has to do with your time in the Marine Corps, doesn't it?"

"Landon has a big mouth." He scowled.

"I overheard you talking during the basketball game. I didn't mean to pry."

He sighed. "Sorry, you didn't. I just…I feel like a loser as it is. Donnigans don't do therapy."

Ava hated that attitude. "Well maybe they should. Getting therapy doesn't mean you're weak. It means you're strong enough to know that you can't do it alone. My friend Lee is an amazing therapist who deals with a lot of veterans. He's really good. He's helped a lot of people."

"I don't want drugs," he warned.

"Lee's not a psychiatrist. He's a psychologist. We can't prescribe medication. We do more with recognizing issues and learning how to deal with them without medication. And he works on a sliding scale. You work it out with him and pay what you can."

Gavin nodded, looking embarrassed. "It's not that I'm broke or anything. I have savings."

"It's not a problem, Gavin," she said softly. "The fact that you want to see someone is healthy. Trust me. Everyone has anxiety."

He grunted. "Not Landon."

"Especially Landon."

Gavin blinked. "Yeah?"

"Sometimes it's the ones who feel the need to bear the weight of the world on their shoulders that stress the most. But Landon being Landon, he'll never talk about it." She gave a wry smile. "I've already been ordered not to shrink him. So the man who thinks he's so smart will stress, while the brother with a brain gets himself some help."

Gavin gave a slow nod, then his smile widened. "You know, I like that. The brother with the brain. You make a lot of sense."

"I know," she said, intentionally sounding smug.

Gavin pulled her in for a hug, and she just stood there, letting him lean on her. After some time, he pulled away. His eyes were shiny, but she made no mention of it, and neither did he.

"Guess I'd better get back before Landon jerks your chain." Gavin snickered. "He's so gone on you, Ava. Be gentle with him."

"Gentle? With Landon? Your brother?"

They both laughed at that. Then Gavin left the room and closeted himself in the bathroom while she rejoined the party.

When Landon saw her, he frowned, but caught in a conversation between his father and mother, he couldn't move. She stuck out her tongue at him, and he relaxed.

Theo arrived, and the conversation soon shifted to his day at the coffee shop.

Landon took the opportunity to scoop Ava up and left with a promise to return—with Ava—for breakfast when they could next arrange it.

In his car, they sat in silence. Then they turned to each other, and at the same time, said, "You owe me."

Landon frowned. "The hell I do." He paused, and his expression turned grim. "Okay, Doc. I want the truth."

"About?"

"What the hell did you and my brother talk about? And why the fuck was he all over you?"

Chapter 16

LANDON COULDN'T CONTAIN THE ACCUSATION. HE knew damn well nothing weird had happened between Gavin and Ava. But having seen his brother hugging her, some jealous instinct had taken over and turned him into an asshole.

She raised a calm, arrogant brow back at him. Damn it all, but he wanted to fuck her and yell at her and kiss her all at the same time.

"Excuse me?"

He groaned and covered his eyes, then looked at her once more. "I know. I sound like a dick. But I need to know. Is he okay?" *Did he shove his tongue down your throat? Did he charm you away from me?*

Such pathetic thoughts, because he thought he knew what Gavin wanted. And what kind of a loser didn't want his brother to get better?

Ava relaxed and put a hand on his arm. "He's going to be okay. I can't talk about it, because I said wouldn't. But I know someone who can help him."

"So not you?" Why he felt relief at that, he couldn't say.

"It wouldn't be right."

"Why not?" Landon started the vehicle and drove them back to her place.

"Because I'm your girlfriend, or at least, that's what you've been telling everyone."

Yeah. Mine.

She continued, "It wouldn't be right to treat him when you and I are involved in a relationship. It would feel odd to me, and I wouldn't want Gavin to think I'm sharing confidences."

"You don't tell me about your patients as it is."

"And I never will," she said smoothly.

He chuckled. "I gotcha."

"And while we're on the subject of who owes whom, what the hell, Landon?" She punched him in the arm.

"Ow." Not bad. That had hurt.

"Why would we just show up at your parents' and you not warn me first?"

"Warn you about what?"

She just looked at him, all intelligent and advanced degrees and fuckin' hot as hell.

"I didn't think it would be a big deal," he tried as an excuse. He'd wanted to see her with his parents. It was stupid, but he'd known she'd fit right in. *Again.* The woman seemed made for him, and it was starting to freak him out. They'd had sex again last night. A long, slow, passionate coming-together that had been more like a religious experience. Jesus, coming inside her, *with her*, was like nothing on earth.

"You think I'm buying that lame excuse? How would you feel if I just dragged you to meet my parents out of the blue? A little pressured, maybe?"

"Nah. Parents love me."

She rolled her eyes, but he saw her slight smile. "You're a pain, you know that?"

"What I know is you got me in the doghouse with my parents because of Claudia." He loved that bite of jealousy she couldn't hide. Mention of Claudia turned Ava's eyes a sharp, possessive green.

"It was childish, I know." She didn't sound repentant at all. "But worth it."

"Worth some discipline, I'm thinking." And like that, he was hard. He'd done his damnedest all evening to think pure thoughts. Being around his parents should have dampened any arousal. And for the most part, it had, turning his sexual feelings for Ava into that deeper emotional bullshit he hated having to face.

He'd swear he'd started to seriously fall for her. Not a crush, not sexual captivation—though God knew she made him come harder than any woman ever had—but soul-deep connection shit.

"I tell you what, Major. You answer some questions for me, and I'll let you push me around at home."

"Deal." Uh-oh. Maybe letting his glands do the talking hadn't been smart. Her obvious satisfaction unnerved him. "Ah, what questions?"

They arrived at her house all too soon. He turned off the SUV and hustled to get her out as well, then rushed into the complex. They were in her unit, the door locked behind them in no time, and he'd already spotted the couch, where he planned to bend her over and…

"Wait a minute." She planted a hand on his chest, stopping him from coming closer. After removing her coat and shoes, she waited for him to do the same. "Hang them up, then come here."

She sat on the couch and turned to wait for him.

He sat, knowing he had his dick to blame for accepting her deal too fast. "Go ahead." He sighed.

"What's going on with your mom and Hope?"

He hadn't been expecting that. "Um, well, Mom expects a lot out of us. And of her kids, Hope and Theo have been the ones she struggles the most with. Gavin and I knew what we wanted from a young age. We joined the Corps. Despite our problems, we loved it."

She watched him, her gaze intense. "But Hope…?"

"She's flitted around from job to job a lot. Like Theo, but she's older. She's been working with our cousin for a while, and she seems to like it. But Mom rides her pretty hard. I think it's a mother-daughter thing."

"Probably." She held her chin in her hand, and he wanted to play doctor patient with her again. Right now. "Tell me something else."

"Yeah?"

"Does this thing between us feel fast?"

He frowned. "Fast?"

"We hooked up pretty fast. It's only been a little over two weeks."

"Nah." It couldn't be. He felt as if he'd always known her.

"I did the math."

"You would." He scoffed, then shut up when she glared at him. Damn. Her mean look totally turned him on.

"It's just… I feel like we're connecting. Or at least, I am. But with you I can't tell."

He glanced down at his erection, saw her follow his gaze, and asked, "Seriously? You can't tell?"

She flushed. "I meant emotionally. When it comes to your feelings, I know nothing about you."

"Oh, come on."

"No. Tell me something about you that isn't about your job, your family, or your cock."

He blinked. When she used those four-letter words, he wanted nothing more than to ride her like a bucking bronco. "Well, since my cock is off limits," he tried to joke. She didn't crack a smile. "Fine. Jesus. You're going to be like all the others, aren't you?"

As soon as he said it, he knew he'd said the wrong thing.

But Ava didn't react the way he thought she might. No tears or anger because he lumped her in with other women. She waited, saying nothing, just watching.

"Something emotional? Fine. I loved the Marine Corps."

"I know that. Something else." She paused, and he had the sense she was testing him. "How did you feel about leaving the service?"

Easy. "I hated it. I loved being in."

"Why did you get out?"

He frowned. "I told you this. I got shot. My knee didn't heal right. Couldn't go back to full duty." Such a bitch, hearing that announcement from medical. He'd been fast-tracking for colonel for sure. Instead, he'd been medically retired a major. Big fuckin' deal.

"Do you miss it?"

"Every damn day. Happy now?" The grief and anger he'd pushed past to get on with his life came rushing back. "Did you get what you needed from me?"

She nodded, surprising him. "Yes. You were honest. Thank you."

He wanted to be angry about her manipulating him, but the pleasure in her gaze stopped him. "So, hold on. You're glad you pissed me off?"

"Anger is a healthy emotion. You shouldn't ignore it. You should accept it. Which you did."

"What about you? What makes you angry?"

"Me?" She bit her lower lip in thought, and his cock twitched. "I don't like being lied to. And I especially dislike being told what to do." She gave him a pointed glance then paused. "But with you, for some reason, I get turned on when we have sex and you order me around."

Music to his ears. "And now it's my turn." He stood. "Get naked and bend over the couch."

She shrugged. "Fine. But it's probably too low for deep penetration."

He forced himself to remain calm, when he wanted nothing more than to shove himself inside her. If she could act cool and collected while talking about *penetration,* so could he. "What would you suggest?"

"My bed downstairs." She shrugged. "But I doubt you can contain yourself. You're pretty quick to get off, aren't you?"

"*What* did you say?" Well hell, his cheeks felt hot.

"It's nothing to be embarrassed about. Sometimes there are medical conditions for—"

"Shut up." He clamped a hand over her mouth, and it took him a moment to realize she was laughing her ass off. "Funny girl, huh?" He lifted her over his shoulder and took her downstairs while she laughed the whole way down.

He stood her on her feet, by her bed.

"Get naked, Doc. Strip."

"My, how creative."

She was in a mood, and he loved it. Waspish, snarky, totally not afraid of him. But she would be, especially when he held her on the brink of orgasm over and over again...

—〰—

Ava begged him to enter her, but the jerk refused.

"You're a brat, you know that?" He grinned down at her. Naked and straddling her waist, he sat on his heels, his dick like a spike, and did *nothing with it.* Not a damn thing. He teased her with the sight of it while he continued to pluck her nipples, kiss her mindless, and finger her all over the place while keeping her pinned down with one hand holding her wrists above her head.

"Are you going to fuck me or what?" she rasped, her body on fire.

"Such language. Tsk, tsk." Landon scooted forward, allowing her to spread her thighs wide once more. "My girlfriend has a potty mouth, doesn't she?"

She groaned. "You're such an asshole." And his dick was too far away to do her any good.

"Yep. Pot-ty."

She tried not to laugh. "I'm wet. My nipples are hard. I'm so ready to come."

"Yes, you are." He sounded way too satisfied for her. She couldn't believe he continued to hold out, especially because he looked to be in pain. His cock was long, thick, and slick at the tip. Flushed and definitely aroused, yet content to drive her insane.

"Okay, I'm sorry I said you're quick on the draw." But she wasn't. Not really. The man had foreplay down to a science, but he needed his ego knocked down a bit.

"You're not sorry."

"*You're* going to be sorry if you don't end my suffering," she snarled and tried to free herself from his grip. His one measly wrist holding both of hers to the bed.

The man's strength impressed the hell out of her, and turned her way, way on.

"Fight harder, my pretty little doc," he murmured, moved back down her body, and stared at her breasts while she tried to free herself.

She watched him lean forward and take a nipple in his mouth. He sucked hard and teethed her sensitive flesh. She arched into him on a cry, squirming on the bed, needing him inside her.

"Please," she moaned and tried harder to get free. That she couldn't ramped her arousal to unimaginable heights.

"Tell me you're sorry."

"I'm sorry. I'm *so* sorry."

He sucked her other nipple, and she swore she felt the start of a climax.

Then he let go, and she cursed.

"Some mouth on you." He shook his head, his eyes so dark they looked black. He lowered his weight, and she felt his balls over her upper belly, his shaft straight and hard. If she could scoot down the bed, she'd be able to take him in her mouth and suck the mean out of him.

But he wouldn't let her.

"The thing is, Ava, you were shrinking me earlier. And you were brutal about it. But I think it's just because you wanted to get punished. You want that, don't you?"

Oh God, she did. "No."

"Yes." He levered himself off her and lay next to her. She missed his heat.

But his hand started moving down her body. He watched her face while his fingers plucked reactions out of her she couldn't help. Her groans, the spasms of pleasure, the shivers as her flesh hardened.

"Yeah, you're nice and wet for me. You want a cock, don't you, baby? A thick cock to pump you full of come."

She was panting and unashamed. "You're killing me."

"You ready for your spanking, Doc?"

"No."

He grinned and moved in for a kiss while his fingers found her sex. He slid through her folds and kissed her, his tongue penetrating where his finger wouldn't. He glided close to her clit but never with enough pressure to fully satisfy her. She followed his mouth, aching for him.

He pulled back, his eyes dark, his blond hair a bright beacon, a pretend angel seducing her into grunts and groans.

"How about that spanking now? Are you sorry yet?"

"I'm sorry I let you do this to me," she bit out. "Okay, okay," she said in a hurry when he started to draw back. "I'm sorry. I need discipline."

"Yes, you do," he practically purred. "You want it, baby?"

She groaned, broken, needy, and falling hard for the stubborn SOB. "I want you."

His eyes narrowed. "That's right. *Me*." He nudged her thighs wider.

"Do I need to turn over?" How he thought a spanking might be sexy, she wasn't sure. She'd never been into pain, and she trusted him not to hurt her. But maybe his kink was spanking. His arousal would surely increase hers.

"Not at all." The amusement should have warned her, but when his hand came down, she was shocked into silence.

For all of a second.

The second gentle "slap" to her clitoris sent her over the edge. She screamed in surprise and ecstasy as her body splintered into a million pieces.

"That's it. You're getting me all wet, sweetheart," she heard him say from a distance.

She couldn't think as she tried to process so much pleasure.

And then he was there, shoving inside her, and she shivered and came harder. Again and again.

"*Fuck.* That's it. Grab me tight. Squeeze me. *Ava,*" he shouted and pumped into her. Her orgasm spurred his own, because he continued to grind into her before he finally ceased moving.

They lay panting together, him on top, and she stroked his shoulders, still amazed this strong man could surrender to her the way he did. He'd been in charge, yes, but at the end, he always released into her. Pushed past his endurance by her warmth, her snug fit.

"What's that look?" he asked, his voice husky.

Before she could answer, he kissed her. The slow, passionate yet tender kiss melted her.

"What's that kiss?" she asked on a breath.

He stared into her eyes, his body still joined with hers. "You have seriously ruined me, you know that?"

"How did I do that, Major?" she teased and caressed the nape of his neck.

He closed his eyes in pleasure, then opened them to glare down at her. Except the glare wasn't real. She saw the mirth he tried to hide. "You're a menace. You seem soft, pliable. But you're not. You make me think I'm in charge, but then you hold me." He paused to gasp when she clenched her body down tight. "And you clamp down around me. I come so hard in you, Doc. So fucking hard." He kissed her again, still so gently. "I want to fuck you, and I want to protect you. I think about you all the time."

His confession startled her, because he was admitting what she'd been feeling. She said nothing, however, letting him get it all out. "Doc, I'm not a fan of lying or hiding things. Yeah, I'm not big on sharing *feelings.*" He sneered. "Seriously? You do tend to talk things to death."

"Hey." She frowned.

"But I have to say I'm falling for you."

Her heart raced. She stared at those eyes, still dark despite the usual honey gold that stared back at her. She saw those eyes day and night, in her dreams, wishing he was near.

"Nothing to say, huh?" He didn't look upset. "That's okay. I see that same whacked-out expression I get when I think of you. It's scary, isn't it?"

"What's scary?" She dared him to admit the feeling.

"You tell me."

Of course he wouldn't. Not Landon "Emotions Are for Pussies" Donnigan.

She sighed. "You know."

"Maybe I do, and maybe I want my girlfriend to meet me halfway." He pushed farther inside her, still half-hard. Then he started to withdraw, and she tried to keep him inside her by drawing down her inner muscles.

He surged back inside her in one deep thrust.

She felt him all the way to her throat. "Landon." She clawed at his shoulders, wanting more.

"Halfway, Ava."

"It makes no sense. We've only been out a few times."

"Nine by my count."

"Eight," she said to be contrary.

"Could be ten, technically, if we call my parents and dinner nine, and this fuckfest ten."

She colored. "Fuckfest? Really?"

"I'm balls deep inside you. I've come so hard already, and I'm gonna do it again real soon." He started moving. "But first you're going to tell me you feel this too."

"Whatever this is," she conceded.

"Yeah. This." He thrust faster, harder. And like their previous play, he worked her into a serious lather before finding his pleasure once more.

She added unselfish to her list of must-haves, not sure when her list had started to revolve around Landon, instead of Landon having to fit her ideal man.

—⁓—

An hour later, she lay in his arms, soothed by his heartbeat and the breadth of muscle holding her safe and tight.

"You always smell like flowers." He sniffed her hair, and she smiled against his chest. "Ava, I really like you. Your dirty talk and your shrinkiness. I even like your cousins."

"Don't lie. I can take it. Sadie's a handful," she teased.

"But not Elliot? Seriously?"

"You have me there."

They both laughed, before Landon said in a more sober tone, "I know what you did for Gavin. You want to help him, because that's who you are. You help people."

"Yeah? So how am I helping you? And if you say one thing about 'draining your snake' again, I'm going to remove your chest hair piece by piece."

He slapped a hand over her fingers and chuckled, the rumble low against her ear. "You make me feel good. Feel needed."

That was surprising. "You're already needed."

"Kind of. But you're different."

She had to see him. Ava leaned up on her hands to see his face. The square jaw, the stubble on that stubborn chin. He had such intense eyes, always focused on hers. "Tell me."

He cupped her cheek, and she saw emotions flare in his gaze. "My family needs help to get along. Landon to the rescue. My boss needs someone with brass balls to keep his people in line, and there I am. But you need me for me."

"For you?"

He nodded and caressed her cheek. "You want me to be strong, because that's who I am. And you're happy with me taking care of you, here, in bed. When you come, I feel ten feet tall. And when I come in you, I feel like I'm more than me." He sighed. "That sounds stupid. See why I don't like sharing my feelings? It's douchey."

"No, it isn't," she was quick to forestall him. "Landon, you're important to me. In a way I'm not sure of. I don't need you."

He frowned.

"But I want you, and I find myself wanting to need you."

His slow smile warmed her. "Is this where I say you complete me?"

"Do it and I'll give you a real purple nurple," she warned.

He laughed. "Ava, you're so funny. Pretty and smart. But your lists... They need to go."

"What?"

"You don't need some moron with seven degrees who wears Gucci loafers. You should have a real man who'll be there for you when you need him."

"And that's you?"

"It can be. If you want it to be." He pulled her down and kissed her. "Now stop talking and get some rest. I know you have patients in the morning. And we have a self-defense class to get to tomorrow night. Last one of the session, so make it count." He hugged her. "I can't go easy on you, or people will talk."

"Oh?"

"Yeah. I have a rep to protect. If I can't kick my own girlfriend's ass, what good am I?"

"You're so full of it."

"No, baby, that would be you. Have I told you how much I love not wearing condoms?"

She sighed. "Too many times to count."

"Well, here's one more. I love not wearing a condom." He sounded so chipper she didn't have the heart to chastise him for sliding inside her once more. Nor did she have the energy to disagree with him.

"I love you not wearing one too," she said sleepily and closed her eyes. *Almost as much as I'm coming to love you, Major Bossy.*

Chapter 17

Landon watched Ava sweep Sadie's leg and throw her to the mat, then give a foot stomp close to her cousin's head.

"Not bad. Faster next time," he critiqued and moved to another pair.

Gavin also threaded through the crowded room, correcting forms and encouraging the participants. Their brief self-defense classes had come to an end, and to his surprise, they had as many attendees tonight as they had when they'd started. His sister, unfortunately, hadn't shown up tonight. Landon planned on talking to her about that.

A glance at the clock overhead told him he needed to wrap things up.

"Thank you all for coming. If you're interested, let Mac know, and we'll see about having another session in a few weeks, after tax season," he announced, mentally getting his shit in gear before he made an appointment to see his accountant.

Groans and moans filled the room.

"I hear you." Landon chuckled.

"Remember, ladies," Gavin added, "your first thought in a fight-or-flight case should be flight—run for help and get somewhere safe. All of what we've shown you should be used *only* in a worst-case scenario. Make sure you continue to practice so it's second nature should you need it. Now get out of here and have a great weekend."

Many women flocked to Gavin for extra help. To Landon's amusement, Michelle, Gavin's Valentine's Day squeeze, was one of them.

He ignored his brother's pleading expression for help and had nearly reached Ava when Claudia stepped in his path.

Damn.

She'd been quiet since their run-in two weeks ago. Attending and following along, but not trying to engage with him. Except for one or two phone calls he'd ignored. Apparently he'd run out of good luck.

"Great class." She smiled up at him.

"Thanks." He tried to keep going, but she refused to move, and the crowd was slow to disperse on this side of the room.

"Landon, can we talk?" Her eyes grew watery.

Shit.

He spotted Ava over Claudia's shoulder. She didn't seem to like him talking with Claudia, but what could he do? He didn't want to hang with her either, but she seemed in genuine distress.

"Sure." He followed her to a corner of the room not occupied by a group of ladies. "Claudia?"

Tears fell. "I miss you."

"Claudia, we talked about this. It's over. Hell, it's been over for months."

"I can't help it." Her breath hitched. "I'm sorry. I don't mean to go on, but we were so good together."

Fortunately, the room started to clear. So at least they wouldn't have a scene. He couldn't care less about himself, but he knew Claudia would be embarrassed later, and Ava didn't like being the center of attention.

"Problem?" came a light, inquisitive voice. Always calm, unless she was begging for an orgasm.

He glanced over his shoulder to see Ava and Sadie. Ava didn't look too pleased, but Sadie wore a big-ass grin. Behind them, Gavin untangled himself from Michelle and darted over, the wide smile on his face annoying in the extreme.

"Gavin, get them out of here." He nodded to the rest of the room paying them some attention.

While Gavin cleared them out, Michelle included, Landon turned back to the scene at hand.

"I don't know what he sees in you," Claudia said to Ava with disdain.

Ava blinked. "Okay. Interesting. Are we supposed to duke it out? Is that what this is? A blatant display of feminine idiocy over a man?"

Claudia frowned.

So did Landon. "Hold on. Are you saying it's stupid to want to fight over someone you care about?"

"Fight *for,* you mean," Sadie added.

"Yeah, fight for. Thanks."

Ava glared at her cousin, then at Landon. "Well?"

"Are you asking me?" He snorted. "Hell, Ava, I don't know. I didn't ask Claudia to get all weepy. You got a problem? Talk to her."

He stepped back, curious to see what she'd do.

Claudia clenched her fists by her sides. Ava shrugged and crossed her arms over her chest, as if bored.

Claudia stared from Ava to Landon. "I'm confused."

So am I.

"I'm not." Sadie waited. "This is Ava's way of letting you know it's your call," she said to him.

"Yeah?"

"You either take up with thunder-breasts or you don't."

Gavin choked at the description.

"*What* did you call me?" Claudia shrieked.

One lady walking by paused at the doorway, watching with wide eyes. *Christ.*

"Look. It was either that or thunder-tits," Sadie was saying, "and I thought that might be a little too crass."

Ava groaned. Gavin laughed out loud, then muffled his mirth when Claudia glared his way.

Landon didn't know what to think. Claudia had never seemed so emotional or clingy when they'd first started hooking up. Hell, it had been her idea for a friends-with-benefits relationship in the first place. But now she acted as if she might die if he didn't attach himself to her permanently.

The thought made him ill.

Claudia looked like she might make a move on Sadie, and Landon didn't know if he should step in or let them battle it out. Would Ava fight for him? Why did the thought of her doing so get him hot and bothered? A glance at her showed her looking removed from the situation.

What the hell?

"Why aren't *you* handling this?" he said to Ava, irritated she didn't seem to want to claim him as her own.

"I shouldn't have to. Intelligent women don't battle over a lover. He makes his choice, she accepts it." Ava gave Claudia a disdainful once-over. "Then again, I did say *intelligent*, didn't I?"

Claudia rushed Ava, and the realization Ava could be hurt shocked him into moving. But before he could interfere, Sadie stepped in front of him. "Not your fight, remember?"

"But…" He watched as Claudia took Ava *to the mat*. Oh hell. Claudia had some weight and height over Ava. And she'd just grabbed onto Ava's silky ponytail.

He cringed and tried to go around Sadie, but she'd reemployed her anaconda hold.

"What the hell, Landon?" Gavin sounded disappointed. "Quit flirting with Sadie and help your girlfriend."

"I'm not flirting, asshole. Sadie, get off." She was worse than a tick and way too curvy to get a handle on. He worried about grabbing her in the wrong spot.

On the floor, Ava and Claudia rolled around. Had this not been a scene between his current girlfriend and his ex-lover, he might have been entertained, like Gavin, watching with glee. But Ava needed him, and he couldn't stand the thought of her being hurt.

Even in his wildest dreams—okay, maybe only there—he never would have imagined buttoned-up Dr. Ava Rosenthal rolling around on a gym mat wrestling with another woman over him.

Damn. I really am the man.

"Get off me, you crazy woman," Ava snarled.

A loud slap froze everyone, even Claudia and Ava on the ground.

Landon gaped at the sight of a hand print on Ava's cheek.

"Are you kidding me?" Ava sounded beyond annoyed. "You *hit* me!"

"Uh-oh." Sadie slowly climbed down his body. "Not good."

"You'd lower yourself, degrade yourself, for a man who clearly rejected you?" Ava huffed. "Have some pride, woman. Quit relying on sex and forced intimacy to avoid your insecurities. Of course you lost his respect and his attention. You don't care about yourself, so why should he?"

Claudia's anger turned to sniffles, and then real tears. But before he could help her or Ava to their feet, he watched in shock as Ava socked Claudia a good one in the gut before standing.

Claudia moaned and held her belly.

"That's for the slap in the face, bitch."

Where the hell has this *woman been hiding?* He wanted to take her home and pay homage to her mind, body, and soul by professing his undying devotion. Man, Ava had layers, sure as shit. He couldn't wait to peel through them all.

She glared down at Claudia. Before Ava could drop-kick the woman into the wall, Landon stepped in.

Mac rushed into the room, obviously alerted to the fight by that interfering woman in the doorway. "What the hell happened?"

"I'll tell you what happened." Ava tried to move, but Landon held her fast. She kept swinging her fists in agitation, so he grabbed those too. Then, in a super calm voice, she explained, "This woman *attacked* me, trying to get 'her man' back." She tilted her head, gesturing toward him. "Pathetic. Claudia, get some help. Your unhealthy obsession with Landon is bordering on stalkerish. And if you strike me again, so help me, I'll do some damage the best plastic surgery in the world won't fix."

Claudia cried harder and got to her feet with Mac's and Gavin's help.

Ava seemed spitting mad, despite her composure. He glanced at Sadie, but she only shrugged and stared at Ava as if she'd never seen her before.

"Uh, Mac? Can we use your office?" Landon asked.

"Yeah, go ahead. Gavin and I will handle Claudia." He sounded stern.

With any luck, he'd kick the woman out on her ass. Granted, Landon was one hunk of man, so he understood her fascination. But come on. He'd clearly broken off with her over two months ago. *And* he'd told her he'd committed to someone else—that same someone else she'd smacked *in the face*.

He still couldn't believe it. A real catfight between two sober women. He would have been titillated had he not been so worried about Ava's sudden serenity. She made him think of a powder keg about to explode.

They walked together through the gym to the back hallway and Mac's office. Once inside, Landon closed and locked the door behind them. He waited for Ava to face him, horrified when he saw tears in her eyes.

"Oh God, honey. Are you okay?" He tried to move closer, but she swore and stepped away.

"I can't believe this! I hit Claudia. I was in a scene with another woman, fighting over *a man*." She said that with such disgust.

"Hey. *I'm* that man."

She didn't seem to care. "I don't do drama. I don't get into fights, and certainly not over men."

"Okay, that's the second time you've mentioned me like I'm slime. What the hell? You're not blaming *me* for this?"

"I am."

"Well, fuck." Now he was mad. "I broke up with that woman months ago. We were clear on the terms. Not my fault she's nuts."

"It's not mine either," she snapped, and he saw another layer of Ava peeled away.

He watched in anger and arousal as she paced around the office, muttering to herself and calling him all kinds of names. *Not so fuckin' calm now, is she?*

"I have a job that means the world to me."

"So what?"

"So what?" She ran up to him and poked him in the chest. "So I looked like a complete idiot in there. No one will come to me for therapy if I can't control myself. God."

"Hey. *She* attacked *you*. You defended yourself. Besides, mostly everyone was gone by that time. Gavin shoved them out the door." *Mostly* being the key word. That one lady had seen. Hopefully she hadn't told anyone but Mac about it.

"It's like I don't know who I am with you."

"Like hell. You're the same shrink who thinks everything through to the nth degree."

"But I wasn't thinking in there. I wanted to rip her lips off," Ava snarled. "And why? Because I was fighting her over you."

Finally. She showed some sense. "Good."

"*Good*?" She poked him again, and the warmth inside him centered between his legs and stayed there. "I don't fight over boyfriends. It's silly and dramatic. A useless waste of energy. If you want her that badly, go get her. We're done."

"Hold on." He grabbed that pointy finger before she

drove it through his sternum. "I don't want her. What *I want* is for you to be pissed about her coming after me."

"I was, but—"

"And you should battle anyone who thinks they can take me away from you."

"That's asinine. And obviously—"

He kissed her to shut her up, and because he couldn't help himself. Their first big fight and he'd resorted to physically overpowering her. *Great job, Landon—you horse's ass.* But before he could apologize and back off, she bit his lip.

He jerked back, stunned. "*Shit.*"

She pounced. Instead of poking him again, she jabbed her hand down his shorts, gripped his dick, and dragged his head down for a fiery kiss.

Totally committed to fucking the mad right out of her, he kissed her back. A hungry, angry dueling of mouths and tongues, and then he was bending her over a nearby table and yanking down her sweats and panties.

"Wh-what—"

"Shut up and bend over," he growled.

"Fuck you," the no-longer-calm doctor spat, even as she thrust her ass out eagerly and spread her legs wider.

He lowered his shorts and yanked aside his jock, then shoved hard into her, not surprised to find her wet. He plowed into her, reaming her as she panted and swore his name, calling him all sorts of awful things in a low, husky voice.

The sex was *fuckin' hot.* Wild and furious and fast. But before he could help her get where she needed to be, he came in a rush.

She didn't seem to care, because her busy little fingers

got herself off while he released. She was grinding back against him before she stilled and clamped down, causing him to shiver uncontrollably.

When he'd ceased and she'd finally stopped squirming, they remained locked tight together.

He panted, stunned and not sure what to do. "Angry sex. Got it. Must do it again. Add that to your checklist." Hell, he still sounded winded.

Ava wriggled to be free, so he pulled away. Handing her a tissue, he waited while she cleaned herself up. She tossed the tissue into the trash and straightened her clothes. Then she glanced up at him.

And he saw more damn tears.

"I'm sorry, but not about that." She sniffed. "I liked our angry sex. I think I'm losing it."

He pulled her into his arms and held her close until she stopped shaking. "You okay?"

She nodded, and once again he noted how much smaller she was than him. "I shouldn't have attacked you."

He swallowed a grin. "No problem." But the reason for their initial fight still bothered him. "Ava, what the hell was that all about?"

"I don't know," she groaned and moved from his arms. "I was angry that Claudia was all over you. And jealous, I guess. That jealousy bothered me a lot. It's such a base, useless emotion."

"Yeah? Well, I kind of like my girlfriend getting jealous. Shows she cares."

"You do?"

"You wouldn't want me to get pissed off if some asshole was coming on to you?"

"No. I wouldn't."

"Why not?"

"Because it's unnecessary. Either I'm committed to you or I'm not, but getting jealous helps no one."

"Bullshit." He didn't like her standoffish attitude. "Look. Do you care about me or not?"

"Yes, I do."

I do.

He could see her wearing a white dress and taking the ring he'd slide over her finger…

What the hell is that? Not the time for weird daydreams, hoss. Jesus, what is wrong with me?

He cleared his throat. "Look, I'm sorry you had to go through all that. But I do hope you were bothered by it. Ava, I'd care if some guy thought he had rights to you. You're mine."

"Yours?"

He frowned. "Yeah, mine. What's the problem?"

"I'm an independent woman, that's the problem."

"So?"

"So I only belong to myself."

"You're overthinking this. Look, the whole situation was weird. Let it go, and let's get out of here. You're coming over to my place this weekend, right?"

"Maybe." She frowned.

"Get out of your head, Doc. My place. Now."

"You can't boss me around all the time. Not if I don't allow it."

"I know. So what's your point?"

She'd been the one to decide to hang out at his place for the weekend.

She sighed. "Fine. We'll go to your house. For now. But only because we'd already made plans."

He was about to suggest she just go home and figure out what she wanted, because he had no idea, but then he thought the better of it. She could stew just as easily by his side as she could at home alone.

They left Mac's office and gathered their things from the gym. He let Gavin know Ava would be staying over. And Ava talked to Sadie before she joined him in the parking lot.

"You sure you're good to come over?" he asked before he could stop himself. He didn't want to give her a chance to say no, but then… *I totally fucked her in Mac's office. Bent her over the table and did her.*

He wanted that again, but this time face to face, so she could see him. Not just feel him, but watch him take her. *Mine? Hell yeah.* She needed to get that fact through her thick, stubborn skull.

Because if she didn't, they'd have a real problem on their hands.

―――↝↜―――

Ava felt as if she was losing her identity. When she'd heard gorgeous Claudia *again* coming on to Landon, she'd wanted to rip the woman's ovaries out. But calm, resourceful, independent women didn't fight over men. A woman sure of herself didn't need to, because she had confidence in her relationship.

And Ava did, to an extent. But seeing a beautiful red-head with double-D breasts crying over her *boyfriend…* It had been all she could do to act civil. Until she hadn't. *Oh God. I hit her. I rolled around on the floor then* hit *her.*

Not sure what had come over her, Ava reviewed her actions on the drive back to Landon's house. She could only be glad none of her clients had witnessed such a public display of insanity. Her actions made her question what she thought she was doing with Landon in the first place.

He's missing half the qualifications you have on your list. The real one, not the modified one. She mulled that over, conscious her cheek throbbed. Crap. What if she had a bruise there? How would she explain that to her patients? To Dennis and the others?

Mortified that she'd rolled around on the ground like a common street brawler, Ava wanted to crawl up inside a hole and hide away until she could figure out why she'd acted that way. It wasn't as if Landon belonged to her. They were dating. Yes, she called him her boyfriend and they'd committed to exclusivity with each other. But to fight for him, that placed him into another realm of importance she wasn't ready to commit to, not yet.

The man had trouble communicating his feelings. He could do sex just fine. Joking, happiness, lust, anger. But love? Could he possibly feel that same emotion she fought every time she pictured his laughing brown eyes?

"We're here." He pulled into his driveway and turned off the car, then faced her. "Ava, let's forget about today, okay? It's over. You're good now." He fingered her cheek and frowned. "Let's ice you up, though, just to keep any potential bruises at bay."

They walked in together, and she let him get an ice pack for her face. Embarrassment took the place of confusion, until she had a difficult time looking him in the eye.

"Hey, what's this?"

She teared up, baffled at her wacky emotions. "I still can't believe I did that."

He nodded. "Never been in a fight before, huh?"

"Of course not."

"You'll be a little shaky 'til the adrenaline wears off. Hey, Ava, it happens. Not often with women, but we both know Claudia's unstable."

That threw Ava into a panic. What if Claudia did worse? What if she got a gun, or made up stories about Landon to get him to come to her? Blackmailed threats that if he didn't date her, she'd lie to the police about him? Ava's imagination went into overdrive.

"Ava?"

"You should report her. What if she gets a gun?"

He blinked. "Ah, honey, I think you're making too much of this. Remember, other people saw what she did. We have witnesses. And frankly, she's not the type. A scuffle with you, sure. A gun? Nah."

Ava didn't know. She'd seen crazy before, and Claudia was verging there.

"But if it'll make you feel better, I'll tell a friend of mine who's in law enforcement, okay?"

"Yes." She felt better. And then she didn't, because even the idea of Landon no longer in this world made her want to cry. "Oh, I'm a mess."

"You got that right. Come on."

He took care of her. Really took care. He ran her a bath, with bubbles, and made her sit while he fetched her a cup of cocoa with marshmallows, the mini ones she liked. Then he waited for her to soak away her troubles. Sometime later, after he'd dried her off and dressed her in one of his T-shirts, he settled her in bed with him, and they watched a movie on TV. And not just any movie, but a Hallmark movie about lost love and sappy, small-town happiness. The kind of movie a guy like Landon would hate.

Ava fell asleep in his arms, felt his kiss on her brow, and knew a sense of peace that would bother her come the morning. She just knew it.

———⁓———

The next morning, she woke to see Landon looking down at her. When he saw her eyes widen, he smiled. "You okay?"

"Um, yeah."

"Your cheek looks fine. No bruising." He gave it a soft kiss, and her heart melted.

Just dropped there and shriveled at his feet. His for the taking.

Panic unfurled.

"You okay?"

"Yes. Um, I'll be right back." She tore out of bed and locked herself in the bathroom. A quick glance around showed it neat and clean. *And the seat is down.* Just one more reason to love the guy—until he dumped her, the way he'd dumped Claudia. And she'd long for him and cry all the time, her dignity and reputation in shreds.

She stopped herself from acting like a complete lunatic and scaled back the alarm. She wasn't and never would be Claudia. So she had a crush on her boyfriend? That was a good thing. Landon seemed to like her as well. She could muddle through this odd happenstance and chalk up her affection to the result of an extreme outpouring of emotion, as well as endorphins from a physical altercation.

With that explanation gratifying her need to

understand her rash behavior, she used the facilities and did a quick brush of her teeth. Landon had been kind enough to take things from her overnight bag and put some of them out on the sink next to his toiletries.

The sight struck her, because it felt as if they'd passed some point in their journey to coupledom that she hadn't anticipated happening this soon. *Only our ninth date, and now we're practically living together?*

She left the bathroom, promising herself to stop making such a big deal out of everything. But when she saw him up on an elbow, his glorious body on top of the sheets, his erection thick and ready for her, she said to hell with keeping control and decided to take advantage of at least one aspect of her boyfriend she had no problem with.

Pure, unadulterated sex.

Chapter 18

LANDON LOVED THE LOOK ON AVA'S FACE. HER LONG brown hair appeared velvety soft as it brushed her shoulders. Her green eyes were wide and witchy and *hungry*—just the way he felt.

She joined him on the bed but wouldn't let him shift over. Instead, she shoved him back, so that he lay flat, and straddled his waist. After she dropped the overlarge shirt he'd dressed her in, she rocked over him, her pussy growing wetter with each pass over his arousal.

"I want you." She stared into his eyes while she ground against him, and he couldn't look away.

She'd been acting so oddly, but their connection here, at least, hadn't changed.

He nodded and cupped her breasts while she moved, until she angled a hand under her to guide him inside. She took him all the way in, and he thrust up into her while gripping her breasts and pinching her nipples, causing her to squirm over him.

She rode him hard, slamming down then lifting up, allowing him to watch himself slide into her each time. The most amazing fantasy, better because it was real, and it spurred his climax until he couldn't stop himself from jetting into her.

He rubbed her clit to help get her off, lost in a haze of pleasure, and she seized around him soon after he came.

They remained locked, joined as one, and he knew he was done for.

She was *it*.

No matter how short a time they'd been together, he knew her. Well, he thought he knew her. Her behavior at the gym still puzzled him, but they'd get through it. He hoped.

Because the more he remembered her saying "I do," the more he wanted to hear it again. He wanted a home with her, sharing their thoughts and *feelings*, even. Having kids. He started at the thought and unconsciously rubbed her belly, wondering what it would feel like for her to carry his child.

A wave of love for her rushed through him so hard, so fast, it left him breathless.

"Landon?" she said, sounding groggy.

He tugged her down to lie on top of him and hugged her. He just held on.

As if she felt the same crazy intensity, she hugged him back, not saying anything, just providing comfort. They stayed that way for some time, until she decided they needed to shower.

But once under the hot spray, his insatiable girlfriend refused to leave him alone.

"On your knees, really?" he teased and groaned when she took him in her mouth and slowly slid those red, ripe lips up his cock, swallowing him whole.

He watched her, enthralled, and let her have her wicked way with him. "Next time, my office," he rasped. "Because yeah, that's a fantasy that's been brewing for a while. Just me, sitting in my chair, while my hot secretary blows me. Right before I eat her out, then fuck her on my desk." He pumped into her mouth and drew closer. "I'm close, baby."

She moaned and fondled his sac, then grazed his thighs with her nails. *So fucking good.*

He gripped the back of her head to hold her steady and swore while he came.

She wouldn't let him return the favor though. Instead, she held him while they finished showering.

He grinned. His dirty doc was a real expert when it came to cleanliness.

———

The next few days passed in a blur. Ava hadn't been avoiding Landon on purpose, but her busy schedule didn't allow for them to spend much time together. They had dinner Tuesday night at his place, where she'd been treated to a visit from a screaming, pink-haired Hope. Apparently the prank wars were well under way, because Gavin also made an appearance to yell at his immature, moronic brother. Something about disgusting Saran Wrap over the toilet. Ava had heard "toilet" and tuned the rest out.

While she'd been amused, she'd also been trying to analyze her fears.

For all that she'd loved spending her evenings with Landon, she was glad for their sudden time apart. The distance gave her leave to understand what Landon really meant to her.

Or at least, she hoped she'd understand during her next break.

Robert Hill had rescheduled his usual Monday appointment for late Friday afternoon.

Ava sat listening to him discuss his latest issues with the world and his place in it while he pondered what new to do with himself. He'd taken a step back in his progress, and she remained patient while he worked through it.

Her gaze strayed to the portrait she'd framed, the one of her smiling.

She wanted that for Rob. To help him find his own sense of self and inner peace.

Serenity—something that had been sorely missing since meeting that blasted Landon. She mentally compared blond Rob to blond Landon and knew it was no contest. Landon had the best personality and best body she'd ever seen, touched, or tasted.

And like that, she was aroused, missing her man.

My man? Oh my God. What is happening to me? I'm turning into Claudia!

Independent Ava had seemingly gone for a long walk and had yet to return.

"My art is everything to me, usually." Rob sighed.

She struggled to remain present, in *Rob's* world, not her own. Time to be a better doctor, she told herself.

"Ava, I can't help myself any longer."

"Rob, what's wrong?" She used her firm but soft voice, in command of the appointment, still providing a safe environment for Rob. He sounded worried, and he needed a comforting, dependable figure.

"I love you, Ava."

Wait. What? Ava? What had happened to calling her Dr. Rosenthal? "Rob, we need to talk."

He watched her with adoration.

She wanted to slap that adoration off his face, then

slap herself for not paying better attention. Then Landon, just for good measure. "Rob, I'm your *therapist*. Not a girlfriend or someone to spend affection on."

"But I love you."

She was kind but clear. "This happens more than you might think, you know."

"It does?"

"It's not your fault. It's easy to transfer emotions. I help you feel better, and you associate that positive feeling to me, personally, instead of to the therapy I'm giving you."

"But I love you," he said again, looking lost.

She truly felt for him. "How can you? You don't know me." And he didn't. Ava didn't share her ideas or interests during a session. She listened—*usually*—and offered advice to best help her patient. It had taken her a while, but now she didn't even have to think about not bringing her home life into discussions, which she'd used to try to build a rapport. Now Ava let the patient talk and only commented on his or her life, as pertained to therapy.

"Ava, you're wrong. I do know you. You're so beautiful." Rob stood. "So kind and thoughtful."

When he crossed to her, she stood and subtly rounded behind the chair, putting it between them. "I'm flattered, Ron, but I have a boyfriend already." A personal fact, but hopefully one that might snap him out of his deluded affections. "Besides which, it would be unethical and even harmful for me to ever date a patient. I care too much for your well-being to harm your psyche that way."

"You have a boyfriend?" Rob looked crushed.

"Yes. I do."

"Oh." He blinked. "But does he really know you, Ava?"

"Dr. Rosenthal," she reminded him. "And yes, he does. There's a person waiting for you out there, Rob. Waiting for you to see how amazing you are, so that you can recognize when she's feeling that same love for you. But that's not me. I'm just your therapist. A person who cares deeply for you. But Rob, this isn't about love. It's about wellness and respect." She gave him a sincere, if distanced, smile.

He sat, his face flushed, and stared at the floor. "I feel so embarrassed."

Whew. Crisis passed. "Don't." She rounded the chair and sat in it again. "This has happened before with patients, and no doubt it will happen again. You just need to realize why you feel this way."

"I do?" He brushed a tear from his cheek, looking like a little boy.

"Yes. Why don't we end this session with what you're planning to do this weekend? Didn't you tell me there was a new exhibit at the art museum?"

He sniffled, and she handed him a box of tissues. Their fingers touched, and he held her hand for a moment. "Thank you, Dr. Rosenthal." He let her go, seeming more at ease with himself. "There's a new collection of contemporary Korean art I wanted to see."

"Will you go with anyone?"

"I was going to take my mom, but I have a new neighbor. She just moved in, and I don't think she knows many people." He cocked his head, studying her. "She looks a little bit like you, actually."

Oh boy. "Will you ask her?"

"I don't know. We haven't really met except to wave at each other. Why would she want to go with me, anyway? She probably has a boyfriend too."

"You could always ask and find out. Worst case she says no, and you go yourself. Best case, you go and find a new friend."

"I don't know if I'll ask her. But I'll think about it."

That he'd mentioned the woman at all gave Ava hope. Rob was noticing the world around him more, not so caught up in his anxiety. They talked for another ten minutes before she wrapped things up.

He'd opened the door to leave, then turned to her. "I'm sorry, Dr. Rosenthal. It won't happen again."

"What won't happen again?" Landon asked, standing right behind Rob in the doorway.

No two ways about it, he dwarfed Rob in every way possible. Including an inability to recognize boundaries. She glared at Landon, but he was too busy scowling at Rob.

"I'm sorry, Rob. Landon, could you please move out of the way so Rob can leave?"

He grunted and moved to the side, but he continued to stare at Rob until he left.

She hurried to his side and yanked him into the office, then closed the door without slamming it, like she wanted to. "What the hell was that?"

"Huh?" He turned to her. "Hey, baby. You look *good.*" He grinned. "I love those skinny skirts you wear."

She felt icy to her toes, so angry she had a hard time holding on to her composure. "You do not. I mean never—*ever*—come to my office and intimidate my patients. Do you understand?"

Landon frowned. "Easy. I was just asking the guy what he had to be sorry about." He looked her over. "You okay?"

"Get out."

"Why? I thought we could do lunch if you had the time. I'm off early today."

She opened her mouth to say something else then noticed what he was wearing. *Holy cow.* She tried to hold on to her anger in the face of his sheer beauty. "You're in a suit and tie." Talk about devastating.

"Yeah." He sighed. "The job, it's a bitch."

She worked to swallow, seriously in lust with the obtuse hunk not comprehending her frustration. "Yeah, well so am I. Do you understand what I said to you?"

He started to look uncomfortable. "I'm sorry, okay? I didn't mean to barge in. The door was open, for Christ's sake. But I'm not sorry for making sure your patients aren't messing with you."

"See, that won't do."

"Won't do what?"

She sighed. "I've seen this coming from a mile away, yet I'm still surprised. And I know better." She'd gone through this song and dance so many times before. She should be used to it by now. Yet she wanted to wallow and cry, because she didn't want it to end like this. But why bother letting something that could never work limp along until it just dragged?

"What the fuck are you talking about? Can we do lunch or not?"

Tension and grief ballooned inside her. She'd made her lists for just this reason, so she could avoid messy entanglements and breakups with men who didn't suit.

She moved back to her chair, where she felt more in control. "Landon, we need to discuss something."

"What?" He crossed to sit on her couch while she stood, and the reminder of their first time playing therapist and patient at her place wasn't lost on her.

Why did he have to make this so difficult? "We're never going to work."

He didn't look upset. Instead, he eased back onto the couch. "Ah. So this is the real breakup scene, huh?" He glanced around. "Nice place. I'm game. Go ahead and give me your spiel."

She blinked. "I'm trying to tell you that we're too different. That this, us, together, is nice now, but it can't possibly last."

"Why? Because I'm not a shrink too? Just because your parents are both medical people doesn't mean everyone has to be in the same field. My parents are way different."

"That is not the point. You try to control everything, but you can't do that with me. I have a brain."

"That you use way too much, if you want my opinion."

"*I don't!*"

He stared. "You're yelling at me."

"You're not getting the point." She felt like she was in another brawl. But instead of Claudia, this time, she fought a losing battle between her mind and heart. "I care for you. Deeply." *I damn well love you, and isn't that a pickle?* "But our personalities will never mesh. You try to take charge of everything, and I can't have that."

"Seriously?" He clasped his hands behind his neck. "That's what you think this is about? Because I wanted to make sure you're okay, that some jerk wasn't hassling you, you think I'm trying to take over your life?"

Put that way, she sounded silly. "No. Wait. That's not what I'm saying. You try to order everyone around, and you don't respect what I do."

He scowled. "Now that's just bullshit." He lowered his hands to his lap. "This is all about you not confronting your feelings."

"What?" She shook off the odd sensation of being counseled by *Landon*. "Since when are you a therapist?"

"Since I led Marines into battle, since I deal with people with problems all day every day." He huffed. "Honey, I don't need a degree to see that you're running scared."

"I am not."

"Yeah, you are." He seemed gleeful about it, the jerk.

"You're not listening to me, and I—"

"Go on. Tell me how you really feel about me. Be honest."

"You first," she sneered. "But no, Landon Donnigan doesn't have emotions. You're good at sex, and you're fun to be around. But you never want to discuss anything meaningful."

"Hey. I told you I was PO'd about leaving the Corps."

"Wow. Big revelation. You want the truth, I think *you're* scared."

He jolted to his feet, looking furious and mean and sexy as all get-out. "First off, I told you not to shrink me. Second, I am scared, okay? You want the truth? You got it."

She hadn't expected that. "What?"

"Yeah, because I feel a lot of stuff for you. I like you. I think about you all the time. I even think about kids and marriage and shit. And I know, I really know, I love you." His eyes looked wild, and he stared at her with intensity. Then he seemed to calm down. "But you don't want me to share, do you? Because then you'll have to realize what you feel for *me*. Your bullshit lists are there to keep you from ever finding a guy.

"A real guy. Not some fucktard who wears Armani or has a doctorate behind his name. But a flesh-and-blood guy who thinks you're terrific and smart and sexy. You can make me laugh, and like now, you make me want to pound my fist through the wall. You're being a real bitch, Ava. And you know it."

"So what if I am? I'm entitled."

He barked a laugh. "So you are. Look, we both know you're in love with me. Just admit it. I did."

She sputtered, "Y-you… I… You can't be… I never…"

"Yeah, I thought so." The smug bastard turned to the door.

"Where are you going?" *Do I really sound that shrill?*

"I'm hungry. So I'm going to eat. I'm a simple guy, Ava. I might not be into architecture and poetry. I hated school and never want to go back. I love beer and football. And I love you." He said it again, seeming almost smug each time he repeated it. "I also love how big those green eyes get each time I say it. You're scared. Damn. Never thought I'd see you running from me, but I guess you really are like all the others."

That was just mean. "Fuck. You."

"Oh, big words, Doc. I'm scared," he mocked. "Tell you what. When you get the gumption to come find me, I won't make you work too hard to apologize. But I will give you a great big 'I told you so.' And you have the gall to accuse *me* of not sharing *my* emotions?" He shook his head. "I poured out my heart to you, and what did I get? Nothing but a big fuck you. You're going to remember that some day when you're telling that to our kid." He walked through the doorway. "Call me when you get yourself together, Doc," he called over his shoulder before leaving through the front door.

She stood there staring at her empty doorway.

Dennis soon filled it. "What was all that yelling?"

"I'm sorry." She felt numb. And confused, but mostly numb.

"No worries. It's just you and me here today, and I'm free until two."

"I have a one o'clock." She blinked and wiped a tear away.

Dennis looked concerned. "Ava, what's wrong?"

"I think I broke up with my boyfriend. But he thinks I'm in love with him and isn't taking it well."

Dennis walked to her and patted her shoulder. "Are you afraid of him? He didn't threaten you or anything, did he?"

She wanted to laugh hysterically. "Landon, threaten me? Only with an 'I told you so.'" The arrogant prick. She started to grow angry. "Dennis, he had the nerve to tell me I'm afraid of my emotions. *Me.* A clinical psychologist unable to handle the fact I might be in love." She snorted. "Whatever."

Dennis's expression surprised her, because he started laughing.

"What's so funny?"

"He nailed it. I want to meet this man."

She wanted to kick Dennis too. "That's ridiculous."

Dennis sat her down on the couch with him. He kept a hand on hers, connecting them, grounding her. "Ava, I want you to listen to me. I'm biased, because I love you like my own daughter. But since your father isn't here to talk some sense into you, I feel it's my duty to."

She groaned.

"That sounds just like my daughter when I talk to her." He squeezed her hand, then let go. "I've known you for nearly three years, and in all that time you've never seemed so happy as you've been lately."

"I don't see any difference."

"Of course not," he said drily. "We never seem to see ourselves as others do from the outside. You've been closed off, emotionally, dealing with a new practice and a new life away from what's familiar."

"It's been over two years. I wouldn't say I'm new."

"New isn't the right word. But I'm not wrong. You're still processing what it means to help others, and at a cost to yourself. It's important in our line of work that we find a happy balance. You devote yourself to the practice. And that's commendable. But what about you?"

"I'm happy. I have a list that I've—"

"No lists. Tell me. What makes you happy?"

"My career. My family." She hated to say it.

"And?" He gave her a knowing look. "Is that all?"

"And Landon," she muttered.

"Why did you suddenly start dating after all this time? Is it because you realized you were missing something? Were you lonely, Ava?"

Exactly. "I'm thirty." She shrugged. "It's only logical I'd start to consider my future. I'd like to have children, and the potential for medical problems gets higher the later in life you have them."

"In English."

She sighed. "Yes, I was lonely. I figured it was time to start dating again, maybe find someone special."

"And have you?"

"I don't know." But she did. "He's great, but we're different."

"Does he not respect you?"

"No, he does. But he's a protector, and he likes to give orders."

"So do you. Sounds to me like you're both more alike than different."

"How do you figure?"

"Ava, you spend your days telling people how to heal themselves. And you're used to being in command of yourself. As therapists, we have to project professionalism. We keep ourselves locked up, not allowed to be human, because we're 'the doctor,'" he said, using air quotes. "But sometimes we live in our heads too much, and we don't see what's right in front of us."

"But Landon and I are so new. How can I know he's The One if we practically just met?" She felt out of sorts. "Geez, Dennis. We've only been out on a dozen dates at most."

Dennis shook his head. "When you know, you know. You do realize you're using 'The One' in conjunction with this man. The last guy you talked about, the only description I heard was that he smelled like corn chips."

"Oh. Aaron." She sighed. "That was a long time ago. I spent so much time investing in my career when I first moved here. But I realized I needed balance, like you said. I've tried online dating, but it's hard. Then I met Landon. He's arrogant, bossy, and big. Different than the type I'd normally go for."

"Ah, your Marine."

My Marine. "We seem to click in so many ways. But we're also different. It just doesn't seem possible it can end well."

Dennis nodded. "It can be difficult sometimes to separate what we see in here from our own lives. So much dysfunction and unhappiness can surround us. But when we communicate and are honest with each other, that's when the magic happens."

"Did you know, with Greta, I mean?"

He smiled. "I fell in love with Greta at first sight. It took her a while to recognize I was The One for her. But like you, I didn't trust my feelings because I had to analyze them to death. Luckily for me, Greta came around before I could talk myself out of loving her." He looked at Ava and paused.

"What?"

"It's scary to open yourself up to someone else. I know. We're so closed up, not supposed to share ourselves while we give so much to others. But Ava, if you don't help yourself, you're no good to your patients. Let's say you open yourself up and let yourself love him. What then? Maybe you last, maybe you don't. You can't keep living with lists and five-year plans. They're great for organizing, but hell on a life worth living."

"Not you too? I love my lists."

Dennis chuckled. "Just don't define yourself by them." He paused. "Dig deep, Ava. Feel, experience love, experience sadness. Yes, we don't share it in here.

But we have to feel it to know it and trust it, don't we? From hate comes love, from fear, trust. Experience emotions. Don't smother them." He patted her knee. "And that's all I have for you. That and trust in your gut, Dr. Rosenthal. It won't steer you wrong." Then he left.

She sat, contemplating all he'd said and all she'd felt. Had Dennis—and Landon—been right? Was she letting fear rule her when she'd been the one accusing Landon of not sharing his feelings?

A reminder for her one o'clock appointment buzzed on her phone. She gathered her files, lost in thought, and realized her next client could be the poster child for salvaging what could have been a doomed relationship. Perhaps she'd pay particular attention to what he had to say.

She gathered her notes in order, then went in search of him in the waiting room. "Brody? Great to see you again. Come on back with me."

Chapter 19

"So how are you and Abby getting along?"

"Great." Brody Singer beamed. He'd come a long way from the tense, wounded man who'd started seeing her a year ago. He came in once a month or more if he felt the need. A victim of child abuse, he'd been carrying around scars that had never healed. But the love of his fiancée and his family had done much to mend the hurt young boy still inside the man.

Brody chuckled. "We're still getting married next month."

She smiled. Brody was a handsome blond—*must be my month for blonds*—and he shone with love when he talked about his fiancée. "Abby's a lucky woman."

"Yeah, I keep telling her that."

She chuckled. "So you and she are living together, and you're feeling okay about that now?"

"Had some nerves at the beginning, but we settled a while ago. Feels like we've never been apart." His knee started bobbing.

It never failed to amaze her how someone who could appear so confident and together could be so shattered within. Anyone looking at Brody would think him a handsome, confident man who let nothing stand in his way. He had a successful plumbing business he ran with his best friend, a woman he loved and who loved him, and a family that would die for him. Another one of the McCauley clan, though not by blood.

Yet Brody had issues he needed therapy to help him resolve.

"But…?" Ava led him.

He blew out a breath. "But we're gonna be *married* next month! Doc, I have to say, I'm freaked out. I mean, I'm happy and fine one minute, a spaz the next."

"By the wedding."

"By *the baby*! Abby's pregnant. She doesn't know that I know, but I saw the test under the bathroom cabinet. And fuck if I can get my head around this." He fidgeted in his seat. Brody had a difficult time sitting still, so she watched him work through it. "I love her. I mean, Abby's my life. I can't imagine being without her." He ran a hand through his golden blond hair. "She's perfect. My life is perfect. Hell, even the damn dog has been behaving. And Hyde's typically a real nightmare."

She bit back a grin. She'd seen pictures. The dog could have passed for a miniature horse. "So what's the problem then?"

"I'm afraid…" He paused and rubbed his chin. "I'm afraid I'll fail my kid. My parents were awful people. They screwed me up. What if I turn out to be like them?" His voice grew hoarse. "Much as I wish it, I'm not a McCauley. Not really. I've still got bad blood in me."

That fear stuck with Brody and would continue to haunt him until he came to peace with his past. They'd talked about it before, but she knew how much he worried about being anything like his family. "Speaking of blood, are you still in contact with Jeremy?" Brody's biological brother.

Brody gave a smile. "Yeah. He's good. Real good.

He's dating a girl right now that's helping him a lot, and his work at the substance abuse place has been therapeutic, I think." He blew out a breath. "I'm an idiot for panicking about the baby, aren't I?"

"Not at all."

"I mean, Jeremy turned his life around, and he didn't have what I have—my brothers, Bitsy, and Pop. They supported me through it all." His grin lit up the room. "And Abby. Man. I can't wait to be a dad." He picked up a stress ball from the table and started squeezing it. "Then I think about it, and I get all freaked out. I'm happy, and I'm nervous. And I'm not supposed to know about it. Flynn thinks I—"

"You told your brother?" Technically his best friend, but Brody and Flynn had grown up together.

Brody shrugged. "I tell him everything. Anyway, he said I should chill the hell out and just focus on the wedding. To not worry about it until Abby tells me."

"Do you think she's holding the information back for a reason?"

"Yeah, because I'm a dumbass who hyperventilates whenever we do something new."

She remembered his panic about moving in with Abby. Then the news they'd become engaged, which had unglued him. Brody shouldered through, though, and Abby had been right by his side throughout it all. She'd even come to a few counseling sessions.

"Tell me, Brody. When you think of a life with Abby, what comes to mind?"

He lost his scared look and smiled. And in that joy, she saw a truth that blinded her. "It's perfect. Everything I want or need, she's there for me. She makes me smile, makes me laugh, turns me on," he said with a chuckle. "She accepts me for who I am. I never take that for granted. Of all the guys she could love in this world, she chose me."

"So if she trusts you to love her and care for her, don't you think you should love yourself as much? That your baby will be fortunate to have a father who won't make the same mistakes his father made? Perhaps you could think of your experiences as a child like that, as a terrible example you'll never, ever follow."

Brody nodded. "I like that. Yeah."

She appreciated the affirmative tilt to his head. "Brody, can you tell me something else?" She wanted to give him this positive reinforcement, and maybe steal some information for herself as well.

"What's that?"

"You and your brothers have all found love. But how did you know Abby was the one for you? How did you know it wasn't just a passing fling?"

He grinned. "Great question. At first, she was just lucky to have me." He laughed at himself. "Well, she was. But who am I kidding? I was lucky to have her. Just being around her put a smile on my face. For me, it was loving our times out of bed more than the ones in bed. I'm not gonna lie. I love sex. But I loved being with Abby more. She gets me, you know? And she's the only person who tolerates Hyde."

"Yes, there is the dog, isn't there?"

"He's great. He finally stopped eating my socks."

"Progress." She smiled. "So tell me about the wedding. And don't leave anything out. This is your chance to vent everything about saying 'I do' in front of all those people."

He groaned. "Man, I was handling that just fine until

you mentioned it." At her look, he muttered, "Well, not really." Then he told her how scared he was that Abby would change her mind.

After Ava talked him through his feelings, she finished her next appointment without much fanfare and called it a day. But she hadn't been inside her condo for two minutes before someone pounded on her door. Both excited and nervous to see Landon again, and wondering if she'd thought through what she planned to say to him, she found herself face to face with Elliot instead.

"Oh my God. I could just *scream*." He stomped past her and flounced onto the couch.

She shut the door behind him and sighed. "Come on in and sit down."

"Do you have any idea what my life is like right now?"

Perfect. Elliot was having one of his moments.

She groaned and flopped next to him. "Tell me, Cousin. What's wrong with your life?"

"I had sex with the man I've been trying to keep at arm's length. But I'm only human, and I couldn't take it anymore. But he wants so much from me. I'm not sure I can handle it, and if I don't get it together, he'll leave. Me! Leave *me!* It's unfathomable." Elliot looked a little wild around the eyes. "Unlike *you*, my hunky banana isn't idolizing my every move, doing whatever he can to make me happy."

At the thought of her hunky banana and her being over, Ava's eyes filled. "Yeah? Well my hunky banana *split.*" She burst into tears, stunning Elliot into silence. "And I didn't even mean that terrible pun. It slipped out of me."

"Split? Slipped? God. You're two for two in the cheesy category. But about your hunky banana, now this I have to hear."

—∿∿—

Landon worked out like crazy. He spent the weekend wondering if anything he'd said had gotten through to his dense, loveable, crazy doc. It didn't help seeing Mac all over his sexy bride, watching couples in love walk hand-in-hand down the street. Having fucking coffee together.

Hell, he and Ava could have been doing that. He knew what she liked to drink. Her favorite foods. That she liked red more than blue and missed her parents, who lived in Cheltenham, Pennsylvania.

He and Ava had done a lot more than fuck all the time. They'd actually had conversations, liked the same stuff, mostly—though he had to admit he didn't like reading as much as she seemed to, but she didn't like sports with his enthusiasm, so it all evened out.

The stubborn woman. He kicked a rock and walked around Queen Anne in the rain Sunday evening, having nothing better to do. His arms ached. He'd really pushed himself, and his guns were bitching. Even Gavin had called him an idiot, and his brother was barely speaking to him since the toilet prank. Apparently being tricked into peeing on oneself left a lasting impression.

Landon felt small joy in knowing he had one sibling left to prank before he'd declare himself king of the prank wars.

Ava would have laughed with him. She'd gotten a kick out of Hope's pink hair.

He sighed. *Ava.* For a brilliant psychologist, she was acting like an utter moron. He'd pulled out all the stops. Gone big. Declared his love *and* hers. Because, come on, he knew she loved him.

The woman watched him when she didn't think he was looking. She stroked his chest, his hair, his cheek, when they lay in bed, recovering from amazing sex. They'd fucking *made love*. As in, soul to soul, staring into each other's eyes while they came. That kind of love.

It had only been two days, but it felt like two years. He couldn't eat. Couldn't sleep. Barked at his family and friends. Even at Sadie. She'd made some smart remark at the gym about Ava and he'd nearly bitten her head off. Then he'd apologized all over himself and left a few hours ago.

There was no way a simple tiff with Ava should end their relationship. Uh-uh. No way he'd let it. That thought in mind, he tried to shake himself out of his funk. He walked with purpose, though he had no destination in mind. He lingered by the corner of Boston and saw something dart into the street.

"Shit." He raced after it and nearly got hit by a car unconcerned with stop signs. "Hey asshole, watch it," he yelled, cradling a shivering puppy to his chest as he hurried to the sidewalk.

"Up yours," the jerk behind the wheel of a BMW yelled back through the crack in his lowered window.

"Yeah? Come on out and say that to my face, motherfucker." Landon was *so* ready to go there, needing a release for his anger, his hurt and tension.

But the guy took a good look at him and drove away. Fast.

"Jackass."

"What do you think you're doing?" a deep voice growled from the sidewalk across the street.

The guy sounded familiar.

"Trying to help this puppy. What's it to you?"

The large man wearing a hoodie ran over to him, and Landon readied to drop the dog and deal with some homeless dude with an attitude. Except the hoodie slipped and he recognized the guy.

"Is this my day for dickheads or what?" Landon swore again, still cradling the shivering puppy. "It's okay, little guy. I won't let this jerk be mean to you."

"Mean to him?" Sam Hamilton, one of the thugs who worked for his cousin Mike's fiancée, glared at Landon. "He's mine." The guy was taller than Landon, and surprisingly more muscular. It was like he'd eaten a steroid factory and was always on a rage.

"Yeah, Hamilton? Way to take care of him. You're doing a bang-up job."

Sam narrowed his eyes. "Oh hell. You're one of those prissy Marines. McCauley's cousin, right? Lancelot, Lenny, something like that."

"It's Landon," Landon said through gritted teeth. "Landon Donnigan."

"Whatever. Gimme my dog." Sam gestured with his head and Landon could see the tattoos running up the guy's thick neck. Probably prison tats in addition to the cars and tribal designs painted over his arms. Sam worked as a mechanic and had the look of a guy fresh out of jail.

"Why? So you can beat him, starve him, then throw him in a ring with a giant Doberman? No fucking way."

Ready for Sam to try to slug him, Landon prepared himself.

Sam's nod of acceptance surprised him. "You know, for a Boy Scout, you're all right, Donnigan."

"Boy Scout, please." Landon soothed the small

puppy. He glanced back at Sam and read the guy's concern. "He's really your dog?"

"I'm fostering him at a friend's house, but he got loose. Come on, Macho. You know you can't break out like that." Sam took the small puppy in his arms, and the little guy licked him, transforming Sam's face from a block of granite into a real human with feelings. Hell, even his eyes looked like they had color, a light blue-gray, and not the demon black Landon had previously associated with him.

He'd met Sam and his mechanic buddies at Mike's engagement party. They'd been assholes, so he and Gavin had tossed them a fair share of attitude until their boss, the guy dating Aunt Sophie, had begged for mercy. Then Landon and Gavin had flirted with their hot dates instead.

But if the guy could care for a foster dog, Sam couldn't be all bad.

"You want to grab a beer?" Sam asked, surprising him.

Landon blinked. "Uh, sure."

They found a bar with a compassionate waitress who fetched a towel and a water dish for the dog. "You out here slumming?" Landon asked him and ordered a beer.

Sam did the same. "Yeah, because us poor folk love nothing better than to lurch around the rich dick types in Queen Anne."

"You don't have much of a sense of humor, do you?"

Sam shrugged and scratched behind the puppy's ears. The little guy was in heaven, rolling his head back. There was one other customer in the bar, the hour near to closing and the rain keeping most folks indoors.

"Why are you out here, Donnigan? Hanging out with all your friends?" Sam smirked.

"Funny guy." Landon thanked the waitress for the beers and took a swig from his bottle. "Nah. Trying to think is all."

Sam watched him, took a long drink himself, then nodded. "Woman problems."

"Yep."

Sam shook his head. "You guys are so easy to spot. Foley, Johnny, McCauley. You all get whipped and don't know what to do with yourselves."

Landon didn't appreciate the observation. "Foley?" He remembered the huge dude and that he and Sam were best friends. "I thought he was your girlfriend?"

Sam gave him one cold-ass stare, one that said Sam would rip out Landon's spine and not think twice.

In the mood to accommodate a fight, Landon stared right back. *Bring it, asshole.*

Then Sam sighed. "You know, you're not as big a pussy as I thought you were. I like you, Donnigan."

"Thanks so much." Landon downed his beer and asked for another.

"So I'm gonna give you some advice."

"You're kidding, right?"

"If you're in love, don't waste your time here with me and Macho. You should be out with your woman getting some."

"You think that's good advice? That's common sense. Except the damn woman doesn't realize she's in love with me," he muttered and took the bottle the waitress handed him.

Sam rubbed the puppy with the towel, watching Landon with what looked like sympathy.

Great. I'm getting lectured and pitied by a guy who

could make a shiv out of his spoon. "Shouldn't you check in with your parole officer before he reports you for being missing?"

Sam grunted. "Good one. No. I'm done with that."

Figured.

"Buddy, you're fuckin' lame. When Foley had problems with Cyn, he didn't let that stop him. Of course, she came back to him, because he's not a moron like you, but still. He would never let anything stop him from making love to his woman."

"How about a restraining order? Would that stop him?"

Sam smirked. "Nah. Not my boy."

"You're kind of obnoxious, but not so much after a few beers."

"So I hear." Sam stroked the puppy into a sound sleep, those big hands so gentle, it was weird. "Look, Lancelot—"

"Landon."

"—get off your ass and see to your lady. It's kind of sad, watching you drown yourself in cheap beer."

"Yeah, you got me there." Landon stood and slapped down a few bills, more than enough to cover their tab, and then some. "For the beer and the dog. Not for you, Hamilton."

Sam raised his bottle in salute. "Good luck, man. Does the poor woman know how clueless you really are?"

"Hell no. I'm not that stupid." *At least, I hope she didn't see through my bravado to what a witless wonder I am at the thought of losing her.*

"Cheers, and good luck."

Landon left without a backward glance, needing to get some closure. Either way, he was tired of Ava avoiding him. Much as Sam irritated him, he had a point. Marines took action. They didn't sit around with their thumbs up their asses.

He walked with purpose, until his knee gave out on him right before a huge puddle.

Now soaking wet, aggravated, and incensed that Ava Rosenthal could think for two seconds that she didn't love him, he limped with purpose past the unlocked gate into her complex and down to her condo. Then he banged on the door.

But he had no idea what waited for him on the other side.

—∿∿∿—

"I just don't understand. He's being so mean," Jason, a handsome redhead currently sobbing onto her shoulder, mumbled. "We were so good together, and then he just wants to turn me away? Why? That's what I want to know." Jason lifted his head from her shoulder, his startlingly blue eyes bright and angry. "Why, Elliot?"

Sadie watched from the chair next to the couch, munching on popcorn as if sitting at the theater. "Yeah, why, Elliot?" she asked her brother.

Elliot glared at them all from his spot standing by the mantel. His entire body language screamed confrontation. From his hands on his hips, to his thrust-out chest and tilted chin. "I told you I didn't want a relationship, Jason. We're friends, damn it."

Ava had to admit, they'd make a nice couple. Elliot and his dark hair and charm. Jason with his stylish auburn hair and ice-blue eyes. He was so handsome, so dreamy. Totally Elliot's type, which made it incredibly interesting that her cousin had put off sleeping with the man. This Jason meant something to Elliot. She could see the torn affection in her cousin's eyes. Saw the way Elliot watched Jason with concern he tried to mask as indifference and even disdain.

"You know, you brought him here to talk. You want me to help you both communicate? Then sit." She pointed to her spot on the couch and disentangled herself, needing to stand. Once Elliot sat some distance from Jason, she said, "This is ridiculous. You feel something for Jason or you'd have dumped him long ago. That, and I distinctly remember you saying you were *not* going to have sex with him."

"Why not? What's wrong with me?" Jason cried.

So much drama.

"Yeah, Elliot. What's wrong with Jason? He's got an amazing build. He's hot, and his blue eyes are just smokin'." Sadie blew him a kiss. "Baby, if you were straight, I'd totally do you."

Jason gave her a watery smile. "Thanks, Sadie."

"You see?" Elliot threw his hands in the air, but before he could jerk to his feet, she snapped at him.

"No, you stay."

Sadie continued to eat her popcorn, staring at the spectacle.

"Now, Jason. Again. From the beginning."

Jason took a deep breath, then let it out slowly. "Elliot's in love with me. I heard him say it after we *made love* last night."

She and Sadie gaped at Elliot, who blushed. And Elliot never blushed. "Elliot? Is this true?" Ava asked.

"He was dreaming."

Sadie exclaimed, "He's lying!"

"Sadie, stop pointing fingers. You're not helping." Ava saw Elliot squirm. "Elliot, why are you lying?"

"What makes you think I am?"

"You're blushing, for one. And you keep twitching. You have a tell."

"Hell." He groaned. "Jason, you're sweet and you're cute. But we're too different. I'm suave, experienced."

"A whore," Sadie translated.

"Sadie, hush." Ava nodded. "Go on."

Jason looked captivated, hanging on Elliot's every word. Oh boy. The poor guy was a lost cause, one more heart broken by her man-eater of a cousin.

"I couldn't help it." Elliot didn't look away from his redhead. "Jason's hot. I had to have him."

Jason left the couch to stand by Ava and hugged her once more. "I need comfort."

She rolled her eyes but gave him a hug. "Continue, Elliot."

Someone knocked at the door.

"I'll get it." Sadie bounced from her chair to the door, while Jason continued to sniffle and Elliot tried not to appear as if mesmerized by his new lover. But he couldn't seem to help himself. Her cousin was smitten.

Ha! Got yourself snagged, didn't you, Elliot?

"What the hell is this?"

Ava whipped her head to the door and saw Landon, soaked through to the skin, glaring at her and Jason hugging.

"Oh boy. This just got *gooooood*," Sadie said with glee.

Chapter 20

AVA FELT SIMULTANEOUSLY FLUSTERED, EXCITED, AND annoyed. He was here. Landon. Her boyfriend. The man she loved. And he was scowling at her and soaking wet.

"I'll get him a towel." Sadie shot down the stairs and returned moments later to hand Landon a bath towel. She hovered around him while everyone watched.

"What's going on?" he asked again and peeled off his sodden jacket. Then his sweater, leaving him in a soaked white T-shirt.

She could have heard a pin drop in the room.

"Don't you think you should take that off too?" Elliot suggested as Landon rubbed his cropped hair dry.

"Wouldn't want to catch cold," Jason added.

Then he and Elliot shared a grin, which quickly turned into another look entirely.

"Ava's helping Elliot and Jason *communicate*," Sadie answered since no one else seemed capable. "See, Elliot's confused about his feelings for Jason. And Jason's obviously in love with the guy." Sadie munched more popcorn, talking around a mouthful. "And now you're here to completely round out the day's entertainment. I love my life."

"Sadie, shut up," Elliot and Ava said at the same time.

She shrugged and reclaimed her seat on the chair.

Landon walked into the room, but he seemed to be limping.

"Are you okay?" Ava asked.

She looked into his eyes and saw a smoldering anger. Terrific. Just what she didn't need.

"Okay?" He glared at Jason and Jason's hands around her waist. "Who the fuck is this *Jason*?"

Jason, like Ava, had a tough time looking away from Landon. Not that she could blame him. Talk about a set of wet-down, washboard abs.

Oh, my pretty, pretty man.

She cleared her throat. "This is Jason, as Sadie already said."

"Hi." Jason sounded shy.

"Jason, this is Landon."

"Her boyfriend," Landon growled.

"Ava likes 'em rough," Sadie commented. "And muscular, and handsome." Sadie nodded. "And a little dense apparently. Jason's gay, Landon. No need to beat him to a pulp in a fit of jealousy."

Elliot spoke up. "He's not going to hurt you, Jason."

"Not now that I know you're gay, though you could take your hands off Ava."

"Seriously, though," Elliot said, "you should really lose the shirt and get warm. It's flu season, you know."

Landon shivered, then must have agreed because he took off his shirt and tossed it to the tiled floor by the door, where his other wet clothes sat. Then he held both ends of the towel around his neck, wrapping it around him like a blanket.

"Oh. Wow." Jason gaped.

"I know," Elliot agreed. Then he shook himself free of Landon's spell and turned back to Ava. "So. Heal us."

Jason nodded, reluctantly turning from Landon as well. "Yes. I don't understand why Elliot's acting so standoffish."

Landon limped to the couch and sat on the towel, rubbing his knee. But that left his chest bare. Unable to concentrate with so much of him staring her smack in the face, Ava fetched a blanket and tossed it to him.

He must have been cold because he wrapped himself in it. "Well, Dr. Rosenthal? Work your magic. Why is Elliot being such a twit?"

"Hey."

"Well," she answered, "he could be pulling away because he doesn't want to lead Jason on. Perhaps his feelings aren't serious for Jason."

"Nah." Sadie nixed that idea and held out the popcorn for Landon, who took a handful. "If he didn't care, he'd have nailed Jason that first night. I mean, come on. Look at that ass."

"Sadie." Jason preened. "She's right though. My ass is fabulous."

Elliot turned even redder.

"But it seems, in this case, knowing my cousin, that Elliot is acting cool because he's scared."

"Oh?" Landon said, sounding interested. "Why? Because Jason seems like a stand-up guy to me."

"I am." Jason nodded. "And I love him."

"Is that right?" Landon cocked his head. "So you told Elliot how you feel, putting yourself out there on the line like that, and he smacked you down?"

"Yes." Jason blinked, and Ava knew more tears would follow. She handed him a tissue box.

Landon continued to stare at *her*. "Not cool, Elliot."

Elliot sighed. "I wasn't expecting this—him. Jason's been a friend for a long time. Hell. He decorated my place."

"Nice job," Sadie said.

"Yeah. I liked it too." Landon nodded.

"I'm an interior designer by trade," Jason said. "That's how Elliot and I first met. I helped with the redesign of Sofa's."

"The coffee shop. Right." Landon kept looking at Ava. "So fear kept Elliot from admitting how he feels?"

"And confusion, I'm sure." Ava frowned. "It's not easy to have your future mapped out in your head, then turned around on you. I'm sure Elliot had specific requirements in what he thought would be a good mate."

Elliot shrugged. "Not really."

"Like someone he can talk with," Ava continued. "Someone he shares common interests with. Someone who respects his work and knows what boundaries he can't cross."

She saw Elliot look at Jason, really look at him.

"I get bored easily," Elliot admitted. "And that boredom is usually because I pick my dates by their looks, not their personalities. But fucking can get old after a while. Then I found you." He blew out a breath. "Jason, you scare the crap out of me. You see the real me, and I'm afraid if you look too hard, you might not like what you see."

"Is that right?" Landon said in a low voice.

Sadie's head whipped back and forth as if watching a Ping-Pong tournament.

"No." Ava wasn't scared of what he might see.

"Yes," Elliot said. "I'm sorry, Jason. Baby, I do have

feelings for you. But I'm not used to this. Getting serious." He paused. "But I want to see where this goes with you. I'm sorry for being such a dick. But honey, you need to get a thicker skin or this will never work."

Jason nodded. "I will, I promise." He hugged Elliot, then gave him a kiss that had everyone staring and Elliot panting like a dog. "Thanks, Ava." Jason sounded smug, and suddenly more in control of himself. "I hope to see you soon." He dragged an unprotesting Elliot out of her condo.

Only Sadie's crunching could be heard in the sudden silence.

"You." Landon pointed to her. "Out." He nodded to the door.

"Man. I never get to have any fun." Sadie winked at him and handed him her popcorn. Then she crossed to Ava and whispered close, "Don't make it too easy on him. Make him work to earn you. You deserve it." She turned to Landon. "You know, you look really cold. You should take off your pants too."

"*Sadie.*"

"I'm just sayin'…" Sadie sauntered to the door, grabbed her coat and umbrella, then left.

"And then there were two." Landon stood and shrugged off the blanket.

"What are you doing?"

"She was right. I'm fucking freezing in these things." He stripped down to nothing. Bare skin and goose-pebbled flesh. And a body that didn't quit. No shrinkage on Major Hottie. Then he sat back in the blanket on the couch and wrapped himself up in it. "Continue."

"What?"

"I'm curious to know why Elliot was such a scared idiot when all he had to do was admit how he felt to Jason in the first place."

Ava didn't like his perception of her cousin—of her. "Elliot isn't a scared idiot. He's protecting himself. Elliot's a smart man. And he's had a long time to be used to men not seeming to get him. They're intimidated. Or they just want him for his body. None of them seem to want him for who he is inside."

"But then he meets Jason, and it's different," Landon said quietly. "Jason sees him. Jason respects him. Hell. Jason even confesses to having feelings and shit."

"But do you?" She was tired of pretending. "You have scars, both inside and out, from your time in the Marine Corps. You lived a life before me. You had girlfriends, relationships. Sex."

"Sex. Seems like so long ago, I can barely remember." He sighed. "So what, Ava? I had a life before you. And…?"

"And you keep that bottled up inside you."

"Yeah, just like you do. You dated guys before me. You went to school, have parents I never met. You have a life I don't know much about. But I'm cool with it, because when you're with me, you're with me. Unless you've been calling out my name while we're in bed, but you're really thinking about some other Landon making you come."

Her cheeks felt hot, especially because she knew exactly what lay beneath that blanket. And she missed him. Missed teasing, arguing, discussing. Kissing.

"You're the only Landon I know, smart-ass. But Landon, this—us—it's scary for me, okay? I'm a contained person. I like to be in control of myself. Around you, I'm not in control at all. I feel happy and sad, aroused, angry. Landon, I fought a woman for you. I don't do things like that."

"Have you ever been in love before?"

She stared at him, getting lost in his amber eyes. "No." She saw him stiffen and had to add, "Not before you."

He relaxed, his firm lips curling into a smile. "Say it, Doc."

"You're such an annoying, aggravating, irritating man."

"You know that all means the same thing, right?"

"Smart too." She chuckled and let go of her fear. "I love you. I'm sorry about before. But I'm not sure how this is supposed to work."

"Come here." He patted his lap, and she went into his arms. "Ava, no one has a blueprint for love. It unfolds or it crumbles. And since I can't see into the future, I have no idea how it will pan out. But I can tell you a few things."

"Go ahead. You seem to be on a roll."

He kissed her forehead. "Now shut up and hold all questions to the end."

"Questions?"

"'Til the end, I said. Ava, before you, I had one great love. The United States Marine Corps. I was going to go all the way. Colonel, general, retirement, then life in Florida on a golf course. Something like that. I'd have the standard Marine Corps wife and two point five kids. Except none of that shit happened.

"I got hit by enemy fire. It tore up my knee pretty good, and I now have compromised range of motion in my left tibio-femoral joint. And let's not talk about my meniscus."

He extended his left knee and sighed. "I've been doing physical therapy, but sometimes my leg just goes out. I would have done anything to stay in the Marines, but they gave me a medical retirement. After only thirteen goddamn years, I was done. I transitioned to civilian life. And it's not what I thought I'd have at this point in my life, but it does make it easier to meet chicks." He grinned to take the sting out of his words.

"Lovely." She pushed aside a hank of wet hair from his forehead, empathizing with such a strong man shoved brutally away from his dream.

"Anyway. I met some women. But I wasn't ready for anything serious. Not until I met you. Hell, I wasn't planning on doing more than fucking you until I went blind, but then you stuck to me. Made me nutty for more of you. We have chemistry, baby. But when I'm with you, I also have all these feelings. I want to be with you in bed and out. I want to see you laugh, watch you smile, wipe your tears.

"You want feelings? You about ripped my heart out when you tried to end us the first time on this very couch."

"I wasn't ending us."

"Lucky for you." He kissed her, a tender touch that made her love him so much more. "And then in your office, it was all I could do to look cocky, when inside I was shaking."

"Oh, Landon. I'm sorry."

"And one more thing—*I told you so.*" He seemed obscenely smug. "You feel that love, don't you?"

"Yes, I do. And I love you right back."

"'I do.' Every time you say that, I get an image of you in a white dress. What's wrong, Doc? Why so pale?" He snickered. "Don't worry. We can take our time getting there. But Ava, it's you. You're it for me. I know it."

"It doesn't make any sense. But you're it for me too. I love so much about you. How you want to take care of me. How you want to make me happy. I actually crave you taking charge in bed."

"But not in life all the time, I know. I learned my lesson," he said.

"My patients know where I draw the line. And you know that now too."

"Yep."

She cupped her hands around his neck, so in love with him. "Landon, we need to go slowly. I can't promise I'll stop panicking about this relationship. I had my life mapped out."

"A boring life with boring men. Elliot told me."

"Did he also tell you I've been changing my list to make your qualities fit what I want in a man?"

"No shit." His wide smile warmed her heart. He shifted her over him, and she felt something else warming her insides. "Tell me."

"Well, my ideal mate has to be big. I like a man who can lift me up without breaking a sweat."

Landon made a muscle, and she stroked his thick biceps. "You know I'm super hard right now, right?"

"And I need a man who's smart and funny. He doesn't have to have an advanced degree, but he has to be good at his job, whatever that might be."

"Another check in the box." He lifted her and slowly

pulled off her pants. Then he tugged down her panties. "Pink. Oh yeah. Keep talking, Doc." Landon pushed aside the blanket and straddled her over his lap. He kept those busy hands moving, stripping her down to nothing but skin.

She sighed when his fingers found the insides of her thighs. "A man who values family and friends. Who's dependable." She groaned when he sank a finger inside her. "Who's willing and able."

"Oh, I am." He kissed her, this time with a hunger he couldn't hide. "What else?"

"He has to be very good in bed."

He smiled and removed his fingers, then eased her over his erection and watched as she slid down, seating himself fully inside her. "So do I have the job?"

"You do, Major Donnigan."

"No, you don't move." He clutched her hips, then drew his hands to her face and cupped her cheeks. "We'll grow to know each other better. I swear, I'll do my best to open up to you. And you do your best not to run when I act like an asshole, because we both know that's gonna happen."

She kissed him, lingering over his neck, his ear. He tasted salty, manly. And that spicy cologne drove her crazy. She wanted to eat him up. "Often, I suppose."

He groaned and swelled inside her. "Fuck. Yeah. But…" He blew out a breath as she nibbled. "I love and trust you. And someday soon, you're going to marry me."

Ava sighed when he lifted her hips and started dragging her up and down over him. "Yes, I probably will." She kissed him again, lost in his touch. "But only if you let me go down on you again. You said something about getting a blowjob in your office?"

He felt so thick in this position, but she loved being able to watch him while they made love.

"You get me so hard." He kept taking her, and she rode him, grinding over him, loving her big, buff man all over.

He groaned. "That crack about my secretary blowing me? All fantasy." He swore and gripped her hips harder. "I don't have an assistant. Just want you…"

He sucked her breasts, biting her nipples then drawing them deep. He rolled the buds, giving her small bursts of painful pleasure to ramp her desire higher. That cock just keep driving, and she felt herself climbing that journey right along with him, lost in desire and love for her perfect man.

"I'm inside you, baby," he said his voice gruff. "So deep inside."

"Deep inside here," she said, bringing his hand to her heart.

"Oh yeah." He kissed her, while he increased his pace, thrusting faster.

"I love you, Doc," he said and yanked her down over him while he spent.

She didn't have time to wish he could go just a little bit longer, because his clever fingers brought her off, and she cried his name as she came. "I love you too," she gasped and clung to him, never wanting to let go.

After some time, they sat together, still joined, and stared into each other's eyes.

"You can always count on me, Ava," he said in all seriousness.

Stable, her sexy rock of trust. "I know." She smiled. "Me too. I'll never let you down."

"I know." He stroked her back. "There's just one more thing."

"What's that?"

"Were you the one who stuck that blow-up doll in my room?"

She blinked. "No. I assumed your brothers or sister did it."

He gave a satisfied smile. "That's what I thought. Don't worry. As we speak, I've made plans to pay back the culprit. And now, you may kiss the grand master and king of this year's prank wars."

She kissed him, demanding details. But he refused to give in until she promised to let him tie her up to her bed later. Then he added a few toys and some oils to spice up the mix. But the hot wax was definitely the cherry on top.

With Landon, she'd never get bored, never want for love. And never, *ever*, get a haircut that wasn't done by a professional stylist. She'd made him swear to that.

Poor, poor Theo.

———∼∼∼———

Monday morning, Theo woke up from a party that had lasted way too long. He scratched his ass as he made his way to the bathroom he shared with his pig of a brother. Freakin' Gavin. After taking a piss in a toilet *not* covered in plastic wrap—obvious much, Landon?—Theo washed his hands and splashed his face with water. But when he glanced into the mirror, he froze in shock.

With trembling hands, he rubbed his head. The

mohawk wasn't as long as it could have been, but the sides of his head were nearly *bald*. And the hair on top…orange. Oregon Beavers orange.

Son of a bitch! *Landon!*

So, big brother had found out he'd left the blow-up doll on his bed. No matter. Because now, it was seriously on. Landon would know so much pain…

The door behind him opened. His new friend from last night entered wearing a half-shirt and panties. "Oh, Theo. I really do love it. Your brother said you wanted a change. You'll fit right in at work, Mohawk Man."

At least he'd gained some cool points with his coffee shop buddies. But he knew the time had come for some payback. Because Gavin had been at that party last night too, egging him on to drink just one more beer. A coalition must have formed. Landon and Gavin against him and Hope. Just as soon as he saw his sister again, he planned on revenge.

But not until he had another go-round with Maya and her pierced tongue.

Chapter 21

SAM WANDERED IN THE RAIN, CONCERNED ABOUT YET another damn dog. He'd found Macho easily enough last week. If that do-gooder Donnigan hadn't picked him up, Sam would have. Typical McCauley. Donnigan, McCauley, Sam lumped them all together. It was as if Del had infected his team by agreeing to marry Mike, because now, everywhere he turned, Sam found himself bumping into a McCauley brother, uncle, or cousin.

Gave him hives being around so much family unity.

The wind blew more rain into his face. *Just awesome.* Another Sunday night spent roaming this damn stretch of Queen Anne looking for a scared puppy.

He idly wondered if Lancelot had fixed things with his chick. Poor bastard had seemed like a lost cause. But whatever. Sam had better things to do than worry about some jackass Marine.

"Hey, Scruffy. Hey, boy." He tried to keep his voice down, because he wasn't supposed to be hanging around the back lots of these particular offices. The cops had already questioned him once for being at the scene of a recent break-in.

That's all I need. To head back to prison. Prison—not jail—where guys did hard time.

He squelched those memories in a hurry and continued to call out for the dog. The animal foster home he'd been helping belonged to a cranky-ass old woman named Willie. A few of her friends had mentioned a stray puppy looking in need of care that they called Scruffy. Sam had already circled the park and the nearby neighborhood. He didn't want the poor thing being dumped at the animal shelter.

He knew all about being a stray, needing a good home.

After a glance around, and spotting no cops, he crossed the tiny lot and slipped past the back gate. The light he could see shining through the window of the office gave him pause, and he decided to hang back in the shadowed courtyard, where he'd seen Macho last week. At least Macho had found a home. But this poor guy out in the freezing rain wouldn't last too long by himself.

"Scruffy," he tried again in a low whisper and glanced down at the bushes, wondering if the dog was hiding back there.

"Oh my God. You're back." The soft, feminine scold startled him. He hadn't seen the woman exit the building.

If she found Sam, he'd be in some serious trouble. Considering he looked like a thug, was too big to escape notice, and too mean, wet, and cold to give a shit about sounding nice, he figured his best course of action would be to keep quiet and hope the chick would go back in.

Then he heard it. A small, trembling yip.

"Oh, sweetie. I'd take care of you if you'd stop running away. Now shush. You're not supposed to be here." She stepped into the light, and Sam stopped breathing.

Then she took that small, wet bundle in her arms and snuck him back inside.

Sam continued to stare at the back of the building, his mind not working right. Because that woman…*damn.*

Talk about a lucky dog tonight. Scruffy had been tucked against a generous rack that gave Sam all kinds of ideas.

Here for the dog, not woman problems. Focus, Hamilton.

The wind blew and knocked over a flower pot that shattered on the ground. The door opened again. "Who's there?" she called out.

He swore under his breath. Opening the door when any psycho could be out stalking was stupid. If he'd been inclined, he could have had her shoved up against a wall in seconds, dangling by her neck, before she could even think of screaming for help.

"I'm calling the police," she warned and slammed the door.

He ducked away, halfway to his car before he realized he couldn't just leave the dog in her care. A woman with those looks, foolish enough to put herself in danger like that, had no regard for safety. Scruffy needed a real protector. Someone like Sam, not some defenseless blond with the sense of a gnat.

He'd come back tomorrow and set her straight. That would be after a long night convincing himself not to gape like a jackass when he saw her again. Her looks shouldn't matter. She was an idiot for opening that door. How the hell could she protect Scruffy when she couldn't protect herself?

It wasn't his job to police the damn city. Just the small, defenseless animals needing his help.

And there was nothing small about that blond. Nothing defenseless about that rockin' body either. Nope. Not his problem.

Or so he kept telling himself.

The Troublemaker Next Door

"But Uncle Flynn, you promised."

Flynn McCauley shook his head, his eyes glued to the television, where the Mariners played out the top of the ninth inning. "Just let me see the highlights from last night's game. I promise I'll turn it back in a minute."

"But, but..." Colin tapered off, and Flynn watched the next few minutes in disbelief. He hadn't thought the Mariners could pull off the win. Damn, he owed Brody twenty bucks.

The frightening sound of a child's tears tore Flynn from the game. He stared at his nephew in shock. "*Colin?*"

Five-and-a-half-year-old Colin McCauley didn't cry when he skinned his knees, when he'd suffered a black eye from a wild pitch, or when his father had mistakenly thrown away his favorite T-shirt just last week, thinking the holey thing a rag. The kid was tougher than a lot of grown men Flynn knew, a mirror image of Mike in too many ways.

"Colin, what's wrong, dude?" Panicked when Colin continued to cry, Flynn hurried to change the channel. Then he offered him some of the soda Colin had been asking for earlier but wasn't allowed to have. Anything to dry up Colin's tears. "It's okay, buddy. Don't cry." He crossed the couch to hug him, concerned there might be something really wrong.

After a few moments, Colin stopped his tears and squirmed to get free so he could see the television. His grief dried up as if it had never been, not even a hiccup to indicate emotional trauma.

A remarkable recovery. "Are you, or are you not, upset about something?"

Colin took a long drag of soda and laughed at the screen. "Not now." He beamed, looking exactly like Mike—smug and annoying.

"Scammed by a kid. This is embarrassing."

"Ubie told me it would work, but I didn't believe him."

"Uncle Brody, right. Now why am I not surprised?" He had his best friend and business partner to thank for Colin's ability to lie with a straight face. "When did he teach you that?"

"At dinner last Sunday. Oh, watch this, Uncle Flynn. See how the monster eats the school? Awesome." Colin dissolved into boyish laughter.

Flynn sighed and sank into the couch. Babysitting duty wasn't so bad, or at least it hadn't been when the kid attended preschool. But if Colin was mastering Brody's tricks now, imagine what he'd be like at eight, ten... hell, as a teenager. Flynn resolved to have a firm talk with good old Ubie. No point in encouraging Colin to scam people if Flynn wasn't allowed to be in on the joke.

Flynn sat next to Colin, enjoying the cartoon despite himself. He rubbed the kid's head. Colin McCauley, future heartbreaker. He had good looks, a great sense of humor, and a quick mind, one that would keep them all on their toes for years to come. Mike had done pretty damn good with the kid, but Flynn liked to think he'd had a hand in Colin's greatness. At least the part of him that kicked ass at sports.

Just as the back door opened and heavy footsteps signaled Mike's return—*thank God*—the phone rang. And rang and rang.

"Flynn, answer the frigging phone, would you?" Mike yelled from the other room.

"What, are his hands broken?" Flynn asked the boy as he reached for the phone. "Can't he tell I'm busy watching you?"

Colin ignored him in favor of a cartoon sponge. Like father like son.

Into the phone, Flynn barked, "Yeah?"

"Um, hello?" A woman's voice. She sounded soft, sexy. Interesting.

Flynn straightened on the couch. "McCauley residence. How can I help you?"

Colin turned to look at him with interest. Flynn never used the good voice on anyone but customers or women.

"Is this Mike?"

"No, but I can get him for you."

"That would be great."

"Hold on." Flynn sought his brother and found him struggling with a tool belt and muddied boots in the kitchen. "Yo, Mike. Phone call."

"Take a message, Einstein. I'm busy here." Mike

struggled with dirt-caked knots on his work boots, the scowl on his face enough to black out the sun.

Flynn flipped him the finger while he spoke to the angel on the phone again. "Sorry, but he's busy right now. Can I take a message?"

Silence, and then a long, drawn-out sigh. "Can you just tell him that we're having a problem with the sink? I hate to bother, but my roommate threatened to cut all my hair off if I don't get this fixed soon. The problem has been going on for a week."

"Ah, hold on." He covered the phone. To his brother, he asked, "Why is some hot-sounding chick asking you to fix her sink?"

Mike groaned. "Hell. That's probably one of the tenants next door."

"Mom and Dad have new renters already? Since when?"

"Been four months now. You aren't that observant, are you? Didn't get the family looks or brains, apparently." Mike's sneer set Flynn's teeth on edge. Arrogant bastard. His brother glanced at the phone and sighed. "Tell her I'll be right over."

Flynn passed the message, then hung up. "I don't remember Mom telling us about renting the house again. All I knew is they had some renovations done since the last bunch trashed the garage. I thought the cars I'd seen in the drive belonged to her fix-it crew."

"Well, in case it's escaped your notice, the garage has been fixed for a while now. She rented the place out to three women who moved in around the middle of February. I think you and Brody were doing that job in the San Juans then. They aren't bad neighbors. Keep to themselves, really quiet, and I think one of them has been working on the flower beds in the front, because they've really taken off this year."

Trust Mike not to come to the heart of the matter. "Any of them hot?"

"And this is why Mom didn't mention them."

Flynn frowned. "Don't be a dick. Just because you refuse to, and I quote, 'open your heart to love again' doesn't mean the rest of us aren't interested."

Mike finally stepped out of his god-awful boots. The things were like boats that had been dipped in muck and rolled over in stink. "First of all, don't quote Mom to me at five o'clock on a Friday after I've spent all…" he glanced around and seeing the kitchen clear, continued, "…*fucking* day working on Jane Risby's kitchen cabinets. The woman changes her mind about what she wants at the drop of a hat, and I'm tired. Second, just because I'm not willing to marry and procreate *again* doesn't mean I'm against getting laid. But you don't piss where you eat, and my neighbors are way too close to deal with in the event a date goes south."

"Hmm, good point. So answer the question already."

Mike rolled his eyes. "The truth? Every one of them is hot. Not cute, or attractive, but one you'd want to bring home and keep around until breakfast the next morning. And the morning after that. So don't even think about hitting on them. I meant it when I said I don't want the fallout of pissed-off neighbors. Find someone else to bone while I find a clean pair of shoes."

"Mike, don't be an ass if you can help it." He ignored the dark look his brother shot him. "Come on, let me take care of this for you. A clogged sink is right up my alley. Hello, plumber here? I swear I won't hit on any of them." Today.

Mike narrowed his eyes but was either too tired to argue or he believed Flynn's crap. "Okay. But as soon as you're done, you come right back here. Leave them alone. I mean it."

"Yeah, yeah. Why don't you go nag your kid? I think he's drinking in the living room."

Flynn left just as he heard his anal-retentive brother yelling at Colin to take his drink back into the kitchen where it belonged. Satisfied he'd at least had a bit of revenge on his nephew, he grabbed a toolbox from his truck and walked next door.

Mike hadn't been kidding about the flowers. Seattle's rich brown dirt made for some killer growth, especially during the summer. Roses, lavender, and poppies scattered the front flower beds like a carpet of color. The grass looked freshly mowed, and the walkway had been swept free of debris. A nice change from the last couple who'd spent more time smoking and letting their bratty kids dig up the yard than tending to anything. The aging Craftsman looked as good now as the pictures he'd seen of it newly built. The slate-blue wooden siding looked fresh against the white columns and rails on the covered porch. A rocking chair sat next to pots of cheery geraniums, and a few pairs of women's sneakers sat by the front door.

He rang the doorbell and waited, wondering what the women who wore the shoes looked like, out of curiosity, not desperation. He had a few female friends he could see when he felt the need for companionship. Nice women he could be casual with, and a few he now stayed away from because the last times he'd visited they'd hinted at wanting something more serious. Casual hookups in bars didn't appeal to him. The threat of disease or waking up next to a woman dimmer than a busted lightbulb made him shudder. If his mother would just stop bugging him about settling down, about how she'd had three children by his age and blah blah blah responsibilities…

"Hello?" Dark brown eyes peered at him through the crack in the door.

"Hi. You just called my brother, Mike. I'm Flynn, here to save your sink." He held up his toolbox.

"Oh. Hold on." She closed the door and he heard her undo the chain. The door opened. "Come on in."

He made sure to wipe his feet on the mat before entering and took in the cheery feel of the foyer. The hardwoods looked clean and polished, comfortable furniture in the open living area neat and decorated like something out of a magazine. Bold splashes of color mixed with eclectic pieces, not at all the traditional style of his mother's place or his stark bachelor pad. Yet the room also felt lived in. Books and magazines scattered the coffee table, and plants thrived in the ledge of the bay window. A cool breeze blew through the window screens in the living room. The light scent of flowers and something delicious mingled, making him hungry and more than a little intrigued about the occupants of the house.

The woman in front of him lived up to Mike's description, and then some. To Flynn's discomfort, she reminded him of Lea, Mike's deceased wife. Short, curvy, and pretty with that same touch of innocence that had always made Flynn want to protect. She had dark hair and deep brown eyes, high cheekbones and full lips. From behind, she and Lea might as well have been twins.

"Name's Flynn McCauley," he said once they reached the kitchen. He put down his tools and held out a hand.

She took it with a smile and a firm grip, surprising him. Not as shy as the softness of her voice would have him believe. "Abby Dunn. Nice to meet you. We've seen Mike a few times, but with us being so busy, we haven't been too neighborly, I'm afraid."

He glanced around. "We?"

"Oh, my roommates Maddie and Vanessa. They should be home soon."

He nodded. She tucked a long strand of dark hair behind her ear, and he noticed the differences between her and Lea. Her eyes had a bit more slant, looking more exotic and less girl-next-door. Her hair was straighter as well, not as wavy as Lea's had been.

Realizing he'd been staring, he apologized. "Sorry. You look a lot like someone I used to know."

She nodded, no longer smiling. "Your brother's wife. Your mother mentioned the resemblance. When Mike first saw me, he looked like he'd seen a ghost. I might have kept my distance because of that too."

"Please don't. It's been years. And Mike would have said something if it bothered him." At least, he thought he would have. "I'm just glad to see my parents renting to people who take care of the place."

She scrunched her nose. "Yeah. When we moved in, there was a faint reek of smoke. Your mother didn't seem happy about that." Abby grinned. "Gave us half off our first month's rent too. I like her. Don't tell her, but she's a soft touch."

Flynn chuckled. "You got that right." He looked at the counter to see a stack of detergents and items normally kept under a sink. On the floor, a few soaked towels absorbed water. "Oh boy. The sink problem."

She nodded. "But I think the water leak is my fault. I knew not to use the sink, but the dishwasher was full, and I forgot. Normally it just clogs up, but today water dripped from underneath." She opened the cabinet under the sink and showed him. "Do you think you can fix this?"

"Better than Mike could. I'm the plumber."

"Good. You're exactly who we need."

"Just let me get under there and I'll have it fixed for you in no time. If you have something else to do, go ahead. Or you can wait and watch if you want."

She bit her lower lip. Lea never used to do that. "If you wouldn't mind, I was right in the middle of something. I'll be down the hall if you need anything."

"Okay." He got to work, grateful the clog would be easy enough to handle. The broken valve, not so much unless he had a spare part in his box. Which he did. Humming under his breath, he lost himself in his work. Once finished, he heard a raised female voice screaming in anger. Odd, because he hadn't heard anyone enter the house.

He slid out from under the sink, curious when he heard Abby try to placate the woman. But she wouldn't stop yelling. Hoping he wouldn't have to break up a catfight, though secretly enthusiastic about the idea, he moved to investigate.

—*—

"Oh my God, Abby! Right there, in the office I visit ten times a day. He had the nerve to drag my hand over his crotch!" Maddie paced back and forth, still in shock about this disastrous turn of events. "I was supposed to be offered a huge job, a step toward a junior partnership, not an opportunity to fuck the boss!"

Abby's eyes were as round as quarters. "I thought you said Fred was gay."

"I thought he was. He's neat, he has a tendency to lisp, and he calls everyone, men and women, *sthweet-heart*. It's all a front so no one feels threatened by him."

"Until he puts your hand over his penis during a business lunch." Abby nodded.

"No, after the lunch. The gourmet meal was to soften me up, play his cards. Dangle the carrot before me and tease me about giving Diane the promotion." Maddie threw her purse against the wall and shrieked. "The man has money coming out his perfectly groomed ass. He can have anyone he wants. Why would he do this to *me*?"

"Maybe because he can," Abby said softly.

Ignoring her, Maddie ranted. "I can't believe this. I had my whole future mapped out. More responsibilities, a major account of my own, then a junior partnership before I'd branch out and start my own design boutique. And now…"

"Now what, exactly? You didn't say what happened after he put your hand over his…you know."

"I squeezed. Hard."

"Ew."

"Tell me about it, it was instinctive. I wanted him to let me go, and he did," she said with some small satisfaction. "Then I dumped his coffee in his lap, told him to kiss my ass, and stalked out of there. I immediately turned in my resignation and told them to expect a call from an attorney."

"You're going to hire a lawyer?"

"No." She felt miserable. "My savings aren't for an attorney, they're for my future. Realistically, by the time I go through with a lawsuit, I'll be broke. The case will have turned into a he said–she said match, and with his money, he'll buy the jury."

"There won't be a jury, just a hearing—"

"Exactly. Not even a jury." She wanted to cry. So angry. Men. "He dicks me over, Ben dicks me over. What the hell is going on with my life?"

Abby stood up and crossed the room to her. "I'm so sorry. So did he say anything after you stormed out?"

"I have no idea. I didn't wait around for the fallout. That ass!"

"Don't worry, you'll get through this." Abby patted her shoulder. "So on top of everything with your boss, what happened with Ben?"

Maddie kicked off her heels, imagining kicking them at Ben's head. "We broke up. He was getting too clingy, so I told him to man up or man out—as in, get out."

"Are you serious? What did he do when you issued that ultimatum?"

"He got out, or rather, he told *me* to get out. Told me it wasn't manning up to want his girlfriend to spend time with him. Oh, like my career doesn't matter because I'm an interior designer? Like being a doctor is so much more important." She saw Abby's wince and snapped, "He's a foot doctor, not a neurosurgeon. Give me a break."

Abby squeezed her shoulder. "I'm sorry, sweetie. I know you liked Ben."

"It's all right. He was wearing on me. They all do." She walked away from Abby and paced back and forth across the room. "Men. Nothing but a bunch of self-absorbed assholes who can't think beyond their dicks."

"Ah, Maddie, you might want to—"

"And really, Fred Hampton? Designer to the stars? Please. Forcing my hand over his lap was a stupid thing to do. His package did not impress. At. All."

Abby flushed.

"Come on. You write a lot worse than that."

"Uh, yeah, but you see, there's someone—"

"All my hard work, for what?" Maddie was on a tear. "I spent ten fucking years working to get to that place. Sure I learned. I interned, paid my way through school, suffered through the chrome years and the faux fur trends, which just won't go away. But this *insult*! In this day and age, with so much bullshit about being PC and sexual harassment has no place in the workplace, and my boss just made me feel him up in his own office during business hours. The perv! I feel like a total—"

She looked up to see a huge, green-eyed hunk filling out a white T-shirt and jeans like he'd stepped out of a Man of the Month calendar. One of *them*. A man. The enemy.

Abby cleared her throat. "Maddie, this is Flynn McCauley, Mike's brother. He was just fixing our kitchen sink."

Mortified but not willing to let him see it, Maddie gave him a disdainful once-over, ignoring the surge of her libido. "How *nice* to meet you. And would you like me to feel you up as well?"

He raised a brow and gave her the same thorough examination, lingering not on her breasts or ass, the way most men did, but on her face. Sure, why should this one be typical when it took all kind of XY degrees of perversion to make the world go 'round?

Annoyed all over again, she tossed her head, grateful her hair stayed out of her eyes, though God knew she had the frizz from hell going on, and stomped out of the room with a low, "And fuck you too." She took the stairs two at a time and slammed the door of her bedroom behind her. After locking the door and turning on the radio to mask any other noise, she lay down on her bed and let the tears fall. Could her life get any worse?

~~~

"Oh man, I'm really sorry." Abby apologized for the fourth time in as many seconds.

"Hey, don't worry about it. Sounds like your friend had the mother of all bad days." Flynn still had a hard time catching his breath.

Had Mike said the women were hot? He was out of his celibate mind. Abby had cute down to a science, and that resemblance to Lea which kind of freaked him out. But Maddie? She of the long legs, killer rack, and sultry face? Sultry, a word he'd never used to describe a woman. But damn, it fit. She wasn't pretty or cute, but with full lips, that flush on her cheeks, and those direct, man-hating eyes so dark they looked like never-ending night, the woman had a knockout punch he still hadn't recovered from.

"Maddie can be a little dramatic, but she had cause." Abby picked up her friend's purse and shoes and put them on the desk next to her computer.

It suddenly struck Flynn that in all the time he'd been standing there listening to Maddie, he hadn't noticed that the women had turned his mother's idea of a sitting room into an office. French doors off the smaller room gave it a bigger feel, and the hardwoods had been covered with a Persian rug in dark red accents. Dark red, reminding him of Maddie's hair. Man, he had a thing for redheads. All that temper… he could only imagine what she'd be like in bed.

"Flynn?"

"Sorry. Hey, you want me to go down to her boss's office and pound some sense into him?"

She blinked. "Probably not a good idea unless you want a lawsuit. Fred Hampton has a lot of money."

He shrugged. "That's okay. I know a lot of people who'd back me up. Heck, my nephew would alibi me with no problem. I'll go kick this Fred guy's ass, and we'll all pretend I was here fixing your sink while Colin watched me the whole time. Kid has the face of angel but can lie like a champ." Was it bad he sounded like he was bragging? Though the thought of beating the shit out of Maddie's boss had real appeal. Who the hell treated a woman like that but real scum?

"Nice offer. I'll pass it on to Maddie when she's in a better mood. Now, about the sink, how much do I owe you for parts or labor or whatever?"

He shook his head. "Your landlord should have handled this when the problem first happened." He made a mental note to talk to his mom and dad after he chewed out Mike.

"It's not their fault. I kind of dragged my feet to get it fixed. Vanessa usually handles the house issues, but she's been busy at work lately."

"Please tell me she doesn't work with Maddie." He liked saying her name. Short for Madison? Madeleine? He'd have to find out.

Abby snorted. "No way. Vanessa is an accountant. Very cut and dry. The woman means business when it comes to numbers. You need a good person to do your taxes, you should call her."

"I would if I didn't make my little brother, I mean, if my little brother hadn't already *offered* to take care of them for me."

She laughed and walked with him to the kitchen to grab his tools. "I have two sisters. They can be a handful. At least mine live on the East Coast."

"Lucky you." Cameron was such a snot. Thought he knew everything when it came to financial planning. From what little Flynn knew, his brother did, but it didn't help Cam's already huge ego to point that out. "If you need anything else, let me know." He fished a business card out of his back pocket.

"You really are a plumber." Her surprise disgruntled him, and she must have seen it, because she blushed. "I know you said you were, but I thought that might have been a little brotherly competition. As in, you're better at plumbing than he is. And besides, you don't look anything like our old neighborhood plumber. He was an older man with a big belly and that problem men get with their pants when they bend over."

It took him a minute. "Ah. Crack, the nonaddictive kind. The pants too low for you?"

She shuddered. "Way too low." So much for thinking the woman was shy. "But yours seem okay. Forgive me for making generalizations."

She walked him to the front door.

"No problem. But if you want, I could wear my pants really low for you the next time your sink clogs."

She winked. "Sounds good to me."

She shut the door behind him, and he heard her faint chuckle. He decided he liked Abby Dunn. Her roommate, on the other hand… That redhead he had no intention of leaving alone. Now that he thought about it, his mother wasn't exactly being neighborly by not inviting her new tenants over for a summer barbecue. He'd have to rectify that, but not until he had a few words with Mike. What had he been thinking to leave a houseful of women like that all alone? God knew what Vanessa looked like. Flynn had a sudden image of the three roommates scrapping around in a ring throwing Jell-O at one another, Maddie leading the match, and hustled back to his brother to yell at him.

*And don't miss the smokin'-hot first book
in the Body Shop Bad Boys series!*

TEST DRIVE

THE OPENING RIFF OF AN OLD-SCHOOL AC/DC SONG
echoed through the garage. Johnny Devlin bit back a
curse when he scraped his knuckles on the pump of the
piece of crap Cadillac he was working on.

The smell of motor oil, sweat, and grease warmed
the interior of Johnny's favorite place in the world.
Webster's Garage boasted a double set of bay doors
and a roomy interior complete with a cement floor and
red-and-brown brick walls, a holdover from the original
Tooley's Auto Shop.

"Hey, asshole," he heard Foley snarl. "We talked
about this. Hands off my stuff."

Best buds Foley and Sam were squared off, staring
holes through each other. When it came to order—and
pretty much everything related to cleanliness—the two
thugs sat on opposite ends of the spectrum. Foley—Mr.
Tall, Dangerous, and Arrogant—was compulsively
neat, while Sam might as well have had the word *chaos*

tattooed on his forehead. Covered in tattoos, Sam was a walking billboard for badassery.

Lou stepped over to the radio near his work station, and soon loud classic rock drowned out the rest of the argument.

Just another day at the office.

A cool breeze made Johnny sigh. Seattle's unseasonably warm autumn temps continued to be a pleasant surprise this year, and they kept the garage doors open to let the air circulate through the sticky auto repair shop. Even at nine thirty in the morning, he had worked himself into a sweat.

Johnny cranked his wrench and stared at a stubborn pump assembly that refused to cooperate. He loosened it, got to the fan belt, then glared down at the problematic power steering pump.

After glancing over his shoulder to make sure he was in the clear, he softly muttered, "Shitty Cadillac."

The sound of someone shaking a familiar glass jar of coins made him tense. He heard it again, even over the blast of AC/DC. Ducking deeper under the Cadillac's hood, Johnny wondered who his sexy-scary boss was going to call out for cursing now. He was sure he hadn't been that loud.

"Seriously, guys?" Delilah Webster held the newly purposed amber glass growler out to Sam and Foley. The woman had a hard-on for swearwords lately.

Such a sad waste of a perfectly good beer container. Once the half-gallon jar had been home to a killer IPA flavored with hops and a hint of citrus. Now, it was nothing but a no-swearing jar filled with goddamn quarters.

As if the shop going clean would prevent Del from slipping up at her wedding.

He imagined her dolled up in a white gown, tats,

piercings, and her hair all done up in some funky twist, looking like a million bucks. She'd be glowing at her behemoth of a fiancé before letting loose with an "I *fucking* do." With a snort, he buried himself back under the hood of the bastard of a car and did his best to calm his frustration. He never had anything pleasant to say before ten a.m. anyway. God knew he needed a jolt of caffeine, and soon, before he took a tire iron to the gray piece of crap he just *knew* was laughing at him.

Sam and Foley bitched about the new no-swear policy even as he heard them drop change into what Johnny had taken to calling the "Rattle of Oppression—ROP." A few clinks of change against glass and everyone seemed to sink into themselves, anxious that their fearsome boss would come storming back in, demanding a quarter for a "hell," "shit," or "damn."

Johnny knew better. Dubbed the smart one of the crew, he kept his nose out of trouble and everyone else on the straight and narrow. Mostly.

He heard Del step in his direction, grazed his already sore knuckle against the frame as he removed the assembly, and let it rip. "*Fudge.*"

"See?" Del yelled to be heard above a man on the radio screeching about shaking all night long. "At least *someone* can keep his friggin' mouth clean." She patted him on the shoulder, and he did his best not to flinch. Woman had hands like rocks. "Thanks, Johnny."

He kept his head down and continued to tinker, listening as her footsteps gradually faded. Then an office door closed, and he found it safe to look up.

"You are *such* a kiss ass." Sam frowned. Then again, Sam did nothing but frown.

Next to him, Foley crossed massive arms over a broad chest and made kissy noises. A glance across the garage showed Lou shaking his head, looking disappointed.

"What?" Johnny tossed up his hands. "Am I the *only* one smart enough to know you catch more bees with honey?" He smirked at the many middle fingers shot his way. "Thought so. Dumbasses."

Of the four of them currently in the shop, Sam was the one whose temper could turn on a dime. He'd gotten better over the years, but everyone knew to avoid the brute when he sank into a rage. Only Foley could talk him down, the pair closer than most brothers. Lou had a sense of humor like Johnny's, but without the quick wit—or so Johnny liked to constantly tell him.

Keeping on Sam's good side would be the smart thing to do.

So of course, Johnny had to prod him. "Hey, McSteroid, you and your boyfriend got plans for tonight?"

Foley sighed. Lou grinned.

Sam's frown darkened. "Why? You got a death wish, stick boy?"

Johnny flexed a greasy arm. "Seriously? Stick boy? Man, I'm ripped. And it's all natural." He raised a brow at Sam and pushed his bicep up from the back, trying to appear bigger.

Even Sam couldn't withstand the Devlin charm. A rare smiled appeared on his face. "Whatever. No, I don't have plans. And Foley—not my boyfriend, dickhead—has his own life."

"So." Lou looked Foley up and down. "No plans for you then?"

"Suck it."

Lou grinned. It took a lot to push the guy's buttons. "Back at you, hombre."

"I thought we'd hang at Ray's if you losers have nothing better to do. Darts rematch?" Johnny offered.

The others agreed.

"You're on." Lou looked eager. The only one of the group who gave Johnny a serious run for his money at the game. Intelligent, a real ladies' man, and he had a steady hand. A useful trait for a guy who painted with great attention to detail.

"Cool." Johnny gave them a thumbs-up. "Winner doesn't pay for drinks. So make sure you idiots bring your wallets."

"Dream on, motherfu—"

"*Foley*," Del snarled from the office door. "What the hell did I say about swearing?" The ROP had returned.

Johnny buried his head back under the hood of the car. He was pretty sure the others did the same. Survival of the fittest worked only if you let the weaker ones, like Foley, take one for the team.

A few hours later, he lounged outside on a picnic table, eating a sandwich Dale, their service writer, had picked up from their favorite shop two doors down. The rare sunshine, not marred by a single cloud, added to the perfection of the moment. A few birds chirped, cars buzzed down Rainier, and only Foley crunching on a huge bag of chips interrupted Johnny's peace.

Foley glanced at Johnny's third sandwich. "Where do you put all that food? You should be really fat."

"You should talk. And just because I don't spend my leisure time jerking off with weights doesn't mean I'm not in shape. I like running."

"From the law," Foley muttered and crunched some more, a sly grin on his face.

"Nah. That's in the past. The trick now is not to get caught." He wiggled his brows, and Foley laughed. "I run after work, if you're interested."

"Nope. I'd rather 'jerk off with weights,'" Foley sneered. "You know, with that smart mouth, it's a wonder no one's rearranged your face lately."

"It's been a few months," Johnny admitted. He had a hard time going without a fight, cursed with an inability to keep his mouth shut around less intelligent, ill-humored people. "I'm not a half-bad boxer. Hence my ability to still breathe on my own."

"I know. That's the only reason Sam and I tolerate you. That and if we're in a fight, we'll throw them the runt and mosey off."

Johnny laughed. Foley and Sam weren't known to *mosey* away from anything. The badass bros, as he and the others called them behind their backs, ended more shit than Johnny ever started. That weird moral code the pair insisted on keeping often had them interfering when a smarter man would steer clear.

"You still dating Alicia?" Foley asked out of the blue.

"Nah. She got a little clingy."

Foley sighed. "They all do."

"I take it you and Sue are quits then."

"Yep."

"Should make tonight at Ray's interesting." Johnny grinned. Sue waitressed at Ray's, and though he'd been curious, he'd been too intimidated by her rough edges to try her on for size. A sweetheart underneath the heavy kohl, many piercings, and fierce tats, Sue nevertheless didn't tolerate horny fools. Fuck with her and meet a bad end. Period.

Granted, Johnny wouldn't typically let a little thing like a woman kicking his ass stop him if he really wanted her. He'd charmed harder cases than Sue. But he didn't want to break her heart, then have to deal with her when he went back to the bar.

"It wasn't like we were serious."

"A little defensive, hoss?"

"Shut up. I am not."

"Uh-huh."

Foley groaned. "It was just supposed to be sex. Then she's texting me all the time. Can I help it if I'm damn good in bed? I mean, Jesus. A little oral foreplay, and the chick's hinting at wedding bells."

"Really?"

"Okay, so I'm exaggerating. But she wanted to go exclusive, so I backed out quick." Foley's ended relationship apparently hadn't dulled his appetite, because he finished the chips and started on a few cookies. Carrying around so much muscle obviously expended energy. "She said she's cool with it, but I haven't been face-to-face with her since Saturday night."

Johnny did the math. "That's nearly a week. Hey, with any luck, she'll be too slammed with orders tonight to notice you. You know how Fridays at Ray's can get." Johnny gave him a fake smile. "Good luck, friend."

Foley frowned at him. "You don't sound all that sincere."

"I'm not. I'll be placing bets on you leaving Ray's with at least one or two darts in your ass. You know Sue holds the bar record, right?"

"Hell."

Johnny snickered. Liam Webster, Del's old man and the other owner of the garage, approached alongside Sam. Before either could sit, Johnny announced the bet. "Okay, gentlemen—and I use that term loosely—ten bucks says Sue tries to attack Foley before we leave Ray's tonight."

Sam considered Foley. "I'll take that bet." To Foley he said, "I told you not to date the chicks at Ray's. You bonehead."

"We're going to Ray's, if you're interested," Johnny told Liam, the rational half of his employers.

Del's father had to be in his late fifties but looked years younger. He had height and muscle on him that Johnny, no matter how hard he worked, would never have. Liam also had an easygoing attitude and knowledge of mechanics that put most auto-thugs to shame. Del was his pride and joy, and J.T., his bruiser of a son, was always good for a laugh when he dropped by.

Liam had grown up poor, worked his tail off to make something of himself, and had raised two fine if aggressive kids. A terrific boss, he didn't judge, knew how difficult it could be to get a second chance, and always gave a guy the benefit of the doubt. Hell, he'd hired Johnny, and Johnny would never claim to be a saint. Not after that pesky felony. Friggin' cops refused to let a guy joyride without making it a huge deal.

Ah, but life at eighteen had seemed so simple back then.

"I'd love to join you boys at Ray's, but I have a date with a lady."

Johnny said kindly, "Blow-up dolls don't count, Liam." Foley and Sam chuckled.

"Shut it, Son, before I shut it for you." Liam made a fist at Johnny, but his amusement was plain to see. They all knew he'd scored big time a few months ago, and ever since, he and Sophie, his lady friend, had been acting like a pair of lovebirds.

Sam shrugged and sat next to Foley, stealing the rest of his cookies.

"Hey."

Sam put an open hand on Foley's face and shoved while inhaling a cookie whole. He talked around his food, opening his mouth to Johnny, especially because the bastard knew it grossed Johnny out. "Still can't believe you got a classy lady like that to give you the time of day, Liam," he said around expelled cookie crumbs.

They all looked at Liam, who puffed up. "I know. Boggles the mind."

They shared a laugh, though Johnny knew they'd all been beyond pleased to see the boss finally get lucky. For thirty years the guy had mourned his true love, raised two hellions, and somehow run a successful garage. Johnny looked up to Liam. Hell, he wanted to *be* Liam, someday. Especially since Liam had scored a fine woman. A mystery to them all.

"So what are your plans? Going to take her ballroom dancing?" Johnny teased.

The whole garage had given Liam shit for the dancing date a month ago.

Liam frowned. "As a matter of fact, we're going fine dining."

Sam stuffed the last cookie in his mouth and mumbled "Good luck" while chewing.

"Sam, close your mouth." Johnny cringed, pushed past his limit. "Just…gross."

Foley snorted. "Hey, at least he's dressed and not

scratching his ass, drinking straight from the milk carton, and busting into your room when you're trying to get lucky."

"With a girl?" Lou asked from behind them. "What happened to Sue?"

Foley growled, "Sue's a girl."

"Yeah, but you already got lucky, right?" Lou shrugged. "Once you're in, you're in. Unless you're doing it wrong." And Lou would know. The guy never hurt for women.

Liam sighed. "You guys are pitiful. Now get back to work."

"Yeah, yeah." Johnny stood with the others and filled Lou in on Foley's dilemma.

"Cool. I'm down for ten. I say she ignores him completely. Kind of the way Lara treats *you*, Johnny."

His face heated, but he pretended not to hear the other guys razzing him and hightailed it back into the garage.

Lara Valley—the lust of his life. He'd been going to Ray's forever, and the first time he'd seen her, four-plus years ago, he'd fallen hard. But his reputation had preceded him: a player and proud of it. He'd teased and flirted his way to learning her name and a few details about the stunning brunette, but little more.

Currently twenty-seven years old and still single, she had her mom, dad, and sister, two nieces she helped care for, and took classes at the community college. For nursing, if he wasn't mistaken. Man, she could help him heal up anytime.

He'd spent many a night at Ray's, discreetly watching her. Long brown hair, deep, chocolate-brown eyes, a slender body curved in all the right places. She worked hard, didn't take shit from anyone, and had a genuinely kind heart for the poor souls sobbing heartache into their beers.

He preferred when she tended bar, because it kept her fine ass away from grabby customers, unlike when she waitressed.

Just the thought of seeing her again made his heart leap, but he knew better. A smart guy didn't shit where he ate. Look at poor Foley and his breakup with Sue. Guaranteed the woman would make him pay in some way tonight. Johnny knew women. He knew what they liked and didn't like. And Sue would be gunning for the guy who'd dumped her, even if she claimed the breakup was no big deal.

He snorted, wondering how Foley could appear so together and be so clueless.

Now take Lara. Johnny wanted her, no question. For a night, a week, a month. Hell, he'd been obsessed with her for a while, and he knew it would take time to get her out of his system. First he had to get her to go out with him.

But Lara? She had a thing about not dating the guys who hung out at Ray's. A smart choice, actually. Johnny loved the joint, but Ray's catered to a rough crowd.

The perfect place for his kind of people, he thought with a grin.

—⁓—

Hours later and a dollar in quarters poorer, having been goaded into a few f-bombs though Sam had *sworn* Del was outside the garage, Johnny sat with his buddies near the darts at Ray's, drinking and preparing for his weekend.

"No plans, guys. For once, I'm a free man for two whole days." He kicked back and sighed with pleasure.

"So no work at your dad's club for you, huh?" Foley asked. "Too bad. I was going to offer to help."

"Me too," Sam added, his voice like the growl of a wounded bear. "Damn. I was hoping to talk to Candy again."

"Sorry, sport. Dear old Dad is Candy's new squeeze."

"Bummer." Sam shrugged. "But the guy's got good taste."

He always had. Johnny had grown up without his mother, but with a bevy of maternal support. His father had a thing for strippers, so it made sense Jack Devlin had finally ponied up and bought his own strip club a few years back. Johnny had never faulted his father's fascination with tits and ass. But it would have been nice to have just *one* set around while growing up, and getting to know more than the girl's stage name before she squirreled.

"So have you seen Sue yet?" he asked Foley.

The others waited. Lou seemed especially amused. Johnny knew that gleam in his friend's eyes.

"Ah, not yet."

Sam snorted. "He's been either hiding in the bathroom or ducking behind Earl."

Earl—a huge-ass bouncer Johnny had no intention of annoying. Ever. And the same went for the other guy, Big J, whom everyone said looked like Mr. Clean.

Foley flushed. "First off, I had to piss. Second, I wasn't ducking behind Earl. I said hi to the guy, and he asked me what I thought about Dodge trucks."

"Uh-huh. Sure you weren't asking him about Sue's

frame of mind?" Johnny teased. Over Foley's shoulder, he saw Lara smiling at a woman over the bar. His heart stuttered, and he did his best to act cool, collected. *She's not interested. She's a nice girl. Leave her alone.*

Like clockwork, his perverse, inner loudmouth had him offering to order the next round. "Be right back. And remember, don't hate the player, hate the game — when *I win*. Suckers."

Grinning, he left the guys at the table swearing, and nabbed a free place at the crowded bar. Lara, Sue, and a few others were hopping, grabbing drinks, and pouring like mad. Behind him he heard a scuffle break out, and he turned to see two guys who used to be friends hammering on each other.

"That's rough," a biker covered in tats next to him said. "But then, Jim should have known better than to hit up Sheila with her new guy right there."

"He really needs to lay off the tequila." Lara sounded exasperated. "I told Earl to keep an eye on him."

Johnny turned and locked gazes with her. She had her long brown hair pulled back in a familiar ponytail. The silky mass reached her lower back, and he was dying to see her hair down just once. She wore minimal makeup, a bit of liner and some thicker mascara. Growing up around women who glammed up for a living, he'd learned early on about a woman's trade secrets. But he doubted the red in her cheeks came from blush. More like from the heat in the place. And damn, it would have been nice if everyone around him cared about personal hygiene as much as he did.

He wrinkled his nose when a new guy replaced the one next to him and leaned toward Lara, wafting his less-than-pleasant scent. Lara wiped her hand over her nose and pretended a cough.

They shared a grin, and his pulse galloped like a racehorse. The sight of her smile, and that heart-stopping dimple, always made it hard for him to breathe. More than physical beauty, Lara possessed a warm inner core that got him hazy and drunk faster than a hometown IPA.

"So, you the bartender?" Smelly Drunk Guy wanted to know.

She glanced at her black T-shirt that read "Bartender" in bold white letters. "Um, yeah." Lara gave Smelly Guy a fake smile. "Another beer?"

"Yep. And keep the change." He slid a grimy twenty her way.

She poured his beer and handed him back a few bills. "You gave me a twenty. You sure about me keeping all that change?" She was so sweet, so honest.

Way too good for you, Devlin. Leave her alone.

The guy belched, then pulled back ten, giving her a few bucks. "Thanks, honey. I'll be back." He stumbled from the barstool, which was quickly occupied by a new customer. Thankfully, this one a woman who smelled like cheap perfume instead of BO.

"What can I get you, Johnny?"

Acknowledgments

I'd like to thank Dr. Elizabeth Leeberg for her generous time in talking with me. Any mistakes I might have made and liberties taken with the characters are solely mine.

And of course, this book would not have been possible without the tremendous efforts of the folks at Sourcebooks. I love working with you!

About the Author

Caffeine addict, boy referee, and romance aficionado, *New York Times* and *USA Today* bestselling author Marie Harte is a confessed bibliophile and devotee of action movies. Whether hiking in Central Oregon, biking around town, or hanging at the local tea shop, she's constantly plotting to give everyone a happily ever after. Visit marieharte.com and fall in love.